T0278875

This Dark Paradise

This Dark Paradise

ERIN LUKEN

BLOOMSBURY

NEW YORK   LONDON   OXFORD   NEW DELHI   SYDNEY

BLOOMSBURY YA
Bloomsbury Publishing Inc., part of Bloomsbury Publishing Plc
1385 Broadway, New York, NY 10018

BLOOMSBURY and the Diana logo are trademarks of Bloomsbury Publishing Plc

First published in the United States of America in October 2024 by Bloomsbury YA

Bloomsbury books may be purchased for business or promotional use.
For information on bulk purchases please contact Macmillan Corporate and
Premium Sales Department at specialmarkets@macmillan.com

LIBRARY OF CONGRESS CATALOGING- IN-PUBLICATION DATA

Names: Luken, Erin, author.
Title: This dark paradise / by Erin Luken.
Description: New York: Bloomsbury, 2024.
Summary: When Lucia tries to steal the magical power source from an enchanted island
to save her brother, she discovers a dark secret that threatens her survival.
Identifiers: LCCN 2024016580 (print) | LCCN 2024016581 (e-book)
ISBN 978-1-5476-1396-0 (hardcover) • ISBN 978-1-5476-1397-7 (ePub)
Subjects: CYAC: Magic—Fiction. | Islands—Fiction. | Love triangles—Fiction. |
Bisexual people—Fiction. | Fantasy. | LCGFT: Fantasy fiction. | Novels.
Classification: LCC PZ7.1.L8427 Th 2024 (print) | LCC PZ7.1.L8427 (e-book) | DDC [Fic]—dc23
LC record available at https://lccn.loc.gov/2024016580

ISBN 978-1-5476-1396-0 (hardcover) • ISBN 978-1-5476-1397-7 (e-book)

Book design by Jeanette Levy
Typeset by Westchester Publishing Services
Printed and bound in the U.S.A.
2 4 6 8 10 9 7 5 3 1

To find out more about our authors and books visit
www.bloomsbury.com and sign up for our newsletters.

To the girls who have lived so long trying to fulfill others'
expectations that they don't know what they want for themselves yet

This Dark Paradise

CHAPTER ONE

The way Signore Naevian's brow furrows as I enter his store says either some nasty stench has followed me inside, or he's not interested in buying from me today. But I could use the money, and I'm the stubborn sort, so I pretend not to notice.

"Good afternoon, Signore Naevian." I bob a small curtsy. Rosana Jandar, the persona of mine he knows, is shy and awkward, so I wobble a little and flash half a smile.

He doesn't smile back. The stone walls behind him sweat trickles of water while a phonograph in the corner screeches out a mournful recording of Verigal City's premier orchestra. All of it picks at the edges of my confidence. If I had any hope that his displeasure *wasn't* because of me, I don't anymore.

He's lined up the last set of Merine luck talismans I sold to him on his scratched counter beside a rusty, dented safe. "Signorina Jandar. I'm glad to see you. I've been hoping to speak with you." His fingers dance over the line of my jewelry in time with the music. Outside, they'd glitter like the gems they're supposed to be, but in here, they're as dull as everything else in his dank shop. In pockets of darkness among the gas lamps, treasures from around the world line the shelves. There are fine porcelain bowls whose elaborate swirling adornments can't be read in the dimness, sitting beside the skulls of foreign beasts whose empty eye sockets stare out from the shadows.

I smile, showing a little bit of teeth this time. "I've got some new pieces for you today, Signore Naevian," I say in Rosana Jandar's lilting accent. "You wanna see them?"

He plucks one of my rings off the counter. "Where do you get these talismans, Signorina Jandar? Are they really from Merine?"

Ah. The situation is worse than him being in a bad mood. But I'd rather not lose his business if I don't have to.

"Can I tell you a secret, signore?" I lower my voice and step closer to the counter, bringing the dark streaks of mold spiderwebbing across the door to his back room into view. The distinct reek of the mold punches right through the faint lemon spritz Signore Naevian has tried to freshen the air with. "I—*found* them."

He spins my ring in his fingers. To my eyes, it looks like an ordinary rock—illusions don't appear to the person who created them. But for him, the light should be perfectly catching the little flecks in the stone, turning them from green to gold just like a real Merine gemstone would. "You found them where?"

If I'd truly stolen them, I wouldn't want to scream that. Still, I have to make him believe I have. That won't ruffle him. I'd bet a good half the items here in Signore Naevian's Bargain Treasures were swiped. "On . . . a stand in the market. Just sitting there. You get me?" I even dare to wink.

Because far better I be a simple thief than a glamorist. Sale of glamoturas except by verified dealers is punishable by death in Verigal City. Once glamoturas leave the city's borders, the illusion dissolves. The city's Board of Merchants can't have goods constantly vanishing en route to their destinations. That wouldn't inspire confidence conducting business here.

Thing is, I *have* a verified permit. But I'd rather face death by the board than let the gang who provided that permit know that I'm selling work on the side. The board'll just kill me. The Silverhands will go after my family.

Signore Naevian clears his throat. "Please wait here, Signorina Jandar. I need to collect your next payment from the back."

There's something awkward in his acceptance of my lie that makes a sliver of suspicion slink through my gut. "Don't you want to see what I've brought you today first before paying?"

"Your work is always so lovely. I'm sure I'll want all of it." His gaze skitters back and forth across his weeping walls and decaying treasures, landing everywhere but on me. What a shame—he doesn't buy my lie after all.

I'm not going to let him out of my sight to fetch someone. Rosana Jandar is a simple, foolish girl, but I, Lucia Arduini, am not.

I move forward, and he steps backward into the door to the back room and taps on it twice.

It flies open, and a man rushes in. He wears the navy double-breasted coat of the polizia, with a red sash draped across his chest signaling the Modian family sponsors him—not an employer I want to find out about this. They often do business with Boss Julius and the Silverhands.

"Don't move!" he shouts.

Apparently, Signore Naevian's not quite the fool I marked him as after all.

He already fetched someone.

The officer lifts a rifle. I hold my hands up, heart leaping into my

3

throat. "Sir, please. I—what's happening?" I could try to run. The crowds are heavy, so maybe I could sneak through. If I can escape, they'll never be able to find me again.

"Hands on your head," the officer orders, and I obey. He *does* recognize some of the real danger I pose. Otherwise, why keep pointing the gun at me, a little, unarmed girl?

He slides around the side of the counter, lowering the rifle with one hand while grabbing handcuffs with the other. Still, I don't move. He extends the cuffs, leaning away from me as he does so.

As soon as the band of metal presses against my skin, he's lost.

I focus on my connection to the magic—a buzzing sensation in my chest. Then I focus on heat, the heat of my own body, the blood thrumming through my veins. To create one sensation, one must give up the same. And I want to make these cuffs *burn*.

I push the sensation of heat into the cuffs before he can close them over my wrist.

The officer's eyes widen for a split second, and then the full effect hits him. He jumps back, howling in pain, clutching his hand, and the price of the glamotura hits me in turn—sudden cold swamping me. My teeth chatter and shivers rack my limbs.

Now for Signore Naevian. He fumbles with the doorknob of the exit. A creator is never affected by their own glamotura, so I easily snatch the handcuffs off the floor with shaking fingers and launch forward, adrenaline sending me flying successfully over the countertop.

I crash into him and press the cuffs into his neck. He lurches back with a gurgling grunt, opening my path out. Clutching the cuffs still, I grasp the doorknob. I don't have much heat left to use before killing myself, but I push anyway. The magic shudders through me, the abrupt loss of heat making my knees shake so violently I almost drop to the floor. But now, if the men touch the knob to come after me, it'll burn them.

Signore Naevian makes to grab me, but I swing the cuffs out, and he leaps away to avoid them.

I open the door and slam it closed.

I'm sure they'll have another way out of the building, so I hurry into the crowd, racing to put distance between us. A canal cuts through the center of the street, pushing all of the pedestrians to the side. Unlike the canals in the tourist district with their delicate drifting gondolas, this one is packed with honking cargo barges. The waterway is almost as jammed as the small cobblestone sidewalk beside it, where young women balancing baskets of fruit on their flat hats dodge older men with hollow eyes, and where little children scamper by, dipping into pockets.

I weave my way through the trudging crowd. The people who slink through the streets of this sector are as hunched as the buildings lining the sides. Tourists never come to the lower quarters, so no one really cares how decrepit it looks, how the wooden buildings have lines of mold across their front and the few stone ones look about to crumble. The smell of the sea mingles with sewage running down from the affluent sections on higher ground.

When Signore Naevian's shop disappears from sight, I duck into an alley. I pull my kerchief from my head and tie it at my waist like a sash. Then I peel the paper-thin glamotura mask of Rosana's features from my face. Last, I drop my satchel with my latest glamotura stones into the mud. It's a sad, unceremonious end to so much work, but I can't keep the satchel. It's evidence of my crimes.

I tuck the mask down the front of my dress. Better Signore Naevian and the polizia think what they saw was my face. I'll burn it tonight. The gang won't be able to definitively link this rogue peddler of glamoturas to me. Not yet.

Farewell, Rosana Jandar.

I keep moving. The surroundings transform abruptly as I step out of the eastern lower quarter and into the Perla Verigaliana. The canal curves away from the streets, carrying the cargo boats into the distance with it, and the street opens up, and everything grows brighter. The pastel colors of the buildings pop, the cobblestones gleam with a polished shine, and the stink of mold gives way to the mouthwatering scents of sweet dough pockets and the bright tomato sauce that drenches cheesy balls of fried rice.

The crowds change, too. No longer are the people I shoulder my way past only other broke Verigalianos like myself in their drab clothes. In the Perla Verigaliana, we're only a few speckles of blight among the far more manicured merchants and tourists from all over with a whole range of coloring from milky white to nearly ebony.

The Perla Verigaliana, which might as well be called the Tourist Sector, cuts through the lower quarters, leading from the harbor to the wealthier sections of the city above. It's a little bubble in the poorest rung of the city, ensuring that visitors disembarking at the docks can travel to their lodgings without witnessing the city's poverty. Markets line the streets, welcoming all the incoming wealth with open arms.

I head for the Cielonarre bridge, the fastest path through the Perla. The gleaming bridge glints high over the marketplace, scattering the sunlight it catches, with every part of its surface wrought in ornate glass. The delicate marvel looks too fragile to exist, let alone hold the vast numbers of people who cross every day, but, of course, it can and does because it's a glamotura.

About halfway up the bridge, I run into a wall of people. Like every day, the bridge is clogged with tourists. Some squat on the ground to stare at the markets below, in awe that they can *see straight through*. They point and exclaim over the merchandise on display beneath them—stalls of leather and lace crafted by the region's finest artisans, stalls of rainbow ceramics and blown glass, stalls of the purest olive oil and the best aged vinegar, stalls of knockoff versions of the most famous Orizzian paintings, stalls of original paintings of the sweeping vistas of the Verigal City cliffs—anything and everything that is Verigal City at its finest.

Others stop to hang over the edge and enjoy the vistas, admiring the view of the city rising behind them up the steep cliffs. As the ground rises, the homes grow brighter, shifting from bright pastels to brighter pastels, then to the iridescent, glittering homes of Verigal City's wealthiest—more glamoturas.

I try to weave my way around the tourist congestion. Usually there's *some* kind of path, however awkward. Today, though, they're lined up practically shoulder to shoulder, a massive clog across most of the bridge. Several people lean over the edge, pointing toward the harbor.

I turn to see what has their attention and my breath catches in my throat.

One of the Estarallan yachts is arriving to pick up tourists for the island.

The almost palpable thrill in the air makes sense now. Even though plenty of the people in the crowd are Verigalianos who see glamoturas all over their city every day, it's still not the same as seeing the Estarallans' arrival. Even *I* used to come out when I could to watch their arrival because the joy is only half about the display itself anyway. It's also a reminder of where these people came from—Estaralla. It's a reminder that unlike the glamoturas here in the city, the people who're putting on this show have come from a place with more magic, powerful magic, magic that can take all unhappiness and hardship away.

I used to feel like the show was a special, magical treat, too. Before what happened four months ago. This time, it's not fascination that freezes my feet but bitterness.

At the mouth of the harbor, a crackling golden haze has amassed. Though nearer the docks the waves are calm, the water in front of the lightning-like fog ripples back and forth, churning in a violent, localized storm.

It feels so real. The air hums, my skin rippling with an unseen current of energy, and a tang of metal and sea sparks on my tongue.

Then, with a *swoosh*, the churning water rises, spinning into a cyclone. Slowly, as though drawn from the air around it, other colors join the blue of the water—black, brown, white—swirling closer and closer until the entire thing morphs from a cyclone into a pair of ships.

The stormy backdrop vanishes. All that remains is the surprisingly clear water of the Verigal City harbor and the ships. The first is large, black-hulled, flying the crimson flag of Verigal City's navy—the standard naval escort provided to all ships (who pay for the privilege, of course) arriving in Verigal City's harbor. It dwarfs the second ship in its shadow. The second ship is white, gold-trimmed, clearly meant for luxury, a yacht that would very much be in trouble without its escort on the seas between the city and its home island. It flies a silvery and sheer flag that vanishes and reappears with each flutter, an obvious glamotura. At the sight of the ship, my insides drop out, leaving only hollowness in the cavity behind.

Around me, people on the bridge applaud in appreciation of the show. Verigal City, of course, encourages these displays. They're not just a reminder to the world of the stunning nature of the Estarallans' magic, but also a reminder that Verigal City is the *only* place the Estarallan ships arrive, the "gateway to Estaralla" as our Board of Merchants calls the city. Estaralla may be the only place in the world offering true magic, but Verigal City is the only other place it can be seen at all, and it's a much cheaper destination.

"Discount Estaralla" some call it, to which I always want to scoff. I've never heard a single tourist return from Estaralla who doesn't say the time on the island was the happiest of their life, and of course, why wouldn't it be? The island of Estaralla houses a source—some object or substance that allows magic to bloom within its radius. Verigal City is lucky enough to be just within that border, but we're far enough away that our magic is limited. Here, glamoturas can only affect the five senses, which makes for flashy, little illusions. In Estaralla, the magic is *real*. It can reach deeper into a person, change their very emotions, access their memories, show their greatest desires and bring them to life. It can create feasts of any and every food to be found in the world, bring mystical creatures only found in legends to life, and even, they say, give the dead a voice to speak to the living.

Bitterness bites the back of my throat, and that's what finally propels me to tear my gaze away from the sight below and get moving again. Most of the crowd stays to watch the ships finish docking— some perhaps hoping for more displays of the magic, others probably curious to see who'll disembark. Verigal City's society papers love to interview returning travelers from the island so the rest of us can read about the wonders—feasts, balls, and impossible sights—we can never afford. Mother often read them to Severin and me when we were little.

She stopped after father left us.

All of these thoughts—memories of hope, the reality of my current desperate situation—swirl violently in my mind as I push my way through the crowds back down the other side of the Cielonarre. I barely feel those I push aside, so caught by the feelings the sight of the Estarallan yacht has brought bubbling back to the surface in me.

The last time I saw that yacht four months ago, the boy I thought I loved had just broken my heart.

CHAPTER TWO

Even though I've rushed across half the city to get here, the final three flights of stairs in the tenement building to my family's room feel just as long as the rest. I take them slowly—*really* slowly—each step squealing the protest I can't voice. Even with the perfume povero so thick it's like moisture on my tongue and the bite of urine coming from the dark, stained corners of the stairwell, it's more pleasant than what waits for me at home.

Mamma's going to be furious.

With every step, I slouch a little more, trying to squish myself into a more appealing shape for her. She likes to see submission, so I'll at least try to give her that since the rest of me is so far from the daughter she wants. The daughter she wants wouldn't continue to risk the family by selling glamoturas behind the gang's back—never mind that it's the only way that our family can eat, since all of the work I do for the gang goes directly toward working off the debt my father left us in.

I slip my key into our door and step inside on my tiptoes, closing it again without a sound as if I'm somehow going to be able to sneak past Mamma in our one-bedroom apartment.

My caution turns out entirely useless anyway.

We've got company.

Felice, one of the Silverhands' enforcers, stands in the middle of the room next to Mamma. Like all of the gang members, he has glamoturas woven like gloves over his hands to give them a silver sheen (silver hands—very creative).

It's a rare circumstance that makes me wish that Mamma and I were alone together, but I'd absolutely take a lengthy lecture from Mamma over whatever Felice has to say to me. My heart beats out the words *He knows, he knows*, but I try to quiet that panic. Does it seem like a highly suspicious coincidence he's waiting for me at home just after I was ambushed by the polizia? Yes, but just because he knows something doesn't mean he knows everything. And if I assume too strongly he does, I'm just as likely to slip up and hand him the key to my execution myself.

Mamma sits at our table in the center of the room, her hands folded on top of the cracking wood. She's set in front of her a proper appetizer—or as close to proper as we have—bread, dipping oil, and our only tiny hunk of cheese. She's plated them on our best dishes, a sparkling set of real Giari crystal, which look a little silly with the meager food offering on our beaten-up table. I was looking forward to that cheese, too, but of course, she's wasting it on our gang visitor. In Verigal City, we say a lousy guest doesn't excuse a lousy host, but honestly, for the gang, I'd like to make an exception.

"Where were you?" Felice's voice is gravelly, like he's trying to growl, but he's trying much too hard. His face is perpetually set in a deep scowl every time he's sent to have a talking with me. He thinks he's above these babysitting duties, but clearly Boss Julius disagrees.

"Today's my day off," I say. "So why does it matter to you?"

Mamma's knuckles turn white as she clenches them. *Don't tempt him*, her narrowed eyes tell me, but if I don't act normally, he'll suspect something.

And normal for me is . . . well, a little mouthy.

"You're still bound by our contract on your days off," Felice says.

"I didn't think my contract said I couldn't leave my own home." I bustle to our icebox in an effort to pretend he's not there.

He steps into my path, sets a hand on the icebox, and slams it closed. "You can't sell glamoturas on your own." He leans over me, wielding his height and hulking body as weapons. His breath stinks of cigars, so thick the smoke might as well be pouring from his mouth.

"Yeah, I know." I fold my arms to stop my hands from shaking. "Wait—are you *accusing* me? I just went for a walk to enjoy my day off."

"Boss got news today there's a rogue girl glamorist in the city."

It's just my luck that the officer Signore Naevian contacted is one in the Silverhands' pockets. But if Boss Julius had any proof it was me, I wouldn't still be standing here. I'd be slung over Felice's shoulder and halfway down the street to their headquarters already.

"And you think that's me?" I widen my eyes and step back. "I wouldn't cross you! Do you think I'm that thoughtless?"

"I think you think you're cleverer than you are."

"Did they say what this girl looked like?" I don't know if I'm as clever as I think, but I'm clever enough to have a response to that.

"We all know you can alter your appearance."

I keep my face straight, but internally I wince. It's a rare glamorist with that level of skill—something I didn't realize when I was forced to start working for the gang five years ago. I was so naive back then. If only I'd known to conceal this ability, my life would be so much easier. "So she didn't look like me."

13

"She was around your height, they think," he says, but we both know that means nothing. I'm a thoroughly average height for a woman with a thoroughly average build, perfect for a con artist.

I purse my lips. "So does the boss want to speak with me about this or not?" I'm getting tired of this conversation, and it's time to make him play his hand or leave. I'm willing to bet they don't have enough on me.

With terrible timing, the door opens. A rancid fog of fish, salt, sweat, and metal sweeps in first. Then my younger brother follows. Clearly, he spent the day at the docks, picking up odd jobs.

"Severin!" Mamma snaps, her fear gone for a brief moment. He flashes me a look of sympathy, face pinched. "What have we said about skipping school?" She loves this argument. It's enough for her to temporarily forget our Silverhands friend in the room.

"Little brother arrives!" Felice steps around me, slamming a shoulder into mine as he does. It's a swift shock of pain, and I clench my teeth.

He knows the fastest way to make Mamma and me fall in line is to threaten the baby of the family. The real reason I work for the gang, creating glamotura after glamotura for them from my own blood, is because if I didn't, they would've taken him instead.

Not only is he my younger brother and my responsibility, but also his ability to do magic isn't good enough for the Silverhands to exploit. Magic is hereditary, so theoretically he should have aptitude. But he has no skill. He's attempted to create glamotura gemstones before, but they turned out dull, soft, and wrong, and he still has the twisted scar on his arm from it.

Unless he suddenly improves, he won't be put to work like me. As much as working for the Silverhands isn't my favorite, my magical talents make me valuable, protecting me from the majority of abuse I could suffer. Sure, I don't enjoy creating glamoturas for them to scam folks with, and I enjoy the dingy stage shows I do for them at night even less, but even in those shows, the audience is forbidden from touching the glamorists. The feats I can perform with my magic are for sale, but I, definitively, am not.

Severin has no such shield.

"What you got there?" Felice grabs Severin's burlap sack and rips it open. He scowls and hurls a wrapped bundle of cured pork round on the table. "Did you waste all your pay on this garbage, or is there any left for me?"

Severin swallows, and his gaze darts to me. Even though he's nearly the same height as Felice, he's so skinny that all it'd take to knock him over would be a strong wind. Felice grabs and shakes him. Coins clink.

"Stop it," I snap.

Felice clicks his tongue, reaches into Severin's pockets, and pulls out two lone copper coins. That's it, the sad wages for his day at the docks. Felice rubs them together. "You owe us, Arduini."

"Fully aware of that, thank you," I say. How could I ever forget?

Our family was wealthy once. We lived high up in the hills on the Verdant Cliffs, where our windows opened to sweeping vistas of the sea instead of a dingy alley and our neighbors' windows, and the air smelled of fresh salt instead of piss. Our concerns, when it came to food, were ensuring we'd had our chef cook sufficient dishes to convince our guests that we were worthy hosts, not whether or not we'd have to skip dinner that night. Severin went to school to learn to manage a business, and I went to school to learn to manage my theoretical future husband's household—and to be the sort of dainty lady who might be able to land a husband above my family's station in the first place. But what I didn't know was that Father had made all kinds of promises to the Silverhands. Promises he couldn't deliver on. And when the bill came due, he vanished into thin air, leaving us scrambling to pay for all he'd done.

Felice's eyes narrow, and he closes his fist over the coins with a horrible grinding noise of metal on metal. "You don't seem aware. Otherwise you wouldn't be taking all these little 'days off' and pretending we don't fully know it's *you* selling shit behind our backs even if we can't prove it."

"I'm not—" I start.

Felice cuts me off with a wave of his fist. "Shut it. The deal was that you work to repay us, and we don't call little brother in to assist in speeding up that debt repayment." He shoots Severin a sidelong smirk. "We won't be able to pay him nearly as much as we pay you because he's got none of your special little magic skills, but we do always have openings for staff to spray down the streets outside of the bars. Somehow, spending nights cleaning up others' excrement isn't a job most people want to take, and then, with the amount of our staff that finds themselves on the wrong end of an angry, drunk patron's knife . . ." He shrugs. "Only the most desperate bother to take that job, but then again, little brother's going to be pretty desperate."

"I'll take fewer days off." I don't want to—the money I make from selling glamoturas on my handful of days off is already barely enough to keep us fed, but I have to say *some*thing.

Felice shakes his head. "Too late. Should've thought of that sooner. You've failed your side of the bargain. Little brother's going to start helping to pay now, too."

There's a roaring in my ears, and their tips burn hot. "You can't *do* this."

Felice shrugs a shoulder. "I can't, no, but I can suggest it to Boss Julius, and he'll approve. He's not pleased one of his glamorists is crossing him." He steps closer, shoving himself into my space again with his horrible odor. "No one crosses the boss. Better learn this now, Arduini, or next time'll be even worse."

"What if I can fulfill the debt?" I draw myself up, because he can threaten me, and he can make me work, but he can't force me to fear him. "Get you what my father promised?"

Felice snorts. "How are *you* going to get to Estaralla? Let alone steal the source?"

My stomach twists. Because that is what my father foolishly promised the Silverhands. He told them that he knew a way to find and take the source, the origin of the liquid magic that runs through the island.

"I can do it," I say, forcing myself to look him in the eyes. "A new ship is about to leave. Give me a month, and I'll get you the source."

Felice flashes a horrible, twisted grin. "Deal," he says. "If you get us the source, the deal's done. You're free. If not . . ." He chortles and heads toward the door. "I'll see *you* in a month," he says ominously to Severin as he steps around him. He continues chortling the whole way out, leaving a cloud of silence behind.

CHAPTER THREE

When Felice's footsteps finally fade, I slump against the icebox and let my head fall into my hands, all the confidence I had to show him draining away. Mamma closes her eyes and breathes out a heavy sigh.

Severin rewraps the pork with care. "At least we still have dinner." He's always the optimist.

Mamma, not so much. She slams her palms flat on the table. "So have you learned your lesson yet, Lucia?" A few of the hairs at the top of her head, falling loose from her swept chignon, are turning gray.

"I'll fix it," I say quietly.

She rises to her feet, the silver buttons down the front of her prim dress winking at me as she trembles. "You will sell yourself to—to whoever you need to before they'll take Severin."

I flinch, can't help it. "I *said* I'll fix it." I'm desperate to protect Severin, too. It still stings, though, hearing Mamma say that. She has high hopes for Severin. He's supposed to stay in school, go to university, start a trading business, and become a respectable merchant. Our family will never be what we once were, but Mamma still has dreams of returning to the middle, if not the top, of the hill for her golden years, with her rich son at her side and a budding trading empire once more.

She sees herself in Severin—kind, innocent, no capability for magic or conning. In me, she sees my father who conned her as thoroughly as he conned the Silverhands. He promised her the world if she'd marry him, promised her profits so high they would be able to buy a vote on the Merchant Council, took her dowry, opened a business, and when he ran that business into the ground, he turned to the gang.

"And how, exactly, do you plan to do that?" Mamma demands.

"The source," I say quietly. "Estaralla."

Mamma snorts, the sound so much more searing from her than Felice. I know she deeply regrets having chosen Father over a safer suitor who didn't offer a steep rise in status but would've kept her perfectly comfortable. But because he's not here to hate anymore, her ire all falls on me. "That con is up, Lucia. You've been talking about getting the source for years. It's time you admit that was always just a lie your father used to swindle a whole bunch of the wrong men out of their money and then you used to keep us all from getting outright murdered."

"I—I didn't . . ." My throat, my tongue, grows numb. I never thought that was a lie. *My* claims, at least, had never been a lie. Were Father's?

"I need to lie down." Mamma thrusts aside the curtain to our bedding area, marches to her canopy bed, and throws herself on it with a petulance she doesn't have the capital for anymore. The bed is decaying as steadily as everything else we own—the gold-plated posters tarnished, the delicate lace canopies fading to the same yellow as the lace of her dress. With each passing year, it's harder and harder for her to pretend we still have our money or that we'll ever get it back.

It was my bed as a child, but Mamma claimed it for herself when we moved out of our villa. Her bed wouldn't fit in this room—or, rather, wouldn't allow anything else to fit—so it couldn't come. But like the few other scraps of our old life we've kept, only Mamma gets to enjoy its comfort. Severin and I sleep on straw mattresses on the floor that collect rat droppings inside and out and make us easy targets for crawling critters in the night.

I pull my gloves from my hands to ready myself for dinner. My skin beneath is graying, peeling, cracked, and rotting away, and I clench my fists over it. Magic always has a price. This is the price I pay for the visual glamoturas I've been making for years. The destroyed skin extends almost to my shoulders now. When I run scams, I hide it beneath gloves because it marks me as a glamorist. Some glamorists start with their faces, so it can't be hidden, so everyone will see and admire them for their power, but I'm obviously of a different mind.

It's the price I pay to keep Severin safe, but I don't mind because he's worth it. Everything I've had to do is worth it—or it will be, as long as I can get the source.

I light the gas stove and set our battered pot of water on top to cook our pasta. Severin nudges me, setting the pork between us. "Don't forget this." Tonight, with the pork to add to our pasta instead of beans, it'll be a veritable feast.

"Thanks," I grind out through my teeth because as frustrated as I am, he's the last person who deserves me screaming at him, and he flashes the smallest of smiles in return. I cut a small amount off, then stuff the rest into the icebox, packing it in tight to make it last.

When dinner's ready, Mamma rejoins us. We eat in silence, but the dirty looks she keeps shooting me speak loud enough for my taste. *You've ruined us all,* she says. *You'll never be able to fix this now.*

But *can't* I? I know exactly what the solution is. She thinks it's impossible, and so does Felice, but she's a narrow-minded, spoiled grown rich girl floundering without the security she thought she'd always have, and he's a thickheaded thug.

After, Severin and I clean, while she retires to her canopy bed with dramatic, dragging steps. Even now, without our maids, I'm not sure she's washed a plate in her whole life.

"Don't waste our gas." She draws her canopies shut for what I can only hope is the final time tonight, and I obediently snuff out our single lamp, leaving Severin and myself in darkness.

Once Mamma begins to snore lightly, he whispers, "Well, we know they don't have any proof it was you illegally selling work, or they would've taken you off to be killed and forced me into work instead."

I know he's trying to look on the bright side, even now. I know he's trying to comfort me. But I don't feel it. Everything is too tight here, too small, and I have to tell myself I'm only imagining my throat closing up as I swallow.

"Felice might be trying to assign me an unpleasant job, but my stomach's not that weak," Severin says, still just trying to make me feel better about it. A growth spurt recently brought him taller than me, and since then, he's started acting like the three years between us mean nothing. He protects me now, too. Or he tries, anyway. My little brother is growing up so fast, too soon. "I'm not afraid of cleaning up piss all the time. I'll be perfectly fine." But the fact that's the best he can say about it isn't great. Plus, the exact job they'll assign him isn't the worst of it—the bigger issue is that if they're taking all of his wages for the debt, as well as mine, I'm not sure how we're expected to feed ourselves. They'll probably "loan" us the money for

21

food, sinking us further and further into a debt we'll never escape. And not only that—they'll force him to work enough that he'll have no choice but to drop out of school, effectively ending his chances of leaving this grim life behind for a better one.

He's not supposed to have to do that. Fixing Father's mistakes, paying off his debt, finishing his plan—that's my responsibility. It always was because while Severin was Mamma's favorite, I was Father's. I sat at his side every night, learning little magic tricks from him as a child. I was the one who begged to hear the story of Estaralla over and over again at bedtime. I was the one, not Mamma, that he told of his plans to steal the source from Estaralla. I was the one he gave his map of the island to. I was the one he gave the little relic he'd bought—or perhaps stolen—from Estaralla itself, a jar he told me was spelled to be able to contain any substance, including Estaralla's liquid magic itself. And I was the last person who saw him before he walked out on us forever.

I don't know what I, a ten-year-old child, could've done to stop it all. But I do know I'm the only one of us with a chance to finish it. Maybe Father was too afraid to try to pull off the heist himself, but he had to have thought it was at least *possible*. That map he'd made—he'd tried to prepare for the heist. Even if he ran instead.

I shove myself to my feet. "No, that's not going to happen. You're not going to work for the Silverhands. I'm going to Estaralla."

The legend of Estaralla's formation says it once was just a rocky island in the middle of the Aeditanian Sea with beautiful vistas and little else—until a storm hurled a tiny boat with a young family onto the shore. The father was a duke and the son of a minor goddess and the mother was his forbidden lover. They had been fleeing to start a new life together in secret with their child.

The duke died a slow death of an infected wound in an unlucky twist of fate. For his mother, Estar, the goddess of beauty, had pursued them, and she could have saved him, if she'd only arrived sooner.

The children's version of the legend says she wept over her son's body, and her tears became the island's source of magic. The other version says she killed herself beside him, and her blood became the source. Both say when her son's lover drank of it, she became the first user of magic, and with it, she was able to create all she needed for her and her daughter to live the life her lover would've wanted for them. His mother's final apology and gift.

Soon, the generous mother decided to share her luck and power with others who'd never had either before in their lives. And so, with other gods' assistance—depending on the version, of course—Estar sent instructions to those who needed and deserved the gift of magic to come to the island, until the magic ran weaker, and she reluctantly cut the outside access off.

Ironic, perhaps, that Estaralla started as a haven for the powerless, and now, only the most powerful can afford to go. Right after Father disappeared, I wished every night that the gods would open a way to the island for me—because I was desperate, because I needed the help, because I was a little girl who'd lost her father, too.

I was one naive kid. If the gods are even real, they aren't going to help me. No path to Estaralla or its magic is going to be gifted to me.

But I *will* claw one out for myself.

CHAPTER FOUR

As I slip down the streets on careful feet, the slouching tenement homes crouch over me, blotting out all but a line of stars overhead. A few streetlamps stand watch, but most are smashed out. They cast only a few patches of amber light that most people avoid. The transport canal down the middle of the street is a dark swath, empty of the honking cargo barges. A few shapes bob down it—maybe garbage, maybe bodies—and the otherwise quiet of the night is drowned out by one person hanging over the edge retching noisily.

Tourists like to swim where this same water passes through the Perla Verigaliana before dumping into the bay, and I always cringe.

I make my way to Rentizia Park in the center of the city, halfway up the hill where poverty meets wealth, close enough to that wealth to be safe at night (mostly). By day, it's a bustling mecca. Carriages circle the park nonstop to parade the affluent to be seen by everyone who matters. Performers from the lower quarters come to juggle or sing or dance to entice pitying rich folk to toss them a few coins. They hope to impress someone enough to attract an actual patron, and the very best of them succeed, but as with every other real opportunity for upward mobility, competition is fierce because there are so many more who want it than will ever attain it.

This park is where I met Antony. Like so many of the performers, I was here to seize my chance for a better future.

And I got it.

Then, I lost it.

I swore I'd never speak to him again after what he did, but I can't get to Estaralla without him.

I slink to a square of benches around a dark fountain. A little cherubic angel carved from marble hovers over the fountain, its arrow a threat, not as cute as it is by day. Shadows blot its eyes, and it looks ready to kill. Around it, water rises up instead of falling into the pool below. It's a popular glamotura. By day, people line up to touch the reverse flow of water, but right now, there's only one other person here, seated on the fountain's edge.

I approach slowly, a part of me hoping it's not Antony at all but a stranger. In the darkness, I can't see his face, only broad shoulders and large hands curled over the sides of the marble. My heart claws its way up my throat—a warning from my body that maybe I'm not ready for this. I can still turn around.

But I don't need to turn around. I must only be nervous because of how much is riding on my performance tonight. I haven't seen Antony for months now, and I'm completely over him.

I whistle twice, a soft sound that could be mistaken for a bird.

The figure sitting on the fountain looks up.

"You came this time," Antony says, his voice soft and longing, and from his phrasing, I know he's been waiting for me.

It's like a hard punch rippling through me, loosening everything I'd locked down. I can't help the sharp exhale—I hope he didn't hear it. Actual pain blooms in my chest, a hand squeezing my heart and lungs.

I thought I was ready for this, but I was *so wrong.*

He stands and steps forward. The moonlight slides over his face, highlighting the strong lines of his jaw and a dark dusting of stubble. One corner of his lip curls into his usual crooked smile.

Breathe, I tell myself. *Just breathe.* It feels too late to whirl around and run. Or maybe I can't. My legs have seized up at the sight of him, and my eyes sting. As if I'm about to cry.

Oh, hell, I'd *better* not cry.

I give him the best smile I can. It wobbles—a betrayal of my true feelings—but maybe that's not entirely out of character for who I am tonight. I have to pretend to reconcile with him at least a little if I want his help. "I wasn't sure you'd come here again."

"Of course I did. I came here every single time I came to the city. You were the one who wasn't here," he says, still soft. "I was starting to doubt you'd ever return, but still, I couldn't make myself stop dropping by to check. I couldn't stand the thought that the one time I didn't bother would be the one time you showed up. I think I would've kept coming here for the rest of my life, even an old man, still hoping. But you're here." The final word is a sigh of relief. Relief! Of all things.

Bile rises in the back of my throat. I hate him for this, that he thinks this could possibly be genuine on my part. That he thinks he can waltz up here, not even offer me an apology or explanation, and think I'll forgive him.

"You were so angry," he continues. "I really thought you'd never show up here again."

And in truth, I hadn't been planning on it because I have some self-respect. He betrayed me. Then he lied to me about it. And still, he hasn't admitted it.

I would *never* want anything at all from a man like that.

He inches closer still, but I can't make myself close the gap. Usually, I'm not quite so bad at getting into character. He's close enough now I can smell him, a salty mix of the ocean and sweat, close enough I feel the warmth from his body, and my face burns. If I move, I'm not sure if I'll try to slap him or kiss him.

Neither of those is going to do shit for me. I have to hang on, stay composed, and get my information. That'll be far more rewarding in the end.

"So what made you come here tonight?" he asks.

Well, silence won't cut it anymore. The cool night breeze tickles the back of my neck, a sharp contrast to the stinging heat in my cheeks. I just need to breathe. And keep it simple. Simple is always better, and even more so now.

I'm not myself. I am a character, a persona no more real than Rosana Jandar. I'll name her . . . Lucia Ignorante. Perfect. And Lucia Ignorante isn't mad. Lucia Ignorante is the part of me that still feels the warm press of his lips against mine as he's speaking. She's the part of me that only cares about that.

"I just—missed you." I reach out a hand and trail it across his forearm. My fingers tingle where they meet his skin, a shock I can only hope he still feels, too. I can't even look at his face. Instead, I stare at his throat.

It bobs as he swallows. "You—did? Really?" I can't tell if it's hope or wariness that slows his speech. He reaches out and tilts my chin up, forcing my gaze to meet his, forcing me to see the softness in his deep brown eyes. It's hope, definitely hope, and I have no idea why.

I'm going to break, one way or another, unless I just throw my hand on the table. Even if it's a little graceless. "You know, we could spend more time together if I went to Estaralla."

Antony jerks back, and the air around me suddenly cools. "Oh, that's all this is about, isn't it? It's not about me at all, but *Estaralla* again."

The knot in my chest finally loosens. With the anger twisting his handsome face, the sharp flushed slashes on his cheekbones, it's easier for me to breathe.

"Tell me, did you ever like me?" Despite the anger on his face, his voice trembles, wounded. "Or did you just look at me and think the Key Vessel's younger brother would get you a place there for sure?"

I want that to be true. So much, it's a gnawing pain inside me. And I would love to spit out agreement right now, see if it would make him crumple. See if it would make him hurt.

But that's not what Lucia Ignorante would do because she did like him. And there comes a point even I can't lie anymore without sliding into delusion. I am Lucia, but I am also Lucia Ignorante. Our relationship might have started as a transaction, but unfortunately, like a weed, it grew beyond that and took over far too much of me.

After Father fled, I sought a way to fix things. Magic is hereditary—passed down through the blood of the original families of Estaralla. But being able to use the magic requires training and practice, and while Father had taught me a few little tricks, they were limited. I needed a lot more training. The magic requires trades to work—and I'd heard stories in the gang of those who'd failed to trade properly, and how they turned catatonic and useless, and I couldn't risk that happening to me.

I needed a teacher, so I wandered the Perla Verigaliana, seeking the most-skilled glamorists putting on shows. What I really wanted was an Estarallan teacher, but aside from those who arrived at the docks to retrieve tourists, there were none. And those Estarallans, of course, were impossible to access unless you were one of those wealthy tourists. The Estarallan yachts were always locked down, of course, heavily guarded for as long as they were in the port. (It's never stopped a handful of people lacking any degree of common sense from trying to sneak aboard, however.)

But my chance came when Estaralla's former Key Vessel passed, and a new Key Vessel was appointed to the island: Keelan. For the sake of relations, the new Key Vessel held a large show here in Rentizia Park. For the public. It was classic tradition for the new Key Vessels to introduce themselves to the city, to prove their power, to indicate that Estaralla remained as it always would. I went to the show, of course. And that's when I saw that this new Key Vessel had brought his younger brother along with him. A younger brother barely older than I was then, at sixteen.

It wasn't unheard of for the Key Vessel to bring a non-Vessel family member along as liaison to the city. In fact, it was fairly standard practice because the Key Vessels were seen as cold and standoffish to the point of being nearly inhospitable, and for the sake of public relations, a family member was usually a better representative to negotiate with the Board of Merchants, to interview and select tourists.

Even though the new Key Vessel and his brother were under guard, I risked myself and used my magic to slip by the guards and throw myself in front of Antony's path—literally—hoping he would find me intriguing enough to interact with. Or at the very least intriguing—or pitiable, whichever worked—enough to not order the guards to imprison me.

It worked. When I threw myself at him, he offered me a hand, pulled me to my feet. And when I offered to show him the *real* Verigal City, hoping this young and ignorant boy who'd never before left his home island would be interested, he agreed.

From then on, whenever Antony visited the city, he would meet me in secret, I would sneak him around the city, and in exchange, he taught me to improve my magical skills. And he was pretty cute. There was nothing bad about our deal.

And as we practiced, as he held my hands and touched my arms to teach me technique, and sparks flew across my skin, there was nothing bad about our deal.

And when one day I turned my head and found his mouth with mine, there was still nothing bad about our deal.

We started meeting at night, here, in the grove. I would drink in the taste of him, the hint of sugar my family could no longer afford. I would slide my hands under his shirt and focus only on the feel of his muscles, hard and solid and present beneath my fingers. I would focus on his hands roaming over me, slowly unlacing my dress until it fell from my shoulders, and I could no longer feel anything else but the moment. In those times, there was nothing bad about our deal.

Then the Estarallan tour guide position was created, and I saw my whole future opening before me. I'd given him what he wanted, so in turn, I thought he'd give me what I needed.

But instead, he sabotaged my chance.

The final stage in the interview for an Estarallan guide is a demonstration of your glamotura skill for the Key Vessel—and Antony himself. I thought that meant I'd have it easy. I would only have to prove myself to one brother, not both. Antony hovered close to me while I worked, and he took the glamotura I created—a lemon, and I thought a perfectly presentable one—when I finished and walked it across the room to Keelan. I was confident I'd be selected; there was no reason not to be.

Then Keelan called me over and rejected me. The lemon was still tinged gray, like the rock it was made from. It was far too hard, and it had no distinct scent. I demanded to see it because it'd had none of those problems when I handed it to Antony, but Keelan was right about each issue. It was embarrassing, sloppy work I *never* would've handed over.

Antony had ruined it.

Then he refused to admit it.

Then I dumped him.

He has no right to be angry with me. "You make it sound like *I* betrayed *you*. You sabotaged my interview—don't deny it! During the demonstration, my perfectly good glamotura was completely messed up after you handled it. I *saw* you."

He shakes his head. "Lucia—"

"Then you told Keelan that I just wasn't the right caliber for the job. I don't even need to hear an apology, you know," I say. "Just admit you did it and say you'll never do it again, and I'll take that as enough."

"Well, I'm never going to do it again because you're never interviewing again. Not tomorrow—not ever." He crosses his arms, his eyes hardening. "You think I want to spend more time with you? I like you fine enough, Lucia, but don't flatter yourself. I never wanted you to go to Estaralla because I never wanted to subject my family to the girl I was slumming with here. You're a broke city rat, and I'm family to one of Estaralla's esteemed Vessels." The moonlight highlights his mouth, but it's no longer an invitation. It curls in a cruel smirk.

How can he say those things when right before he was looking at me with such hope? Is this really what he's thought of me all along?

"Wow," I say, breathless. He's given me an all but perfect opening with that, but I can't even muster the ability to feel smug through the sting. "Thing is, Antony, I wasn't going to ask to interview tomorrow. I was going to tell you that I'm going to Estaralla. This *broke rat* you were *slumming* with."

He blinks and recoils. "What? No, you're not."

I straighten. "Yes, I am. Don't you know who the tourists are? I am one." As much as he knows what I say is untrue, enough of him believes me. Confusion swirls across his eyes.

"Of course I know, and you're not. It's an ammiralia and her daughter, and don't say that's you because her name is Oriana, and there's no way—" He stops. Understanding dawns.

I smile. Indeed, there's no way it's me. But he's given me what I wanted. Even if I can't get him to interview me again, there are other ways to get that position. The tourists get the final say in all things regarding their tour. If *they* want me, Antony can't reject me. I just have to find them and make that happen.

"Lucia," he pleads. "Please tell me you're not going to cause problems for them tomorrow."

I step back, done here and done with him. "I'm not going to cause problems for them." I bat my lashes. They're going to love me. That's the whole point.

"Why are you so obsessed with Estaralla? Whatever you think it is, you're wrong. It isn't what it once was."

I have no idea what he means. As far as I know, Estaralla is still as luxurious and as exclusive as it ever was. The rich still desperately bribe anyone they can, including the Silverhands, to move them closer to the top of the waiting list.

I throw Antony a final scowl over my shoulder. "Maybe I wouldn't be if I didn't feel my chance had been stolen." Then I march away and leave the memories and the whispering trees of the grove—our grove—behind.

We were so close once. I loved him. And I might've come here tonight hoping that somehow he felt the same. That he would apologize. That we could be close again. That he would help me with what I need to do to save my brother.

But he won't.

So he's nothing to me now but in my way.

CHAPTER FIVE

A massive crowd spills across the dock in front of the bobbing Estar-allan yacht, a cloud of gray desperation smothering them all. The boat rises above, a brilliant white nearly blinding in the sun, with golden trim and golden railings, while the archway over the dock announces in winding vines and flowers that this is The Gateway to Estaralla, as if anyone had doubts. It's a modern yacht, powered by steam, built for a comfortable and exclusive ride to the island for its passengers. Beside it, its Verigal City naval escort bobs, the deck lined by officers with guns not so subtly trained on the dock of hopefuls, a warning should anyone get aggressive.

Even though I don't plan to do this the proper way at all, the sight still sucks the moisture from my mouth until all that remains is the bite of salty air. There are so many of them.

Ever since the Estarallans started hiring glamorists as guides to accompany the tourists last year after one of the tourists tragically and mysteriously disappeared, hundreds of middle-class folks who'd never touched their magic or needed it for anything suddenly started practicing. Of course. Because while they may have owned a profit-able small shop or restaurant or what have you, and never needed to use magic to perform on the street for tips or work for the gangs, they would never be able to save enough money in their lifetimes to be a tourist on the island. The job is their only way to the island just as much as it is mine.

Even if I need it far more.

A man appears by the railing, dressed in as sharp a suit as can be, the tail of his coat snapping in the wind, and a mask covering his face. With gold lining the eyes and fake golden lips, it looks like it might've been chosen to match the boat. This has to be Keelan, Key Vessel and leader of Estaralla, since it's known tradition that the Vessels always wear masks when they leave the island.

While everyone on the island is connected to the magic, the Vessels go through a second ceremony to absorb additional magic, and with that extra power, they run the island. There are seven in total, all descendants of some of the first inhabitants, and the secret of becoming a Vessel is kept within these families, making it not so different, I think, from the hereditary nobility of the Tottian peninsula. The Key Vessel is, as implied, the leader of the Vessels and the protector and maintainer of the magic itself as, according to legend, he or she is descended from the very first user of magic, the duke's secret lover.

No one's ever explained to me why the Key Vessels always wear a mask while visiting the city, while on the island, the Vessels and tourists are the only people who don't wear masks. When I asked Antony, he said stiffly, "It's tradition." Given how short he was, I've since wondered if *tradition* is really cover for something more distasteful. Since the Vessels use powerful magic to rule the island, my theory is that the masks are to hide the cost of magic, like I use my gloves to hide my hands.

"Welcome, welcome." Keelan's voice is airy, yet carries easily over the hum of the people and hiss of the sea. There's a mechanical cadence to his speech, an evenness, a lack of emphasis on any particular word or vowel—every time I've heard him, it's clear within one sentence why the Key Vessels are considered notoriously aloof. "Thank you all so much for turning out today."

Antony slides into place beside him, a taller, angrier form. He doesn't wear a mask but a dark scowl, doing a pretty crappy job performing his duty of being the personable representative to the city today.

"I'm pleased to see so many of you have passed our prescreening tests," Keelan continues, though I must say, unless they altered the tests, they're quite basic, so of course they're easy to pass. There's an actual test on Estarallan history, which is probably the hardest part, a few questions on how you use magic in your life and how extensive your experience with it is, plus a personal statement in which the way to success is to simply wax poetic about how much you wish to see real magic, but that seems superfluous because everyone feels that way. "Please form an orderly line. My brother here will bring you in for your demonstration for me." With that, he claps Antony's shoulder and vanishes below the deck.

The jostling begins, a frantic swirl of bodies like a crashing storm while I stand back and watch. I've got a long time to wait. By underestimating the number of hopeful guides who'd be here, I've underestimated what time I needed to arrive. I alternate between watching the interviewees on the docks, and the crowds milling about the Perla Verigaliana's market, trying to spot the ammiralia so I can approach. My legs grow stiff, and I shift back and forth.

By the time the sun has risen to its highest point and the city clock tower chimes for noon, the line barely looks shorter, and I still haven't seen anyone who's likely to be my tourist mark. My stomach growls as scents swirl over from the market—powdered sugar, baked dough, fried cheese, and tangy tomato sauce.

The food here is horrifically overpriced, but maybe I can bargain for something stale.

I wander toward the markets, passing Verigal City's welcome fountain at the main entrance. It's an ancient marble fountain that's a sculpture of the old god of the sea with water pouring from his hands, enhanced with a glamotura that makes the water appear like liquid gold. A powerful past and a golden future—the image of Verigal City that the Board of Merchants wants all our visitors to take away.

After the fountain, the street opens into a wide plaza lined with food vendors. A quick look around says not a single stall has a line fewer than five people deep, which means they'll never sell to me.

This is the most popular area, of course, so I keep walking. There's a chance, however small and sad, with vendors who receive less traffic. My stomach screams for the small chance with every person I pass who's got tomato sauce dribbling out of their mouth and a box of fried rice balls in hand, a pork roast sandwich with a small slice of the roast dangling, so close to where I could snatch it, or a fried pastry tube with the cream filling oozing right out.

In the next section, I pass a few carnival games, manned by Silverhands glamorists. People can throw knives at fake animals or people—whatever they choose—and if they hit, it bleeds fake blood. It's supremely morbid and supremely popular.

And that's when I see them approaching—a pair of women with dark hair piled high and artful tendrils escaping their updos. One is clearly older—middle-aged with a common Verigaliana golden olive complexion—and the other looks around my age with copper skin a shade darker, but they look nearly identical aside from that. The skirts of their dark green and cream dresses are gathered in the back in a large, artfully draped bustle. Unlike my mother's old dress, theirs are the height of modern fashion, announcing them as women of wealth and importance. But the bright silver epaulets on the shoulders and silver chains crossing the bodice mark them not as nobility, but as a family of the navy.

An ammiralia and her daughter.

And in case that wasn't enough to prove they're my tourists, a man follows closely behind them, struggling with a large traveling trunk.

Time to assess what kind of guide they'd want to see. I need them to love me so much and so quickly they'll tell Antony they want me as their guide without even meeting the other candidates. Then, he'll have no choice but to accept me. No one wants tourists to be disappointed. It's better to break the rules than to let guests down.

The older one walks with her nose in the air with the kind of haughtiness that only money breeds. But the younger one watches the games closely, something hungry on her face, and she lags a few steps behind her mother. And that's something interesting and unusual enough to make her the better mark. The older one will probably take anyone who's deferential and polite, but I can make a connection with the younger one.

I head for her. "Are you interested in playing?"

She eyes me with a cold degree of suspicion. Intelligent, really. "Oh, no," she says. "I was just wondering how anatomically correct you glamorists make the animals. Are they like animal-shaped balloons that ooze blood-like liquid, or do you make them correctly, such that if I cut one open, the muscles and organs would all be in their proper places as well?"

I bite back my outright laugh at the gruesome bluntness of her question, but don't stop the smile. "More like animal-shaped balloons. Most people who play just want to see the blood burst, and it would take more effort to make them anatomically correct. But I can make one for you."

"No, I was just curious." Her gaze flicks ahead to her mother, who's now looking back at us with a curled lip. "I have to be going, and anyway, it would be unbecoming of me to play." She grimaces slightly at the last, and there's my opening.

"It could just be our secret." I lean in slightly, conspiratorially.

"My mother is watching." She starts off, taking long, easy strides despite her thick skirts. I follow, and now alarm widens her eyes. "No, I'm not interested," she says firmly. She thinks I'm a hustler, I'm sure. And I suppose I am, but not in the way she assumes.

I step back, lifting my hands. "Oh, I'm sorry! I'm not working these streets. I didn't introduce myself properly. Ammiraligna Oriana, I'm Lucia Arduini, your tour companion for Estaralla."

She lifts her eyebrows. "You are? I thought our companion wasn't assigned yet, and we were to select her from the finalists today." Then she frowns, probably considering the likelihood I'm not the companion and yet still know her name and where she's going. Thanks, Antony.

"Well, you can reject me if you think I'm unsuitable," I say. "Then another guide will be provided. But I've been selected because the Key Vessel thinks I'd be best suited to provide the ideal experience for your mother *and* for you. Estaralla is a place of dreams, and I'm here to make the experience perfect." I spread my hands wide and beam my brightest smile. Mostly, I'm counting on her being intrigued that I included her in that statement, not just her mother. She has to believe I've seen something in her beyond her wealthy surface and that I'm going to make her tour interesting, too, even if it's not something her mother would enjoy. "I really can make anatomically correct animals for you to dissect, if you want."

"I see," she says, but a faint smile flickers. She then jerks her head. "Mother's coming this way. She booked the tour, not me. She's the one who'll make the final decision on you."

For the ammiralia's sake, I lift my head like Mamma would and pinch my shoulders back as she always does for me. I've worn my very nicest dress today, and for once, I'm glad Mother insisted on keeping *one* nice item of clothing for all of us. It's several years out-of-date, now, and is a plain blue color, lacking the beautiful and delicate embroidery that swirls down the bodice of the ammiralia's dress, or the flowerlike drapes of the bustle, but it looks generally respectable. With my salt-sticky fingers, I tuck the rebellious strands of my hair behind my ear, neat as I can make them.

When she's close, I sweep my best attempt at a curtsy. "Good afternoon, *lumina.*" She gives me such an empty look in return I hastily add, "That is an address of nobility in Estaralla." It's also the best cover I have for the fact that while I know her daughter's name, I don't know hers.

The ammiralia lifts her brows—a brighter mirror of her daughter's expression—and beams at me. "Oh, is it? Good afternoon, little sparrow."

A few of my nerves dissolve with her smile, even if the pet name irks me some. I *thought* she might like to be called a nobility's title.

It's a well-known fact that a perpetual sore point among the

Verigaliano admirals and their families is that, while they have more money than many of the old Verigaliano High Council families, they will never bear the title *nobility* since they're not on the council. Nor can they even buy a seat for themselves on the Board of Merchants, despite being easily able to afford one of those as well. It's explicitly forbidden for the admirals or their families to sit on either of those two governing bodies of the city—separation of power, or some such. Without that political seat, there's continual resentment from the admirals that they are never respected enough. So I'm sure the ammiralia here will appreciate if I lay my flattery on thick.

"Your dress is so beautiful," I say. "I assume it must be custom. Who designed it for you?"

It's a question that would've made Mamma beam and smooth down the folds, but this woman simply sighs. "It was designed by Philipe Meriman. Are you familiar?"

"Yes, *lumina*." Of course I was. Am. When we had money, Mamma used to interrogate me on such topics. I was required to know every big designer's name and what they were known for so I could keep up with conversation at any party I might secure an invite for. "His eye for color and detail is only rivaled by Alessandro Herass." I struggle to keep the monotone from my voice. I know Mamma's correct answer by rote, but that doesn't mean I don't hate it. "But you, of course, add even more luminosity to the dress."

That brings out a small smile from the ammiralia. "Oh, aren't you an elegant little charmer? Who schooled you on designers?"

I shrug and smile. "A tour guide must know such things to make good company, wouldn't you agree?" It's a small thing I still own, the capital of being able to speak these people's language.

The ammiralia smiles back. "Are you our companion, then?"

"Well," I say, even though my tongue is so thick and dry in my mouth it's a miracle I don't stumble over the lie. "If you will accept me, *lumina*."

"Of course!" The ammiralia claps a hand on her daughter's shoulder. "I was expecting someone older, I'll admit, but I find it so thoughtful they sent someone near your age as our companion, Oriana, don't you think? Do you like her?" There's something a little desperate in her tone.

Oriana glances between her mother and me, with slightly narrowed eyes, but then, she shrugs. "Sure, I like her."

"It's settled, then." The ammiralia claps her hands.

Step one, completed.

I extend a hand to the man carrying the trunk. "I can assist. Why don't I just take this the rest of the way?" The uniform he wears suggests he works elsewhere, a private driver, and I'm going to guess he isn't going along to the island.

He passes the trunk over. It's heavy, but I manage to hoist it. For now, I need to appear as a porter so everyone waiting in line will have no reason to stop me or realize I'm sneaking aboard.

It turns out to be a smart choice since glares from those in line still blister my back as I walk past them all, down to the dock and up a plank onto the gilded steamboat. But no one yells at me to turn around.

They'll be even more furious once they find out what I'm really doing. Smugness warms my chest.

Step two, completed.

Only one step left to go: facing Antony's fury.

CHAPTER SIX

While we wait on the deck, I set their trunk down to rest my arms. The yacht sways gently beneath my feet. It's a grand creature—sails stretching tall above us, a smokestack tucked between them for extra propulsion. I pointedly study the gold trimming, trying to determine if it's a glamotura or not, but even my attempt at distracting myself doesn't cancel out the burning stares from everyone down on the docks. While I'm used to conning folks well enough, I usually don't have such an audience, and I'm not sure if the prickling of the skin on my neck is guilt or just nerves.

It doesn't take long before Keelan reappears from below, leading a girl up the sloping staircase. Her lower lip trembles, and she valiantly fights not to cry. Even if she's a rival, the pain in her expression is too familiar to not bring a little pity welling to the surface in me. I've been her.

I won't be her again.

The Vessel approaches and bows deeply to the ammiralia. Up close, the silver of the cuff links on his suit wink. "Good afternoon. You must be Ammiralia Rubellian. And Oriana." The bow he offers the younger one is shallower but perfectly polite. "I am Vessel Keelan."

The ammiralia sweeps a curtsy now that she knows he's important. "It's lovely to meet you—*lumino?*" She throws a small smile my way, and I return it with a nod.

"Let me show you to your rooms." He reaches for the trunk.

I snatch it up. "Let me."

He narrows his eyes. "No need. We will take it from here. You're dismissed."

I widen my eyes, channel all the innocence I can while keeping my insides steel. "But I'm their tour companion." I glance at the ammiralia and nod, a silent plea.

"Yes, we accepted her," Ammiralia Rubellian says, perfect in her ignorance.

Even up close, I can't get any sense of the emotions behind Keelan's mask. His eyes remain narrowed, and I'm sure he's not happy, but beyond that it's a bit like trying to guess if a rock is angry or confused. I don't love it—too much of my entire position involves needing to know what people are feeling in order to play off them, and staring at Keelan, I feel a little like I've stepped into a fog.

But though I can't be sure, I'm counting on him not wanting to argue in front of his customers. He can't want to let them know how foolish they are. That'd be embarrassing—not a flattering start to a vacation of dreams.

His throat bobs as he swallows. "Follow me, then, please." With the same mechanical cadence as always, his voice betrays no emotion either.

I beam at Ammiralia Rubellian and Oriana with all the innocence I've got. Oriana's eyes remain narrowed, not the best sign. Hauling their trunk along, I follow their swishing skirts down the stairs into the ship's belly.

The first area we enter is a sitting room of sorts. Light pours through the open windows, gauzy curtains drawn back, and spills across the couches on the sides. A wooden table with a crystal center occupies the middle of the room, and a painting of a sunset glows over the next doorway.

Keelan opens a door at the end and ushers the two of them in. As I pass, he says, "I need to speak to you. Now."

I smile, nod, and deliver the trunk to the women's room. It's small, but lit by a deep blue light that seems to come from the glass walls. They're full of water and the most beautiful, colorful fish flash around them, as though the room sees straight through to the ocean outside. Amid the splendor of the ocean are two full beds tucked in either corner.

Outside, Keelan clears his throat.

"Excuse me, please." I curtsy. "It was lovely to meet you two. See you shortly." I latch the door firmly behind myself. My game is over if they hear any of this conversation.

"Who even are you?" The sun from the windows catches the gold on Keelan's mask, and it flares bright like a halo around him, though his voice remains stiff and chilly. I wouldn't know from his tone alone he's mad. I can only guess as much from that rude phrasing. And the fact that—well, he probably should be.

"My name is Lucia Arduini." I bob a little curtsy, just for the sake of it. The crystal in the table sparkles at me, tempting in its luxury. I'm so close.

"Why exactly do you think you're their tour companion? I don't even recall your name from the interview list for today."

The corner of my mouth twitches, a smirk threatening, but I force it back. I am polite. I am innocent. I am *not* smug. I need to get

Keelan on my side because Antony is going to be firmly against me. Keelan, even if he may be frustrated with my unconventional approach, won't be blinded by whatever nasty emotions Antony has. And even though I wish I could read Keelan's emotions a little better, as the Key Vessel, I don't need to read him to guess what's important to him. Happy guests and a competent guide. I offer both. "I've been training with Antony for months now. I really thought today would be my day." Vague, but it conveys what I need to: I know Antony and am skilled.

"You do understand today is merely the final step in a process?" Keelan asks. "The interviewers today have already done a written questionnaire with us on some basic information about the island and its history and passed the city's background checks."

"Of course," I say. "I went through those checks months ago. You do maintain the records and allow those who make it to the final stage to reinterview without redoing a new round of the same paperwork, don't you?"

That's enough. "Come with me." Keelan marches me back out of the sitting room, past the stairs to the deck, and to another sitting room, this one without the table in the middle, that overlooks the bow. But we don't stay here. He shifts the rug on the floor, revealing a trapdoor.

We climb down into a hall without any windows, dark and dank as the worst of the tenement buildings. Four doors sit across from each other in the hall, and Keelan raps on one of them.

"Antony, when you finish, I need a word."

Antony pokes his head out. "What? Lucia," he breathes, and his gaze darts between Keelan and me, a caged wild animal. "Oh."

"So you do know her." I'm not sure if I'm imagining the note of interest in Keelan's voice, but I like to think it's there.

"No—I—" Antony starts.

"As I told you," I cut in, "we've been training together for months." I throw a little smile at Antony, and the satisfaction I feel almost blocks the chilly flip of my stomach from the sight of his handsome face bent with fury.

"No, that's a lie," Antony says, but he's so caught off guard it's all too easy to walk right over him.

I turn to Keelan, flashing my smile at him. "Why don't I show you my skill? You can judge for yourself."

"*No.*" Antony steps out, closing the door behind him, and then stands with his arms folded as if that alone can block me. "Keelan, you don't want to let Lucia do anything. I told her very specifically not to cause problems for our tourists today, and, you see, that's exactly what she's done. She's reckless and unprofessional and will inevitably be an embarrassment if we hire her."

Even though I have the upper hand still, it's all I can do to not breathe *wow* in response to that lashing. I can't believe that for so long I thought this boy loved me.

"I'm not causing problems. I'm the best choice for the guide, and I'm here to prove it." I keep my gaze pinned on Keelan. "Just let me show you."

My heart beats heavy in my throat as I wait for his judgment. His mask gives me no hints as to what's coming.

"Antony, does the latest interviewee show promise? Otherwise, I'm going to escort her out." He says it so blandly I barely dare to hope this is success for me. The way he says it sounds more like he's completely forgotten my presence. There's no hint of curiosity, of irritation, of anything.

"Escort her out," Antony mumbles. He stares at his shoes while Keelan skirts behind him, opens the door again, and exits with a young woman whose head is bowed. She knows her time is up, that she's failed.

"Step in." Keelan gestures to me. "I'm going to verify your paperwork as well. Full name?"

"Lucia Arduini." I beam, not hiding the hope that blooms in me. Keelan gives me a single nod and leads the other woman away.

I'm not thrilled to be alone with Antony, so I quickly step away from him and into the testing room. I try to focus on what's there and consider what I can use in my upcoming test—and keep my head clear from Antony-related thoughts as much as I can. It smells rancid. Rotting garbage dots the edge of the room, but that'll make the test easier. There's no way to create something sweet without a vile reality.

"Did you see the line outside, Lucia?" Antony stares at his shoes in the doorway, the awkwardness on his face and in his pose undercutting the anger tearing into his voice. "It's rude of you to be trying to cut in here."

I shrug a shoulder even though he's not watching me. "You're one to talk. A lot of what you've said to me was pretty rude, too. Some might think that makes us even." The words feel good to spit out, a release of the heartbreak I've kept bottled up for too long.

He sighs, posture deflating. "Are you trying to get back at me for saying I didn't want you last night? If I said that was a lie, would you turn around now?"

"No, I would tell you that you're an arrogant ass to be thinking this has anything to do with you—or my feelings about you. I'm getting myself a prime job. That's it."

Antony finally looks at me, glares with darkened eyes, but in their depths, there's more than fury. He looks hurt, of all the ridiculous things to feel. But why should *he* be hurt? He made it perfectly clear last night that he doesn't care about me. Still, it makes my chest ache to see him in pain. I want to feel nothing when I look at him, I should feel nothing when I look at him with how cruel he's been, so why can't I?

Keelan reenters with a slam of the door, steps hard and clipped, even while his voice remains monotone, none of the anger that his movements imply. "The ammiralia is already asking about you. She asked me if anything was wrong, if the 'sweet girl' was in trouble."

I wipe the smirk from my face, replace it with a vacant smile to match that descriptor. "They liked me. The ammiralia did seem so hopeful I could connect with Oriana since we're a similar age. You see, I told you, I'm really the best candidate you have for their companion. Give me a chance, and I'll prove that to you, too, *lumino*. If you don't think I'm good enough, I'll leave without protest. Although I can't promise Ammiralia Rubellian won't be a little disappointed."

Antony bows his head and closes his eyes so his lashes skim the top of his cheeks. Silence stretches, and neither of them say anything.

Finally, Keelan nods. "I'll see a demonstration."

Antony's eyes fly open. "You can't be serious."

"The ammiralia likes her," Keelan says—exactly as I hoped. "Her opinion matters the most. And I, at least, am curious to see what she can do."

I bob a curtsy. "Thank you, *lumino*. You won't regret it." This time, Antony won't be able to ruin my illusion, and I'm far more skilled than I was last year. Working in the stuffy, windowless rooms day after day crafting jewels from rocks for the gangs and night after night in their smoky parlors crafting glamoturas for shows has done something to help me after all. "What do you want to see?"

"What about the fact Lucia has shown she'll blatantly ignore all protocol when it suits her?" Antony demands, still not done. "Do we really want a guide like that?"

"Since her paperwork was indeed in good order, there's no good reason she shouldn't have been on our interview list for today. She's not the only one ignoring protocol." The edge of ice in Keelan's voice is so satisfying I want to pump my fist into the air and scream. Serves Antony right. "Lucia, create an item for me that looks natural. Anything you want. It only needs to be realistic."

I walk to the pile of garbage in the corner of the room, pulling my gloves from my hands because I'll need my skin for this, and pluck a glass bottle out. A thin film of, well, *something* rotted clings to it and sticks to my fingers in turn.

First, I fix the appearance. I reshape the space around the bottle, less like drawing, more like folding the vision into something new. Appearance is easiest to change, of all the senses, even if it also causes the most lasting damage. As I work, the skin on my fingers flakes off, seemingly vanishing into the air. Exchanging a piece of my own beauty for the beauty of my creation. Oddly enough, it doesn't hurt, despite the strange wounds it leaves behind, wounds that leave even stranger scars. As I work, I can see a thin outline of my new creation, like it's overlaying the original.

Touch must be next. It's no good if Keelan holds my flower and feels a bottle. The bottle is firm, and that makes a good start for some soft petals. I focus on its solidness beneath my fingertips and *push* any subtle softness of the smooth glass away until I can no longer feel it, passing all of my sensations of softness into the petal glamotura. My fingertips go almost numb from the sensation, like they've turned to rocks themselves, and that's how I know it's ready.

For the stem and thorns, I select what appears to be a rotting peach from the pile. It collapses between my fingers into mush, and with focus, my fingers feel like they dissolve beneath it, too.

For the final touch, of course, to really be convincing, it needs to smell like a flower, too. I close my eyes and focus just on the stench in the room. The smell is rancid, churns in my gut, and curdles on my tongue. I give up all the sweetness I can smell in the room, which is easy enough when it's barely there to begin with. I don't really have to *push* the magic out of me. It just flows.

Of course, I have no real way to test what I've done. The bottle still smells like a bottle to me, still looks like a bottle, still feels like a bottle, although the annoying squish I feel on my fingers says I did something to it. I have to believe in my abilities. So I do.

I hand the bottle-flower to Keelan. "Done."

He gives an approving nod and twirls the flower. "It's beautiful in appearance." He skims a finger over one of the thorns, and blood immediately springs to the surface. He yanks away, studying the blood welling on his skin before he smears it between thumb and forefinger. Then he takes a sniff. "Very well done. I could believe it's real."

Antony stands frozen, his shoulders stiff and eyes wide with horror.

"Please wait here. We are going to have a word." Keelan catches Antony's arm and pulls him out, shutting me inside alone.

Once the door has been closed, all the nerves hit me in a flood. I let out a sigh while my whole body shudders, and struggle to fumble my gloves back on over my jittering fingers.

It'll be harder to walk away now that I've thrown everything I have into this, tricked my way this far, and come so close to success. To then have to retreat as a failure would be crushing. I've done the best I can to show Keelan exactly what he wants to see, to be exactly what he wants me to be, and if I've not done that well enough now, I'll never be good enough. I'll never be able to get the one thing I need more than anything—the source. And without that, I'll never be able to repay our debt, and I'll have failed my family—Severin most of all. He and I both will spend the rest of our lives locked into working grimy jobs for the gang.

The door opens, and it's Antony again. I lock my hands together behind my back, trying to hide their shaking.

"I hope you're happy," he snarls, low, a caged animal's growl. "Keelan was impressed with your display, and Ammiralia Rubellian still thinks you're a charming girl. You're hired."

A hideous squeal escapes from me, and I smack a hand over my mouth to cover it. It's a good thing, I suppose, that Keelan didn't deliver the news himself because it's such an unbecoming reaction. It's nothing like the innocent tour companion I'm supposed to be.

"You're going to regret this." He scrubs a hand hard over his face, fury rapidly deflating into something more like desperation. "You don't understand. I—*please* don't do this. Please, Lucia, I'm begging you. Go home. Whatever you think you'll find on Estaralla isn't there."

He reaches for me, but I yank myself beyond his range.

"Why?" I say. "Why are you so determined to keep me away?" My voice cracks. I could just as easily be asking him why he stopped caring about me, after all the promises he made.

"It's not—" He cuts off and looks around, as if checking we're alone. Then he says, in a lowered voice, "The island isn't safe."

"Not safe?" I repeat. "Tourists have been going there for years. You're going to have to explain why if you want me to believe that."

Distress twists his expression. "I can't, okay? I shouldn't have even said that. But you have to believe me anyway."

I snort. "That's convenient. Why do you have such a vendetta against me?"

"Lucia." He clasps his hands in front of him like he's begging. "I don't have a vendetta against you. You think I would've done this— *any* of this—if I didn't care about you?"

"I don't see how any of this means you care. Just last night you told me you never loved me at all."

Antony groans. "Because I needed you to stay here where you'll be safe! I didn't mean it. Any of it. I wish you could come to the island with me, Lucia. I wish you could come there and stay with me forever. But you can't, and it has nothing to do with me or what I want. Because if I could—I want *you*." He steps forward and reaches for me, his gaze burning fervently into mine. "I want all of you."

There's a deep, naive and traitorous part of me that's tempted. It would be so easy to fall for this again. I've missed him so much. Missed his beautiful smile and his scent of cedar and summer and the way I used to feel warm and safe inside his arms.

But I can't. As much as I want him, I can't afford the consequences of following my heart here. It puts Severin in even greater danger, and he's already been put at risk because of my love for Antony. If not for that, I would've been on this boat months ago.

I can't make the same mistake twice. Protecting Severin is the most important thing.

"You had me," I point out coldly. "Then you threw me away."

With that, I step around his outstretched arms and march out the door, leaving him alone behind me.

CHAPTER SEVEN

My cabin in the lower deck of the yacht makes my family's room in the tenement building look like a mansion. The thing reeks of fish and mildew, and all that fits is the small hammock, which I can't quite lie flat on. It folds around me, and the crusty salt clinging to the cloth scrapes over my skin—at least, I certainly hope it's salt.

I squeeze my eyes shut because I need to make sure I'm rested, but my heart and thoughts race. I can barely believe it—I'm *finally* on my way to Estaralla. Finally on my way to the source. Finally on my way to freeing my family and myself from our debt.

But I can't tell if the warmth I feel is thrill that I've managed this first step or fury that it took me this long. I should've been on this boat months ago if not for Antony's interference. The image of the hurt in his eyes keeps popping back into my mind, entirely unwanted, because I still, truly, don't understand why, and, more importantly, what it all means for me when we reach the island.

Eventually I'm tired enough that sleep, thankfully, overtakes me.

———————————————

A hand clamps around my ankle.

I shriek and twist to reach my attacker. Antony looms over me, but as soon as our eyes meet he releases my foot and leaps backward with a sheepish downturn to his lips. "Sorry for grabbing you, but you didn't respond when I called your name."

All I manage is a wordless snarl in return. Somehow, the feigned shyness in the way he won't quite meet my gaze only serves to make me more infuriated. I pull my foot back and attempt to curl it under me, but it tangles the hammock, which spins and promptly spits me out onto the floor.

"We're arriving. Thought you'd want to know," Antony says, and then pauses. Maybe he's waiting for my agreement or thanks, but I'm not interested in giving it. I don't want to give him anything while my thoughts are muddled by the morning. I need to have my head on much straighter before I can engage.

I flop over on the floor to show him my back.

Antony heaves a sigh and says, "This is for you."

Another pause lingers. He's really going to make me turn to see what he's offering. I sullenly turn back and sit up, bringing my knees to my chest.

Two eyeholes set in a beige ceramic plate dangling from one of Antony's hands stare back at me. A mask. His other hand clutches a paper.

I snatch the paper first as he says, "This is the Rubellians' schedule for the trip." I stuff it into my satchel and then turn my attention to his second offering: the mask.

Even though Keelan wore a mask in the city, the Vessels and tourists are the only people on Estaralla who don't wear masks. As a tour guide, I've been gifted the plainest of the plain.

"You should wear this at all times on the island. Even asleep."

I take the mask from him. At least it's lightweight, so it probably won't be too uncomfortable, but I eye it with suspicion. "Why would I have to wear it when I'm not in front of people? Isn't it just to be polite?" General rumor says wearing a mask, hiding your face, is a gesture of respect to the Vessels who are "faceless" themselves, whatever that means.

"No. It's for protection," Antony says, so harshly my mouth struggles over words of protest.

"From what?"

Antony curls a hand, a motion for me to stand. "Try it on."

"Why?" I clutch it close to my chest.

Antony scrubs his hand over his face. "Ugh, Lucia, are you going to resist everything I suggest now? To check that it fits properly."

The morning fog is lifting from my mind, but not quite fast enough. Thoughts swirl: *I trusted you. You betrayed me. How are you pretending that didn't happen?* But saying any of that is far too much vulnerability, especially when it's all so irrelevant to his reasonable current request.

"I'm not your enemy." Antony kneels, bringing himself to my level. With the room as small as it is, I can *feel* his presence in front of me, warm and solid, and the look in his eyes right now is softer than anything I saw from him yesterday or the night before. His lips part, and I feel the shudder of the breath he takes.

I shove myself to my feet, away from his gaze. "You haven't given me a lot of reason to believe that recently." Then I fumble with the mask's strings. It's a good use for the energy that's thrumming through me, and one more barrier between us seems like a good idea. The ceramic is welcomingly cool against my cheeks as I press it into my face.

Unfortunately, my shaking hands do a poor job of tying a tight knot in the back of my head, and the mask slips down, pressing heavy on the bridge of my nose. Antony steps forward. "I can help you."

The finger of space between us somehow doesn't stop me from feeling the racing of his heart—or maybe, the pounding is all my own. It certainly doesn't stop me from feeling his fingers skim my hair as he reaches behind me to take the mask's strings in hand. I freeze. My body acts of its own accord, some horrible, base instinct—or, even worse, a memory—and I let his hands bow my head toward him. It's only the mask that stops my face from pressing against his shoulder. It unfortunately does absolutely nothing for the way his scent of summer rain envelops me. I breathe deeply and feel—relief. I could collapse here into his arms so easily. And I wouldn't even hate it.

Not at first, anyway.

Somehow, that weakness is what jolts my control back to me.

"I *do not* need your help," I snarl, ducking under his arms and staggering back as far as I can get. It's not far.

Antony steps back, lifting his hands, cheeks a bashful pink. "Sorry. I—uh, well, if you don't want my help, you should consider asking someone whose help you will accept so that the mask can be snug. Remember, you need to wear it all the time, so make sure it's comfortable."

"Yeah, I remember." The mask dangles awkwardly, askew over my nose at this point, but I don't want to try again to tie it, and I don't want to take it off to give him a view of my flustered face. He watches me too intently, hands still half lifted, as though with enough time I'll change my mind and let him tie it. I flap my hand as a dismissal. "I'll fix it later. You can go now."

Antony drops his hands, and I hate the way my own insides lurch as his hopeful expression falls. "And don't trust anything anyone on the island tells you. You can trust the Rubellians. That's it."

I flap my hand again. "Fine. I'm not inclined to trust anyone. You don't need to worry about that." Everyone on the island *is* going to be my enemy, even if Antony doesn't have the right reason why.

He steps away, but there's not even time for me to take in a fresh breath of clean, Antony-free air when he turns back. "You should also limit your magic use."

"What? Isn't that a large part of my job?" I can't help but snap. He can't think these vague and ominous pronouncements with no explanation are helpful.

"I'm sure you can find a way around it. See you above deck when you're ready." Antony finally exits. I slam the door closed behind him and slump back against the wall.

Maybe I should be more afraid of his declaration of the danger, but I can't get past the nagging voice asking if this is just another lie, another attempt to stop me. I don't get what he's playing at. A person's deepest desires are key to a con, so I'm usually very good at guessing those, but I don't even understand what he wants here. Until I do, I can't trust him.

He has it all wrong anyway. I don't care if I don't make it through the tour. I only care that I make it long enough to locate and take the source. If he kicks me off the island after that, it'll only make my life easier, reducing the number of days I have to keep up my tour guide charade or risk getting caught with my real prize.

With that, I take the schedule he's given me back out from my satchel, unfold it, and place my father's map beside it. My heart gives a little stutter seeing the five days listed out—only five days to manage the impossible—before I smooth the map with a gentle hand to even out my breathing. I blame the messy morning I've had so far for the panic. I knew full well coming into this that timing would be tight.

Besides, Father already highlighted the four areas on the map he personally suspected were most likely to have the source nearby, and several are front-loaded into the first days of the Rubellians' tour. The fact that I'm supposed to visit these places will make my job much easier. Instead of having to find them, I can just test the magic while I'm visiting each of them, see which has the legendary power of the source. I'll have to figure out a way to do it without the ammiralia or Oriana noticing—or if I have to make it obvious, I'll need a cover story for what I'm doing—but those sorts of things are my specialty.

Father's highlighted "Pool of Dreams," which is listed for Day One, tomorrow. Day Two is the "Cave of Ghosts," also highlighted, plus the Island Ball, which is listed to take place at "Teresta's Treasure (palace)." Father has a palace marked, and I can only hope it's the same. The area Father's highlighted that's missing from the tour is "the Forest of Transformation," but three of four at least puts the odds on my side.

Sort of.

There's always the possibility that Father's guesses are all wrong—maybe inadvertently, or maybe on purpose. Maybe Mamma was right, and every single one was selected not because he believed in any but because of the story they allowed him to tell others for his con.

I need some kind of backup plan, but the tour's given me a potential option there, too. At the top of the schedule is listed, "Host: Vessel Dionne," and while I don't know how many of the islanders know exactly where the source of magic is, the Vessels do. Theoretically, they've each visited it and drunk from its waters in the same way all of the original islanders once did, as a part of the ritual that makes them into the esteemed leaders of the island. In the accounts I've read, they all describe touching the source as feeling an electric shock, a burning, a tingling, and a power. Which should make it easy to know I'm at the source once I've found it.

Even if this map doesn't have the answer, my host definitely does. All I have to do is figure out how to get it from her.

The second half of my plan is also shaky. I have Father's enchanted jar tucked inside my satchel, of course, and there's no reason to think they're going to search me when I leave the island. The bigger risk will be if there's too much time between when I find it and fill my jar, and when I get on the return boat. Because these yachts are the only transport off the island. I'm going to have to see the tour to its end to return.

I tuck the map and schedule away, sling the satchel over my shoulder, fix my mask, and make my way to the upper deck.

The room I emerge into is empty, and I follow the mutterings of voices into the adjacent room.

Luckily, Antony's not there. Keelan sits on one side of the table, Ammiralia Rubellian and Oriana on the other. Oriana's dress is plainer than yesterday, a simple dark blue wool, though the diamond-studded buttons on the bodice make sure it still shouts *money*. The ammiralia looks to be wearing a gown of entirely peach-pink lace, which seems an absurd choice to me, but I suppose this is a vacation for her. She lounges on the velvet cushion with a flair her stiff daughter doesn't have.

A feast is arranged artfully on the table. A frittata is the center-piece, with baskets of biscuits and cream-filled pastries placed on either side. Both of the women hold mugs, which must be coffee and steamed milk, because its rich, earthy scent fills the air and makes my mouth water, and I can see the milk foam peeking right over the top.

Oriana spots me first, and immediately her expression drops into a deep frown. A few strands of her dark hair have escaped from her chignon, and they float around her face, glowing in the light in sharp contrast to the dark expression she wears. I'm not sure what I've done to earn it.

Ammiralia Rubellian turns around, following Oriana's scowl with all the sunshine that her daughter lacks. "Good morning, little sparrow!"

The pet name still makes my skin crawl a little, but it's a small price to pay for friendliness. "Good morning."

Then Keelan turns to me, and my heart jumps.

He has no face.

This morning, he's not wearing the mask from yesterday, and now I know what the books meant when they said the Vessels are "faceless." The skin over his face is flat, lacking a nose, lacking lips, even lacking eyes—completely and flawlessly blank. No wonder he wears a mask in the city. People would run screaming. They would be even more terrified of magic than they are. They'd no longer be intrigued, just disturbed. And then they'd never want to visit Estaralla.

He gives me a nod, no real acknowledgment of how *creepy* he is. "Good morning, Lucia." His "face" doesn't move as he speaks, and it sends shivers crawling down my spine. Where exactly is the slightly raspy, monotone sound of his voice coming from? "Please feel free to take some of the breakfast." He gestures at the table. "I can fetch you a cappuccino, too."

Without money, living in the tenement building, I haven't had the luxury of milk in months. I want it, but part of me doesn't really want to take anything at all from him right now. Still, it's not like he's going to give me something that'd poison me, right? So I nod.

A cappuccino would be nice.

He stands, but then quickly adds, "Miss Rubellian, this refusal isn't a reflection on you or even that you aren't from our island. Even we Vessels don't visit the source unless we are inducting a new one of our number."

Then he leaves, and my head spins in his wake. "What was that—" I start.

Oriana sits back, folding her arms, scowling deeper still, and even though she's definitely not going to answer me, the ammiralia quickly does. "Oh! You see, Oriana was curious if the source of magic had ever been offered as a tour destination on the island. You walked in right at the end of the Key Vessel explaining it's not an attraction but a sacred place, only the Vessels know its location, and apparently also, they don't visit all that often either." She beams.

I eye Oriana, who meets my gaze with a dragging reluctance. "You want to visit the source?" I don't know what to make of that, if her interest is something I can use, or something best avoided.

She sighs, picking at a sleeve. "One of my friends—Rita"—she throws a puffed lip in her mother's direction at that—"claims she visited on her tour."

"Well, it sounds to me like Rita is just a big fat liar." The ammiralia strokes the curve of her teacup with a finger. "You really shouldn't let her get to you, Oriana. I swear, just laugh at her, and she'll stop. She only keeps lying because you listen, and it bothers you."

Ah, the drama of the wealthy, always trying to one-up each other with the exclusivity of their experiences or items. I do pity her, though. I remember my friends like that—they were actually the last to drop me after Father disappeared. Everyone else vanished immediately, but they stayed for just one more visit, to ensure they rubbed my fate in my face, before disappearing, too.

I lean back against the wall. It's probably best I don't mention the source again, then, since it sounds like Oriana was never interested in it, just in impressing her "friend." Still, I send her a silent mental *thanks* because, although she has no idea, she's just made my life so much easier. That was information I needed, wasn't sure how to obtain in a non-suspicious manner, and now, I have it.

Oriana and the ammiralia leave to enjoy the air shortly, giving me some time to savor my own cappuccino and quiet. While I could join them above deck, I prefer taking these final moments to myself. Besides, Antony might be up there.

When shouting sounds above me and footsteps pound, I settle my mask back into place and hurry up the stairs onto the deck. The atmosphere has changed, an electric charge running through the air, pulsing with energy. A few of the sailors I hadn't seen yet rush around, and the air rings with their calls of instructions.

I sidle up to the railing beside Ammiralia Rubellian, finishing off the crumbs of what was probably a lunch I entirely missed, and ready myself for my first view of Estaralla.

But there's no mystical island ahead of me. Instead there's a wall of water—a massive, towering wave. And we're heading straight toward it.

My heart skips a beat. That wave is going to destroy us. Even if it doesn't crack the boat in two, surely we'll all be swept off the deck. My luck has never been good, but it seems wildly unfair I'm so unlucky as to have gotten this close to Estaralla only to die at sea.

My gaze swings around the ship. Beside me, the ammiralia clutches her daughter's arm, but Oriana looks ahead at the wave with more boredom than fear, and the sailors around us aren't even bothering to look at it.

And it hits me, though I should've realized the moment I saw it, that the wave isn't real.

This is going to take some getting used to for me. Verigal City, with its tight regulations on glamoturas, forbids them to be outside specific glamotura zones so that no one is ever stuck afraid and questioning reality. But on Estaralla, even I may have no way of knowing what's real or not.

The new knowledge that it's probably just for show still doesn't stop my heart from beating double time as we draw closer, doesn't stop my eyes from threatening to close, and doesn't stop my body from flinching as we hit the image of the wave.

No water slams into me, but the air chills sharply. It darkens all around us to a swirling deep gray. Sharp streaks of white light crackle around like lightning, like we've entered the center of a storm, and even though no droplets touch my skin, every breath I suck in tastes like rain.

Then, as quickly as we entered the dark vortex, we exit. The sunlight is so sharp and so sudden that I squint. And my vision settles into place.

It's a view so perfect it looks more like a painting than reality. The blue of the ocean, the green on the rising hills of the island ahead of us, and the golden sand of the beach surrounding the inlet we're aiming for are all so bright they seem rendered by an artist's hand. The few visible homes are little pops of color among the green, their bright shades of reds, blues, oranges, and purples what Verigal City's homes wish they could be. They're so bright they almost seem to glow like more jewel than house—I can't tell if I'm only imagining it or there really is an added shine there. Far in the distance, iridescent spires with a shifting rainbow sheen rise behind the rolling hills, a reminder that the island doesn't just offer beauty but *magic* as well.

Ammiralia Rubellian releases her daughter's arm and leans forward, hanging on to the railing with a childlike glow on her face. Even Oriana's stiffness relents, a small, uncertain smile tugging at her mouth.

Then a shadow falls as Antony steps up behind me, and my own enjoyment is ruined. All of my nerves seize up, readying for a fight. He wears a strange mask with what looks like feathers all arranged vertically, including fraying edges over the eyeholes. There's an immediate positive to this strange custom—at least I won't have to see his face for the remainder of this trip. But the mask does nothing to hide his tightly gripped fists and stiff shoulders.

A rumbling sounds on either side of the ship. It lurches, and I stumble into the railing. Two silver-scaled sea serpents shoot from the water. They leap above us, dark forms that block out the sun. Ammiralia Rubellian yelps and grabs her daughter's arm once again. I flinch, but the water that should pour from their bodies onto our heads doesn't hit. Makes sense—they're fake. One of the activities offered to tourists is to ride on the back of a sea serpent, which means they *must* be fake, because the real beasts of legends could never be tamed.

The ammiralia releases Oriana with a little laugh, smoothing her daughter's hair down, making sure no strands have slipped astray from her bun, and then her own.

"Excited to be here?" Antony asks.

"Oh, *yes*." The ammiralia spins toward him, clasping her hands in front of her chest. "Where's everyone else, though?"

A bright silver dock juts into the inlet with only one person standing on it. It's too far to make out much aside from the fact she has pale skin, long, dark hair, and a rippling blue gown. But even if our welcome party there is small, the dock itself welcomes us. Water spirals above it like a gateway, a misty rainbow haze surrounding its spray that I've no doubt we won't feel at all when we walk beneath it. And written within the water itself are the words

Welcome, Rubellian Family.

"Everyone else?" Antony echoes. "The—islanders? We allow you a private entrance to the island."

"No, the other tourists," Ammiralia Rubellian says.

"We pride ourselves on the exclusivity of the trips." Antony sounds more annoyed than proud. I wonder if Keelan knows what a terrible advertisement for the island his little brother really is—it can't be the attitude a Vessel's sibling is supposed to have. "Tourists are never double-scheduled. You won't even know they're on the island—except at the Island Ball, of course."

"Ah, of course." The ammiralia's chipper tone doesn't make it into her eyes. "So, who's that?" She nods toward the woman on the dock. Closer, now, I can see the details of her dress—the fabric rippling like running water, a gown of waterfall—and the total lack of features on her face. Another Vessel, then.

"That's your host, our Vessel Dionne Eliades," Antony responds as the boat drifts to a stop beside the dock. The ammiralia loops her arm around her daughter's and pulls her away. I move to follow, but Antony catches my shoulder, darting in to whisper.

"Be polite, but speak as little as you can with Vessel Dionne." Even with his mask on, I can feel his breath against the back of my neck, against the shell of my ear, and I shiver and curl my shoulders away from him.

Another useless warning. That's the exact opposite of what I need to do.

"Don't worry, I'll make sure she's charmed." I turn to him, and even though my mask hides my smirk, he cowers away from me behind his colorful feathers.

"That's not really—" he starts, but the gangplank lowers with a *thunk,* and Keelan's already leading the Rubellian women down to the dock, beneath their welcome archway, so I scramble after them because I won't be left behind. I've got an impression to uphold for the Rubellians—and one to make on the Vessel.

Keelan stops before the Vessel woman and gives a flourish of his wrist. "Cosima Rubellian, and her daughter, Oriana, this is Vessel Dionne, your host."

"Charmed to meet you," says Vessel Dionne, but her voice is tight and nasally—and with the exact same mechanical cadence of Keelan's. She offers both hands to the ammiralia, who accepts them with a stunning amount of stoicism, and allows the Vessel to pull her in and offer a kiss to each cheek with her lack of mouth.

"Thank you," says Ammiralia Rubellian. "We are so excited you've selected us to visit and stay with your family."

"It is my pleasure." Her voice has a certain empty quality to it—more like a bell chiming than human speech—certainly nothing that suggests she even knows the meaning of the word pleasure. I don't like to doubt myself before I've even had the chance to open my mouth, but if I'd had the opportunity to choose, I certainly wouldn't pick Dionne as my mark. "Antony, please escort our guests to their ride. Keelan will introduce me to my next guide girl."

I'm up. I straighten as her blank skin swivels in my direction, and try my best not to let my gaze follow Antony away, even though in the corner of my eye, I see him repeatedly turning back to look at me.

I wish I could see the expression in Dionne's eyes as she studies me, to gain a hint of what she might think of what she sees. She seems like a formal sort, though, so I bob a curtsy for her.

"Charmed, *lumina*," I try.

She doesn't make any noise, and her blank sheet of a face shows no shift. For all I know, she didn't even hear me. My skin itches in frustration. The movement of her watery dress keeps tugging at my gaze, offering something to look at that isn't her empty face, but I fight to meet her lack of gaze evenly. Rudeness or fear isn't going to make her give up the information of the source's location to me, surely.

"This is Lucia Arduini," Keelan says. "Her demonstration was one of the most impressive I have seen in a long time. She is going to improve the island experience, I am sure. We are lucky to have located her."

Vessel Dionne taps the bottom of her face, around where her mouth might've been, if she had one, with a finger. Her skin is smooth—no sign of age anywhere. I'm not sure if she is young, or just as ageless as she is faceless. "And you're very sure she is . . . suitable?"

"You know you can trust me, *lumina*," says Keelan. "You should worry more about Calista than Lucia's competence."

69

"Calista is just fine, now. You can trust me, too." A perfect bite of haughtiness briefly lends humanity to her tone, and she whirls away and glides toward the end of the dock. As she moves, she snaps her fingers, and just like that, the watery archway vanishes. I stare at the empty air where it was—I'd expected something beneath it, the way the Cielonarre bridge is merely painted over real stone, but there's nothing. I'm not sure if anyone else is as impressed as I am by this display, but they should be, because while I know perfectly well how to make a glamotura, that I can't do. Create an illusion from nothing? That's *real* magic.

I can't help the giddy smile that briefly dances over my lips. I'm really, truly, in Estaralla, the land of magic I've dreamed of visiting since I was a little girl.

Then I shake myself loose from awe's grip and scramble after her. Nothing about her says she's going to wait for me if I'm still standing on the dock gawking.

At the end of the dock, Antony waits beside a floating box. It looks a bit like a litter, with waterfall curtains across the sides like the gown Vessel Dionne wears, but nothing holds it up. It hovers in the air on its own.

Despite the way it hovers, the litter stays stable as I climb in, ignoring Antony's offered hand of assistance, and sit beside Oriana. Inside, the water glows all around like we sit behind a waterfall, surrounded by its glory. It smells like fresh water, too, cool and calming.

Vessel Dionne takes the seat beside the ammiralia, and I barely have the opportunity to wonder where their trunks will fit when Antony adds, "You'll find your luggage waiting for you at the manor when you arrive. Have a pleasant journey."

We jerk into motion, an unknown force propelling.

"Do you wonder what this material is?" Vessel Dionne asks, and she skims her fingers over the waterfall curtain. Her nails are shockingly long, filed to little spikes, and they look as though they're plated with gold.

"Of course," says Ammiralia Rubellian.

"We call it silken water," Vessel Dionne says, and I must say, that's not very creative. "If you touch it, it will make your skin look soft and young again."

As a con artist, I like to think of myself as pretty good at spotting a con, and "water to make you look young" has all the elements. Especially as it seems to hit her mark's insecurity with the way Ammiralia Rubellian reacts, sliding her hand through. A good con always appeals to a mark's pride or insecurity—those are the fastest ways to blind them.

The ammiralia retracts her hand then, and it's flawlessly smooth, wrinkles and years erased from her skin. Her mouth opens in soft awe. Mine does, too. It's not a con. This is Estaralla, and such things *can* be real here. Oriana just bites her lip and folds her arms around herself.

I brush my hands over the curtain, curious what will happen to me, and it's a soft, cool touch, not like water at all, no matter how it looks. I'm about to slide my hand through when a sudden sickness snakes into my gut, and I yank my hand back. Bile slides up my throat, and I gag.

All three women look to me, and I press the back of my hand over my mouth. I swallow the bile down. "I'm sorry," I say. "I don't know—"

Oriana touches my shoulder, so swift her touch is there and gone, but at least there was kindness in it. Her mother's eyes are wide, and she shifts a little farther from me. But as swiftly as the nausea hit, now it's gone. And they ignore me again.

Except Vessel Dionne.

She watches me still. The skin over her skull shifts, so there's a crease in the middle of it. Where her mouth might be. A little like a smile.

CHAPTER EIGHT

As lovely as the litter is, and as soothing as the silken water should be, there's a tremor in my hands by the time we come to a halt. I cover it as well as I can, knotting my fingers in my lap. At least the nausea hasn't come back full force, but queasiness still clenches my stomach.

Vessel Dionne exits first, not even looking back for the rest of us. Ammiralia Rubellian pushes Oriana out next, and I follow.

We stand before a golden gate and a golden fence around a mansion behind it. The mansion shines, a clear color that looks like sculpted ice. Around, instead of a green yard, the entire place looks as though it's been bathed in soft flakes of white.

It's like how I've heard snow described, not that it snows in Verigal City. And this can't be snow, regardless, because the air still holds soft warmth. It must be some sort of glamotura created to look like snow without any of the unpleasant chill.

A girl waits beside the golden gate, her hands folded primly, a silver-blue mask over her face. Her matching gown fluffs out from her hips, the design an older fashion much like my mother's dresses, even though the material looks unreal, like spun candy.

"Welcome to our home, dear guests," she says, and as stiff as that phrasing is, her voice is soft and melodic and human with none of the hard edges of Dionne's. Her mask is the most elaborate I've seen yet—a silvery blue with navy swirls across the forehead and beneath the eyes. In each curve sits a small crystal stone, and a few more silver metal strands circle around behind the mask at the base of her neck, like a necklace. Or a chain. Her long dark hair wraps around the top of the metal behind her head, then tumbles down her back.

"My daughter, Calista," says Vessel Dionne, and after Calista's voice, hers sounds even more like a hollow thud.

Cold shocks me. So this is the Calista Keelan mentioned. I wonder why he said Dionne should worry about her. She doesn't exactly look like an object of worry. She looks like a masked porcelain doll. She's easy on the eyes, her voice easy on the ears.

Calista extends both hands to the ammiralia, who takes them with a smile, and Calista pulls her in for the standard two kisses. It's a bit of a familiar greeting to be given to a total stranger, but common enough when trying to imply a closeness, even if a false one.

"What a beauty!" the ammiralia exclaims.

"Thank you so much," Calista coos, although I highly doubt it's the first time anyone has said as much to her. Even though her dress is an older style, I can easily imagine Verigal City's rags writing a gushing piece in the people or fashion section about its fit. She's got the sort of beauty that stops a person in their tracks on the street—the sort of beauty the papers make their darling.

Ammiralia Rubellian flicks her fingers, and Oriana slinks to her side. "This is my daughter, Oriana."

Oriana slouches, mumbles, "Hello."

Calista offers her hands to Oriana in turn, though Oriana looks substantially less thrilled than her mother to receive Calista's demure air-kiss greeting.

"Pleasure to meet you," Calista says to Oriana, and then doesn't even acknowledge me as she turns, takes her mother's arm, and they walk through the gates. The ammiralia and Oriana follow, and I bring up the rear, appropriately.

I shouldn't be surprised Calista said nothing to me. She's here to make an impression on the guests, not me. So I don't really know where the strange tug of disappointment comes from. It seems she's one of those people whose attention feels like a beam of sunlight we all wish we could have for ourselves.

Or maybe I'm jealous. That kind of charisma makes running cons so much easier than having to work to make people like you.

Soft music drifts through the air as we step into the home, although there's nowhere in particular it would be coming from. It's an ethereal sound, somewhere between a woman's whispering voice and a flute, and it hums alone. As I walk, a soothing warmth travels up from my toes to the very top of my head, the sensation of stepping into a hot bath. I have to bite my lip to stop the little sigh—but at least it's not just me. The ammiralia and Oriana both wear small, goofy smiles on their faces.

There's nothing to worry about. It's *fine* if I allow myself to relax right now, to drift away. There's nothing I need to do anyway. There's a distant part of me that screams that's *not right at all*, but it's quiet, growing fainter with every step and every note.

Then, slowly, illness trickles through me, as though it seeps in at my eyes, dripping down my sinuses, down my throat, like contaminated fog. My vision swirls, and nausea builds in the pit of my stomach.

I can't be getting ill. Of all the times for my body to betray me. I want to ask for the night off, to see if early rest can stave off sickness, but this is the very first night of the tour. I can't bail now. I've just got to do the best I can.

Calista ushers the Rubellians through a doorway, but when I move to follow, she thrusts a hand out across the frame. I pause, waiting for whatever instructions she's stopped me for, but the silence gapes between us.

"So, you're the next guide." It's the sort of bland, obvious sentiment stated just for the sake of filling space, and it doesn't match the intensity with which her gaze grips me.

"Uh, yeah." I immediately kick myself internally. That was my chance to make an impression, and instead I'm barely more than a grunting lamppost.

"What did you say your name was, again?"

"I mean, I didn't say it. To you. Uh." Another mental kick to my kneecaps. Picking apart someone's phrasing of a perfectly innocent question still isn't the charming opening I want to have—even if it *is* my natural inclination. "It's Lucia."

"I'm Calista, as mentioned. How are you . . . feeling?"

For this, at least, I manage to get my feet under me and say with all the enthusiasm I can, "Oh, I'm so excited to be here! It's an absolute dream to be able to come to Estaralla—even working." I let out a little laugh.

"Mmm, of course." I'm not sure if I imagine the narrowing of her eyes in the slits of her mask. "Well, welcome to our legendary island." I'm fairly sure I don't imagine the acidic bite in her tone.

She pulls her hand from the frame and offers it to me, palm up. I stare a beat too long, once again reduced to confusion, because it looks like she wants me to give her my hand, and I've no idea why. She greeted the ammiralia with kisses, of course, but that's always a two-hand offer, and besides, she shouldn't offer me such a familiar greeting when I'm way below her in rank.

But even if strange, it is a friendly gesture. And with Vessel Dionne as cold as she is, I could use someone friendly. Someone easier to win over. Someone, who, as the child of a Vessel, well might know where the source of the magic is, and be willing to let it slip to this sweet new friend she's made in a tour guide.

I place my gloved hand in hers.

Smoothly and without a beat of hesitation, she lifts my hand and presses it to the mask's painted lips. Heat from shock floods me, and I'm glad, at least, that my mask hides the way my eyebrows lift and my mouth gapes. I drop my gaze, telling myself, *This is fine; this is Estaralla*. But not only is this greeting reserved for equals in Verigal City; it's also a greeting only a man would give a woman. It's flirtatious.

She releases my hand, and I look again at her unreadable silver-blue mask while my flush slowly subsides. She gestures at the open doorway. "We shouldn't be late for dinner."

My hand tingles, and I absently rub it. But as my gaze drops to my glove, I see far more skin there than should've been exposed. The top of the glove has been pushed down far enough that the edges of my cracked skin peek out and my sleeve has been pushed up. I straighten both, unease coiling in my chest as I do, and my gaze snaps up to Calista. She strides ahead of me, oblivious to my stare. *She* did that, I'm sure, and using a classic technique to distract me so I didn't even notice she was moving my sleeves around as she kissed my hand.

I can't believe I fell for that. This is absolutely not the start I need with my potential mark.

I wonder what she was looking for on my wrist.

I walk into a domed room, the ceiling sweeping above painted a deep, dark blue with glimmering lights like a more vibrant version of the beginning of night. The music still plays, and both Oriana and Ammiralia Rubellian still have their slackened expressions of joy. I think I'm supposed to feel relaxed, too, but my mind just feels fogged and heavy, and queasiness churns in my stomach.

Three chairs are arranged in a semicircle behind a round table, and I'm not sure who the third chair is meant for until Calista heads for a different door. Dionne says, "Please do not be offended; I will not join you for dinner. I hope you will enjoy the food all the same—it is only that I cannot." She taps her blank face. "In place of my company, please enjoy the show."

She snaps her fingers, and sparkling lights spring to life on the wall opposite the table. Then she sweeps herself away. I settle into the third chair and set my satchel on the ground beside me—perhaps this is part of my purpose. To be a host and keep company when our island hosts cannot. In Verigal City, being a good host is a crucial part of one's reputation, and one of the key tenets is dining with your guests. And while Dionne is providing us food, it would be extremely strange for a host not to keep company with the guests. *Good food and good company are the keys to longevity*, they say in the city.

But that seems not to be the case, as the little sparkling light show of mini fireworks holds all of Oriana's and the ammiralia's attention for now. It even holds mine—I barely see flickers of shadows as Dionne and Calista deliver our dishes.

One moment, the table is empty, and the next, it's strewn with all kinds of dishes, the likes of which I haven't seen in years. Or ever. There's a plate of pheasant glazed with pomegranate sauce, grape-stuffed meatballs in broth, a salad of fresh herbs and capers, and, of course, fresh bread that's warm when I pluck it from the basket. It's been a long time since I've seen any food that looks this luxurious, much less been the one to get to eat it.

In the back of my mind looms the pasta and beans my family eats so frequently. Brief guilt chokes me. I wish Severin could be here to eat this with me, too. He deserves to enjoy this more than I do— especially because my queasiness threatens to rob me of quite a bit of my own enjoyment. I hope, wherever he is, he's fine.

I press my nails into my palms. The Silverhands had better not be harassing him already.

My guilt dissolves into only confusion, however, when I grab a forkful and then realize I can't put it into my mouth with the mask there. Feeling quite ignorant, I lift a hand, trying to catch either of our hosts' attention before they leave.

Calista comes over, and I tap the bottom of my mask. "Uh," I say quietly, trying as best I can to not scream my cluelessness to the ammiralia and Oriana if I can help it. "I don't want to be rude."

"Oh. It's fine to just shift it. It's not rude." She reaches out, pauses just a second, and then pushes the bottom of my mask up to expose just my bottom lip. That will work fine for the food, I suppose, but leaves me no visibility.

By the time I twist the entire thing so that I can see out one eyehole while my mouth is still exposed, she's gone.

I'm ready to dive into the food. But as beautiful as the meal looks, my first bite of pheasant is oddly dry and bitter, and my stomach clenches.

I force another bite, but this time, my stomach heaves in full rebellion, and I drop my fork. There's absolutely no way I'm going to be able to continue eating and keep it all down. As it is, my stomach rolls in threat. I close my eyes and take slow, deep breaths. I don't know what the ammiralia will do if she realizes I'm ill. I can't afford to risk being dismissed on the very first night here.

I have to be fine; I have to be fine, I chant to myself.

When the churning in my stomach has eased at least to the point I'm sure I'm not going to vomit right then and there, I open my eyes. It's a shame I'm unable to enjoy this feast—but as I stare at it more, the food begins to swim in my vision. The glaze on the pheasant looks more like a rotten gel across the too-gray skin, and I press my eyes closed again.

Keeping my eyes closed allows me to make it through dinner at least. I open them a few times to check that neither Oriana nor the ammiralia has noticed something's off with me, but the food and show have them thoroughly distracted.

Once they've finished off the food, I briefly fear they're going to want to linger, and with Calista and Vessel Dionne gone, it'll fall to me to entertain them. I poke phrases around in my mind, trying to find the most polite and least suspicious way to say, *I want to just go to bed to see if I can sleep off whatever's wrong with me.* But in the end, I don't need to. The ammiralia wants to retire so she can be completely rested for tomorrow, and as though they'd been listening the entire time, Vessel Dionne and Calista appear in the doorway.

"I can show Lucia her quarters," Calista says, but Vessel Dionne puts a hand on her arm and says, "No, no, please take our guests. I will take the guide."

If I'd felt better, I would've been annoyed, but only relief washes over me as I shoulder my satchel once more. Vessel Dionne is far less likely to try interacting with me, and while I needed to get it together to befriend Calista later, right now I just need sleep. I'd hate to slip into rudeness and blow my chances with her.

Dionne brings me to a closet-like little room far at the end of the hall. "There is no adjoining lavatory," she warns. "But there is a small washbasin for you in the room, and you can use the main hall's lavatory in the morning. There is a chamber pot beneath the bed if you need it by night."

I know it doesn't matter, but still, the insult stings. The house obviously has indoor plumbing. Why dump me with a pot?

"I can use the lavatory at night, can't I?" I ask.

"Mmm." Vessel Dionne gives a pinched hum. "I would not advise it. It gets very dark here, and it is far. We provide the pot for your comfort."

At least I don't really have the energy to scoff, and she leaves me peacefully. It doesn't matter anyway. I just want to sleep the sleep of the dead. With any luck, I will.

I've been waiting for this moment all day. To finally have the opportunity to test the island's magic. To experience for myself the theory Father thought might help direct him to the source: that the closer you are, the easier using magic is. But of course, now that the opportunity is here, all I want to do is collapse.

Still, I only have five days. I can't waste *any* moment.

I yank a hair from my head and then pinch around it in my now-instinctual motion of creating petals because I've practiced *so many damn* flowers in my time. Power hits me like a wave, a flood, crashing down over my head, and I drop the petal, gasping. It *is* a petal lying on the floor now. I can see its hazy outline over my hair, and it's large, and it's . . . glowing?

I drop onto the bed with a shaky laugh and kick the odd creation under the bed. Father was definitely right about that. At least about it being easier to use magic in Estaralla than in Verigal City. I suppose it'll still remain to be seen if I can feel the difference between locations on the island.

As I tuck myself into bed and curl up, I'm all too aware of the slick sweat on my forehead and cheeks beneath the stifling mask. I'm tempted to toss Antony's vague warnings aside and take it off anyway so that I can get some better sleep, but there's just enough of a voice in the back of my mind that whispers, *What if he's right?* that I can't do it. I consider offering up a coin to the goddess of luck and begging to be fine again by tomorrow in return—but I don't have any coins with me, and even if I did, they probably wouldn't be enough to win the goddess of luck's favor.

She really seems to hate me. That, or she's just a childish superstition who has no real power in this world anyway.

Almost as though Fortuna wanted to prove her existence to me with a big slap to the face, I wake abruptly in the night with a hot flash of nausea gripping me. I'm not fine, I'm not fine, *I'm not fine.*

I stumble to my feet, tearing the blankets with me, and stagger for the door. Each step jolts through me, bile rising higher. Maybe I just need to accept the chamber pot, but if I vomit there, and someone sees it when I empty it, they'll wonder why. I can't let anyone know I'm ill in case it gets me fired.

So I fling the door open and run into the hall—or, well, it's more like an attempt to run. I careen into the wall, the world spinning. I manage two more steps, leaning on the wall, and then my stomach contents force themselves past my lips. Tearing my mask from my face, I bend and retch.

Little comes up, just a strange, inky dribble of something thick and dark and viscous. It tastes deep and coppery, a little like blood, and I wipe my mouth while tears sting my eyes.

The hair on the back of my neck prickles. I'm not alone.

I spin.

A shadow flickers, warped against the wall at the end of the hall. And it's gliding in my direction.

CHAPTER NINE

Panic flares in me—there's a very primal terror in seeing a shadow approaching you in a dark hallway in an unfamiliar home. I straighten, attempting to order my body into behaving because no matter who it is, I can't be caught. If anyone finds me ill, it's the end of my tour. And the end of my chance for the magic.

This sort of sickness is so common from the filth of the slums. I have plenty of practice working while queasy. I can do this. I can hide it. As long as I'm not caught right here, right now.

My stomach lurches in protest, and I retch again.

So much for running.

The shadow draws closer, shape solidifying into Calista's silhouette. She drifts toward me, so smoothly it's like she floats above the floor.

"I am so sorry about this," I croak as I hold my mask in place over my face, a not ideal attempt to take control. Of all the options, Calista's probably the best. I just need to convince her not to tell anyone else about this, and it'll be fine. "I don't know what's happened. I'm not really sick. I mean, I was completely fine before I boarded the boat—I think the sea messed with my stomach."

Calista stops beside me and seizes my free hand. This time, she doesn't bother to hide it when she yanks my sleeve up and stares at my skin.

"What are you looking for?" I ask.

Calista lets out a huff that might be relief and drops my hand. "A sign of a . . . bad illness. But you're fine. For now."

I lean against the wall, shaking while I redo the ties on my mask, not feeling *fine*.

"Don't eat anything else." She kneels on the floor beside the inky vomit, her thin night robe fluttering around her with a grace entirely unsuited to this ugly situation. She pinches the space on all sides of the inky stain, folding it right into the plain walls, making it invisible. She has real talent for magic to have done that so quickly. Maybe that's just how everyone is here on the island.

I wonder what else has been hidden that swiftly.

"Why?" My throat is aching and raw. "This can't have been the dinner. I felt sick before it, and besides, I assume the ammiralia and Oriana are fine." They'd better be, anyway. I need this tour to continue.

Calista stands, running her hands over her robe. Even though it's a casual, loose garment with no more form than a sash at her waist, she still manages to make it look elegant. Then it hits me—it's odd and quite rude to be staring at this girl I don't know *in her night-clothes*, so I force myself to look at her face.

Or, well, mask. Because she's still wearing one, too. So Antony's advice to wear them even at night maybe isn't that strange after all.

"Some people—well, they don't react well to the food here on the island," Calista says. "You're one of them, I'm sure."

"Why are you sure?" I demand because something about this isn't really adding up.

Calista gestures at the wall, now perfectly pristine, no hint of the nastiness that's sitting there in what should've been plain sight. "The color of the vomit. You just have to trust me on this. *Please*. Don't eat anything I don't give you. And no one else can know about this. Any of it. Don't tell anyone you were ever ill, don't tell them I warned you away from the food, and don't let them see you're avoiding it."

Luckily, I'm not exactly inclined to repeat any of what's happened to anyone else, but none of my many reasons should concern her. "Why? What'll happen then?"

"Nothing you want to experience." With that, she retreats into the darkness.

Don't trust anything anyone on the island tells you, Antony's voice whispers in the back of my mind, and I don't trust Calista, not really, but I also really need to find a way to not continue to be sick.

I can give her advice a try without trusting her.

The next morning, I wake with a heavy tension in my stomach and a tickle in the back of my throat. I have to sit at the edge of my bed a few moments and gasp for breath before I can stand.

A small and very hard piece of bread waits for me on a plate along with a note in front of my door. I wrinkle my nose because whoever set it there must've opened my door while I slept last night, and that's creepy.

The handwriting on the note is neat and tiny.

Eat. This will help. —Calista

I need *some* food to make it through today, so I obey, and at least I don't vomit again. As long as what she gives me doesn't make me sicker, I'll continue to take it. Then I dress for the day in the provided outfit: a white blouse, traditional red-and-green flounce skirt, and white apron, tying the fitted bodice as loosely as I can.

Breakfast is held outside at a small table in a courtyard. Weeping trees bend around us, rustling in the breeze. They're a stark contrast against the white ground, and a fountain in the center glitters like gold. Dionne is nowhere to be seen, and even though it's clear already her absence doesn't mean the same as it would in Verigal City, I can't help but feel as though she's being extremely rude. But we're not completely unattended.

Calista lounges in a nearby hammock, swinging back and forth and humming. Her long hair spills over the sides, unbound, and as the light passes through, it ripples between dark red and brown and back. It's pretty—somewhat entrancing, even. Any of the ladies in Verigal City would love to know how she's made it look so soft, I'm sure. A very odd, very small part of me wants to touch it to see.

Oriana gulps down the first few bites of her peach-stuffed crepe. I don't miss the scathing look her mother shoots her, and neither does she. After that, she slows, picking the dough into shreds with her fork.

I resort to the safest and dullest line of conversation I have to fill the space instead of eating any of the food myself. "Ammiralia, your gown today looks different than any designers I'm familiar with. Is it someone new? Who's designed this one?"

I barely listen to her response. The point isn't to listen. It's to get her talking.

Calista drifts over and places a small cup of espresso in front of me. She bends close to me, her mask brushing against my hair and sending a shiver down my spine. "Even here, everyone knows no breakfast is complete without it."

It's an innocuous enough statement, so I'm not exactly sure why my face flushes. I sip the drink—can't not after that—and it's strong and bitter. If I wasn't feeling off already, I'd probably appreciate it, but now it curdles a bit in my stomach. Still, with the bread and espresso in me, I'm gradually feeling less and less shaky.

After a time the ammiralia mostly fills with her thrilled chatter about the latest designers, Vessel Dionne reappears, as good a signal as any the meal has ended. She leads us back out the front to the same litter as before.

"It will take you to the Pool of Dreams," she promises while she twists her fingers in the pouring curtains and smiles, an expression as sharp as her pointed nails. She pats the top of it, like it's a pet. "It has been instructed."

Even though I fully knew this was our first stop because of the schedule, the words still send a thrill through me. The Pool of Dreams might just be the source. This might just be *it* for me. While Oriana and the ammiralia bathe in the pool, I, of course, dutiful guide, will monitor them outside. And while the pool engulfs their senses with their dreams of whatever they want most, my own actions will be completely unmonitored. I'll be free to take my enchanted jar, fill it, and tuck it away again well before they exit the pool and return to reality. It would almost be a too perfect opportunity.

Ammiralia Rubellian keeps her face pressed against the silken water curtain throughout our whole ride. Oriana picks at the curtain with a finger for a while, then scoots herself to the center and sits with her arms folded.

I can't let my rising hope take over my logic, though. The chance the Pool of Dreams isn't the source is greater than the chance it is. So I squint, attempting to peer outside to gather more of my bearings here, but the rippling of the water thoroughly obscures whatever we're passing. While the Pool of Dreams is marked on Father's map, Vessel Dionne's home isn't, and I could really use the understanding of where exactly my home base is on the island. That's real misfortune for me—though at least my mask hides my irritation.

We glide to a halt, and I step out first. It's one of my major duties as companion to prepare their destination, to ensure it looks as it should, and make their experience as perfect as can be.

We're alone in a grove. The ground rises in front of me into a sharp cliff from which a waterfall tumbles, the pool at the base such a bright blue it nearly glows. It's not as large as I expected—a size fit only for lounging, not for swimming. A soft mist rises from the waterfall, and the air rings with the buzzing of insects and the distant shrilling songs of what I think are birds.

I unfold their schedule and review the instructions for this location: It is a natural pool in a jungle-like setting. Ensure vegetation is vibrant and thick and water is clear and pure. A cliff is behind with a pristine waterfall.

I frown. So, basically, the scene is already set. I have no real purpose here. I suppose, if this is what I'm going to get the whole time, I will easily be able to follow Antony's order to limit my use of magic. Maybe he even knew this.

But in that case, what *am* I here for?

I kick aside the creeping sensation across my skin that follows that question. It doesn't matter why I was hired as a guide or what my role is supposed to be anyway.

And I have a few moments to myself, since as far as the ammiralia and Oriana know, I am getting the area ready for them.

Removing my gloves, I approach the pool's burbling blue liquid, barely able to breathe because it would just be *so lucky* if this could be the source, and my journey could simply end here.

I kneel beside the pool and dip my fingers into its water. They feel . . . wet. The source should have reacted to my skin. The accounts of those who took it into their body, all of those years ago, describe it as stinging and burning. Still, in case that information is wrong, I do a tiny test, create just the visuals of petals in my palm. I'm ready for the gushing flow of the way the magic strikes me this time, and it's still just as easy, but it doesn't feel different than at Vessel Dionne's home.

Fair. I suppose it would've been mighty bold of Estaralla to really allow all its tourists to bathe in its precious source. Pool of Dreams is off the list.

"It's ready," I announce, and slide my gloves back on.

Ammiralia Rubellian and Oriana exit the litter. The ammiralia's eyes grow wide as she takes in the view, perfectly entranced as she should be. Oriana fidgets, gaze darting.

I gesture toward the pool with my best performer's flair because even if I know I'm a useless accessory here, they don't need to know it, too. "Welcome to the Pool of Dreams. Better than any hot springs, you'll find the next level of comfort here. While relaxing in the pool, you'll live the moment you want most to live."

As I say the words, even I can't help but marvel a little at the possibilities. I've done many a glamotura show for the Silverhands in the city, and it's not like this at all. I can use the magic to reshape everyone's five senses, but it's a little like staging a play, and everyone sees my work the exact same.

The fact that, here, the magic can be set to interact with each individual separately, play off their own emotions, their own wishes, their own fears, well, that really feels like *magic*. And it could have far more dangerous applications.

It's little wonder that when Father promised the Silverhands the source, they fell for the chance so they too could create this level of magic.

Ammiralia Rubellian sucks in a sharp breath and hurries for it. She glances back at me once. "We won't be bothered here, will we?"

"Of course not," I say. "This is ours for the day."

"Help me remove my dress, then," she commands, and I obey. I lift the metal cage of epaulets from her shoulders and then untie the bodice's tight knots that keep her contained. She unfolds from it, sighing when she steps free, and descends the steps into the pool in her chemise and drawers and sinks neck-deep into the water.

"Can we see each other's dreams?" Oriana stops at my side to ask. Her voice rings low, barely audible beneath the hiss of the waterfall.

"I don't think so," I say, and she presses her lips together.

"I need to know." Her gaze flicks to the pool where her mother's already sunk in. "For sure."

This is hardly the first time Oriana's expressed discomfort with her mother on this trip, though most of the other times have been no more than fleeting glances, but it is the first time she's given up the hint why.

"You won't." No accounts I read said anything about that, and plus, this is one of the most popular tourist attractions. There's no way that would happen and not have been mentioned anywhere. I can't imagine it would be as popular if everyone saw each other's dreams. That could definitely lead to awkward moments.

Oriana's lips thin. "You're just saying that. You don't know for sure, do you? That's fine. I don't care enough to participate. I'm just going to sit out." She settles on a rock, placing her chin in her hands. She looks so uncomfortable, so out of place in the lush greenery and humid island air as her gaze sweeps the area over and over. She still wears her thick gown with gleaming metal pressing down on her shoulders, chains draping down her back, the velvet dragging in the dirt, and her constrained chest heaves. Sweat beads at the top of her forehead and around the edges of her collar, and her eyes glisten as she watches the pool.

The curiosity that rises in me is like an itch. I really can't figure out what would be so bad she doesn't even want to take the chance of her mother seeing. And Oriana may not be my first target on this island for information, but having a little blackmail to hang over someone's head is always useful. I could foreseeably need her to help or for her to cover for me at some point.

"Your mother would hate your dream so much?" I sit beside her, the edge of the rock scratching my back.

She laughs, shrill and pained. "You have no idea."

"You could tell me." I nudge her shoulder. It's meant to be friendly, but she turns away.

"I don't know you."

I've pushed too far for now, so I don't try again. We sit in silence. I close my eyes, focus on the sharp whistling of what I assume are birds, and the whispering of the waterfall. The air is thick and warm and wraps me in a suffocating hug. Sweat collects along my collarbone, along my forehead, beneath my hair, an irritating prickle.

It's more rotten luck for me that Oriana refuses to get into the pool. If she were distracted along with her mother, I could have a little wander around the area. I don't think the source is here, but that doesn't mean I couldn't experiment a little with the magic to see if I could determine which direction it's coming from.

"Well, while we're sitting here, I can put on a show for you." I wish I could conduct tests while moving around to slightly different locations, but I'll do what I can. "What do you want me to make?"

Oriana waves a hand in dismissal. "I'm not interested. I don't mind just sitting with my thoughts."

At least she can't see the way my lips twitch in frustration beneath my mask. "It's my job to provide you with a satisfactory experience, *lumina*."

"If anyone asks my opinion, I'm happy to tell them you are." If it weren't so currently disruptive to my plans, I might've respected the cold practicality infusing her words. But I suppose if she truly doesn't care what I'm doing, maybe I can do a little exploring anyway.

"Will you tell them as much even if I take a little stroll around the area? I want to . . . familiarize myself with all of it so I can offer an even better experience on my next tour."

Oriana flicks her hand. "Of course. Go ahead."

I wander to the edge of the clearing, where there's such a knot of brambles it almost looks like a fence, and then look back to Oriana just to check once more. She flicks her hand again, and that's good enough for me. I shove my way into the crush of branches, so thick it almost feels like they're trying to push me back, push me out. It means I don't quite get the distance I want from the clearing before I lose patience. I need to stay close for the ammiralia's exit.

I fold petals from nothingness into my palm again, concentrating with everything I have on the sensation, trying to stem the flow, trying to feel something, anything to tell me the direction. My vision narrows, everything but what matters—the petals—growing blurry, until there's nothing left in my world but them.

"Lucia!" Oriana's scream abruptly shatters my focus. "Help!"

Terror seizes my chest with a cold, tight hand. If anything's happened to her, if anything's happened to the ammiralia, my time here is up. I hoist my skirts and sprint back to her, fast as I possibly can through the underbrush. I never should've wandered away.

I break through the thicket, and my stomach lurches.

Oriana's not alone in the grotto anymore. A girl staggers toward her, black veins crisscrossing her face and arms, nearly popping from her skin. Under her feet, the vivid green grass crumbles to brown ashes.

I rush forward between the girl and Oriana, a shield I'm not really sure I want to be. The girl stops walking, lifts her hand in my direction, and her lips part. They're black as her veins, and my heart races because I don't want to hear what she'll say.

I don't get to.

Darkness pools in her eyes and drowns her green irises.

Then her eyes burst, black-red liquid pours from the sockets like bloody tears, and she collapses.

CHAPTER TEN

My heart rises to my throat as I bend and jam my fingers into the girl's neck. I don't know why I bother. The dark ooze from her hollowed eye sockets dries swiftly on her cheeks, crusting already.

No pulse.

I sit back.

"What's wrong with her?" Oriana whimpers behind me.

I whirl. I'd forgotten I wasn't alone. Oriana's still here. So's her mother. The only small mercy is her mother still floats in the Pool of Dreams, oblivious to all this gore.

"Is she dead?" Oriana gasps. "What do we do? We need to go back to Vessel Dionne right now."

Oh, no, this isn't good. People—rich people—come to Estaralla to see their dreams come alive. To see magic. To see beauty. To feel young and alive and happy.

No one comes to Estaralla to see dead people.

"We need to tell Antony and Vessel Keelan," Oriana rattles on. "I wonder if we can get our money back."

My mind races while Oriana's shadow above me fidgets. If the tour ends, so will my time here. I can't go back now. Not yet.

I won't go back.

I can't let Oriana tell anyone about this. I wish I could just erase her memory, but—well, this is an island of illusions. Maybe I can convince her this is one of them.

I take one last look at the girl, my own panic and desperation screaming this can't *really* have happened. This girl can't be real; she can't be dead. I would also like to believe she's just a glamotura.

Her eyes are sunken black pits, cheeks streaked with the stains of it. Her lips are pale, chapped, and open over her final words. My stomach heaves, and I have to briefly look away.

She's most certainly dead.

I look at the rest of her, avoiding her face this time, studying her white blouse and apron. And red-and-green flounce skirt. In my initial panic, I didn't even notice her entire outfit is identical to mine.

She is—*was*—a tour guide like me.

A chill sinks through me. I'm not sure if that's just a coincidence or if it means something awful, but I can't dwell. Right now, I've got a tour to save.

I rise, slowly and solemnly, and turn, holding my hands out. Somehow, they don't shake. "I've seen this before."

People come to Estaralla to live magic. To dance with the Vessels and bathe in beauty and pretend they're even more than they already are.

Some come to be heroes. They come to ride the backs of sea monsters or climb across rainbows in the sky or battle monsters of legends.

Obviously, that's not at all the tour Ammiralia Rubellian booked, but Oriana's already shown she's very much not her mother. And I've already implied, too, she'll get a different tour as a result.

I set this up even without meaning to. Now, all I have to do is deliver it.

"I told you your tour would be different, see?" I wink. "There's a monster that haunts the island." Shows and stories are better with monsters. They feel safer when the villain isn't human, when the villain and hero are nothing alike, and it's clear which is which. "When it kills its victims, their eyes bleed like this." If she thinks it's part of a story, perhaps she'll doubt this girl is real, that she was *really* alive and *really* now dead. That's better.

"Is that so?" Oriana's eyebrows lift, but there's some level of interest within her skepticism.

"Of course," I lie. "And I think we can catch the monster. If you want to, that is."

"How?" Oriana asks, but her hold on herself is loosening. I have her attention, and I've diverted her from the real panic. I just can't lose her now.

My brain stumbles for an explanation, one both believable and advantageous, and while my vision goes blurry, the dark streak left in the girl's wake sears across the swirl of the rest. "The last time they caught the monster, they found its lair by following the trail it leaves behind." I gesture to the scorched grass. "It kills everything it touches, you see. So it's easy to track."

The scorch will also be easy enough for me to replicate to lead Oriana wherever I want to go.

While I speak, the potential of this storyline unfolds in my mind alongside it. Maybe I don't need to lose Oriana and her mother to go to the source. Maybe I can trick Oriana into coming with me, a wealthy shield and potential alibi should we be caught. She can flash those diamond-laden wrists of hers and say innocently, *Oh, we're not trespassing; we're here because it's part of my tour!*

Oriana nods. "Should we follow its track, then?"

"Not yet." I bite back a nervous laugh. I'm glad she's eager, but I'm far from ready, and I really don't think I do want to know what waits at the end of the trail of death left by the girl. "We need a weapon to fight it first, don't we?"

Oriana's lips part in an O. She nods quickly.

"We'll get one." I hold out a hand to her. "And train you, if you want to be the one to kill it. Kinda like throwing a knife at a fake animal, right? But better."

She takes my outstretched hand and squeezes tight, a promise between us.

I have no idea if it'll be one I can keep.

"We probably shouldn't tell your mother." I glance back to the pool. The ammiralia floats still, face tilted up to the sky, and her expression is so slack it should bring me comfort, but it only makes my heart give a little skip because she doesn't exactly look alive in this moment either.

"I won't tell her," Oriana says sharply, and I smile. Of course, she would like this. Another secret from her mother. Something that can belong to her alone, something her mother wouldn't approve of.

"This stays between us, then," I say, and Oriana grins. The horror of this, of the corpse at my feet, has been wiped away. For her at least. My blood still rushes like lightning through my veins.

It's time for me to hide the girl. I grab her by the shoulders, and an unnatural cold quickly seeps through my skin. Death oozes from it, a sickening taste flooding all my senses. My mouth goes dry, and a thick stench of rot blooms in my nostrils.

Briefly, I wonder, if I *pushed* the magic now, would it bring her back to some kind of twisted life?

I'd rather not.

Instead, I haul the body off to the trees and out of the path so I don't have to bother with adding a tactile glamotura. I fold a visual of foliage about the body, hiding it from sight. I still see it, of course, but Oriana gives me a nod. "I don't see it anymore. Shall I get Mother? Is our time here done?"

I nod. I think we're cutting our time here a little short, but I'm not interested in sticking around to see if something else is going to come stumbling into our clearing. Better to return to the Eliades Estate where I'm slightly more convinced nothing bad will happen.

Oriana squats by the side of the water and awkwardly heaves her mother from the pool. The ammiralia lies on the grass a few moments, focusing, and then she lets out a soft sigh.

"That was lovely. Oriana, did you love it, too?"

Oriana glances at me, and a smile plays on her lips. "Yes, Mother. Actually, I did."

When the floating litter returns us to Vessel Dionne's mansion, Calista waits for us at the gate.

"Welcome back." She bobs a curtsy as we exit. "Did you enjoy your visit to the Pool of Dreams?"

Any words I might have stick in my throat, but luckily, it's not me she's asking.

"It was lovely." Ammiralia Rubellian beams. "Have you ever visited?"

"I haven't." The top half of Calista's face is covered in a new, delicate metal half mask, the portion beneath colored to match the golden olive of her hands. But when she speaks, the bright red lips don't move, betraying that the part beneath the half mask is still not real. "But I don't need to. I already live the life of my dreams." If her voice were a pastry, I'd gag on that sweetness.

The ammiralia inclines her head. "A lucky girl you are, then, as well as so pretty."

"How could I be anything but grateful to live on Estaralla, island of dreams, and have the chance to serve my island and its magic?" I can barely believe this is the same girl who spoke to me in the dark last night. Her voice doesn't even sound the same, all breathy and light, now.

"Your mother is lucky, then, too," the ammiralia says without a second glance at how Oriana's face crumples at those words. But I notice. So the ammiralia and Oriana clash over whether or not Oriana is grateful.

Calista opens the gate and motions us inside. I go last, as always, and she touches my elbow as I pass, a ghost of a touch that makes me shiver.

"How was it?" she asks me in her low voice again. "Any problems?"

A vision of the corpse with its bleeding black eyes flashes in my mind. My mouth goes dry. But I won't reveal the truth. I've got it under control. I don't know what Calista will do with the information. I don't know why she's asking in the first place.

"No, it was fine." I glance back at her. Her mask hovers

shockingly close to mine, close enough I don't miss the way her eyes narrow in the slits. "Why, should there have been?"

"Of course not," Calista says, but she's back to speaking with her breathy coo. "We just like to check in with our esteemed guests."

I don't believe that, but if I continue to push, I doubt she'll continue to believe that nothing happened. And I'm not ready to let that slip yet.

CHAPTER ELEVEN

Ammiralia Rubellian and Oriana take turns in the bathhouse with its magically heated water and glass-like walls that somehow allow no sight of anyone enjoying those waters from the exterior. As I'm hovering outside, waiting for Oriana to finish so it can be my turn, Calista takes my arm. "Let me show you somewhere else to bathe."

"I can wait," I say because that's the polite thing to say, but I do my best to infuse my words with a sort of reluctance that'll hopefully betray that if Calista has a different option for me, I'll take it. Any moment I can spend alone with her is to my benefit. I've got a lot of work to do to make sure I win her as a source of information.

"No, this will be better," Calista says, and I gladly let her guide me down the hall.

The door she opens leads to a small bedroom. It's shockingly plain, the plainest thing I've seen here yet. There's a basic wooden bed with what's clearly a handwoven quilt—the imprecise stitches give it away—and a bookshelf lined with so many books that some sit on the floor in front of it. The titles are eclectic and random: *Basic Yzzeran*, *World's Deadliest Creatures*, *Seafaring*, *Best of Alia Merantis*.

It takes a moment for it to click. "This is your room."

"Mm-hmm." Calista's already tugging me across it quickly to a tiny washroom attached, but this is an opportunity to understand her I don't want to pass up.

"It's so—" I start, then realize it might be rude to call it plain. "Uh, you don't have glamoturas?"

"Nope," she says cheerfully with a note that might even be pride. "None at all. You're forgetting—for you, glamoturas are rare, but here, they're ordinary. Here, the rarest thing of all is something completely real." She pushes the door to the washroom open. "Even the water in my tub is unaltered. Sorry, it'll be pretty cold as a result."

I dawdle in the doorway. Aside from its plain nature, there's little to comment on to get her talking. Except the books. I consider commenting on Alia Merantis's poetry—after all, I've read plenty because even when I was a ten-year-old child, Mamma made sure I knew who the famous artists were. To be worldly was a critically desirable trait in a merchant's wife.

Looking at the books, I feel like I'm back in the society I barely missed out on, trying to decide which comment will make me seem the most sophisticated. But everyone knows Alia Merantis. The Yzzeran is more interesting, more unusual. It's both something that will make me seem more impressive and yield something more specific about Calista. It's not one of the standard trio of languages I was schooled on, but I once sold fake Yzzeran silks and learned a few somewhat random phrases to be able to pretend to be a merchant with proper Yzzeran connections. So even though I can hardly hold an ordinary conversation, I launch in as best I can in Yzzeran, "I don't mind. The cold brightens the soul."

Calista blinks, and I realize perhaps she hasn't actually read the books on her shelves. I don't exactly know why she has them.

"Uh," I say, and go simpler. "Do you speak Yzzeran?"

"Oh!" Calista lifts a hand to her mask. "You actually speak Yzzeran?" She asks it still using our shared Tottiano language, but her voice has brightened.

"Some," I say. "Not perfectly, but I've met Yzzeran traders in the past."

Calista laughs. It's a light sound, but with an entirely different tone than the sugary laugh she uses around the ammiralia. "Oh, you're so lucky. I feel so silly now. I didn't even realize what you were saying. No one's ever tried to speak Yzzeran to me before. There've been a few Yzzeran tourists on the island, but they've never stayed with us, and even if they did, tourists from beyond the peninsula always bring along a translator, so I doubt they'd bother trying." With her mask, it's rather hard to tell because her outer appearance is as flawless as it ever is, but the high pitch of her voice, the way she's sped up speaking—I think I might have embarrassed her.

"You could always try speaking to them first," I say.

Calista shakes her head swiftly. "I don't think so. I'd only make a fool of myself." She marches into the washroom and flips the faucet on the tub. She's trying to get rid of me. I've misstepped.

"How come you have that book, then?" I ask. "Was it a . . . gift from someone?"

Calista breathes out, the sound turning at first from sigh to heavy hiss and then back again. She bows her shoulders, setting her hands on the edge of the tub. "You sure ask a lot of questions."

Big misstep. I want to appear friendly, not pushy. I flip through options, but I think backing down now will make it seem more calculated, not less. Without entirely meaning to, I've roped myself into a chatty persona, so there's only onward with the act now. "I'm sorry. I can't help it sometimes. I just love learning what makes people tick." It's not even a lie, even if it's only interest in learning to better manipulate them. "And your books are such an interesting collection I thought there might be a story somewhere in there."

"Mmm." I'm noticing she uses this hum as a response somewhat frequently, though I'm not sure it's a good response, and she stares into the tub as the water rises.

The rising water seems like time slipping through my fingers, but I hesitate, grasping for what might be a safe topic to keep prattling on about without annoying her more.

She spares me, giving another sigh, releasing her hold on the tub's edge and straightening up. "There's no interesting story around that book. I bought it at the market. So what about you and those Yzzeran traders?"

Not ideal, but if I refuse to answer questions about myself, it's not exactly going to encourage her to share more about herself. I force a laugh. "Oh, well, that's not that interesting either. I've done work as a—merchant of sorts—reselling goods, and, uh, I worked with some Yzzeran traders to sell their silks. They didn't like me too much, though. Didn't think I got them good enough prices."

"Not that interesting?" At least a little energy has returned to Calista's voice. "But how did you meet them?"

"They had a stall in the Perla Verigaliana. It wasn't doing well, and so I approached them with my own offer." I shrug. It's close enough to the real story that it's easy to tell. I *did* meet Yzzeran merchants at the Perla, chatted extensively with them trying to learn how to pretend to have been working with them. That they didn't like me much was also true. They used to often spit words I didn't understand but could easily guess were nasty, and one day, their stall up and disappeared. I'm sure they thought I was wasting their time, ruining their business, scaring away real customers, or something like that—and, well, I probably wasn't helping.

"What's the Perla Verigaliana like?" Calista asks. "I've heard it stretches farther than you can see all at once, that the entirety of it is packed with stalls from all around the world. That you can find anything at all you could ever think to want."

My instinct is to scoff and say that it's jammed, smelly, and, sure, you can find an awful lot there to buy, but only if you're willing to shell out heaps of gold. As far as I'm concerned, the best part about the Perla Verigaliana is how packed with pickpocketing marks it is. But Calista's leaning forward now. Something about this fascinates her, so I don't want to shut it down.

I have to dig deep, back into the past, to before Father left us. When we did, sometimes, go to the Perla Verigaliana as a family. When that was a special outing for me, when it was a place that filled me with awe. "You really can find everything. Some of it—well, you'd probably rather *not* see." I laugh a little. Calista returns the laugh, but it's a little flat, so I instead reach back for what I loved. "When I was younger and my family . . . hadn't yet fallen on hard times, my very favorite thing to get there were the Narguestan egg custard tarts. Not *the* most exotic thing there, but delicious all the same."

"I've never had a Narguestan egg custard tart," Calista says softly, and I kick myself yet again for implying they were something ordinary. It's not really something I've thought much about—how many things I've been exposed to just by virtue of being born in Verigal City that so many other people in this world might not have seen.

My life in the city isn't perfect, far from it, but that doesn't mean it hasn't also conferred some advantages.

"You live on Estaralla, though." I attempt to salvage this conversation. The tub's nearly full now, and I need to end this on a positive note so Calista doesn't leave hoping she never has to speak with me alone again. "You see incredible magic every day, don't you? You could literally see anything you can imagine."

Calista laughs again, but this time it's cutting. "Not quite. The magic, the glamour, the shine—it's for the visitors, not us. Obviously, it's not like I can use magic to do anything for myself, and no one else here is going to waste their effort and pay the price to do something for another islander. There's no point."

"Oh." It's all I can manage, which might be for the better, because everything I say keeps being wrong.

Calista waves her hand in a vague, circular gesture. "It's a little like being a performer in a show. The audience, our visitors, see the spectacle, but we—we're the ones creating it, not experiencing it."

"Oh," I say again, as heat strikes me, the memory of working the Silverhands' glamotura shows so vivid it instantly floods me. The stage lights beat down on my skin, and I have to squint into the glare, and while the audience oohs and aahs and claps, all I smell is sweat and grease, and my skin flakes from my arm with every beautiful item I show them.

That *is* the experience of a glamorist in Verigal City. The glamoturas there are for others to enjoy, not us. I don't know why I thought Estaralla would be different. I feel—well, I feel like I've been conned.

"I'm sorry," I say sincerely. "I've done magic stage shows in the city, and I should've made the connection."

Calista shrugs, but her voice softens, dropping into its lower pitch. "I don't know about should. No one does. I know how the world thinks of the island, of course. It's the image we've created. I'm sorry to have shattered the illusion for you."

In the back of my mind, I see the girl's eyes bleed again, and I flinch. "No, I—the illusion was already gone anyway."

"Mmm." There's that hum again. "Before you arrived, though." She leans a little closer, gaze suddenly intent. "You assumed it would be magical? Is that why you wanted to take this job?"

My mind shrieks, but if I don't give her an answer, I've lost her. If I give her the wrong answer, I've also probably lost her. I mentally replay our conversation, fast as I can. She's expressed jealousy over experiencing food from around the world; she's intrigued by the trade in Verigal City. She was angry when I praised the island. I don't think flattery's the right route. But it snagged her most when I expressed commiseration. Of course—it is always a good ploy to build a sense of shared identity with a mark. To tell them we're the same. It builds trust.

"As I said, I've been doing stage shows in the city," I say. "I had to take the job when my family fell on hard times. My father made a bad business decision, and we lost everything." I pause, trying to assess how she's receiving this, if the sob story is the way to go. As much as I'm a fan of the mask hiding *my* face, not being able to see hers is making this a lot more difficult. Her eyes are locked on to mine, though, so at least I'm holding her interest. "We used to be merchants, see, but in Verigal City, so much is dependent on your reputation, and my father destroyed his. So I had to take a job as a performer instead. It was the only option left so we didn't starve. People overlook your reputation if you're talented enough with magic because it's rare. But it's exhausting, and I was tired of seeing that gray warehouse ceiling and staring into nothing but bright lights night after night." I pause because sweat is beading under my mask, and my muscles are coiling tight, and the tension is starting to squeeze my voice, too, because I feel like I'm back there, now. But it's not just about the shows—though I hate them—but the fact that I have to do them because if I ever don't show up, the Silverhands will come take Severin away instead. I was trapped, I was powerless, and so of course, *of course*, I came to Estaralla because it's the only way I could take control back.

I set a hand on the edge of the tub to ground myself. A little vulnerability, a little sincerity is good, of course, because it makes it convincing. But I have to always maintain that this is an act. I am a character, a version of Lucia that's not quite real, the version that Calista will like best and want to help by telling me where the magic is. I can't bring too much reality in. I have to *seem* vulnerable but not *be* vulnerable.

Calista leans forward and covers my hand with her own. It's truly a sign of how much I've slipped because her touch startles me, a shock traveling up my arm, even through my glove.

"Anyway," I conclude swiftly. "I thought Estaralla'd be better. That if I had to take a job using magic, it should be the one that would bring me to see the most exclusive island in the world." I look at the tub. Full enough. I turn the water off. I think I've redeemed the conversation, so now, it's time to end it.

"That's why you wear the gloves all the time." Calista's fingers shift up my wrist, peeling at the edge of the glove. I fight the urge to yank back at the brush of her fingertips against my bare skin.

"Huh?" I swallow, my mind a useless swirl. Parts of thoughts arise, swiftly bitten off again by the press of her fingertips, and it must be just how infrequently people ever touch my skin that's making it take over so much of my focus.

"The gloves. If you work shows, you're probably destroying your skin to do it, aren't you?" Calista asks.

"Oh. Yeah." Part of me wants to just plunge right into the bath now, clothes and all, because at least that would end this. But that's even more graceless than the one-word grunt answers I'm managing now.

"You can take them off, you know." Calista's speaking softer again, her voice low and gentle, but I can't even feel the triumph I should feel in this moment. I've turned the conversation around. She doesn't hate me. "I've seen it before."

"The Rubellians haven't," I squeeze out. Obviously, plenty of people have the peeling skin of magic use in the city. Plenty of them don't hide it either. But I—I don't like people looking at me and instantly knowing things about me, my abilities.

And maybe, just maybe, though I've not really thought about it before now, I'm bitter that I had to do it. If it'd been up to me, I wouldn't do the shows, wouldn't make the glamoturas, wouldn't have those markings at all—or if I did, they'd be much smaller, more subtle. They're a literal, constant reminder of the fact my choices aren't my own.

"The Rubellians aren't here right now," Calista says, but she steps back, lifting her hands. "But you can keep them on if you're more comfortable that way. Just thought you should know the sight of the price of magic is nothing new to me. You don't need to hide in front of me—unless you want to, that is."

The air hangs still, while I remain uselessly frozen. Part of me screams this is my chance. I'll take the gloves off, show her I trust her, and she'll trust me more in turn. *I don't want to hide in front of you.* The words are right there on the tip of my tongue.

But I can't get them out.

Maybe because in the end, I *do* want to hide.

Calista taps the edge of the tub. "I'll leave you to your bath. I know you're waiting, and telling you that you can remove your gloves in front of me is quite a lot different than telling you that you're free to disrobe completely after all. We're certainly not there." She gives a little laugh that oddly makes me shiver, glides away, and *clicks* the door shut.

It takes several breaths after she's gone to force my limbs to move. I peel my gloves off first, hands shaking as I do, and I find myself studying my bare skin, thoughts flitting back and forth, trying to imagine what Calista would do. Realistically, probably nothing, but I can't stop imagining her fingers brushing my own the way she briefly touched my wrist.

I strip the rest of the way and plunge into the bath. It's not miserably cold, at least, but a tepid sort of temperature. Another time, I might've found it chilly and unpleasant, but my skin is so hot, hotter than I'd realized—and the chill is a relief.

At least, by some absolute miracle, the queasiness that'd been plaguing me has let up. Or—well, I suppose it's not a miracle; it's whatever Calista has done for me. She's even allowed me into her own room, trusted me alone here. Even in Verigal City, where being a host is an essential part of your reputation, this would extend well beyond what would be normally expected. A host should show grace in all public spaces in the home, but a person's own room is still a private sort of place, not a place anyone is ever required to show a guest. I don't know if it's different here on the island, but it sure does feel

111

private, with how very different, how sequestered and plain, it is. It's a level of kindness I can't entirely dismiss—although I also don't know what to make of it.

I sink deeper into the water, plunging my face into the cold, too.

Dinner is a quiet affair in the courtyard with the bending trees and the icy background. For our entertainment tonight, a sheet of water springs from the ground and, in the ever-shifting liquid, moving pictures flash. It's a silent production of the entire play of *Stella and Giovanni*, but everyone knows that tale well enough to not need the dialogue anyway. I'm a bit bored—the way the images flash in the water is entertaining for all of a minute—but the ammiralia is enraptured, and that's what matters, anyway.

"This is my very favorite show," she murmurs at one point to me. "It's like they knew."

At first, I think *Stella and Giovanni* is quite a popular play, so it's an easy guess to make that plenty of people will enjoy it. But then again, this is Estaralla. They probably did use something to determine her favorite show.

Clearly, they focused on the ammiralia, though, because Oriana's boredom leaks from her expression uncontained. When I stare at her for long enough, she spits out, "I hate this show. I think it's utterly ridiculous how Stella throws her entire life away because she thinks she loves Giovanni."

The ammiralia clicks her tongue. "You'll understand it one day, when you fall in love, my little Ri."

"I won't." Oriana sits back and folds her arms defiantly. The ammiralia merely sighs. This seems like a well-worn argument.

Calista and Dionne serve us again, bringing out more platters of fresh fruit, roasted vegetables, and a main dish of roasted fish.

Calista slips me another single hard slice of bread. So far, I haven't seen any servants or help belonging to their family. It's odd to see—in Verigal City, anyone with even the beginnings of money hires help.

"Did you cook this all?" I dare to ask Calista as she dips by, dropping off a final bowl of peaches swimming in juice. The ammiralia pauses at that, looking up with an expected, yet patronizing, form of pity for them.

"We prepared it all," Calista says evenly. This can't have been the first time she's been asked by guests. "But, you know, we on the island have our own form of help." She takes a hand and runs it over the rim of the bowl. From beneath the touch of her fingers, tiny flowers bloom instantly. Even being able to create glamoturas myself, I'm impressed. My workings are nothing like hers. She makes it look like, well, magic.

But wait. Is she implying that the food everyone—or, everyone but me—is eating is just glamoturas?

My bite of bread sticks a bit, and I push hard to swallow without a choke. If the food is really glamoturas, what are they eating?

It must be something plain like my hard bread altered to taste like something luxurious. I don't want to contemplate the other, creepier options, and certainly, the blithe expressions on both the ammiralia's and Oriana's faces say those darker thoughts haven't even brushed by them. Of course not. This tour is expensive, exclusive, and they can't imagine being terrorized on it. The Estarallans would surely not harm guests who paid them so much.

But I can't cling to that line of thought. I saw someone *die* in front of me today.

A soft whistling sound echoes around us from nowhere. The hairs on the back of my neck rise. It's such an eerie noise. I don't know why so many noises here have to sound so unnatural. Or rather, I do—it's probably to emphasize the fact they're glamoturas, but it's long lost its charm for me.

A moment later, Vessel Dionne reappears in the courtyard, leading Antony.

CHAPTER TWELVE

I hate that I recognize Antony even with his face covered with a mask of glass shards, hate that I know him from just his body. My fury—at myself, and at him—is enough to briefly distract me from the fact another person's arrived with him and Vessel Dionne: a squat, middle-aged woman I don't recognize. She wears a bright, colorful mask a bit like patchwork, but her dress is a simple and drab gray with full long sleeves despite the warmth in the air.

I focus on her as much as I can, trying to ignore Antony at her side because the sight of him is making my mouth go dry and my stomach fluttery. I don't really want to consider if it's panic or thrill at the sight of him causing that. Instead, I focus on the part of me that's demanding to know *why he's here*. Clearly, he's escorting this woman. He's the tour liaison, here to visit the tourists, but I can't shake the feeling he's here to cause problems for me.

"This is Signora Sabella," Antony says. "Ammiralia, ammiraligna, she's here to take your measurements and design requests for your ballgowns for tomorrow night. She's going to create them for you."

"Oh!" Ammiralia Rubellian rises and gives a sharp clap of her hands. "How wonderful!" She gives an expectant look down at Oriana.

Oriana lurches to her feet and plasters a smile that barely even looks like she's trying onto her face.

Signora Sabella bobs a little curtsy. "I'm honored to serve you, *lumina*. If you would follow me to some privacy." She gives a small flick of her wrist, drawing my brief attention to the fact she's got her hands completely covered with gloves, and leads them away.

With the ammiralia and Oriana gone, the air grows thicker, draws a little tighter around me. With the Rubellians, I was perfectly safe. They were a shield from anything strange. With the Vessel and Antony—I don't feel good about what might happen. I'm not keen on any more unwanted conversations about my suitability. Even with Calista hanging in a corner.

My bad gut feeling is confirmed when Antony turns to Vessel Dionne. "*Lumina*, Keelan's hoping to have a private word with Lucia. May I?"

Vessel Dionne's blank face swivels in my direction, giving a loaded but empty pause, before she turns back to Antony. "Very well."

At least my mask hides my grimace. I drag myself over to him slowly, as if the delay will do anything to help. It doesn't, of course, and then he marches me right on out, through the house, and out the front gate toward a waiting litter.

He steps toward me and asks in a low voice, "How is everything going?" My traitorous body freezes, remembering other times when he spoke to me softly. When he put his arms around me and whispered that he had never known anyone like me.

It takes me several long seconds to remember that I'm not supposed to want him to stand so close anymore. I step back as it dawns on me why he's speaking so quietly.

"Keelan's not here," I realize.

"No, I said that so Vessel Dionne would let you go. *I* have little reason or authority to speak with you privately, but Keelan . . ." He shrugs to finish that off. "So, how is everything going?"

I let out a long, slow breath, while in my mind, the girl falls in front of me, again and again, her eyes bleeding black. I bet he'd know what happened to her, why she died. He told me Estaralla was dangerous, so he must know *something*.

But even if he knows, that doesn't mean he's going to tell me. And I don't know exactly what he will do, and I certainly don't know that it'll be helpful. He might well just pack us up onto a ship and send us back to the city in the name of protection, and I can't have that.

I wish I could trust him. But he's already shown me I can't.

I'm not going to show my hand to him unless he shows me his first. "It's been fine," I say, bland as I can.

Antony's gaze sharpens, eyes glimmering dark against the bright glass of his mask, like he's trying to dissolve my mask to see the truth beneath it. "Everything's gone smoothly?"

"Of course. Is there a reason it shouldn't have?" As I speak the words, part of me aches. *Please, Antony, just tell me.* He suspects I'm lying. Of course he does. If he'll tell me the truth now, it'll show me I was wrong about him. If he tells me the truth, I'll know he cares. Maybe he can help me. Maybe we can go back to the way things were before.

But he shakes his head, and my heart sinks. Even though I knew that's what he'd do.

When it counts, he always lets me down.

"Not necessarily. Everything will probably be fine if you're following my instructions. I just wanted to check in." He leans a little closer, sets a hand on my elbow that I should probably shake off. But it's gentle, it's steadying, and it's everything I wish I could really have from him. "You *are* following my instructions, right?"

I only manage an eye roll as an answer before a crackling sounds behind me, from the direction of the Eliades Estate. Antony swiftly steps around me toward the noise, and I turn. The gate is scraping closed, but Antony lunges forward, thrusting his hand into it, and flinging it open again.

Calista stands behind and folds her arms.

"Oh, Calista," Antony says. "What are you—"

"Where's Keelan?" She steps out of the estate and closes the gate behind her.

Antony spreads his hands, but his answer's clear enough. Calista hums.

"What are *you* doing here?" Antony asks.

"I was concerned about what Keelan might want from Lucia. I'm sure you understand," Calista says.

"*I* don't understand," I cut in because there is definitely a private exchange occurring here I'm not a part of, and I want someone to tell me something.

"It's not important," Antony says, voice growing tighter with every word.

At the same time Calista says, "Keelan might ask you to stretch beyond your capabilities with the magic, which would be dangerous for you."

Antony gives a sharp flick of his hand, his voice near a growl now. "Which is obviously not happening right now, Calista, so you can go."

Calista's gaze swings between Antony and me, and once again I can only wish I knew what calculations are running through her mind.

"I brought Lucia out here to speak with her," Antony continues. "*Alone.*"

Calista lifts her hands at that, but it's impossible to tell if it's real apology or mocking, then backs away and closes the gate without another word, giving me nothing to add context to her final gesture.

Antony sighs heavily and shakes his head.

"I think she was just trying to help me," I say, as much a prompt to him as a defense of her. I don't know if he's going to be as close-lipped and useless about whatever irritates him about Calista as he has been about everything else.

"Maybe," Antony says, but his annoyance lingers as a weight in his voice. Once again, there's a portion of this conversation happening silently and without my complete understanding. "Has she talked to you much?"

"Some." For as long as I don't understand the real questions, I'm not going to give real answers. "Do you have a problem with her?"

"*Problem* is strong." Antony sighs again. "She's just . . . irresponsible. Careless. Ignores the rules of this island because she thinks they only apply to everyone else and not her, which in some ways, they don't because she's a future Vessel, and we need her. But that just means anyone else she's involved with takes the brunt of the punishment that should've been for her. And she's got her own—let's say grudge— against the rest of us. So you just—you should be wary of any help she offers you."

The words ring in my head. Irresponsible. Careless. Ignores the rules. Antony might think this is a warning, but instead, for me, it's a bright sign announcing, *Full steam ahead.* If Calista's known to break the rules, that'll make it that much easier to convince her to tell me where the source of the magic is. All I have to do is give her good enough reason to do so.

"I'll be careful," I say blandly. I can't tip Antony off to how thrilled his so-called warning has made me.

"Really, Lucia." He sets a hand on my shoulder, fingers curling over me with more warmth and protection than I want to feel. "I mean it. You're not always careful, but you really need to be now. The best thing you can do is just keep your head down. Do your job, keep your mask on, keep to yourself aside from interacting with the Rubellians."

"It would help a lot if I knew exactly what I'm supposed to be hiding from."

"It wouldn't," Antony says. "Because if anyone realized you knew, and this island has ways of knowing things it shouldn't, you would only make yourself that much more of a target. Please. It's just four more days, and I'm going to check on you as much as I can." He reaches his free hand up toward my mask, as though perhaps he's going to touch it.

Part of me tries to hold still for his touch, his brush of affection. I can still remember all too well the way he would cup my face in his hand, still remember the heat, the thrill with which my body would respond. I can't help missing that.

The smarter part of me jerks away from him at the last moment. He drops his hand quickly and releases his grip on my shoulder, stepping back. "See you tomorrow at the Island Ball."

After everyone's retired separately to their rooms, I wait several minutes, and then, I take my newly created glamotura to Calista's room and knock on her door.

Calista opens it, still masked, with narrowed eyes. "Lucia. Is something wrong? Are you feeling ill again?"

I'd walked to her door feeling my usual easy confidence, certain this was a clever way to win her trust and appreciation, but somehow, standing before her, my confidence begins to dissolve. "No—I uh—" She's once again in her night robe, but even in such plain clothing, she has a presence that feels regal. It manages to make me too aware of the way I lean on one foot, the way I slouch, the way my hair hasn't been combed since I left home. "I brought you a gift. From our conversation earlier."

"A . . . gift?" she says slowly. She wasn't expecting this. Of course she wasn't, but she's supposed to be flattered by it. It's supposed to give me the advantage. It's going to, but right now, I feel as though I'm groveling at her feet, begging for approval, instead of cunningly winning her interest—and her information.

Still, I've come this far, so I pull it out from behind my back. The plain cloth feels heavy in my hands, but in hers, it should feel light as a feather—I am confident, after all, I can make very convincing fake Yzzeran silks. And I've left my gloves off, the mottled gray a sharp contrast to the shimmering material, but I don't dare any more deliberate attention to the fact I've done that, can only hope she notices. "They're not real," I clarify. "It's not like I brought any Yzzeran silk with me to the island, but you *did* say no one makes you glamoturas either. And look." I give the cloth a little shake, and it ripples into a new form, a scroll of Yzzeran phrases. "The fastest way to convince someone you know more of a language than you really do is to know some slang. I can help you with pronunciation if you want. So you could more easily convince Yzzeran tourists to speak with you in the future."

When she doesn't immediately step aside to usher me into her room, I realize I've shown up late at night while she's in her nightclothes, and even though she welcomed me inside earlier today, this may have been a large overstep. *I* would hardly invite a girl I'd known for all of a day into my room at night. My determination to win her over has apparently wiped away my entire sense of decorum. It's only Fortuna's blessing she's another girl because a man might've seen this as practically solicitation.

"Uh, I can teach you tomorrow, of course, or another day—during the day—whenever you have time to spare," I push out.

Calista steps aside then, sweeps a hand in gesture for me to enter, and closes the door behind us. A single candle burns low on her bedside table, light cast across an upturned book and rumpled blankets, and I flush again, wishing a little that she'd sent me away.

"I'm sorry about Antony," she said. "I hadn't put it together yet. I probably should've."

"Put—what—together?" The fake silk hangs limply in my hands.

"Keelan has been quite sure for a while now Antony had a girl back in Verigal City he was seeing. Antony repeatedly denied it, but no one really believed him. Several of the Vessels, to be blunt, have been waiting for her to arrive on the island for as long as that rumor lasted in hopes of her talent being . . . valuable. To the island. I should've realized sooner that was you."

I didn't think my face could grow hotter, but it does. I press the edges of my mask to ensure none of my embarrassment can bleed through. "Um, why would you think that?" I don't think that it's strategic for me to deny it. In fact, it would probably be a big mistake. I need her to trust me. Lying about something she can very easily determine for herself is thoughtless.

But still, something about *Calista* knowing this, *Calista* having put this together, of all people, makes my stomach bubble in unhappy ways.

She giggles, but it's the same frothy sort of laugh she uses with the ammiralia. Fake. "Well, if it's not you, I'm quite embarrassed on her behalf. I saw the way he looked at you. Are you saying it's not?"

"He wears a mask. How can you see anything?" Finally, my gaze slides away. I can't look at her anymore, and I know I've given the answer away. "Fine, it *was* me, but I'm not 'Antony's girl' anymore. We haven't been together in months. I hope that got reported back to all of you here, too."

"It didn't," Calista says, clipped and hard. "As I said, none of this came from Antony himself, and Keelan is certainly unaware that anything's changed. Does Antony know about this change, even?"

I bristle at her insinuation. I may be a liar, but I've no reason to lie about any of this. "I can't see how he wouldn't. Honestly, with some of what he's said to me, I thought the disinterest was mutual."

Calista hums, but at least her brief frustration has lifted from her tone. "I don't think that's quite true."

With those words, I feel the weight of Antony's hand on my shoulder again and give a little shiver to shake it off. "Well, Antony can feel whatever he wants about the whole thing, I suppose. But mutual or not, we're done. Because I'm done." Even as I speak the words, there's a heaviness that sinks into my chest. *Are* we done? Right now, we are. But if Antony came tomorrow, told me where the source was, and helped me, actually helped me, instead of giving me cryptic warnings and messing with my plans behind my back . . . what would I do then? Would I still yank away when he reached out to me?

I'm not sure.

It's irrelevant, though, because with each passing day, I'm more and more sure he'll never do any of that.

"Anyway." I thrust the fake silks back out at Calista. "I came here to give these to you, not to talk about Antony. So just take them, and I'll see myself back to my room."

Calista extends a hand, hovering it for a brief moment, before she closes her fingers over mine. It feels like an agreement, a promise, though I don't know of what. "I thought you offered to teach me the pronunciation."

Something about the way she says it brings the warm flush that I *finally* lost right back to my cheeks. "Tomorrow?" I squeak.

"I had thought maybe you initially showed up thinking right now," Calista says.

"I realized that might've been an imposition." I wish now that I had my gloves because the warmth of Calista's hand is distracting me from what I'm supposed to be doing.

Calista laughs, her bright, chiming real one. "Oh, no, not from you. I would never consider your presence an imposition, not when you brought me such a thoughtful gift." Still without releasing my hand, she guides me to the chair and then drops herself onto her bed across from me. Her words should feel like triumph. She likes my gift. She likes *me*. Antony may be too loyal to the island to give me useful information, but Calista's not, and I'm drawing ever closer to the point where I can start asking her real questions.

But somehow, I feel more unsteady than ever as I clear my throat and say, "Well, let's begin, then."

CHAPTER THIRTEEN

If I could've figured out a way to do it without arousing suspicion, I might've canceled our expedition to the Cave of Ghosts. Even if there's a chance the source might be nearby, it's the last place I want to be. If yesterday, a tortured girl stumbled into the beautiful, well-lit clearing of the Pool of Dreams, who knows what we'll run into in the dark underground that stories say is *so close to the underworld you can hear your dead loved ones speak.*

Yeah, I'd rather not.

When I join Ammiralia Rubellian and Oriana at the gates where the litter awaits, none of us are the cheerful party from yesterday. Oriana somehow manages to look as though she slept even worse than me, and I slept very little after leaving Calista, too much nervous energy coursing through me. Oriana has dark circles that are pits under her eyes, and her skin has an odd yellow sheen. The ammiralia doesn't look quite as beat down, but is the picture of somber in a long and plain black gown as though she's going to a funeral.

As we begin the ride, the ammiralia continues to fidget uncharacteristically, twisting her hands back and forth in her lap, periodically dabbing her cheeks with a handkerchief even though I see no tears there.

"Are you expecting someone?" I dare to ask.

"Probably the love of her life," Oriana mutters with the disdainful sort of boredom of a story told too many times. "Little Pasqual Guzzo, right? Poor Pasqual, the fisherman's son she fell in love with, who died early, just a few years after she married my father. Because she honors her family."

"Oriana," her mother snarls.

Oriana slouches and folds her arms across her chest, the picture of surliness.

Ammiralia Rubellian sighs heavily and stares at the curtains. But, unless she's a better actor than I realized, there's true wistfulness in her gaze.

The litter comes to a halt, and although I don't entirely want to step out, I have to. This area's a thicker jungle, heavy branches crossing every which way, the underbrush spilling onto the path. The air is thick with a humidity that sticks in the back of my throat as I breathe.

The entrance to the cave lies ahead in the middle of the trees. Glowing white flowers outline its edges in a ring I suspect is meant to make it welcoming, but it doesn't conceal the gaping mouth of the cave itself. Staring into it, I can't help but feel a chill. It looks so dark, so endless, so ready to swallow me.

I must still be jumpy from yesterday's scare. This is one of the most popular attractions on the island, so, as ominous as it may look, it can't be dangerous.

I push the curtain back and offer a hand. Ammiralia Rubellian takes it, takes one whiff of the air, and coughs.

"Are you not well?" I jump on the chance. "Shall we return?"

"No, no." She waves me away, pushes my hand off her. "I'm absolutely fine." She covers her mouth with her handkerchief as she turns. Sweat beads along her forehead and collarbone, above the thick lace edging of her dress. "I've just never been to such a place as—this." She waves a hand.

"Wow. It's stuffy." Oriana exits the litter last. The litter falls to the ground, done with its trip, and I wonder if I could command it to rise, and it would obey. At the Pool of Dreams, it'd automatically risen as the ammiralia exited the pool, and then, I'd found it so convenient. Now, I eye it, suspicious that it was instructed beforehand and we're stuck here until it deems our stay complete.

"I'm sure inside the cave won't be." Ammiralia Rubellian lifts her skirts and sweeps forward. The end of her dress catches on the thorns of a bush, and it tears. She hisses and lifts her skirts higher. I reluctantly follow.

"She's really determined to go to this miserable cave," Oriana mutters and falls into step beside me. "Pasqual's been dead for years. I don't know why she hasn't let him go by now."

"So you think she really did love him?" I ask, and Oriana shrugs.

"I don't know," she says. "She certainly felt something for him at the time. But I don't know if she really loved him or is just bitter she had to lose him."

"Or is using it to guilt you into sacrificing for her," I guess. "Reminding you how much *she* sacrificed for her family is an easy way to remind you of what you owe her, too."

Oriana stops walking and leans back, sweeping sharp appraisal over me. I'm not sure if maybe I've pushed too hard, too fast again. I wanted her to see I understood her, but she might only take it as a guide poking her nose into things that don't concern her.

Finally, she offers a smile. Thin-lipped, but a smile nonetheless. "There's always that, too."

Even though she's relented, the next thing I say is still critical in order to not lose the little progress I've made. It's time to show that my understanding is born of something genuine, not just nosiness. "You know, my father's gone, so I have to support my family entirely. Mother won't work, and she wants my younger brother to stay in school, so I work, or we starve. So I'm well acquainted with guilting tactics." I laugh a little, trying to make it lighter.

Oriana's brows lift. "I didn't know that." She hikes her skirts and starts trudging again toward the cave. "You must think of me as such a wealthy little brat."

"I don't," I say. "I mean, sure, if I don't sacrifice, my consequences are high, but I also have a lot more freedom in every other way as long as I keep us fed. I mean, even the fact that I can make money and not be considered a complete disgrace to my family by holding a job. I know it's seen as shameful for wealthy women." It's part of why Mamma constantly refuses to work. She makes me be the one to take the reputation hit. She still dreams of returning to a place where her reputation means something. Never mind that it's also shameful for a wealthy woman to be unmarried. I'm not sure how she plans to snag herself a respectable husband with her past. "I can walk the city without a chaperone because I've no value to preserve, and Mamma isn't going to matchmake me for the same reason. I can marry who I want."

"*If* you want?" Oriana asks.

I shrug. "Yeah, I suppose Mamma wouldn't really care." My marriage will gain her nothing anyway, and that's all she cares about in the end, so she won't care if it never happens.

Oriana sighs, once again abruptly stopping. "You know that's why we're here, right?"

I tilt my head. "I didn't."

Oriana huffs, smoothing her frizzing hair down with a frantic hand, but there's an animation to her annoyance now. "We're here to get me a match. There's a young conte who's visiting the island this week from Tottia-Delan. He just inherited his father's estate. He's named—well, actually, I've forgotten his name because, let's be honest, his name doesn't matter anyway, just the fact he's a young and unmarried conte. Mother heard gossip he would be touring here this week and *had* to get us a slot. She's rather irritated we'll only see him tonight at the Island Ball, so I've basically been told I have to charm him so very much in possibly only a few minutes that he'll request to see me again." She rolls her eyes. "It's never going to work."

"It's not impossible, though. That'd be a logical match." I try to encourage her. It's not an uncommon marriage: nobility of Tottia-Delan and the children of Verigal City's highest naval officers. Tottia-Delan is the conglomerate of the remaining states on the Tottian peninsula, aside from the independent states of Verigal and Estaralla, and they're always eager to bring members of the holdouts into their fold. Plus, a lot of the nobility titling of Tottia-Delan is purely hereditary in nature and rather broke in reality, so it's a mutually beneficial match. They receive money while the Verigaliano naval family receives political power and a title.

Oriana's mouth twists.

"Unless you're hoping it won't work," I say.

Oriana sighs then, and her expression opens, a gate finally unlatched for me. "I don't know. I don't really want it to. I don't want to marry this conte. But that still doesn't mean I want to face Mother's disappointment if I deliberately ruin things. Not with how much money I know she paid to take over this particular tour slot from Keristilli nobility."

I place a hand on her arm gently, a gesture I hope says to her that's something I understand. Because I do. Guilt and familial obligations aren't restricted by class.

Oriana smiles, and I assume she's gotten the message well enough. "Well, for what it's worth, I'm impressed with the hiring process that led to you—I didn't think there'd be any way we would end up with someone I wouldn't hate."

I smile in victory, the smugness probably staining the expression thankfully buried beneath my mask. We're both lucky in our own ways. If Oriana had been different, maybe I wouldn't have been able to snare her as well as I have so far.

She loops her arm around mine. The touch startles me enough that I jump, but one corner of her lips lift, and I relax. We walk like that the rest of the way to the cave. Almost as though we're friends.

"Do you think you'll speak to anyone in the cave?" I ask.

"I fucking hope not," Oriana says so quickly the bark of laughter slips free of my lips, entirely unintentional and entirely real.

Our conversation ends there, though, because we reach the ammiralia at the entrance of the cave. She peers into the dark mouth. There are only a few steps visible before everything turns to black.

As excited as the ammiralia is, even she's wary.

"Should I enter?" she asks.

"Go ahead. We're not supposed to take any lights because it will disturb the spirits. They'll be less likely to talk to us, then." Honestly, the more I think about that, the more I'm not thrilled by it. Yesterday's encounter might've turned me a bit paranoid, but the "don't bring lights" sounds more to me like there's something in the cave the islanders don't want its visitors to see.

Ammiralia Rubellian pinches her lips at that but turns and steps into the mouth of the cave.

"You should follow the sides and keep your hand on the wall at all times," I say. "It'll keep you from accidentally getting turned around."

She wrinkles her nose, but obeys. A few steps, and she's vanished into the dimness, and Oriana and I are alone.

"I don't suppose I can just wait outside again for this one, can I?" Oriana asks.

The part of me not keen on entering myself wants to agree and say we'll both just wait out here. But the magic veins are supposed to run within the cave, not outside it, so I need to go in to verify that it's not really my source.

And I certainly won't leave Oriana alone out here. The cave has to be safe because it's such a major tourist attraction, but out here, I'm not as convinced. I can't have anything happen to Ammiralia Rubellian because it'll get me prematurely sent back to the city. But, Oriana I need in other ways. I need her as a potential ally, a potential decoy. She's of even more value to me. And perhaps against my better judgment, I like her. She doesn't have much classical charm—in fact, she's pretty surly—but she has a practicality and dry wit that *I* appreciate. She deserves better than an unknown gruesome ending.

"I don't think you should," I say. "It's not safe out here alone."

"The monster?" Oriana raises an eyebrow.

"Yeah." The great thing about a made-up monster is that it can be whatever I need it to be in a given moment. "The magic within the cave is so powerful the monster is weakened if it enters, so it won't." I shoot her a sidelong glance. "In fact, if we took some of the cave's stone out, I bet we could figure out a way to use it against the monster."

Oriana nods solemnly with an "I see," and though I'm not exactly sure I've convinced her, it's enough for her to step into the cave, pulling me along.

Instantly, the temperature plummets. The air hangs wet and cold, and the wall so slick beneath my hand the sensation even seems to leak right through my gloves. I regret the instructions I have to keep a hand on it, but as unpleasant as it is, I guess it's still better than getting utterly lost in the dark. The hairs on my arms rise, my skin turning to gooseflesh.

"Ugh." Oriana shudders into me.

I lie through clenched teeth, "You'll get used to it." For all I really know, we're going to walk into the darkness and vanish forever.

Soon, I see nothing, not even the curve of the mask's nose in front of my face. Oriana's grip on my arm tightens, and I lean into the little warmth she provides. The air tastes like earth, and it clings to my tongue, no matter how much I swallow and lick my lips. Oriana's and my footsteps crackle on the ground—at least, I hope it's our feet making the crackling sound I hear—while something hisses like running water.

A cool gust of wind whips by, sudden and unexpected.

I gasp.

Oriana yanks us both to a stop. "Can we go back?" she whispers.

"I don't think that's a good idea," I whisper back, and the corners of my eyes sting. Her other hand curls around my arm and holds tight. I blink furiously, trying to clear the darkness. I want to see, *need* to.

Someone—something?—whimpers.

"But maybe we don't need to go any farther either," I add. Cool air slides down the wall beside me, and the ends of my fingers turn numb in the dampness that's seeped through my gloves. A churning in my gut says that I really don't want to try pulling magic from this area to test its proximity to the source, that the eeriness present in this cave isn't all for show.

But what if the eeriness is in part to frighten people away from figuring out this is the source? What if it's merely a protective facade? If I avoid this out of fear, and then nothing else turns out to be the source, I will kick myself for all the sad remainder of my life.

I take a deep breath and pull my hand free of Oriana's arm. "Hold on a moment." I have no interest in trying to pick up a rock from the ground to work with, so I simply place a hand on my dress. Even though I can't see its color, it doesn't exactly matter. I swipe a hand over a swath, transforming it to brown.

Magic rushes in, making the transformation easy. But as soon as the sparks touch the fabric, the stone wall *grabs* my other hand, wrapping my fingers in slippery cold. I yelp and tug at it, but I can't get free.

The stone has wrapped around my hand.

I'm stuck.

CHAPTER FOURTEEN

I yank and yank at my hand, but I'm trapped.

"It's so dark," a voice whispers on my left.

Oriana was to my right.

"I'm afraid."

I can't tell if the second whisper is the same or a different voice.

I flail my free arm into the darkness. "Oriana!" But only cool wind slides over my outstretched arm, running over and around it, thousands of hands of death touching me all at once.

"I want to speak to you," a voice hisses.

It's impossible to tell if this voice is the same as either of the first ones. A gust of cold wind slides over my left side, as if the wall exhales on me, and my left ear tingles.

Maybe the owner of the voice lives in the wall. Maybe that's the real reason I was supposed to be touching the stone this entire time.

"Don't listen to her!" another voice—and this time I'm sure it's a different voice—whispers. Too bad I'm trapped by the wall and have no choice but to listen. "She lies!"

"I want to go home," someone whines. "How do I get home? I never wanted to be on this island!"

A buzzing sensation burns in my lungs. I try to step, but my feet are frozen, too. My legs won't even bend. They don't belong to me anymore.

"One of us! She's one of us!" another voice whispers. "Come here; come be with us." I shove to try to push myself free of the wall, but my hand sinks in deeper, a tug dragging me up to my elbow. Where my arm's buried, numbness sinks in.

"Please, talk to me," the first spirit says.

"Can I not?" I ask.

"You should talk to me. I'll keep the rest away," the ghost says. And really, who am I to say no to that? Especially with the way the wall of the cave has my hand clamped still.

"Grandma?" I ask because if I must talk to this thing, I want to know who it is. To know why it's talking to me. To make it stop. "I didn't think you'd care enough to reach me here."

"My name is Teresta," the spirit says, and although the name sounds familiar, I can't quite remember who in my life had that name. I'm still picking my way through memories when the spirit adds, "You've never met me."

A trickle of freezing sweat slides down my forehead and into my eye. I thought that maybe the Cave of Ghosts drew from people's memories to create its ghosts, to allow people to talk to their actual loved ones. But then—who am I speaking with? What is happening? Is this a *real* spirit I'm speaking with? If it is, it doesn't seem fair that the ghost of someone I've never met would choose to corner me like this.

"Why are you talking to me?" I ask. "Have I hurt someone you love or something?"

"Not exactly," Teresta says, and I shudder. The last thing I want to have done is become a target for a ghost's vengeance. "Are you afraid of me? I'm not going to hurt you."

I give my arm, the one trapped in stone up to my elbow, a little tug in response. It doesn't budge. "Then why's the wall practically entombed my arm?"

"You just pulled on the magic, didn't you? It's pulled on you back, that's all." She says this as if it's a perfectly normal occurrence, but my heartbeat skips.

"I've used magic a lot, and I've never had that happen before."

"You're not an islander, I can tell," Teresta says. "So I assume you've never tried to draw on the magic while you were so close to a vein of it. The veins run through these walls, you know."

"Is this the source, then?" I ask. My heart beats hard, as I'm not even sure what I want the answer to be. I'd like for my search to be over, but I also don't really want to have to dig into these walls to get what I want. I'd really prefer the source to be in a nice location. Somewhere sunny and warm with lots of life.

Teresta laughs, not quite a pleasant sound. "Oh, no. If you'd tried to use magic at the source, it would've simply swallowed you whole. But it *is* how you're speaking with me now. I'm one of Estaralla's Key Vessels. We all live on in the magic."

Did all of the voices I just heard come from Vessels, then? The one who whined about wanting to go home doesn't really fit. "So how do I get my arm back?" I have so many questions I could ask, but I need to start with the practical because they're all irrelevant if I can never move from this spot again.

Silence stretches. I give my arm another hard tug, try to wiggle my fingers, but I get nothing from either. I can't feel my hand anymore. "*Hello?* Look, I'm aware there's a price to all glamoturas, but

I've never had my arm swallowed by a rock for creation of a tiny little swath of color. Can't you let me go?" I don't know if it's smart to bargain with this spirit, but brute force is getting me nowhere. And if the magic is what's holding me, surely, it can release me, too.

"It is an abnormal price, but our magic is weakening. It's desperate for your energy," Teresta says. "I can't just let you go. It needs you."

Tingling begins to prick something that feels disconnected from the rest of my body—my encased hand. It's like I've grasped a branch of thorns, and I hiss. I'm not sure I like this better.

"Why is the magic weakening?" It's not quite as urgent as my hand, but I need to know this, too. I don't want to think about what the Silverhands will do to me, to *Severin*, if I end up giving them magic that doesn't even work.

"There's a . . . person—if someone so wicked and cruel could be called that—poisoning it," Teresta snaps, and it's almost like each word echoes in my bones.

My stomach sinks, and I attempt to clench my frozen hand. The Silverhands aren't going to thank me for poisoned magic. If I bring them magic that doesn't function, they won't consider my promise fulfilled, and I can't imagine I'll be able to convince them to accept that I did what they asked, at least by the technical definition. They'll be more than happy to fulfill their promise to me to force Severin to work to pay for it. "And you can't . . . do anything?"

"What do you think I'm going to do? I'm not even alive. There might be something to be done if I knew who was poisoning the magic because then, I could tell the current Vessels, and they could handle it, but of course, this person wears a mask. We call them the Shadow."

I don't entirely want to get involved in whatever this is, but if I want to steal the magic, I may have to. "So . . . you need to know who the Shadow is. Under the mask. Will that fix the magic?" That's what I need to know.

"Once we find the poisoner, we will sacrifice this person at the source," Teresta says. "It should restore the magic."

My heart skips a beat. *The source.* The idea of participating in a sacrifice doesn't exactly appeal to me, but *the source.* My conscience is irrelevant here. I need the magic, and I need it fully functional. "But you haven't found this person yet. Must be hard being . . . incorporeal. But I could help you."

"Would you?" Teresta asks, and I let out a little breath, trying to keep my voice steady. It's nothing more than a con, even if this is the first time I'm trying to con a ghost—or whatever Teresta is—instead of a human. She has something she needs. Badly. I offer to provide it. How hard can it be?

"Of course I would," I say. "It—it breaks my heart to hear this special, one-of-a-kind place is in danger. I'll do anything I can to help you. I'll unmask this poisoner for you and bring them to the source, if you'll just tell me where it is."

"I won't need you to bring them anywhere," Teresta says. "Once we know who it is, I can send the Vessels to fetch them and perform the sacrifice."

Not ideal. "I know this might be against protocol, but . . . could you at least let me see them sacrificed? I just—it'd really bring me satisfaction to see justice served." I fight the urge to tug at my hand more while I wait for Teresta's answer.

"It is against protocol. But also, I am the protocol. So, very well. You have your deal. Unmask my poisoner, and in addition to getting to keep your life, I'll allow you to view the execution."

"So where exactly do I have to be to unmask them?" I ask. "So that you can see?"

"We can see everything from anywhere magic rises. I am magic. Anywhere it runs, that will do."

"Right." The words slide down my spine. I'm watched in a lot more places than I realized, then. I'll need to be very careful to not make my plans obvious even when completely seemingly alone.

Ahead, someone screams, long and high and pained. I can't tell if it's one of us or another ghost. Then I hear, loud and clear, Ammiralia Rubellian's voice whimpering, "No, please no. Don't hurt him more."

I jerk uselessly against my walled prison. "*Lumina?*"

She screams again, and the wall under my hand vibrates around my trapped forearm. If something happens to her, I'll never get to fulfill this bargain, never get to find the source any other way.

"Ammiralia!" I wriggle my stinging fingers.

Suddenly, a pulse of energy ripples through the wall like a wave. I tug with the momentum, and the rock spits me free. I stagger away from it.

Then I start forward. "Oriana! Ammiralia! Speak to me!" I need to hear them to place them in the dark.

"Lucia!" Oriana yells. I hold my hands out and stagger along. The air feels too hollow, too empty around me, and shivers crawl up and down my outstretched arms.

"Oriana?" I call again.

"Here." Her voice sounds beside me now, and a hand reaches out, brushing over my right shoulder before I grasp it. A cold breeze passes by, a strange whistling near my left ear.

"Ammiralia?" I call out. "Where are you?" Oriana and I begin to shuffle forward, hands linked.

"I brought matches and a candle," she says. "I know I wasn't supposed to, but I couldn't not. Can I light it?"

My instructions said we shouldn't use lights because it'll frighten the spirits so they won't talk to us. But I want them gone. "Do it." That was smart preparation. I should've thought of something like it.

The match scrapes, and a tiny flame bursts to life at my side. Oriana's face flickers behind it, and she extends it out.

It's a tiny light, but even still, it turns the tunnel a little less terrifying. The walls are just stone. The path, just broken gravel. Whatever lies beyond that may be supernatural, but ahead is just the tunnel of a cave.

At the edge of the light, where it fades to gray and then to black, a body is sprawled on the ground. "Ammiralia!" I lurch forward. Oriana hurries after me, eyes wide.

We reach the body. Ammiralia Rubellian lies crumpled on her side. Her eyes are open, but they stare out, unseeing. A glassy film coats them, making them a milky white. And she's curled around her hands, where her veins pop out like black spiderwebs, crisscrossing her skin.

Like the dead girl.

Oriana gives a soft whimper.

"Was it here?" she whispers. "The monster?"

"It must have been." Each word slices up the back of my throat a little more. I shouldn't have brought them here today. Maybe I shouldn't have told Oriana that lie. I shouldn't have pretended everything was fine, that this was no more than a twist on the tour.

That this was all just a game.

"We need to get her up and out of here. Can you help me?" I'm so weak, so useless, I can't even carry her alone. We are so unprepared for this.

Even still, I don't tell Oriana the truth.

Oriana grabs her mother's hands in one of hers. With her other, she holds our small, flickering light against this endless dark. I grab the ammiralia's feet.

With her stretched between us awkwardly, we make our way back out of the cave and to the waiting litter.

CHAPTER FIFTEEN

Partway through the ride back to Vessel Dionne's manor, Ammiralia Rubellian's eyes uncloud. Her eyelashes flutter, and she stirs and licks her lips. The milky film over her irises recedes, and she's back again.

Mostly.

The black veins crossing her arms remain.

"Mamma!" Oriana leans in, hands fluttering over her mother's. There's fear and concern in her eyes and a connection between them I haven't seen before.

No matter how much they don't get along, they are still family.

Ammiralia Rubellian blinks a few times. She lifts a hand to her mouth. "I don't—feel—" Her eyes widen. "Oh. Oh. Stop." She lunges for the curtain.

Oriana catches her mother's arm as the ammiralia hangs out the side and retches. With her other hand, she rubs circles over her mother's back and watches me, brow furrowed.

I can't offer anything.

When Ammiralia Rubellian finishes, Oriana helps her lean back against the seat. She huddles, wrapping her arms around herself and shivering. If I were a better person, perhaps I'd have words to comfort her, but for once, I'm honest with us all and don't try.

"What happened?" I ask. "What's the last thing you remember?"

Ammiralia Rubellian licks her lips, and her tongue is oddly dark. "I—the cave. It was—" She glances at her daughter, and there might even be shame in her eyes. "It was Pasqual."

Oriana purses her lips and nods. "I know." This time, there's no eye roll and no judgment in her tone.

"I reached forward," Ammiralia Rubellian says, and her voice is thick and breaking. "Because he told me to. He said he was trapped, but he wanted to . . . hold me. For warmth. I reached out and touched the wall and it—it sank beneath my hand and then enveloped it in stone. It was cold, so cold, I lost feeling in my arm, and then suddenly it came back in with horrible pain and that's it." She bends over, still shaking. "That's it."

Absently, I massage my own hand that was trapped. I dare to peel the edge of my sleeve up, checking for any matching marks on my own skin, but my wrist and forearm, at least, are fine. Whatever happened to me, I guess it happened to her, too, but worse.

I wish I knew why.

When we arrive at Vessel Dionne's home, Oriana and I exit first, each holding out an arm to support the ammiralia as she steps down. As her hand touches my arm, I flinch. The black-veined skin is freezing and slippery, living ice against my skin.

Calista waits at the gate, as she always has, this time in a shimmering dress of gold paired with a plain golden mirror of a mask to match.

She hurries forward when she sees us, a little of her usual grace lost, hands outstretched. The ammiralia staggers back, placing Oriana between herself and Calista.

"What's happened?" Despite the abrupt concern clear in her movements, her voice is still its sugary coo. "*Lumina*, are you ill?"

"No, no, it's nothing," the ammiralia says, even though I can see how she grips Oriana to both keep hidden and keep herself upright. "Just a little—chill. From that cave." She clicks her tongue, haughty wealth lifted as a shield. "You really should consider warning your guests how unpleasant that interior is. Or better yet, simply make it nicer. Surely something as basic as a little extra warmth is possible here."

"Uh, it shouldn't have been that cold," Calista says mildly. "*Lumina*, is there something I can do for you now?"

Ammiralia Rubellian flaps a hand. "You can fetch some tea. I'll take it in my room."

Calista's gaze drops to the ammiralia's hand, dark spiderweb veins and all, and she makes a soft noise. Unfortunately, I can't decipher the meaning with her expression hidden by the mask. The ammiralia sharply clears her throat, and Calista takes a step back.

"Yes, please, the tea, like a doll," the ammiralia repeats, and with that, Calista leaves us, though I can feel her reluctance. I didn't really want to see her go either. We have a lot to talk about. All of my questions rattle around in my brain, beating to get out.

Oriana and I help Ammiralia Rubellian back into her room, a sweeping suite in the mansion I haven't yet seen. Small rivers with delicate stone bridges pop out in corners, and the entire floor is glass to show the colorful fish swimming beneath. We ease her onto the bed, a canopied monstrosity that might just be as large as my entire room here, and she rolls herself up in the blankets. Oriana kneels beside her, a hand on her shoulder.

"Is there anything I can fetch for you?" I ask. "Additional blankets?" Even Calista's quilt looked heavier than the thin, silver silk sheath glimmering on the bed right now.

The ammiralia looks to Oriana, who gives a small nod in return in a silent exchange. "Yes, little sparrow. You're so thoughtful."

I'm glad the mask means I don't need to force a smile at that. My motives are entirely selfish—I just want to speak with Calista. I want answers, and I want them *now*. I back out of the room with some degree of patience, but once I'm in the hall, I jog down.

Calista's at least not hard to find—she's behind the only door cracked open, almost as though she wanted to make it easy for me. The room isn't one I've seen before. It's plain, clearly not intended for guests, with a large, stained, and cut-up table in the middle, a block of knives on top, and various ice boxes and pantries lining the shelves. It looks like a kitchen, sink included, except, distinctly, without any sort of oven or stove in sight.

She whirls at my crashing entrance with only a thin flash of surprise in her eyes as I march toward her.

"What happened to her?"

I catch a waft of vanilla, and I can only think *of course* she would smell so saccharine. She leans back, her stormy gray-blue eyes wide in their slits. The reflective surface of her mask's gold plating shows me nothing but my own simple mask. The anger roiling in me is invisible. "That's tough for me to say since I wasn't even there. Why don't you give me more information first? She obviously didn't want to."

"I didn't see what happened exactly because it was dark. She said she reached toward the wall because it was speaking to her as some dead lover and then—then the wall encased her arm, which went numb, and it hurt and spat her out and she collapsed, and now she's like this." The words pour out of me, the rush half fury and half fear. This is the second day something horrible has happened to us. Antony warned me the island was dangerous, but since I'd heard nothing else, I didn't think it could be that terrible. I don't understand if it's this bad how this information hasn't spread the whole world over yet.

Calista's exhale whistles against her mask. "That shouldn't have happened to her."

"Yeah, doesn't seem like an ideal vacation experience," I say. "The wall tried to eat my arm, too. I don't know why it didn't mess me up as much as it did her."

Calista sets the mug of presumably steeping tea on the table and takes my hand in both of hers, lifting it between us. "Your arm?"

"It's fine. I discreetly checked."

"Under the gloves, too?"

"I—no." I'd been doing so well in not stumbling over my words like I do so often around her, but there I go again.

"May I?" Calista gives the end of the glove a small tug, and all I can do is nod.

She peels the glove from my hand, one finger at a time, her other hand wrapped entirely around my wrist. I don't know why I can't watch her do it. My gaze drops to the floor, tongue feeling thick and dry in my throat.

She hisses again, and with that, I look back. Black spiderwebs cross my fingers, not quite making it to my palm, abruptly and unevenly ending as though whatever created them was cut off partway.

I pull my hand from hers and give it a little flex. "It doesn't hurt," I say, but when she doesn't give any kind of encouragement, I add, "It's bad, isn't it? What *is* it?"

"I don't know." But she says it fast, too fast to have put any thought into what it might be.

I narrow my eyes. "But you're acting like it's something bad. If you don't know what it is, why are you afraid of it?"

"The ammiralia is waiting for her tea." She extends the mug to me. "Deliver this. I'll find her blankets."

I fold my arms, ensuring it's impossible for her to force the mug into my hand. "What do I need to be afraid of?" *Is it poison?* The words hang on the tip of my tongue, but I can't let them out because that'll only raise the question for Calista of why I would ever leap to that conclusion. I want, no, *need*, her to be the one to bring that into the conversation if I'm to ask about it.

She sighs heavily, a rough whistle of frustration. "Yes, Lucia, I have a theory on what it is, but I don't—I don't want to share yet because I'm not sure. You don't have anything to be afraid of, though. At least in the immediate future."

That's far from reassuring, but, still, when she presses the mug closer to me, I accept it. And when she starts off, I don't stop her. I stand alone in the stuffy kitchen, mug burning against my skin.

Calista said she wasn't sure. But I don't know if that means she's unsure about what's going on—or if she's just not sure she should share the truth with me.

CHAPTER SIXTEEN

As I approach the ammiralia's suite with the steaming mug of tea, sharp, raised voices drift toward me, though muffled enough by the walls I can't make out any words. Just the furious tone.

I knock on the door, politeness winning over the sheer curiosity of wanting to know what they're saying. It's only the Rubellians, so I doubt it's useful enough to be worth the possible repercussions of hearing something they don't want me to.

They fall silent.

I step inside. "*Lumina*, I brought your tea. Calista is bringing blankets."

The ammiralia has apparently found enough strength to sit, as she's bolt upright. Oriana sits on the edge of the bed, angled away from her mother, arms folded. A flush darkens the ammiralia's cheeks, while Oriana's jaw is clenched tight enough the strain is visible.

"Thank you, little sparrow." The ammiralia's voice is a little roughened, but the brightness she infuses wouldn't otherwise have me guess I'd walked right into the middle of an argument. She extends her hands, and I deliver her tea, trying not to look at the marks on her arms, or the way her fingers tremble. She takes a sip and lets out a little sigh.

"This is lovely," she says to Oriana. Oriana doesn't turn around. "With a little hot drink and a little rest, I'll be right in no time."

Oriana grunts. I'm not sure if she's about to break into argument again because Calista enters next, giving a little nod before she drapes the blanket—a monstrously white fluffy thing that's probably a glamotura—across the ammiralia's legs.

The ammiralia catches Calista's arm, halting her. "This won't change our attendance at the Island Ball tonight, will it?"

Ah. My gaze flashes to Oriana, and her lifted eyebrows confirm this is definitely what they'd been arguing about.

Calista extracts her arm from the ammiralia's, taking the ammiralia's hand between her own instead. "That's entirely up to you, *lumina*, and how you're feeling. It will be, of course, impossible to reschedule, but you absolutely do not need to attend."

"Oh, no." The ammiralia takes her hand from Calista to fan herself instead. "I just wanted to ensure that you hadn't already canceled on my behalf. I'm already feeling so much better. We'll be fine."

"I could always go by myself, Mother," Oriana says stiffly. "Leave you to get some additional rest. It would be tragic if you were stuck in bed for the entire rest of our trip from having pushed yourself so hard tonight."

"Nonsense." The ammiralia covers the harshness with a little titter. "Besides, if that's what happens, it will be worth it." She turns to Calista. "The ball, you see, is what I'm most excited for."

Behind the ammiralia's shoulder, Oriana rolls her eyes.

"The only thing I do need to know, *lumina*, is about the magic." Calista says. "In your booking, you swore you've never touched it.

If that was, perhaps, an exaggeration of the truth, I very much need to know that now. There won't be consequences, but we need to know."

"It was completely the truth." The ammiralia gives a little sniff to the insult to her integrity. "I swear it."

Calista nods. "The dressmaker should be here soon with your gowns, and I'll send her in when she arrives. She'll assist you in the final fittings." With that, she exits the room. Sounds like my cue to leave as well, so I follow.

She's paused outside the door, giving me the opportunity to approach and murmur, "Is it safe? For them to go?"

"Honestly?" Calista absently touches the bottom of her mask with a finger. "I don't know. It's probably fine. As long as the ammiralia is telling the truth about not using magic, nothing should happen. Do you trust her on that?"

I purse my lips. I don't trust anyone here—including the ammiralia. If she's lied about having used magic, though, I'm sure that'll be the immediate end to the tour. I don't entirely like how Calista has put this on me. If the ammiralia lied, it was her choice to—twice. I can't have this tour end. I'm not going to change the decision she's already made. Besides, I don't really understand why it's a problem if the ammiralia has used magic. The guides all have, including me, and there's obviously no rule against *us* visiting. "Yes," I say.

Calista shrugs. "The dress fittings should be a while. Do you want to—to come teach me any more Yzzeran in the meantime?" There's something so shy, so uncertain, in her voice that my stomach drops out a little bit.

Because I don't think it's the right use of my time. I was teaching her to win her trust, her interest, her friendship, so that she'd tell me where the source is.

But I have another way to find the source, now—find this Shadow and unmask them for the Vessels to deal with. And as much as there's a part of me that might rather get the information from Calista just because it means spending more time with her, I can't just take the magic as it is now. I need the Vessels to deal with this Shadow and purify the poison from the magic.

Calista waves her hand swiftly. I've waited too long, and she correctly interpreted my silence as a no. "Never mind, actually. I'm sure you're also looking to prepare for the ball." She spins and stalks off, so fast it's like she's fleeing. Part of me wants to reach after her and say, *Wait, I do want to talk with you!* I don't want to have hurt her feelings, and I think I might've.

But I can make it up to her later. I may or may not get another opportunity like this one to explore alone. I don't have a lead on the Shadow exactly, but I do have a logical place to start looking—the place where horror struck. Whatever happened to that girl yesterday at the Pool of Dreams, the Shadow has to have been involved.

So I'm going to return to the Pool of Dreams. To the corpse and her strange, dark tears.

I slink out of the mansion and close the golden gate behind me on my way. The latch clicks, a thunderous noise in the quiet. The sun's already set, leaving only the gray light of dusk behind. In some ways, this is a relief. Since it's dark, I'm all but certain if any tourists were visiting the pool today, they should be long gone, and I'll be alone.

But otherwise, it's just creepy.

There's only one path in front of me from the gate of Vessel Dionne's home. I follow it. The gravel crunches beneath my feet, no matter how light I try to step, and trees arch over the pathway, the gray twilight slicing through their branches like bars. I lick my lips, but my mouth stays dry as paper.

Something soft hums behind me, and I spin. I search the dark path, scanning the shadows for anything that moves. But it's so dark, and even as I squint, I see nothing.

The path forks ahead, one side descending out of the forest and toward a few scattered lights. The other turns up a hill into a dark grove. I waste a few seconds trying to convince myself the right way must be heading into the town.

It's not, of course.

The trees of this path are denser, the few little beams of light gone. I pick my way along slowly because if there's something in front of me, I probably will run right into it. It's never been this dark in the city anywhere; there are always gas lamps glowing faintly. This is like a bottomless pit. My footsteps are finally silent on the dirt, but if someone is following, I'll never hear over my own raspy breath.

The hair on the back of my neck rises. So does the hair on my arms. Something hums again behind me.

A bird, a bird, I tell myself, and this time I don't turn around. I'm too far already to run back, so I speed up and keep going.

The Pool of Dreams is in a gap in the trees where the rising moonlight pours through, giving me at least a little view. The dew on the grass glows, and the whole place shines silver.

Except the water in the pool and waterfall is pitch black. It doesn't reflect any of the light, not like the day, where it's such a clear blue. Even the little light there is should reflect from it, but instead, it looks like a dark pit.

The realization hits me—it must be illusioned to look blue and clear. Whatever it is, it isn't water, and the illusion has only been constructed to look convincing during the day.

I head for the trees, still careful, pushing my feet along to feel for roots. I find most of them gently. Only one catches me by surprise and sends me stumbling.

I peel the thick curtains of the tree's weeping branches aside to find the body. In the darkness, it's just a lump. My heart races, and I swallow a few times to try to get myself back under control. It shouldn't scare me that much. I can't even make out the details in the darkness.

I don't know what I was expecting, that the body would be gone? That perhaps I'd only imagined it all yesterday? That it'd been a horrible hallucination given to me by the pool itself? (Putting aside the lack of logic in thinking it would be my dream to stumble across a corpse.)

Perhaps I wasn't expecting anything, only hoping.

I steel myself and shove the branches aside again. With my other hand, I reach forward and grab the dead girl's wrist. It's hard beneath my fingers, and when I yank, she slides out easily because her arm is so stiff it stays pinned to her side.

The light makes her pale skin seem to glow like the dewy grass around us, which has the unfortunate effect of making the dark pits of her eye sockets all the more stark. I squat to touch the black crust on her cheeks. It crumbles beneath my gloved fingers.

My stomach heaves, and I throw myself away from her, sucking in deep breaths through my mouth only, until I'm sure I'm not going to vomit all over her.

I wanted to smell the black crust, to see if it had any particular scent, any particular hint to what it might be.

Before I can steel myself enough to try again, something crunches to my left. I whip in that direction, praying it's just a ghost like all of the other noises I've heard.

But a dark, humanoid form stands there.

My heart lurches into my throat. I scramble to my feet and dive behind one of the curtains of the tree's thick branches, then peer out. I blink furiously, as if maybe, if I blink enough, the illusion of a person will vanish. I'm just imagining there's someone else here with me.

But the shadow moves forward into the moonlight and doesn't vanish. They're tall and slender, which is clear even with their loose black shirt and flowing pants. Their mask—I regret being able to see it clearly. It's hideous, looks like it's crumbling, decaying, with three dark streaks down the front like it's been torn by giant claws.

They approach, movements so fluid it's more like floating, and fall beside the corpse. Gloved hands touch the dead girl's cheeks, skimming the blackened crust there.

I press my hand against my mask to push it against my mouth and stifle any sound I might make, willing my breathing to be soft and silent, gentler than the rustling of the trees.

They pick up the girl's hand, squeezing it between their gloved ones. Their dark hair, tied in a tail behind their back, swings over their hunched shoulder.

The tree behind me shifts. One of its branches arcs down and twists around my bicep. I gasp and wrench free—and tumble right out from my hiding spot.

Not fair. Even the trees here are my enemies.

"Lucia." The masked person gives a tired sigh, and though Calista's voice is deeper and softer than it usually is, I recognize it. "Want to tell me what you're doing here?"

Busted. I lick my papery lips, trying to whip up a story that's not going to get me into trouble with her. Unfortunately, I don't think there's any way to spin this strange little expedition as part of my getting ready for the ball. And I'm certainly not ready to breathe a word of my bargain with Teresta.

But the answer—or an answer, at least—lies dead between us. There's no sense in continuing to hide the fact I found this body because Calista fully and clearly sees that right now.

"The girl." I gesture to her, and even without seeing Calista's expression, some degree of shock, or perhaps panic, bleeds right through her mask as her head whips up to me, down to the girl, and then up at me again. "You wouldn't tell me anything about the markings, but I'd seen them before—on her. She collapsed in front of me when I was here yesterday, and I—I couldn't save her. I didn't know what was even happening. So I hid her."

Calista sharply inhales. "Why didn't you tell me this yesterday?"

"I didn't trust you. I didn't know you! I didn't know if—if I'd be blamed for this girl's death. If I'd be sent away. You know I need this job. Because she was already dead. If I thought I could've saved her, I would've said something." I'm not completely sure if that's true. Really, there's a part of me that's glad I didn't get the opportunity to have to face that choice—trying to save the girl's life at my own risk. "But it's not like there was anything left to do here."

"No, there wasn't. You're right that you couldn't have saved her. If that helps to know." Calista's words feel like they should be kind, reassuring that this wasn't my fault, but she sounds like she's spitting ice.

"A little." I shift my weight between my feet, and the ground squishes beneath my boots, a simple sound that manages to make me flinch. I don't exactly want to keep dwelling on the whole thing. "Anyway, why are *you* here?"

"I went to your room to ask if you wanted to borrow jewelry or hair ornaments from me for the ball, but you weren't there. So I left to look for you and started my search with the places I knew you'd been before."

"Am I not allowed to leave the estate?" I ask, because if not, I need to know to be far more careful sneaking out in the future.

"Not really," Calista says. "Mother and I are . . . responsible for you—and your actions."

"So, the Vessel hosts are supposed to protect the tour guides? Why aren't you doing a better job?" I gesture at the corpse between us.

I know it means something because Calista's shoulders flinch and she steps back with a sharp squelch from the ground. "No. I said we're responsible for you. The Vessels aren't supposed to protect the tour guides from anything." Her eyes widen abruptly, gaze dropping to her feet. I glance down at my own in response. A thin layer of water coats them that definitely wasn't there before, as though the ground's flooding, though I don't know from where. "You need to get away from the body. *Now.*" She reaches for me, seizing my arm and giving it a tug.

I stumble right into her, but she holds us both steady, her body a solid pillar of support. I turn back to the corpse—now seeing that the water seeping across the ground has come from the pool itself. It's a dark stain, rapidly rising, and I don't fight as Calista pulls us both a few steps farther from it.

Suddenly, tiny waves rise across the water all around the corpse, like a thousand tiny fingers scrabbling at its side, propelling it toward the pool. The dark water of the pool slips over the body, staining cracks, the pockets of her face, the bend at her elbows, before it gurgles and swallows her completely.

I let out a noise of protest, tugging against Calista's grip, but she holds tight. And quicker than it appeared, the water recedes from the ground, rushing like a mini river into the pool, and then it's gone as well.

"What *was* that?" I demand. "Was that normal?" People swim in there. How many decaying corpses lie at the bottom of the pool?

"It happens," Calista says lightly, entirely too composed for this whole thing. "The magic was simply reclaiming its debt. The bodies of all glamorists belong to it—that's the price we all pay for using it. And you know you always have to pay the price, right?"

I stare at the darkness where the body vanished. Something cold twists around my fingertips and numbs them. I didn't really know that. I suppose it makes sense. All magic has a price, and if I only have to pay that one after I'm dead, that's not so bad. I shouldn't care what happens to my corpse.

Calista releases me, leaving nothing but cold behind. "We shouldn't stay out here. There is a ball we need to prepare for, isn't there?"

I cast one final look at where the body sank. The water—or whatever the liquid really is—has stilled, and there's no trace remaining of what's now beneath that surface. "Do you need to report that girl missing or anything?" I'm not exactly the sentimental sort, but something's locked my feet down, thinking of how that girl is simply gone. Someone should want to know. Someone should care. Otherwise all she's got for mourners right now are Calista and me, and while I think we're both sorry she's dead, *I* at least am more disturbed by the manner than I am saddened.

Calista crosses the space between us and sets one of her gloved hands on my forearm. The little warmth from her seeps through the fabric, seeps through my skin and down to my bones, and I shiver. "I'm sure the Vessel she was with has already noticed she's missing. They'll bring in a replacement—if they haven't already."

I frown at her hand instead of the creepy ripped mask she wears now. "A replacement," I say slowly. In Verigal City, the bottom rung of workers are just cogs in a larger machine, not people to care about, and when a machine breaks, it's not lovingly nursed back to function, but simply replaced by another. Because there are always more who are desperate to take their place. I'd thought of the guides here as different—elites, winners of a rare and coveted position. But they're also, I realize for the first time, completely replaceable. Thousands more wait in the wings back in the city, eager to step in. "But do they care what's happened to her?"

Calista's silence brings to mind what she'd said earlier, words I really didn't pay enough attention to the first time she spoke them: *The Vessels aren't supposed to protect the tour guides from anything.*

And with a deep sinking feeling, I know that's the answer here, too. There's a lot of turnover among the guides—I know this quite well because that's why they keep hiring more. I also know it's pretty much impossible to find a former guide in Verigal City because I tried to. At the time, I'd assumed they stayed on the island, or moved on to bigger and better positions after this job. Estaralla is an island of magic and dreams. Nothing bad is supposed to happen here.

But Estaralla is here to serve its tourists. Estaralla guarantees *them* they'll have the time of their lives, guarantees *their* safety, and it follows through.

No one's made that promise to the guides. And based on what just happened to this poor, now forever lost guide, they aren't safe from whatever's happening on this island with the poison and magic.

I am not safe.

CHAPTER SEVENTEEN

Once again, Vessel Dionne's litter is our transportation, carrying us locked behind shimmering curtains to the palace for the Island Ball. When it comes to a stop, Antony unfortunately waits on the other side to greet us. He peels the shimmering curtain back and offers a hand to Ammiralia Rubellian first. She wears a pair of matching gloves, and other than the faint blue tinge that's still in the whites of her eyes, all signs of her earlier illness are gone. Her bright red lipstick buries the off coloring of her lips, and the rouge gives her cheeks a golden glow.

She places her hand in his, and he helps her out.

She hides any discomfort so well I'd never think she was sick earlier. She must have more practice at living a lie than I realized. Maybe she doesn't love her role as a wealthy, prim, and spoiled lady, even though she wears the role with perfection. Maybe she's not so different from her daughter after all.

Finally, there's no one left in the litter but me. I'd entertained hopes Antony would ignore me, but he holds out a hand, an offer for me, too. It'd look petty to ignore him, so I take it. His grip's as strong as I remembered. He holds on a second too long as I step away from the litter, and I give a forceful tug to get my hand back.

The others already stride a few steps ahead. From the front, Calista's dress had been plain, the color of dark smoke, but the view from the back is entirely different. She glows in the middle of the rest of them, the bustle of her gown like trailing flames. Unlike many of the other styles she's worn, this one would be right at home in Verigal City with its large bustle—except for how very low it dips on her back, exposing her shoulder blades, curved and sharp. It has to be the fact that it'd be such a scandal in the city that makes me unable to stop staring at the line of her spine where the fabric ends.

Oriana glances back and gives a swift jerk of her head. I fall into step beside her.

She's a gray cloud in her golden gown, which complements the golden tones in her skin perfectly. It's a beautifully constructed piece—it looks as though she's wearing metal, except for the bustle, which is like mist more than fabric. I'd compliment her on it, except I'm pretty sure she'd hate that. "Don't fall behind," she mutters. "I need someone here whose voice I can stand."

"I wasn't falling behind," I say. "Calista's dress is just—pretty."

"Calista's *dress?*" Oriana's mouth twitches in a small smirk.

"It's very eye-catching. Don't you think?" I don't know why I need her to agree, but I do. Perhaps because, if I wasn't entranced by her dress, what else was it that had me completely forget what I was doing? Calista herself?

"If you say so," Oriana mutters, but there's an edge in her tone that's not really agreement.

The palace, what must be the palace, sprawls before us, nestled between the high walls of a ravine. Glittering blue water cascades from both sides of the gorge with the hazy rainbow building at their center, almost as though it's merely the rainbow at the center of the falls' mist. I remember the beauty of its ever-shifting coloration from the distance, but up close, it's even harder to look away from its entrancing glow. The building is near translucent except for its bright shine and tiny pinpricks like a thousand stars, with the fluctuating colors almost an overlay, as though a rainbow had been wrapped around its spires as a cloak. It's gorgeous, and the changing of the colors is hypnotizing, and I can barely look away.

I force myself to anyway.

It can't possibly be real.

The whole thing has been created from magic—it's one massive glamotura. It's an obvious glamotura at least. I don't know how much of this island is all just glamoturas hiding something else beneath them. For the first time, I understand some folks' distrust of magic back in the city. I can't trust anything I sense here because none of my senses will tell me the truth.

We approach the double doors, Vessel Dionne and Calista first, followed by Ammiralia Rubellian, then Oriana and me, while Antony brings up the end of the procession. The doors open when we reach them, seemingly of their own accord. They grind open slowly, and we step inside.

The entire building glows, and the ceiling sweeps above us, an entire twinkling crystal with a depth and darkness that mimics the night sky so well I could absolutely believe I was still outside, but it's so empty, so vast, and so cold.

The door grinds closed behind us on its own and closes with a final *click*.

I flinch.

We walk down the entire hallway alone, our footsteps echoing in the emptiness. They call out, a soft beat of a song, but I can't tell if it's a march to our funeral. While the ceiling above is the night sky, the walls beside us appear wrought entirely of metal that transitions from gold to pink, upon which the silhouettes of people have been carved, standing in a line, to watch our march.

"This is the hall of Vessels," Antony explains. "All the people you see carved here were the island's past Vessels."

I pause, studying one, and I could swear one of its fingers twitches. I scuttle onward.

Theoretically, this palace belongs specifically to the Key Vessel. He always hosts the Island Ball, since he doesn't have any guests who he hosts on tour. I shouldn't really care, but my gaze sneaks its way to Antony behind me.

"Antony, did you grow up here?"

"Of course," he says, and ahead of us, the ammiralia gives an appreciative "ooh."

I feel cold. Maybe I'm just overreacting, more skeptical of everything here because of the horrors I've already seen, but this place has such an eerie feeling to it. Oppressive and impossibly vast at the same time. I want to still just be mad at Antony, but that feeling's getting harder and harder to grasp. I don't really know that I'd be a great person either if I'd grown up in this creepy place.

"Thank you, *lumina*," Antony says. "I do assure you, you've got your own set of luxuries in your life the likes of which I've never really seen either."

"Such a gentleman," she coos, and I regret starting this at all.

At least the conversation is short-lived. We pass through a second set of doors, back outside into a courtyard. And here, there are people, and a little bit more warmth that lingers in the air. Here, life moves. It exists.

Waterfalls surround the place, spilling around the beautiful grass from cliffs high above, rivulets running all around like a web, coalescing into a singular pond that's also the basin for the largest tumbling crystal-blue falls. The ground is coated in something silver and shining, the icelike material that's also all over Vessel Dionne's manor. It's so much that the air itself seems to shimmer, a gleam that touches everyone and everything here.

Around the area, people drift, movements made ethereal against the backdrop's glamor. The women wear elegant and dainty gowns, some like the gown of spun candy Calista wore the first day I met her, some that more closely resemble smoke, and some that look like Dionne's waterfall, while the men mostly wear dark and metallic tunics. And I see more masks than I've seen before. All are beautiful in their own way. Some have artful swirls and glittering jewels for lips or adorning the foreheads, with tassels hanging from their sides or metal edges curling out. Others wear masks that are meant to look like faces, beautiful faces, so beautiful they could never truly be real, but it's still hard to pull my gaze away from them.

A white balcony hangs from one of the cliffs, dipping over the party, and two faceless people—Vessels—sit on it and watch us all below them.

"Please enjoy the ball," Vessel Dionne says curtly and leaves us, heading in that direction.

"Where are the other guests?" Ammiralia Rubellian turns to Antony and asks—not surprisingly. "It's harder to spot them in this crowd than I thought it might be."

"There's a whole bunch of them at that large pool." Oriana lifts a hand in the direction of the basin into which all the water is draining. I follow her pointing to see several people, easy to identify as guests because they're the only ones who are maskless. They're kneeling at the pond's edge, splashing themselves and one another with the water. I grimace. There's probably no corpses in Antony's backyard, but I still can't look at any of the water on this island the same way.

"That's because they're looking to get a little taste of our magic." Keelan speaks beside my ear. I jump aside. "That pool, Ammiraligna, is one of our many little treats for you tonight. It's not just water you see there. Some of it comes directly from our source of magic. Don't get any wild ideas about drinking it to acquire powers, of course"— the bottom of his face crinkles in what might be a smile—"because the amounts are too trace for that. But you still might be able to feel it on your skin."

"Interesting." Oriana doesn't sound that sincere, but she still starts in the pool's direction. The ammiralia seizes her arm, yanking her back.

"Interesting, indeed, but I don't see Conte Niccolo over there. Perhaps he's looking for a dance partner." The ammiralia begins to drag Oriana away.

I barely hear her. My mind is still replaying what Keelan said: *Some of it comes directly from our source of magic.*

Direct.

From the source.

I could scream.

It's the biggest hint I've gotten so far. This is the closest I've been. It's also the closest I may ever be, the biggest hint I may ever get. And, of course, it's also while I'm in the biggest crowd I've seen on this island.

The crowd might be an advantage, though. It may make it easier to slip away without those who'd follow me—namely, Calista—noticing.

Oriana flings a desperate look over her shoulder at me, and it jolts me out of my thoughts. This is *it*. I need a plan. And the first decision is: alone, or with my wealthy shield, Oriana?

I haven't entirely decided when a hand lands on my shoulder. I turn to see who and barely stop myself from rudely leaping away when Keelan's blank sheet of a face leers close to mine. Up close, he's not any easier to look at. In fact, it's worse, because while at a distance, his skin appears mostly smooth, up close, I can see the faintest of shadows marking where his eyes, nose, and mouth might've otherwise been. As though they are still there—buried beneath a stretched, thin skin.

"Lucia," he says, "I regret not having the opportunity to have caught up with you just yet. Come, tell me how you are finding our humble little island so far."

CHAPTER EIGHTEEN

I don't have much of a choice but to walk as Keelan propels me forward with a push of his hand. "Oh," I say lightly with a giggle that's not nearly as convincing as Calista's bubbly laugh. "Well, it's been just *marvelous*, of course. I'm still so honored you recognized my abilities and allowed me this position."

Keelan throws a look over his shoulder. Calista and Antony trail behind the two of us like shadows. "There is no need for you to stay."

Calista and Antony exchange a long look, yet another I know has far more meaning than I'm able to glean, and then Calista gives a small bob, chirps, "Consider saving at least one dance for me, Lucia," and skitters off.

"I meant you as well, Antony," Keelan says.

"Lucia was complaining on the way here that she's quite hungry," Antony says, and I'm glad my mask hides the way my nose wrinkles because definitely not. I don't know for sure that the food here is bad for me, but I haven't felt sick since two nights ago, so I'm not keen on testing it out here, in the middle of this ball. "I was going to show her the food."

"You can fetch her some, then, while the two of us chat," Keelan says. Cold seeps into my skin where his hand grips my shoulder. He's very determined to have me alone. And Calista and Antony both very much expressed concern about that.

But what can he possibly do to me in the middle of this crowd? Locked in a remote room alone, perhaps I'd fear him. I just want to get this over with, give him whatever he's looking to get from me so he'll leave me alone for the rest of the night.

"That sounds great. Go fetch me some food." I flick a hand at Antony. It doesn't feel terrible to rudely boss him around.

Antony hesitates, but obeys after a moment. I can't help but notice, though, the large, loping strides he takes away. He's going to rush back as quickly as he can. So I turn to Keelan. "Is there something you're looking for from me?"

"No, not much," Keelan says. "I just sent the others away to ensure you would be honest. Not pressured by anyone else's presence to lie to me. This is my island, and I am responsible for it all. So. How has everything been for you so far? Have your activities gone smoothly?"

"Yes," I lie, because if I didn't trust Antony enough to tell him the truth about the corpse and what's happened to the ammiralia, I'll tell Keelan only when the Aeditanian Sea freezes over. "It's all been marvelous. I love getting to see the sights with the Rubellians."

"I see." Keelan doesn't sound at all interested, but then, I don't know why else he's asked me that. "And how have you found your hosts? I trust Calista has been polite?"

"Oh, so polite," I say. "She's a most gracious host and person. I think the Verigal City society papers would love her for her hosting skills."

"I see." Keelan steps in front of me. "She has said nothing alarming?"

In my mind, I laugh long and loud, which is what stops me from doing so really. "Not at all. Why would she?"

Keelan's face crinkles at the shadow of his mouth. "Oh, Calista loves to get attention, and sometimes, she seeks it out in negative ways." He sounds like he's talking about a toddler.

He lifts my hands between us, a thumb brushing over the base of my gloves, but unlike when Calista did the same, I only feel a vague, cold queasiness in my stomach. For one ordinary moment, I think he might be about to comment on them. And then he says, "Are you afraid of death, Lucia?"

"What?" I sputter, because—well, I have no idea what to say to that. Half of me thinks I must've heard him wrong, but I also have no idea what ordinary question I could've mistaken that for.

"Are you afraid of death?" he repeats, monotone, as if that's a perfectly normal question to have posed.

Since I can't continue under the delusion that I simply heard wrong, I try to pull my hands free of his. But his fingers lock down, tight and icy cold as the walls of the cave, and I guess I'm not getting out of this. "Why are you asking me that?" I need to understand because it feels like there's a wrong answer to his question, and I really, really don't want to give it to him. Is he asking as a strange way of alluding to the corpse I found, of telling me he knows? Is this a threat?

Keelan shrugs. "Curiosity, I suppose. I will not die—not really, because I'm a part of this island's magic. So I do not remember much what it is like to even consider it."

"Well, to be honest, I don't think about my own death all that much," I say. Cold crawls down my fingertips, up my palms, and I try to breathe evenly, to remind myself that Keelan can't possibly do anything to me in front of everyone here. Right?

Keelan tilts his blank face. "No? You do not feel it coming for you? Creeping ever closer, reaching for you now?"

"Not . . . really." I cast a sidelong look into the crowd, searching for Antony, Calista, Oriana, even the ammiralia—anyone I can shoot a desperate look at to beg them to come over here and interrupt this.

"Interesting."

"Should I?" No one's out there to help me, so perhaps, I just need to be direct. "Are you threatening me?" At the very least, if he is, I want to know why.

"Threatening?" Keelan's blank face crinkles with what might be amusement. Or shock. Very hard to tell without features. "Oh, no. I told you I am only curious. I only wonder if you were given the chance to escape death forever, how interested you would be."

"Probably interested," I say slowly because I still have no idea what he's getting at. "I think most of us humans would be. But there's no such thing as immortality."

"I just told you that I am, though," Keelan says.

"Yeah," I say, "but that's different. You're a Vessel, and I—"

"Lucia!" Antony lopes back to us, a skewer of some unknown sort of meat in hand, and for the first time in a long time, I'm not angry to see him. Instead, the warmth of relief washes over me, easing the ice in my hand.

Keelan releases my hands. Even though he has no eyes for me to follow, I could swear he's still staring at them.

"The ammiralia has been asking where her guide is," Antony says. "May I, Keelan?"

Keelan inclines his head, and Antony wraps his arm over my shoulder and steers me away from his brother. The touch isn't entirely necessary, but this time, I let it slide. I'm shakier than I realized, only feeling how I'm trembling against his steadying, sure, and solid grip. I throw one last glance over my shoulder. Keelan hasn't moved. He stares silently as we walk away.

"Thanks for that. Has your brother always been so . . . awkward?" It's the nicest way I can phrase my feelings because Keelan *is* Antony's brother after all. I don't need to insult him. Of course, Antony's the one who didn't want me stuck alone with him in the first place.

Antony gives a short bark of laughter. "Awkward. Right. No, not really."

I open my mouth to ask, *So what happened?* but quickly snap it shut again because I should be trying to get on with my night, not sink into conversation with Antony.

"I know you wanted to ask what happened." Antony shoots me a sidelong look. "I know you, you know. You're too curious about everything."

His arm on my shoulder is too heavy then, and I quickly toss it off, spinning to face him. "Fine, I did, but I was trying not to be rude."

He extends one of the skewers to me, but I shake my head. "I'm really not hungry. Thanks, though. And thanks for . . ." I can't bring myself to say *rescuing me.*

Antony twirls the skewer, studying it, before dropping his hand to his side. "Keelan was actually very charismatic. I was the awkward kid between us. Before he became a Vessel, I mean."

I can't believe it. I sneak a look over at the creepy Key Vessel before I can stop myself, and Antony gives a soft, sad laugh. "I know you can't believe it."

"Being a Vessel really changes someone that much?" I ask. "I know they become part of the magic and all, but . . . I thought they were still there."

Antony pauses, closes his eyes, and then shakes his head slowly. "I thought so, too. Before. That's what everyone says, isn't it? But it—" His voice grows thick, choked. "It doesn't feel like that, actually seeing it happen to someone I loved. He doesn't even remember so many things we did as children. My favorite days we shared—they don't mean anything at all to him anymore, but they used to." He shakes his head again. "It feels most often like a faceless monster is puppeteering my brother's body." He opens his eyes, and their soft brown glistens.

I can't help myself. I reach out and set a hand on his shoulder, even though I probably shouldn't. But I can't even imagine how I would feel if I woke up and one day, Severin didn't even remember our times together, if he saw me as a stranger all of a sudden, and he felt like one to me, too. "I'm sorry."

Antony shrugs, the movement tossing my hand aside, and that's how I know more than anything he's truly distressed. "I shouldn't feel upset about it. It's the life he was always destined to have, and I grew up knowing that, too."

"But you didn't know exactly what it was going to mean."

He shrugs again, the motion too fast to convey the detachment he probably wants it to.

"Have you ever thought about not being the liaison to the city?" It can't help him to constantly be around this body that doesn't belong to the boy he remembers anymore. "Surely there's some other Vessel's sibling that could do it." Bitterness, bitterness that really shouldn't be there, seeps into my words. Because if that's true, why didn't he already do it? He could've stayed in the city with me. Maybe he would've been able to help me pay the debt with actual coins instead of me having to make this final, desperate gamble to get the source.

He shakes his head. "Keelan's destiny was to be a Vessel, and this was mine. And . . . I promised him. If there's any part of him that's still in there, and I left him behind—" His voice grows thicker again, cutting off his words, but I don't need to hear more, even though I don't know what else I can possibly say.

Part of me wants to hug him. Part of me wants to shove him. I hate him for the way he's jerked me around, hate him for the fact that he clearly puts his duty to this lousy island far above whatever we had, and yet, this is the man, the one who would never break the promise he made to his brother, who kept me coming back night after night.

"I only feel sorry for the family of whoever they pick as the additional Vessel, since they won't have prepared their whole life to lose their child and sibling."

I tilt my head. "Additional Vessel?"

Antony steps back, eyes suddenly growing clear. He blinks, and their softness, their pain, vanishes. "You aren't supposed to know any of that."

"I'm perfectly capable of keeping a secret." Before I can stop myself, I even wink. I want to think it's just trying to put him at ease, not some wild grasp for the past we had, the past I *don't want* any-more. I step back in turn, drawing the curtain of reality down between us. "You said the ammiralia asked for me?"

"She didn't," Antony says. "I said that to take you from Keelan. But you should stay with her and the ammiraligna as much as you can manage tonight."

"For my sake or theirs?" I ask.

"Because it's your job," he says coldly. "And as of fairly recently, you told me you cared about doing that properly."

I wave a hand at him. "And I do. Obviously. Which is why I'm going to them. Right now."

He doesn't stop me as I scuttle around him. And I'm not sure if I appreciate that—or hate that he doesn't try to stop me once again. The threads of our conversation tug at me as I walk away, almost tempting me to be the one to stop. It feels unfinished. It feels as though we were just on the brink of . . . *something*. A real apology from him, perhaps.

But I don't know if he did offer a real apology, if he did begin to offer me the truth, what that would mean. Would I want to be with him again? Could I actually trust him?

So I ignore the lingering feeling. It's easier to walk away. I have a theft to plan.

CHAPTER NINETEEN

Antony trails behind me as I walk off to find the Rubellians, passing a large patio with stones of all colors, constantly shifting. Some sort of music begins as we walk by, and people clear away from it, making it obvious the area is a dance floor. It's a sound a little like a woman's croon—except wordless and distorted—and seems to be emanating from the waterfalls themselves, rising like steam where they hit the pools. It's got to be something altered with magic, some special sort of song we can only hear on Estaralla, but like the music that's drifted through Vessel Dionne's home, it gives me the creeps. In my opinion, this sort of noise can stay here on the island, and everyone is better off for it.

"Another word of advice," Antony says, catching up to me. "I hope Calista wasn't serious about a dance and said that to irritate Keelan, but if she asks, you absolutely should not dance with her tonight." A snappish edge hardens Antony's voice, and all of my own muscles clench up in preparation to fight back.

"I don't need your advice," I say, but I also can't help but notice he's singled Calista out as the problem. Not, *don't dance*, but *don't dance with Calista*. "But why? Do you think Calista is a threat to me?"

"Not an intentional one," Antony says. "But if Calista asks you to dance, she's aggressively flouting the rules put down for her, and the Vessels won't be happy. And as I told you already, you'll be the one punished because she's untouchable. Trust me. I'm just trying to look out for you."

A few sets of partners trickle their way back onto the dance floor. The dance, at least, appears to be a standard partner Prenician waltz—although some of the couples seem to be following an entirely different beat than others, and I'm not sure any of them are truly in time with the strange music.

"I have zero reason to trust you. It's not like you're reliable in telling the truth." A bit of fury boils in my belly, but my chest stays ice-cold. Even though I don't trust Antony, Keelan also told Vessel Dionne to worry more about Calista than my competence when we first arrived on the island, and I'm fed up with no one telling me what's supposedly wrong with her, especially when I'm putting trust in her. "The rules that were put down for *her*? Does Calista have additional rules around dancing?"

Antony sighs. "Don't repeat this story. It's . . . not a secret, exactly, but Dionne naturally doesn't like it being talked about. About a year ago, the tour guide who was staying with her and Vessel Dionne was killed. Calista was . . . very close to the girl. Rumors said they were lovers."

My mouth parts. At least my slack jaw is hidden beneath the mask. Antony's blunt words answer the question that's been flickering at the edges of my mind—does Calista like other women? It's the sort of thing that's only hinted at in Verigal City, two women like that.

"When her lover died, she turned paranoid and angry. She

terrified the next girl sent to stay with them so badly they weren't allowed to host another for a full year. Vessel Dionne says she's better now, but the rest of the Vessels are still concerned. You're the first people who've stayed with them since. Understand now?"

My mouth's gone dry, and I don't trust myself to speak, so all I can manage is a silent nod. I don't even know how to pick through all the emotions that rise in its wake. A little bit of horror, a little bit of pity for her, and something—ugly and twisted. Maybe even jealous. I've been flattered by Calista trying to protect me. I thought maybe that meant I was special, but obviously, she's been closer to other guides in the past. That probably shouldn't bother me, though, since it's not like *I* want Calista like that.

The only decent thing about my silence is that it effectively ends the conversation. Antony, apparently, takes it as understanding.

I spot Oriana and Ammiralia Rubellian at the edge of the floor, standing partially beneath a hunched tree with tumbling green branches. Wrapped into a few coiled branches sit wineglasses full of red liquid that I assume is wine, but don't trust. Nor do I trust how the tree appears to hold them in its twisting tendrils. But the ammiralia has no fear, yanking one out as I hustle away from Antony and cross the final steps to them alone.

"Evening, *lumina*." I hope the scowl on the ammiralia's face isn't because of me as she hurls her wine back rather quickly. "Are you not enjoying the party so far?"

Oriana stands jauntily, hand propped on a hip. "It's perfectly fine. She's just in a mood because *shockingly* someone else had the same idea as she did regarding the conte, and he already has another partner for this first dance." Now I see why she looks like she's hiding glee—and poorly.

"Oriana." It's a snap that turns into a sigh, and the ammiralia takes another sip, a little less egregious than the first.

"She'd been hoping we'd be the only ones," Oriana continues, leaning closer to me and lowering her voice. "Because now, I have to compete with other women to win his interest, and she doesn't trust I can."

The ammiralia sighs again. "That's not entirely true, sweet. You know you're quite a beautiful girl when made up properly, and most men do appreciate a wife with a bit of a wit. It's helpful for entertaining your guests. You could be a catch if you just tried."

Oriana's lips thin, and she raises her eyebrows at me. "There it is."

I sling an arm over her shoulder, hoping perhaps to her mother it looks like some kind of consolation. Or persuasion. Whichever works for me. I lean in and whisper, "Well, I know you aren't interested in this ball at all tonight, so I set up another little excursion for us. I've found a—a clue. To the monster's lair."

"Is that so?" Oriana murmurs.

I nod. "Don't you hear that?"

Oriana cocks her head. "No?"

I use magic to throw a little sound, a sort of rumbling growl, far off in the distance, hoping it's bland enough to not draw anyone else's attention here. I watch the crowd, but nobody's head turns. A small smile pulls Oriana's mouth, though.

Her gaze flicks just beyond me. "What about Mother?"

"We can excuse ourselves to the lavatory," I suggest. It's a classic way to sneak off, not terribly creative, but a classic for a reason.

"Not a good plan. Mother will murder me if I walk away before this foolish dance. She'd probably prefer I wet myself and hope the magic in this dress will cover the stench." She wrinkles her nose. "After?"

It's far from my preference, but as I'm scrambling for something I can say to her or a lie to feed the ammiralia, the music halts, and my opportunity is lost.

A young man approaches the three of us, wearing a tailored suit that's in mild taste compared to most of the costumes, but would fit in well in the rest of the peninsula. It's not hard to guess who he is because he's one of the few people with his face exposed. It's a relatively handsome face, too, with sun-kissed golden skin, a carved jaw, and full lips, and he has a rather pretty way of smiling as he bows to Oriana. His gaze flickers to a small card, which he then hastily stuffs away.

"I believe you are Ammiraligna Rubellian? Next on my dance card?"

Oriana curtsies, lowering her head, which I think is strategic on her part to hide her face. "That's me." She barely manages to sound more bored than angry.

The conte extends a hand to her, and as if on cue, the next song begins, which unfortunately for me is no less eerie than the first. Ammiralia Rubellian gives Oriana a small push forward. Oriana sighs, still as bad an actress as always, and he intones, "The honor of this dance is mine."

He pulls her into motion, guides her through sweeping turns and spins. He looks an impeccable dancer, and Oriana does admirably. It might've been a beautiful sight if she wasn't scowling. They're a handsome couple—even though it feels a bit like a betrayal to think as much because Oriana's so clearly unhappy about the whole thing.

I turn to wander the perimeter—might as well see what kind of options we have for an exit while Oriana's dancing—and determine which direction we need to be headed. I run the same test I ran at both the Pool of Dreams and Cave of Ghosts, the creation of a little flower. I check that no one's watching me, but no one is—too caught up either in the swirl of the dance or the glamor of the party. Even still, I do it quickly, one hand covering my other wrist, from which I pinch the flower into existence.

This test isn't like the ones before. The magic slams into me still, but this time, it's not like a tidal wave, but a punch straight through my chest and to my heart. It's not just diffuse, hitting me from every direction—it's coming from somewhere specific.

I turn slowly while my heartbeat speeds up, both from the steady pounding stream of energy that hits me and the realization that I'm close for once. The traces of magic here aren't just direct from the source as Keelan said—it's somewhere near here.

I face the palace itself first because, well, it would make plenty of sense for the Vessels to have built their own home over it. But as I stare at the shimmering rainbow of a building, close my eyes, and focus, I can feel—the beam isn't before me. It's coming from behind.

So I turn again and find myself staring up the face of a cliff, from where the waterfalls tumble. I don't love that I have to figure out how to get up there. Hopefully there's a back path of some kind—I'm not going to be able to climb that cliff, let alone in front of this entire gathering.

I start to head to the side, keeping the cliff face to my right, to see if I can find an alternate trail when Calista steps into my path. Her mask matches the fiery ends of her gown, a beautiful half mask of curling flames over a fake face with dark red lips, and as I see it, I wonder how closely the painted mouth resembles her own beneath it.

"Lucia?" She extends a hand, palm up.

As though I've no memory of anything whatsoever, because it's a perfectly scripted gesture I've seen countless times before, I glance down and ask, "What are you doing?"

Calista laughs, and it's like the first sip of wine, sweeping away all the rest of my thoughts about how I should be scouting out the area and filling me only with effervescent warmth. "I told you to save me a dance, did I not?"

"Oh." My voice is a squeak, and my heart gives a hard kick. Antony's warning bubbles up, but I'm not entirely sure it's only that making my pulse beat faster. There's a familiar fluster setting in that I've experienced before with Calista, turning my mind all but blank. "Um, but, *can* you? Dance with me?"

"I'm an excellent leader, I promise. As good as any man." She speaks in her lower voice, the voice I've come to think of as her real voice, although there's an edge I've never heard before. It's something both lightly teasing and darkly suggestive, a caress made into words. Like when she kissed my hand in greeting, it feels like she's flirting with me. Maybe, even, she is. I'd thought that an impossible explanation at first, but based on what Antony said, maybe it's not.

That wasn't at all what I was asking, but a wave of something new rises in me, drowning Antony's warning under its crush. What do I care if the Vessels are annoyed? "I didn't mean it as an insult. I meant . . . I've never danced with a girl before."

"Well, I'd be more than happy to be your first. All you have to do is follow my lead."

Oh. She is *definitely* flirting.

The one small mercy is that my mask hides how red my face must be. My cheeks burn as though all her flames are real. It's ridiculous how flustered I am. It's not like I'm inexperienced with romance even if I've never been with another girl. I'd never considered other girls an option.

If I want to turn her down, I have the easy excuse that Antony did tell me to stay with the Rubellians—although claiming I need to keep the ammiralia company would ruin my chance of scouting the area later. But curiosity pushes me forward, and I take that excuse itself as rationale. If I'm not going to be able to scout the area right now either way, I'd rather spend the time dancing with Calista than standing with the grumpy ammiralia. I *am* curious. I can't deny it. If I don't try, a part of me will always wonder what it would've been like. So I give her my hand.

She lifts my hand and sets her other at my waist, and then we tumble into the music. Her movements are ethereal, as is the pressure of her hand at my waist and her grip on my hand. Despite the lightness of her touch—or perhaps because of it—everything around fades away. My senses dull, until all that's left is the brush of her fingers, and so she guides me through the dance steps with the most effortless strokes of her hands.

She *is* a good leader. Not that I expected anything else. She doesn't seem like she's bad at much of anything.

With each curl of her fingers into the small of my back, a flush crawls its way across my body, and it's distracting. I feel like I'm about to trip any moment now, so I grasp for words, something to focus on besides her. "Ammiralia Rubellian seems to be handling her illness well."

"I think she's just good at hiding discomfort," Calista says. "She's been doing it all her life, you know. We all wear our masks. Some of us wear them better than others."

She lifts an arm and twirls me, leaving those words to echo in my ears.

And you? I want to ask. *How well do you wear yours? Do I see behind it now, or is it still there?*

She pulls me back in, and inadvertently, I let out a soft gasp as her body presses against mine once again. "Uh," I say quickly as if I could *possibly* cover that, "how did you learn to lead, anyway?"

"My dance teacher, of course," she says. "We're all instructed here because of these balls. I insisted mine teach me to lead as well. Mother was furious, but it was already done when she found out. Nothing she could do." I can hear her glee, hear the smile in her voice, and a thrill snakes through me.

She glances up suddenly, and I follow her gaze to the overhang where the Vessels except for Keelan stand watch. The warmth drains from me as I stare at the six of them, their blank faces. Somehow, even though they don't have gazes that I can track, I just know they're watching the two of us. Calista must've felt it, too, that sensation of being watched, even if these people are without eyes. And the longer I look at them, the more everything else fades, a blur, a tunnel, leading me straight to them. The sound of the music quiets, and instead, a low, frantic whispering of nothingness begins to hiss in my ears.

Calista tightens her grasp on me and leans in, jolting me back into my own skin with the brush of her mask against my bare shoulder. "Look, I need to warn you." The music covers our conversation well enough, as her mask hovers close to mine. "My instructions not to eat anything—it's *critical* you follow them tonight. Touch nothing. And if—if anything strange should start to happen, don't move, and you'll be fine."

"Why do you think something bad is going to happen?"

"It may not. We are at the Island Ball after all. But there's a lot of magic in the air, and it feels unstable. And that can lead to bad things."

This close to her, it's all too obvious that her gaze drops from mine as she says the last sentence. She's lying. Or hiding something. "Why would the magic be unstable?" I press because this is a perfect time to. She's not going to want to draw the attention of walking away from me in the middle of a dance.

Her gaze focuses somewhere distant over my shoulder, and her arm around my waist stiffens, but she says nothing. But I can find out if she knows about Teresta's poisoner and isn't telling me about it. I can't make her speak, but she also can't hide her reaction this close. "Is it because of the poison?"

Her gaze snaps up to mine immediately. "What do you know about the poison? Did Antony tell you?"

I bristle. "Antony doesn't tell me anything. It was a creepy voice in the Cave of Ghosts, actually."

"And what did this creepy voice say?" She's still looking at me, at least, but it doesn't feel like victory. Her grip on me is just as stiff, and in fact, I actually think she's trying to turn the interrogation around on *me* now.

"That the magic's getting poisoned, but they don't know who's doing it, except that they call the perpetrator the Shadow. That's it." It's enough of the truth I'm confident my delivery'll be convincing, even under her scrutiny. "So if you knew about the poison, why didn't you warn me about it?"

Calista sighs, her grip and body softening against mine in a way that makes me want to soften, too, when I need to stay focused. "I did warn you, you know. Indirectly. But perhaps it won't shock you to hear that the islanders have all agreed to keep the fact that the magic is getting poisoned to ourselves. If that information made it off the island, we'd be in huge trouble, wouldn't we?"

"So then why would the weird, creepy cave voice tell me about it?" I ask. "Why would she want to put the island at risk?"

"I really don't know. As the one who actually spoke to this cave voice, you're in a better position to answer that than me." She lifts an arm, turns me halfway, leaving our arms crossed over my chest, my back pressed to her. This isn't a common step in the Prenician waltz—one, it's rather impossible for the wealthy in their bustled dresses, and two, as a result, it's considered rather scandalous. "Can you follow the steps without my lead for a moment?" Calista murmurs at my ear. "And keep your arms crossed, as though mine are still there?"

"I'll try." Before we lost our money, I attended some dance lessons as a child to try to ensure I wouldn't be a clumsy embarrassment at a ball, but it's been a long time. So much for that theory, Mamma. Then again, if we hadn't lost all our meager fortune, I probably would've had to endure plenty more years of lessons and might not be as unsteady now.

I focus on my feet as hard as I can, mutter the count beneath my breath, while Calista's hands brush against the side of my neck. I trip, missing the step, but somehow Calista follows me in my missed step anyway, hands a weight against the back of my neck now, making the timing of this dance swirl in my mind. What is she doing?

"One, two, three," I mutter louder now, and Calista's arms lock around me, spinning me back out and into the standard position just as the music winds to a close.

Calista releases me and gives a little bow, as any proper leader would. I'm supposed to curtsy back, but my legs are surprisingly weak, so I barely manage a bob, not wanting to risk my knees dumping me on the ground.

"Thank you for the dance," I say at least, my own proper response.

Calista extends a hand again, an offer of another. "My pleasure."

I can't. Even though I can't say there's not a part of me that's tempted. But Oriana will be done dancing now, too, and we've got a search to sneak away to conduct. "I should return to the Rubellians, I think. This ball's for their enjoyment—not mine."

Calista inclines her head. "So dutiful. You can find me if you get bored of that." She steps forward, and as she passes, she murmurs, "Tuck it beneath your dress." My hand rises to my neck to find what she gave me, locking around a chain there. On the front, there's a thin metal disk as the only adornment.

"Why?" I ask. "What is it exactly?"

"It's protection," Calista says. "The strongest we have, gifted only to those of us the island can't afford to lose, and I'm not supposed to loan it to anyone else. If the Vessels see it, they'll take it from you."

I shove it down the front of my shirt, best as its somewhat low cut allows anyway, a million more questions rising on my tongue that I don't have time for—like why she would give it to me, what that means about her safety. Because even if I want to know these things, they're not as important right now as my hunt for the Shadow or the source.

I watch her flickering flames move away from me and drift among the others in the crowd. No one else is as bright as she is, and no one else moves quite like she does. She has a grace and a subtle sway of her hips that makes it hard to look anywhere else, and my side and my hand still tingle from her touch.

I force myself to turn back to the little copse where I left the ammiralia. I'm not going to find the source by gawking after Calista.

Oriana's already back and lifts a hand, spotting me. "Lucia!"

The ammiralia turns, too, absolutely beaming now, and chirps, "Little sparrow!"

She's altogether too satisfied, and given how the conte hovers just over Oriana's shoulder, it's not hard to guess why. I gnash my teeth. This was not what I needed. Oriana sidles up to me.

"I was hoping you'd be my escort while Niccolo and I go for a little stroll." She's smiling, and it takes a lot for me to not angrily snap, *I thought you weren't interested in the conte?*

There's no way for me to say *no*, though. I'll just have to reformulate a plan on this walk. Perhaps I can abandon Oriana and the conte at some point along the way. The walk does at least give me an excuse to slip away from the main gathering.

I nod. "Of course."

Oriana loops her arm through mine and drags me away, down a small path into the copse of trees. The glasses hanging from these trees sparkle in the darkness, a light illuminating the bright red liquid within them that may or may not be wine.

"I thought you weren't interested in the conte," I murmur to Oriana, a little bold, since she's still clinging to my arm while the conte merely drifts along behind us, a strangely silent shadow trailing.

"Oh, I'm absolutely not," Oriana chirps. "But you see, this is by far the most effective way to leave Mother behind and have her not start to make a fuss about how long we've been away."

I blink and stifle the flash of laughter. My chest loosens, relief flooding into the cracks. "*Oh*. That's—smart." I have to focus on that, not how betrayed I briefly felt when I'd thought Oriana had lied to me, been misleading me about her attitude toward the conte all along.

"I told you, your lavatory plan was bad. I improved it," Oriana says with a little sniff, and I give her a little shove, untangling our arms.

"Aren't you a proud one."

She gives a flourish of her hand and half a bow while still walking.

"But what about him?" I give a nod back in his direction. I suppose if I must, I can make this foolish thing a game for him, too, distract both him and Oriana while I seek out the magic. The plan's not ruined. Not ruined at all.

Oriana shrugs. "He just didn't want to stay at the party. Said he came to the island to get *away* from balls and suitors."

At that, he bounds up to us. "It's never-ending. Exhausting." He offers a broad grin, but I'm glad the mask means I don't need to offer him one. This may be something he and Oriana can connect over, but I personally find ripping my hands to shreds during midnight magic shows in the gang's casinos and brothels to be far more exhausting.

He stops walking again—abruptly. "Did you hear that?"

That's my line. Except I haven't thrown a sound out there yet. I consider just using the opportunity anyway so that I don't need to bother, but then I hear it, too.

Somewhere above us, a deep rumble vibrates, the sound rattling all the way down to my bones.

CHAPTER TWENTY

Part of me wants to ignore the sound, stick to the plan. I've gotten away from the crowd; I'm on my way to try to find the magic. I can't afford to turn back now. But a cold queasiness slips through me with the rumbling, a familiar feeling of illness, and I remember Calista's warning.

Bad things happen on nights like these.

I don't obey her warning, though, and stay still. The trees leer over us on either side with their crimson-red goblets, and I don't want the three of us to be alone if something is coming.

I hike my skirts and jog back in the direction of the ball. As soon as I can see the courtyard again, I follow the line of the sparkling, winking cliffs up to the top, toward the sky.

At the top of the waterfalls, the water doesn't glitter a gray blue as it does the rest of the way down. It gleams a molten black. I blink a few times, and when it doesn't change, I scrub at my eyes as best I can with the tips of my fingers.

Still, it gleams black.

Scuffling sounds behind me, Oriana appearing at my side and the conte a beat later.

The darkness creeps forward in the water. A few black streaks escape the top of the cliff and plummet into the pools nearby. They curl in the crystal blue like snakes.

Above, a crack like thunder sounds. It's the sound of fabric ripping somewhere high in the sky. More and more black tendrils slip down the falls.

"Lucia!" Oriana clamps a hand around my upper arm, yanking me from my stillness. "What's happening? Is this the monster? Were we too slow?"

Oh, I wish. That'd mean I was in control.

Ahead of us, the crowd on the dance floor has stilled. The music falls silent, leaving only the rumbling above and the hissing of water and a few whispers darting around between people.

"The Shadow," I hear someone whisper.

It's the first time I've heard whispers of the Shadow at large, but I have no idea what it means right now. Is the Shadow here?

If the Shadow is here, this might be my chance. All I have to do is run, rip the mask off, and I'm done with this island forever. My gaze darts around the crowd. How am I even supposed to know which one of these masks hides this so-called Shadow?

Plus, Calista told me to stay still if something started to happen, and something is definitely happening.

"It's not the monster. Something's coming, but if we stay still, we'll be fine," I tell Oriana, placing one of my hands over hers on my arm. I need her to be fine. *I* need to be fine, and Calista hasn't given me bad advice yet.

But if it becomes clear to me which person here's the Shadow, then I'll move.

Above us, a silver mist coalesces around the top of the falls. It shimmers and glows with its own light, but beneath it, the green grass curls in on itself.

The ammiralia stands a few steps away, her glass raised in hand, and she calls to me, "Is this a show?"

"No." I barely stop myself from giving a panicked laugh. The fear hangs heavy in the air, so thick it's like a palpable vibration of the heartbeats of everyone in the crowd. How can the ammiralia not sense it? How can she still believe everything's fine here with what happened to her in the caves? Truly, that is the gift of money. It buys an unwavering belief that you're untouchable. Because most of the time, you are. "Just don't move, *lumina*. Until it passes."

Oriana's fingers tighten around my upper arm, squeezing the blood and warmth from my veins. "Are you sure?" she whispers, and no, no, I'm definitely not. All I can do is trust Calista.

I can't even force the lie out through my dry throat, so I simply nod.

The mist spills over the top of the edge and crawls down the cliffs. The vines winding up the cliff crumble beneath it, shriveling first to brown, then to gray, then dissolving beneath the mist. A few of the revelers on the edge of the dance floor slowly back away from it, but those closest stay utterly still. That's both a slight comfort—if they're doing what Calista advised, her advice is probably sound—and an eerie sight. A flash of movement ahead shows only one lone person jogging, weaving through the rest who've frozen, as though a spell has been cast on them all, except the unfortunately ignorant one.

Deep in my chest, behind my heart, the space where I feel magic begins to burn. The taste of ashes fills my mouth, and my tongue is dry as sand. I squeeze Oriana's shoulder. Her fear wraps around us both, twining with mine into an icy and bitter mix.

Antony emerges from the crowd, jogging the final steps toward us. *He* was the one moving through the crowd, which surprises me because he must know the reasons behind the warning Calista gave me. He stops before us, breathing not quite even.

"What's going on?" I demand, although I don't expect an answer from him.

He shakes his head. "Just stay still. Think of it like you're being hunted. You don't want it to see you. Okay?"

Even if it's not as much information as I'd like, it's something and it corroborates Calista's advice.

He extends a hand. I eye it, and I'm sure my gaze contains enough skepticism even with my face hidden, because he says, "Look, I can help to . . . confuse it."

The mist reaches the bottom of the cliffs, swallowing those around the pool at the base first before it continues to curl outward. It draws nearer. I swallow my pride because humiliation is better than death and seize Antony's hand.

He steps in, not quite pulling me into his chest, leaving a small space between us, but still positioning himself as a shield.

The mist curls around our ankles. Its edges peel away, small fingers of gray that stroke our feet and the bottoms of our legs. My calves tingle, and in my chest, there's a deep, dark hole that's been opened.

Oriana yells, something harsh and indistinct, but then the mist swallows us.

She falls silent.

I can't see her at my side.

I can't see Antony in front.

I only see where our hands our joined, where Oriana clutches my arm with hers, and I hold Antony's.

A second *crack* splits the air, a flash of light somewhere deep in the gray. Sparks fly across my vision, currents of energy crackling in the air. Dark figures flicker in the light. They look like hooded humans, tall and relatively shapeless.

I glance down at Oriana's fingers again near my shoulder.

Black veins crawl across the back of her hands.

No.

On my other side, Antony's skin glows gold against the darkness.

And my own skin—it's got the same golden shimmer, the glow dimmer where it disappears into my gloves, growing brighter up my arms, brightest still at my collarbone where Calista's necklace hangs just below the edge of my shirt. I peel Oriana's fingers from my arm, and hold them tight in my own. They leave searing red burn marks behind.

What feels like cold fingers scrabble at my neck, picking along the edges of the mask. The sharp tang of metal slides into my mouth, and my mouth fills with hot liquid, like I've taken a large swallow of blood.

I open my mouth, and whatever it is pours out, sliding down my chin. It burns against my skin. A sizzle and the smell of ash fills the air.

The mask there has melted away.

A third *crack* tears through the silence, followed by a burning wind. It strikes my face, then hits my chest like a punch to the gut. Magic flares in me, a rush of energy I've never felt before. It races through my blood, hums high in my ears, like a shrilling bird. I feel

I could simply leap and lift off from the ground and never come back down.

Then it fades.

As quickly as it came, the mist recedes, leaving the wreckage behind it. Oriana appears at my side, and she drops to her knees, a soft whimper, while my hand still crushes hers. The same black veins that afflicted her mother wind up her arms, all the way to her elbow. They bulge and pulse with what must be every beat of her heart.

"Oriana." I break out of Antony's grasp and drop beside her, grabbing her chin in one hand. As I turn her face toward me, her eyes don't quite meet mine. A glassy sheen covers them, and I don't think she sees any of the reality before her.

The ground is gray ash. It crumbles beneath my knees, rising about us, a swirl of death. A chill coats the air. I glance to the side, seeking the ammiralia to see if she can help her daughter—but she's gone. And where she'd stood, there's a glossy red swipe. Maybe it's her drink, spilled.

It also looks a little like blood.

As the mist vanishes, everything suddenly returns to how it'd been, swift as a blink, so thorough and so sudden I could almost think I imagined the ash and blood. The landscape is all lush green-ery and flowers once more. The pools are bright blue again, a shim-mering, sharp color that glows with its own light.

The ammiralia is still gone.

Oriana stirs in my grasp, her eyes clearing. "Oh," she murmurs, and presses a hand to her forehead, and I wrap an arm around her shoulder to try to keep her steady while she trembles. "I feel horrible."

I scan the crowd, desperately now, for the ammiralia. Maybe she disobeyed and moved. But if she did, where did she go? I look up at Antony and realize with the way my mask's cracked, he can see my lips, so I mouth, "The ammiralia," and give a jerk of my head to indicate where she'd been. Where the stain had been. Where now, there's only grass, tall and proud and without any imprints of someone having stood there not long ago.

Antony spins away, leaving me stroking Oriana's back while my heart pounds hard. Whispers of other conversations drift toward me.

"Shadow attack—"

"Who's missing?"

"—never been so bold before."

"Is everyone here?"

Oriana lifts her head, untangling herself from me, and staggers to her feet. Her gaze lands on the last place the ammiralia had been, and she frowns. "Mother?"

She whips toward the crowd with surprising energy for how much she's still shaking and takes several lurching steps forward. A group of three masked women near us back away as she approaches, gasps stinging the air.

"The Shadow's marks!"

I stalk after Oriana, plant myself in front of them. "What does that mean—the Shadow's marks?"

They glance at one another, and then one says quietly, "The Shadow is corrupting magic, making people disappear. When he wants to take you next, *those* marks appear." She waves a gloved hand in the direction of Oriana's hands. Oriana lifts them, studies them, and her eyes grow wide. Her lips part, and she wheezes.

A cold, hard lump settles in my stomach.

Those marks. Ammiralia Rubellian had the same ones.

"Take you?" I demand, because Oriana has frozen. "Take you where? How? When?" Teresta had only said this person was poisoning magic, not also kidnapping people.

The woman shrugs. "We don't know where. People just disappear. No one's ever found anyone he's taken. And he takes them— like this." She lifts both hands and twirls them. "The mist." She pins Oriana with a stare. "You'd better leave the island quickly, or the next time the mist comes, it'll be for you."

Oriana's gaze whips toward me and clings, desperately pleading. I want to look away, to dodge the question, dodge the truth. "Mother? Do you think—"

I consider the lies I could give. The story I could spin about the monster. But under the beating of Oriana's stare, I can't do it. Because it sounds like there *is* a monster on the island. It's real, and my pretend one will never stand a chance now.

"I think she's gone," I say softly.

Oriana drops to the ground with a wrenching sob.

CHAPTER TWENTY-ONE

In no time at all, Vessel Dionne marches through the crowd, trailed by Calista, and wastes little time in seizing Oriana by the arm. She leads us out of the palace even while Oriana screams, "Where's my mother? You have to do something!" She thrashes in Dionne's grasp, but the one time she manages to break free, she only manages three steps before she collapses. Calista says nothing at all. I look back at her several times, but her unbroken mask gives me nothing.

Vessel Dionne packs us into the litter. "I know you are worried, Ammiraligna Rubellian, but you will be much safer in my home. Calista will protect you. Please let us begin the search for your mother ourselves." Her lack of face is far from a comfort with those words.

The three of us return to the mansion in a grim cloud of silence. A few tears silently slide down Oriana's cheeks, and I rub circles into her back. She's slumped, her weakness more than grief. Shivers run through her body, and the darkened veins in her arm periodically give a few jumping twitches beneath her skin. In the early twilight, the flaming edges of Calista's mask glow. It buries any emotion she might have and makes her look like a god, judging our mortal frailty.

Oriana leans heavily on me as I lead her to bed. Calista stands in the doorway, silent and half in darkness, our own personal shadow.

"Do you really think they'll find her?" Oriana slides beneath the blankets I hold for her and curls onto her side, making herself very small. "Is she going to be okay?"

"Of course. They're going to do everything they can, I'm sure," I say.

It's true enough. They should be motivated to try to find her. It won't be good for their business if another tourist goes missing. But they've certainly explained away a disappearance before, and this time, well, this time, they've got a "guide" to take the blame.

Me.

Not that I'm sure how much that matters. The blame the Estarallans may or may not try to dump on me isn't even the biggest problem I have right now.

It's this Shadow. With that creepy voice in the Cave of Ghosts, the mist, the marks on my and Oriana's arms that Calista claims is the poisoned magic, the fear from everyone at the ball—it's definitely not enough to just steal the magic now.

I need to ensure the magic is restored to its original, not poisoned state. Because I have to give the Silverhands what they want, and that's the magic. If I can't do that, I'll never be free of them. It feels unfair that my already not-easy task is growing, warping into something even worse than it originally was. It makes it almost feel impossible—because what if the sacrifice doesn't work? Or what if I think it does, but then, there are still problems with the magic in the city? The Silverhands will blame me. Even if the problems happen years from now. They'll come back, come after me, ruin whatever happiness I've managed to scrape together for myself away from them.

I can't think about that now. The next few days will be difficult enough as it is.

With two days of the tour down, I only have three left.

I stay with Oriana until her breathing turns easy, and gentle waves of sleep flutter against my skin like feathers. Calista stands in the doorway, our guard, as the world grows darker and darker, and she becomes nothing more than a silhouette.

We step out together into the hall. There's no light at all here except a single silver sliver from the end, and we are alone in a dream world. While everyone else has gone to sleep, the ghosts have come out to play, and soft whispers drift up and down the corridor. It might be the wind. Or perhaps the Cave of Ghosts isn't the only place the spirits of magic wander.

"Tell me what happened to Ammiralia Rubellian," I say. "Is it because of the poisoning? Or was it something else that took her?"

"I don't know." Calista's voice rings low. I always used to think Antony's voice was made for night, but his is a bright and sunny day compared to Calista's.

"Some of the women at the ball talked about the Shadow," I say. "They seemed to think that's what took the ammiralia. What do you know about him?"

Calista sighs. "Very little. Including gender. The Shadow is . . . currently the one blamed for all the disruptions happening on the island, but it's all just rumors and speculation. Some people will tell you the Shadow is poisoning magic, some people say they're corrupting it, some people say they control it now, some people say they've birthed their own strange form of shadow magic that is the mist you saw." She shrugs. "No one really understands. But people have seen a mysterious figure in a dark cloak wandering the island, and what better way to tie all the tragedies occurring than a story of a villain?"

"So you don't think this Shadow took the ammiralia?"

"I don't. I'm sure we'll find her, though."

"If you don't even know what happened to her, then what makes you sure of anything?" I demand.

"I'll *make* sure of it." A breeze twists down the hall, and Calista's skirts lift and billow about her, making her a monstrous silhouette. And somehow, skeptical as I am, the words to argue stick in my throat. "And I'll be getting you a new mask in the morning."

Tomorrow. A new day to bring new horrors. My fingers find the jagged edges of my broken mask along my cheek, and Antony's warning to never take it off rings in my ears. "Do we need the masks?"

"You're safer with one," she says. "Masks hide you after all."

It's such an obvious statement that I hope there's a hidden insight in it I'm not understanding yet. "From what?" The air tickles the unprotected skin on my face.

"From everything." She touches my cheek, her fingers soft, but cold, and the touch tingles all the way down my spine. Suddenly, I realize, she's never seen any part of my face before now.

"No, but really." I pull her hand from my cheek. If she stays hidden, so do I. "Why do you wear masks here? The books say it's to honor the Vessels, but I don't believe that."

"You're right not to. They hide you from the magic trying to reclaim you early." She looms above me with those curling flames that glow in the darkness, only slightly dimmer than true fire would be.

"Reclaim like it reclaimed the tour guide?" I say slowly, and I can't help but wonder—the tour guide was dead, but would the magic take someone alive?

She inclines her head in what's probably a nod.

"So you never take off your mask?" I confirm.

"Very rarely. But a few seconds won't hurt." Before I have time to breathe, she lifts her other hand to her face and removes the mask.

I don't know really what I expected her to be underneath, but the girl who stares back at me is just that—a girl. Her eyes are rounder, and her cheeks are softer, while her lips are paler and fuller than the version painted on her mask. A smile flickers, and she drops her gaze, almost shy.

She extends her mask to me. "You should wear this tonight."

I lift my own mask from my face. "Are you sure? Don't you need it?"

Her gaze flickers over my now bare skin, studying me, skimming the curves of my cheeks and my lips. My breath comes in short puffs. I have to remind myself it's normal for someone to see my face. People have been looking at my face for years. It's not like I've just ripped all my clothes off, no matter how my nerves sing like I might as well have. I just hope my face looks . . . well, nice. I hope she's not disappointed with what she sees.

"You don't have to worry about me." She smiles broader, the corners of her eyes crinkling in a very alive sort of way that's hidden beneath the mask. How many times has she smiled at me like this before, and I missed it? It makes me oddly disappointed to wonder. "I have plenty of other masks to wear."

She steps closer, and my breath comes fast and shallow, and I don't know what I want to happen.

That's not true. I *do*. Her lips part slightly, and I want to know what they'll feel like, what they'll taste like. She lifts her hand to my cheek, and I lean in.

She presses her mask against my face. "And it's much more dangerous for you to be exposed so long," she murmurs.

Disappointment lashes my cheeks, but at least the mask hides their flush. I don't even want to think about the look I must've just given her. I'm sure she saw it, too—sure as if I'd just dropped at her feet. I'd try to hold on to the fact that I can't be the first girl who's swooned for her, but I know I'm not. And that doesn't help. It makes it worse.

The mask folds against my skin, adjusting tight. There's a lingering scent of something like singed sugar that I can only assume is her.

She pulls my mask from my hand and slides it over her face. The broken edge leaves her mouth exposed, and I can't help but watch the exact way her lips form the words, "Good night, then, Lucia."

I'm not sure if it's something I'll ever see again.

The next morning, I head to the dining room for breakfast, but it's empty. Only a breeze blows through the open window, silent and hollow. It drifts around the room, lifting the lacy drapes, and they flutter, telling me to get out.

Calista?

Oriana.

I run to Oriana's room, my heart stuck in my throat. Fear pulses in my veins, even as the remainder of my logic, trapped in an increasingly smaller corner of my mind, asks what it really matters if Oriana's gone. I'm here in Estaralla for one thing, and it's not her.

She sits cross-legged on top of her sheets, her face an ashen gray and covered in a thin sheen of sweat. She picks at the top of the covers, glaring at them, both furious and lost in the world.

"Oriana," I say.

The veins in her hand still bulge from her skin. "Is that you, Lucia?"

"Of course. Why . . ." I hesitate, then remember why she might be confused. I still wear Calista's mask, complete with its flaming edges. "Calista let me borrow her mask."

"So I see." Half a smile, half a smirk flits across Oriana's face.

"We're supposed to go to the Cloud Gardens today. But I thought we should discuss a change in schedule in light of . . . everything." I certainly don't want to be wasting my limited time traipsing around some set of gardens on clouds in the sky with rainbow waterfalls and panoramic views of the island. Especially since with our luck, the clouds might dissolve beneath our feet and send us plummeting to our deaths. And Oriana's so far proven quite reasonable. I can't imagine she'll enjoy herself with her mother missing and her own arms marked up in threat.

Oriana's brief amusement drops. "Yeah. We do have something to discuss. We going monster hunting today? Got all the clues lined up and ready for me to find my mother? The Vessels are just pretending to tell me not to do anything about it, right?"

"Uh." I was perfectly ready to go with that spin, but Oriana's tone comes in slicing, already on attack, and it knocks the words right out of my mouth.

"You guarantee I'll find her, right?" Oriana continues. "She's not really in danger? Just like that guide didn't really die—she was just a prop for a story, right?"

"Of course," I say, at least getting myself under control enough to say that with conviction.

Oriana unfolds and hops off the bed and onto the floor. "Okay. So you must know where she is right now. If I can cancel the trip to the Cloud Gardens, I can cancel this miserable monster-hunting portion of the tour, right? No one's told me we can't cancel any excursion we please. So I want to cancel it."

Shit. I wasn't ready for that. I grapple for an explanation. "It's—uh, very hard to cancel a storyline already in progress, but I'll see what I can do."

"Bullshit." Oriana takes a step closer, her chin jutting forward. "Mother paid over a million cincs for this thing. You know where Mother's located, so what's so hard about canceling? All you have to do is tell me where she is. Go on."

I weigh another lie against the truth. The way Oriana's talking, she's confident she's got me trapped. She's not *willing* to believe in this anymore. If I keep lying, I'm only going to keep eroding her trust. If I tell the truth, it's a hard blow to that trust, but I might be able to keep her hanging on enough to not fire me.

I shake my head. "You know I can't."

"Yeah, I knew it." Oriana folds her arms across her chest. "You lied to me. All along. When we found that tour guide, she was really dead. She wasn't some special portion of the tour just for me. There is no damn monster, or if there is, you haven't the slightest clue what to do about it."

I bow my head. "I'm sorry."

"Yeah, you should be!" Oriana marches forward until she's right in front of me, only her folded arms a barrier between her anger and myself. "If you'd told me the truth from the start, my mother might still be here. I might not be 'marked by the Shadow' to be next or whatever." She lifts her arms, pushing them into my face as if I haven't already been staring at the ominous markings there.

I lift my hands. "Look, I swear I didn't think anything was going to happen to your mother—or you. When the guide died in front of us, I thought it was just some freak accident. I had no idea it was part of a larger pattern, that it was something that'd happened before and would happen again. Much less something that was going to happen to one of the tourists!"

"So that's why you did it?" Oriana demands. "Because you thought we'd be fine? Good thinking, there!"

"Come on. You know you thought the same way. Even if you'd known that was a real girl who'd died and not a glamotura, you can't tell me you would've made the leap to thinking that you were in danger, too."

"No, I wouldn't have," Oriana says. "But I still would've told my mother about it, and we still would've ended the tour even if we weren't terrified for our own safety because we paid for a pleasant vacation, and pleasant vacations don't include corpses!"

I wince. "Yeah, but that's also why I did it. I couldn't have the tour end. I told you how I'm the one who has to support my entire family. I couldn't afford to get sent home without the full payment, and I wasn't going to get that if it ended early."

"So you want my pity? For your choice to endanger *my* family?"

I'd make the choice again, but the guilt still grips my throat. "No, I'm not asking for pity. It's up to you what you want to do now. I just wanted you to understand. It wasn't about blowing off the threat of danger. I needed this. More than you and your million cincs may ever know."

Oriana smiles sourly. "Ah, yes. So you do see me as a spoiled rich girl. Fat load of help that million cincs is giving me now."

"I don't! I thought of your money as a shield for you and your mother—that's different than being spoiled. This wasn't out of spite. You really think, even from a selfish perspective, I would've wanted you to stay if I knew your mother was in danger of vanishing? Have you realized who's going to be blamed for her disappearance? Me! It's me. They made the guide position to ensure another guest doesn't vanish ever again. It's my job to stop that. And, well." I spread my hands and shrug. "You could probably even push to have me executed back in the city if you wanted."

Oriana's nasty smile falters. Her gaze drops. "I don't want you executed." She spits the words out. "I want you to feel guilt, because you should, but I'm not a monster."

"I do feel guilt." The fact it's true somehow makes that harder to say.

Oriana narrows her eyes, a sly, sidelong glance. "So then did you have a plan to find my mother today? Or were you going to lead me in circles to keep me distracted?"

I clear my throat. "I did. A few, actually." She doesn't need to know that I've thought extensively about this not because of the guilt I do feel, but because if the Shadow is who made Oriana's mother disappear, finding Oriana's mother will very likely lead me to them in turn. "The magic on Estaralla can do anything. When you booked the tour, you had the opportunity to buy additional items, as well as book the locations you were visiting, right?"

Oriana nods. "All kinds of things. Most of them sounded rather creepy and invasive to me, actually. Love lockets, truth perfumes, garbage like that. I wasn't paying a lot of attention there, though, because I mostly read the list and was concerned Mother was going to try to buy a love locket for me. The good news, though, was that the items don't function beyond the borders of the island, too far from magic, or Mother just might've bought me a locket to force me to fall in love." She wrinkles her nose. "What were you thinking?"

I kick aside the small knot forming in my gut considering her words. She's right that it's currently a good thing the magic is limited in its borders. In the wrong hands—like the Silverhands'—the kind of magic that could alter feelings would be very bad. But I can't dwell on that because I'm not willing to throw myself and Severin on the execution block just to stop it. "If we could last-minute book you an item to point you to the person you love most," I say, "I'm pretty confident that's something that could be made. You could go ask Calista about it. We could—if I'm not fired."

"You're not fired." Oriana turns and props a hand on her hip. "I'm practical, Lucia, not spiteful. Right now, I just want to find my mother. I can't see how firing you is going to help that. I don't believe you really thought she was going to disappear, you have an idea on how to find her, and you should be pretty damn motivated to do so. So. *Should* I fire you?"

"No!" At least that answer's easy enough.

"You won't lie to me again?"

"I won't." I will. I am even now. But at least these lies shouldn't end up hurting either of the Rubellians, and they shouldn't be revealed until I've already fled.

I want to feel triumph in Oriana's refusal to let me go. Even if she's being practical, at worst, it means she thinks I'm intelligent and not spiteful myself. Better, she may even feel somewhat sorry for me, like me enough to not want to hurt me. But it's hard to feel good about any of this because none of it's true. I don't even feel competent right now. This entire heist has veered so violently off course, and I haven't even gotten to what was supposed to be the hard part—the actual theft and escape.

Oriana inclines her head. "Then let's go."

We find Calista outside, sitting on the patio with a cup of espresso on the table in front of her. She wears her reflective gold mask today, my broken one gone, and it currently tilts up, exposing her mouth. It's probably just so she can drink, but still, something fluttery in my chest rises. As we approach, she slams her mask back into place again, boots crushing my little butterflies' wings.

She stands, grabbing a white mask from the table. "A new mask for you." She slips it into my hand as she passes briskly, heading for Oriana. I am the afterthought.

I kick that petty jealousy away. Oriana's given me no reason to think she's a threat to Calista's interest in me. And, well, then there's the fact I probably shouldn't hold out any sort of hope about Calista's interest in me at all, because despite her flirtatious moments, she all but rejected me last night while our masks were off.

I flush at the memory, half embarrassment and half . . . something else. That delusional hope I have, I guess.

Calista takes Oriana's hands, flips both of them over, and inspects her palms. Then she sighs. "You, too."

"Yes?" says Oriana, and I feel much like her and that small, hesitant question mark at the end of her words.

"You were affected like your mother," Calista says.

Oriana's face flushes faintly. "I—does it have something to do with having used magic in the past?"

Calista recoils. "What? We asked you if you lied about that! Now you want to tell the truth?"

Oriana lifts her chin defiantly. "Mother knew we would've been thrown from the island. So it *is* that."

I consider announcing it seems like it wasn't just my lies that led to this, but Oriana obviously knows that already with the way she avoids looking at me as she says it. Maybe that's even part of why she rejected firing me. Either way, I'll win more points with her by keeping this to myself instead of being gleeful. I need to be repentant, not smug.

"Yes, it is. But if you'd told us sooner, we could've protected you. If you'd told us sooner, your mother wouldn't be gone right now." Calista's words are a whip, and even I feel their lash, but Oriana barely bends.

Only her chin trembles. "Mother thought it would ruin our reputation to get kicked off the island. We'd be the subject of ridiculous gossip. Plus, she was obsessed with being able to introduce me to Conte Niccolo at the Island Ball. I think she might've opted to tell you the truth this morning. If she were here."

Calista shakes her head. "That's hardly helpful. Lucia, give her my mask." To Oriana, she says, "You're going to wear one from now on, too. At all times, even to bed. Understand?"

Oriana nods, a stiff acceptance of the judgment cast on her choices in the gesture, all the more reason for me not to leap to defend myself further. If Oriana simply bears the consequences, so will I.

I swap my masks out, removing Calista's for the new plain one.

The new one smells overwhelmingly of ammonia and plaster, and I wrinkle my nose. The fragile intimacy of our moment last night is gone as I pass her mask on to Oriana. In fact, everything this morning has made me doubt there'd been something between us last night at all.

"We came to you to ask if it would be possible to book the creation of an item for Oriana," I say. "I thought we might be able to order something to help Oriana locate her mother."

Calista taps the bottom of her mask. "You know the Vessels are conducting a search for Oriana's mother. They don't want you to interfere. My mother put me in charge of ensuring nothing else happens to you. You're not to leave the estate grounds for the remainder of your time here."

Dread blooms in my chest. "And are you going to stop us if we try?"

Calista steps in close to me, and my heart lifts, then sinks as she beckons Oriana in as well. With our heads bowed together, she speaks in a low voice, "No. I shouldn't even admit that, but, no. You can make your own choices, but I will *very strongly* warn you that if the Vessels catch you interfering, I can't promise your safety anymore."

It's amazing how her tune has changed. First, we would be safe if we stayed on the right path. Now, the illusion has fallen, revealing the ugly truth beneath—there is no safety here, not even for Oriana.

"Do you think we need to conduct our own search?" Oriana asks. "If the Vessels don't want us interfering, can we trust them to find her?"

Calista pauses, presses a finger to the carved mouth of her mask, and shakes her head. Then she withdraws from our circle of safety. "I'll see if I can commission something for you. No promises."

She starts away, while my thoughts swirl, a whirlpool of unease spinning around and around until my next question solidifies in my mind.

"I'll be right back," I tell Oriana, and chase down Calista, who's just stepped inside and is closing the door behind her. I slip in the crack before she closes it entirely.

"If the Vessels don't want us searching, are you going to be able to commission something?" I ask.

"They're not all-powerful, but no promises," Calista repeats stiffly, and I guess, that's answer enough. She turns away again, and there's a sudden surge in me, and I reach for her before I can think the better of it.

She turns back. "Something else you need?" I hate the aloofness in her tone as she asks it. I don't need anything. I just want acknowledgment. My cheeks heat, as I scramble for an actual question for her, to pretend there was something more than me just not wanting her to go quite yet.

My hand flutters up to where her necklace still lies against my collarbone, exposed by the blouse I wear today. "Do you want this back?"

There's a long pause in which she stands utterly still, and at the slight distance, I can't even see her eyes in the slits of her mask. She's blank, empty. And then she steps forward. "Yes, I suppose."

"Thanks, by the way. You were right I was going to need it." The laugh I attempt is nasal and forced. "But why didn't you give it to the ammiralia instead?"

I half expect her to ignore that question like she ignores so many, but instead, she continues forward, closing the distance between us, reaching for the necklace. Her fingers skim my skin, a chill that's not entirely unpleasant, and come to rest where the pendant of the necklace lies as she lifts it up. I barely hear her words—it's like the entire world's gone muffled. "Since she'd repeatedly claimed to never use magic, I wasn't sure she'd be a target. You were definitely in danger."

My throat's gone dry. It's hard to look at the hollowness of her mask, and more, I don't want her to see whatever rawness is in my own eyes right now, so I watch the way she twists the pendant back and forth. Its mirror surface catches the light, flashing it into my eyes.

"Besides." She steps around behind me, standing close enough I can feel the hint of the shape of her body where there's pressure and warmth against my back and where there's a chilly emptiness. "I know I'm supposed to care more about protecting my guests, but I'm personally a little more invested in you."

A laugh escapes me, something weak and breathy and entirely awkward. Part of me wants to ask *why*—but enough of me knows there's no good answer. Last night's rejection was humiliating enough—I don't want to hear in plain words that she doesn't feel that way about me. But if she were to say the opposite, that she actually does like me, what could I do with that? I'm still only here to steal magic from her island and send it into upheaval. There could only ever be something brief and meaningless between us, and I don't even know if I want that, because it'll be guilt to carry onward I don't need.

"Well, thanks," I manage instead. "I appreciate you . . . looking out for me."

Calista hums, the sound close to my ear, so close my skin tingles as if from the reverberations. She runs her hand from the pendant she's lifted along the chain around my neck, sweeping my hair to the side as she does so, leaving my skin tingling in a warm sort of delicious way in its wake. Part of me wants to demand if she's doing this on purpose, but it's another answer I'm not sure I want.

The hair on the back of my neck stands, cold and exposed, as her fingers work the clasp, and she lifts the weight of the pendant from my neck.

"Will I be safe now? Without it?" I turn around to her, hand outstretched to take the necklace from her and lay it on her neck in turn, but she's already got her hands behind her head, fiddling.

"You should be." She drops her hands, necklace in place, and I feel foolishly robbed. "The mist shouldn't strike again before you leave in a few days, but I'm at risk all the time." She presses her thumb against the flat surface without a smudge. "It's my gift—and curse, you see—as a Vessel's child. This pendant ensures I'll stay safe, just so I can be given away to the magic later."

"Oh." I hear Antony's words echo, *We need her.* I remember how we both glowed gold in the mist while Oriana suffered. He must have one, too. "I'm sorry. Is it not an honor to be a Vessel?"

Calista snorts, but it's a gentle tease more than a slice. "I would've thought some of the idealized shine to this island would've worn off for you by now. It's an honor, but it's also—the end." Her gaze and her hand drop.

"What do you mean 'the end'?" Cold crawls into the tips of my fingers, my gloves no shield. Even if I don't have anything good planned for Calista myself, the thought of her actually hurt, the vibrant glow of life she carries so easily with her snuffed out, is painful. "It doesn't kill you, does it?"

"Not exactly," Calista says. "My body will live on, but not really

213

as mine anymore. It'll be, well, a vessel of magic. I won't be *me*. Everything I do will only be in service of the magic."

The image of the Vessels' blank faces flashes in my mind, and Antony's words about Keelan not being his brother anymore ring in my ears, and I shudder. No wonder she's unhappy. If I had to live my life knowing I only had so long before I became a shell of myself, I'd do whatever I could to try to escape it. No wonder she's known for breaking the rules, doing whatever she feels like. I would, too. If I couldn't escape, I'd at the very least want to experience whatever I wanted, as much as I could. Antony's judgment there seems more unfair than ever now.

But then—is the life waiting for me if I fail all that better than the one that waits for her? I'm bound in service to the Silverhands. I rip my body apart to do their crappy illusion shows every night. My mind is still my own at least, but the money I make, the choices in front of me, aren't. Even this damn island trip. I'm doing it because it's my only potential escape from them, yes, but ultimately, it's still *for them*.

"Is there no way out?" I ask softly.

"Not really," Calista says. "I'm my mother's only child—not that, I think, I would want a sibling to have to take my place anyway."

"Maybe if they were terrible," I say, and she gives a soft laugh in return. "I would never, though. My brother's one of very few people I actually like in my life." I don't know why I say it. It's so far from an important mention, so far from anything relevant. I just want her to know.

She laughs a little harder at that.

"Do you wish you had a sibling?" I want to pretend this is

somehow still reconnaissance to find out what the best way is to get her to tell me where the source is located, but that excuse is getting flimsier with each word we continue to exchange.

She shrugs. "In some ways, yes. Others, no. It's complicated. I think it might be nice to have someone, but with the Vesselhood looming, if they were older, and it would fall to them, I think I'd forever feel a little guilty. But if it was still my duty—even if I loved them, and even if I didn't want to pawn it off on them—I'd be jealous. Our relationship would always be a little . . . tainted."

I can't help but think back to Antony. I wonder if he ever felt the same about Keelan in the past. Last night was the most he'd ever said about his brother and, well, it was clear there were a lot of tangled feelings around that subject.

"Is your brother older or younger?" Calista asks, and in that moment, a knock sharply raps on the door behind me. I jump, but it's just Oriana who pushes it open.

"Just coming back inside." Even with her mask over her face, I don't miss how her gaze flicks between Calista and me, and it's clear she chose to knock specifically as a warning. Maybe I should tell her that if she thinks we were back here making out behind the closed door, she's wildly wrong, but I can't bring myself to. Because even though she is wrong, I sort of wish she wasn't.

Calista nods sharply. "I should get going to see what I can do for you."

Part of me still wants to stop her, but with Oriana at my side, the pull of reality is stronger. The reality is that time is ticking. I have a Shadow to find, magic to steal, and talking about Severin, of all useless topics, with Calista is so far from helping me on that path. But as

215

she walks away from us, I can't help but add, "My brother's younger. His name's Severin."

———————————————

Oriana and I stand in silence until Calista's gone, at which point, Oriana turns to me. "Do you know of anything for us to do around here?"

I press a finger to my mask, lean in, and whisper, "We're not staying here."

"Okay," Oriana says slowly.

"Look," I say. "If the Vessels don't want you involved in searching, there's some chance they might interfere with Calista's attempt to commission something for us. But I've got a backup plan." I've already considered it extensively, decided, no matter what, I would try. The only question was whether or not to involve Oriana. But something tells me I don't want to go alone. I don't know if it's a logical gut instinct, or simply fear, but I'll listen.

If I'm going to go in search of her mother, she might as well be there, too.

"We know where your mother went missing. Right below those waterfalls in the palace grounds. So the most logical area to investigate while we have no other information is the scene of the incident. See if there's any hint of where she might've gone. Footprints, items she might've left behind."

"Are we going to be able to enter the palace grounds again?" Oriana asks, wary, but right.

"I doubt it, but I wasn't planning on it anyway," I say. "The waterfalls came from above, and so, if your mother was taken somewhere, it was probably in that direction. Remember, Keelan said those waters came from the source." I certainly don't know enough to know why the Shadow would haul their victims closer to the source, but it makes some sense. If they're poisoning magic, they're probably sticking close to the areas it runs. "So. Do you want to come along?"

Oriana draws in a shuddering breath, and even though I wasn't sold on inviting her along in the first place, I find myself holding my own breath while I wait to hear her decision. She may not be as much of a shield against danger as I'd initially hoped, but I'd still much rather not be alone.

She nods.

CHAPTER TWENTY-TWO

By day, the path that terrified me last night is shockingly plain. The trees arch above, but they aren't hulking and monstrous shadows about to snatch me from the path and devour me.

They are, however, nothing like the lush greenery around the Pool of Dreams or the entrance to the Cave of Ghosts. Barely any leaves cling to these spindly trees. Their naked branches twine together in a weird, desperate sort of way that reminds me of lovers clutching each other in a final embrace.

The path beneath us is gravel, and for a while, the only sound is its crunch beneath our feet. It's eerie—even more when I realize if there were other animals out there, they should've been making some kind of noise. There might be nothing alive in this forest but us.

Oriana traces the tops of the trees with her gaze. "Do you know if the trees are designed to look dead?"

"I don't," I say, catching her gaze, a silent communication of my agreement with her unspoken words, *This is really weird.*

She gives a small *hmph*, and in that moment, it's almost like we're friends, as though my betrayal's erased, and my future betrayals won't ever have to come.

We round a corner and step out of the woods onto the top of a hill looking down over the town.

Unlike Vessel Dionne's golden mansion and icelike sculptures, unlike the lush pool and mysterious cave we visited, the town is full of crumbling stone buildings. Moss runs through the cracks between the cobblestones we walk on. It's not a town of magic. It's a town nearing ruination.

Oriana narrows her eyes within the slits of her mask, her gaze scanning, as she takes it all in. It's nothing like the Estaralla we're promised, little like the Estaralla we've seen.

"Are you—" I start to ask Oriana if she's seeing what I am, but then I blink, and the town shifts before my eyes. It transforms from the crumbling stone into bright, vibrant colors, all of the homes different: deep rich purple, greener than the forest, bluer than the crystal waters. Some are framed by bright, healthy green vines, others by arches of flowers, and still others with edges trimmed in gold. Even the air around the town looks clearer, the sky a little bluer, and the cobblestones beneath our feet are no longer cracked, dirty, or in disrepair, but gleaming stone of a rich shade of ivory that, if I didn't think the price exorbitantly impossible, I'd believe was marble. Everything, the houses, the street, the ocean beyond, has a bold gleam to it, like someone swiped gloss over every single surface, and they nearly sparkle in the sunlight.

"Am I—" Oriana repeats. She blinks rapidly, and I wonder what she's seeing. If she's seen the colors all along. If she still sees the ruins.

"Never mind," I say because I don't know what good the confirmation will do either of us. I'm not going to turn around, so I don't want to accidentally scare Oriana into doing so. "Let's just go."

We descend the winding path. If I didn't trust my eyes, I'd think

I just imagined the ruined town I saw at first, as now there's no hint of it remaining. The houses glitter brightly with their colors, so bright I squint as we pass them. Some have balconies jutting out over the path, and a few even have people sitting on them in lacy gowns and flowing silk shirts sipping from mugs and watching us.

But there's something unnatural about it.

Maybe it's all a glamotura, I realize. Glamoturas aren't supposed to crumble or flicker on their own, but maybe they could if there's something wrong with the magic. And I already know there is. It's getting poisoned by the Shadow. Just before a glamotura completely vanishes, when it goes too far from the source of magic, it does tend to flicker in and out of existence. So perhaps that's happening here—the magic's range is decreasing because of whatever the Shadow has done, and all the glamoturas that are painted all over this island can't hold like they should.

The spires of the palace gleam in the distance past the town. It may not be ideal to be bumbling our way down an unfamiliar path, but I don't know where the litter is, much less trust it to take us to our desired destination.

The sun is almost at its zenith, and the muggy air smothers me like a hot, wet blanket. As we walk, and the sweat drip-drip-drips down my neck and back in a steady stream and Oriana's breathing rasps loud and uneven beside me, I wonder if I should've asked Calista for assistance getting to the palace, if I could've trusted her to help us since this walk sure is unpleasant. I twist our interactions in my mind over and over again. Every time my thoughts wander to her face—the curve of her lips, the softness at the corners of her eyes—I kick those useless memories away. It's obvious she's hiding something. Antony thinks she's dangerous, but I don't know that I trust him either.

Still, there's a small, hollow spot that wonders why she won't trust me. Why she will give me her pendant in the night to save me, but she won't tell me what she knows about the island.

It takes a liar to spot a liar, but I don't know if one can ever convince the other to tell the truth. If I'm not ready to tell her about my real reasons for being on Estaralla, why should she tell me anything either?

If my honesty is the only way to encourage her own, she can keep her secrets.

And I will keep mine.

There is no footpath leading in the direction of the cliffs above the palace, at least not that I see. So as we approach the palace gates, Oriana and I are forced to leave the path behind and fight our way through the forest.

It's thicker than I expected. Roots and vines tangle across the forest floor, an uneven mess of underbrush we wade through. It rises almost to our ankles. I have to lift my skirts to move, and Oriana follows suit.

The black veins in her arm throb with every step, but if she feels pain, her mask doesn't show it.

"Look," I say for the sake of the prickles of guilt crawling up and down the back of my neck as Oriana walks behind me. "I really am sorry about what's happened to your mother."

"I know that," she says with a heave of a sigh. "And, look, I also know she made some really stubborn choices that didn't help the situation. As did I. I sort of wish it was all your fault, but it's not. I forgive you. For your part in this."

Somehow, that doesn't help. The guilt burrows deeper into the back of my neck, and I grimace. She shouldn't offer such an apology. Not when she doesn't yet know the half of what I'm really doing. How I'm really trying to use her and her mother. Still, I have to say something, so I force out, "Thanks. That means a lot."

The roots squirm, shifting beneath our feet as we walk. Thorns prick my legs, small spikes of pain as we pass them.

A particularly painful jab makes me pause, bend down to see if something's embedded in my skin. A hiss slides past my lips.

A small trickle of blood oozes from a pinprick mark. There's nothing stuck in my skin—but the area around it has black lines radiating out.

I lower my skirt. Let the thorns tear my clothing, not my skin. "Oriana," I say. "Don't let anything cut you."

She wipes her hairline with the back of her hand and nods.

At last, we crest the top of the hill, which should mean we're above the palace cliffs. The trees part, the thick canopy above us finally ending. An open area beckons us ahead, glowing with light. It should be welcoming—but the air twists around us, thick with a choking stench that's definitely not. I pause just before the opening, breathing deeply through my mouth while I try to place the smell. I don't think it's just my rancid, sweat-drenched dress. Despite the heat, goose bumps break out on my skin.

Beside me, Oriana sways. I grab her arm to steady her, and she murmurs a small, "Thanks."

I take in another breath through my nose and gag this time.

It smells like rot.

It smells like death.

"Wait here a second," I say. "Let me see what's ahead."

"If you think that's better," Oriana manages to push out.

I nod. "Stay here. Just a moment." Then I push the branches aside and dare to step into the light.

I hadn't realized just how dark the forest was until I step into the clearing. The sunlight burns, and I squint against it while my eyes tear up. I shield them with one hand, blinking quickly to try to adjust. It's a moment of weakness I can't have.

Then the clearing slides into focus.

I'm alone.

Or rather I'm the only living thing here.

At the edge of the clearing, a thick fog hovers. In front of it, the ground is a collection of bodies and bones and old blood. The bones have been arranged in an outer circle around a pool of water, with an inner circle of decaying bodies. The arrangement is precise—all their heads pointing in the same direction, into the pool. Some are fresh, the skin a bloated greenish gray, but still human-shaped. Others are old, the skin sloughing, hanging, and flapping from the bones. The ground around them is darker, stained with dried blood. All that still have some semblance of skin have slit marks on their throats.

And one looks brand new. His skin is still pale, and his head hangs into the pool, wisps of dark hair wriggling like worms. The slice in his throat oozes blood in a fresh stream that trickles down his neck and into the water. His face is twisted into an expression of pain, so dramatic it's unnatural and almost looks like a mask.

"Oh, shit." The words escape me. My hand falls to the knife I tied to my waist, taken from the kitchen before we left. It's suddenly so tiny in my grip, and even though there's no one to fight here, I wonder abruptly if it's not going to be enough.

Branches crackle, and Oriana steps into the clearing. "What is it?"

Then she gasps, a sound wrenched from the back of her throat. She retches. My stomach churns, and I squeeze my hands tight, digging my nails into my palms to keep from joining her.

"Mamma!" she cries and starts forward.

I thrust a hand out and block her. I don't think we should approach the mess of corpses. "She's not here."

"What *is* this?" Oriana whispers.

"I wish I knew." And to think, this was above us the whole time last night. This is what feeds into those crystal waterfalls, into that bright blue pool. It makes me wonder if all water here harbors corpses.

"If this is where the Shadow takes his victims, shouldn't my mother be here?" Oriana sidesteps my arm and begins to slowly walk beside the river, studying the ground along the way, downstream from the pool of death, close to the roar of the falls where it hurtles from the cliff.

I follow behind her. "I would think so, too."

Oriana leans over the water, peering into the rushing stream, almost as if she expects to see her mother at the bottom of it. She places a hand on top of the water, skimming the surface. It parts beneath her touch, and she asks, perhaps even to the water, "Where would the Shadow take my mother instead?"

"Don't touch that." I drop to her side and yank her hand out of the water.

Oriana pulls her hand out of my grip and massages the ends of her fingertips. "But it was—nice," she murmurs, the sharp edge of her voice replaced by something soft, nearly slurring.

Definitely not water, as I've suspected. She reaches for it again, but I shove her hand aside. "It's not safe to touch anything here." I've been assuming it's all basic glamoturas, simple sensory changes like we'd see in Verigal City. But now it hits me—that might not be the case. This is Estaralla. Whatever this is could have more spells on it than I know of. Spells to mess with Oriana's mind or emotions. I have no idea what's here.

"I thought I saw my mother," she cries, and I wince. "It was like looking through a window to her. She's looking into some water somewhere, too. She's out there—somewhere out in the mist."

I hate to do this because it feels like a mistake. It feels like the move of some gullible fool who will fall into the water and drown and never be heard from again, but still, I let my fingers skim the surface.

The liquid is cold, ice-cold, and it jolts up my arm in a crawling numbness as though my glove isn't even there. Inside my mouth, my tongue turns thick and dead. I see nothing but a blur, though, nothing but a thick gray fog that swallows everything. I squint into it, but there's no life to be found.

A crackling noise sounds, and I yank my hand from the stream.

My vision snaps back to the grotto, to the clear liquid running beneath my fingertips, and Oriana at my side. She tugs at my sleeve.

Because rising up the flowing waterfall, ascending the cliff at a rapid pace, almost as though the river itself lifts him against its own current, is Keelan.

"Hello, Lucia, I wasn't expecting to hear your voice up here. What are you doing trespassing?"

CHAPTER TWENTY-THREE

I weigh our choices. We've only really got three: run, fight, or feign total ignorance, and I'm not confident in any of them. Run—I have no idea how fast Keelan is, but I know neither Oriana nor I are in the best shape after having trekked through the forest all day in full dresses. Plus, even if we did evade him, where would we go? He'd surely keep watch over the Eliades Estate, so we'd have to go into hiding, and that just doesn't seem like a great plan in these semi-sentient and not-nice forests. Fight—well, it may come to that, but as of right now, I know that Keelan can't be trusted, but I'm not sure he's outright our enemy. At least in this moment. And I *am* allied with the cave ghost voice, who's part of the magic, and Keelan's a part of the magic, too. If I fight him, I can probably kiss that alliance goodbye.

Ignorance it is.

"Oriana was desperate to search for her mother—she's so worried." I don't even have to nudge her for her to nod along and even add a little sniffle. "I thought the most logical place to come looking was the place she was last seen."

"Yes, the rest of the Vessels and I have been working on trying to locate her all day, which we'll be far more effective at than you." His unmoving face as he says those words gives me chills. "Didn't Calista tell you you're not supposed to leave the Eliades Estate? It won't help us much if we locate the ammiralia, and you immediately go missing in turn, Ammiraligna Rubellian." That's definitely a threat—and I can't tell if it's even meant as a direct one. "Why did you think the ammiralia would be here, anyway? Don't you think, if she were so close, we would have already located her?"

I at least manage to resist saying, *I'd only think that if I thought you were putting any effort into the search.* Instead, I give a little nod over my shoulder to the collection of corpses. "So you knew about . . . this?" When in doubt, I answer a question with a question, and something really isn't adding up here. If the Shadow is dumping bodies right above the Key Vessel's home, shouldn't they have already caught them? Keelan should've been able to organize the Vessels to ambush them during their regular drop-bys, mask on or not. Why would Teresta need my help?

He pauses—a long pause, I've got him here—then finally says, "Knew? Yes. But you're not just asking if I knew; you're asking if I knew, why it's still here, aren't you?"

"That would be the next logical question, yes," I say with maybe just a little more bite than is tactful. Unfortunately, the more someone threatens me, the ruder I get. It may not always be smart, but I can't help it.

Keelan lifts his blank face up to the sky, and the sunlight catches, gleaming on its flat surface. "Yes and no, but this isn't the place to have a conversation. Why don't you come inside?"

Even though I should probably be a whole lot more worried

about this entire situation—both Antony and Calista explicitly didn't want me alone with Keelan, and the last conversation I had with him was thoroughly unnerving—I can't help but feel the thrill shiver through me. No one has yet given me any good information on who this Shadow is and what they want. But maybe Keelan will.

I'm not sure I feel any more comfortable being in the palace than I did standing mere feet from a ritualistic pile of corpses.

Keelan brings us to a very small and very plain room that feels a bit like a cage. It doesn't even have any windows—just stone walls and a wooden table. The light in the room is provided by a single gas lamp in the center of the table, bathing it in an orange haze that'd be right at home in Verigal City's tenements. At least the chairs around the table are plushly padded with what might be real leather. Since there are so few items in the room, I wonder if this is a private room, one in which everything is real, and, therefore, valuable to the Estarallans. But since we're not Estarallans, I don't have a great grasp on if he's trying to be genuine and polite or subtly rude by putting us in here.

I reluctantly sit in the offered chair. Oriana sits beside me, and Keelan takes the seat facing us.

Even though he has no eyes for me to observe, I can tell that Keelan watches us intently as he says, "Now, before I tell you about the Shadow, I'd like you to tell me one more thing, too. Why are you wearing a tour guide mask, Ammiraligna?"

Oriana's shoulders hunch. "Uh, I was told it might make me safer while we wandered around the island."

"By whom?" Keelan asks.

"Me," I say quickly, because it'll be better to maintain that Calista knows nothing about any of this.

"Take it off," Keelan says, a quiet threat in his voice. "It won't help you, Ammiraligna. The masks are only for people who've used magic, and it's insulting for you to wear one otherwise."

Oriana obeys without a single suspicious glance in my direction. With the mask removed, she looks worse than the last time I saw her. Her face appears more gaunt, dark pits forming beneath her eyes, and a sheen of sweat shimmers across her cheeks and forehead, while her lips look very nearly gray.

"Why is that?" I ask, not because I expect any sort of truth, but because maybe his lie will tell me something all the same.

He doesn't even give me some interesting horse shit. "I'm glad to see you take the mask off. I briefly feared that was indicating perhaps you and your mother lied about using magic—and the thing is, if that was the case, we could no longer guarantee your safety or your mother's safe recovery."

My skin prickles. If the Vessels have genuinely been looking into the ammiralia's disappearance, maybe he already knows full well that she did use magic. And he's telling us now she'll never be found. "But if the Shadow's taken her, why is that relevant?"

"The Shadow only takes those who have used magic, and we have never recovered one of his victims."

I lean forward and study the flat planes that are sort of his face, hoping I don't appear too eager as I try to wheedle additional information out of him. "And do you know why? You don't think it's just coincidence because most people on this island have used magic?"

"I do not think it's coincidence," Keelan says. "We believe it may be a part of his overall plot against magic, against the island. Perhaps he merely has a vendetta against magic and all its users. Or he uses his victims in whatever he is doing to poison the magic. None of us know."

"You don't know how he's poisoning magic?" I ask. "Doesn't the magic have eyes? Wherever it is?"

"Yes, wherever it is," Keelan says. "But it is not everywhere on this island, and the Shadow seems to know where it is absent quite well, which is why we have never seen him remove the mask. If we had, we would not need you, now, would we?"

His knowledge jolts me, a zing that makes me recoil, even though I shouldn't be surprised. Of course—Teresta already told me she communicates with the current Vessels through the magic, and it would only make sense to tell Keelan about our deal.

"What do you mean *need her*?" Oriana, who'd a moment ago been swaying listlessly, eyes half closed, cuts in sharply. "What do you need from Lucia?"

"He means that I—uh—" I say before Keelan can speak because I don't want her to know of the deal. I need her to want my help finding her mother, and if she knows I have a hidden agenda, I'm not sure she will anymore. "Antony asked me to track the locations of the magic." Vague as I can be, and she's probably seen Antony pull me aside enough. If anything, he's a more believable other half to the "we" than some weird disembodied voice that spoke to me in the cave.

I'm saved from having to try to say more. The door crashes open, and Antony enters in a whirlwind, Calista on his heels. She marches to the end of the table and slams her palms down on it, as she snaps,

"Lucia!" Antony takes up the place beside her, folding his arms across his chest, the heat of his glare burning even through his mask.

I wince.

"What were you thinking?" she snarls. "I told you you're not allowed to leave the estate anymore!"

"Lucia only left because of me." Oriana drags her fingertip along the table. "I had a new idea on where to look for my mother."

Calista's gaze sweeps between the discarded mask beside Oriana's hand on the table and Keelan. Her own mask hides whatever calculations race through her mind as she sweeps a curtsy quickly.

"I'm so sorry, *lumino*, that I failed to keep control of them. Thank you for finding them. I'll do better going forward." She glances sidelong at Antony. "And thank you, Antony, for letting me in here to retrieve them."

"Not a problem," Antony says gruffly, but he doesn't look at her. His gaze remains locked, leaking fury, on me.

Keelan's not as gentle. His voice is hard. "You really need to. They had a very close call."

"With?" Calista asks, rather boldly when everything about Keelan's posture and tone demands nothing but apologetic groveling from us all. Antony shifts beside her, running a clearly frustrated hand through his hair.

"They found the Shadow's circle of victims," Keelan says. "Are you going to also ask me to explain how dangerous that is, how they risked coming across the Shadow himself in being there?"

Calista shakes her head swiftly. "See, Lucia! That's why you can't just wander around on your own."

I tilt back in my chair, assessing the scene before me. I'm

absolutely going to keep wandering around on my own. But I gain nothing by tipping my hand, and, in fact, protesting will only make them work harder to block me.

"Okay," I say. "I'm sorry. I'm not going to do it again."

Luckily for Oriana, Calista brought the litter to retrieve us, so we don't need to walk all the way back to the Eliades Estate. Unluckily for me, Antony chooses to follow us out to it, and as soon as we cross the threshold of the gates, snaps at Calista, "You really need to do a better job keeping track of them. This cannot happen again." Irritation lashes out from him in waves.

"I'm aware of my responsibilities," Calista says with a chilly calm I've never managed in the face of one of Antony's lectures. "But I want to remind you they're both perfectly autonomous individuals. There's only so much I can do. What do you expect me to do—chain them up every time I'm not in the same room with them?"

"If that's what it takes," Antony says.

Oriana, swaying lightly in place beside the litter, raises her eyebrows at that. I clench my teeth. Antony is giving me such emotional whiplash. Not long ago, I was starting to thaw toward him again, having realized just what a messed-up life he's led on this island, the fact that he wasn't lying at all about the danger, and that he clearly tried to protect me last night at the ball. But now he suggests making me a prisoner?

"I'm not going to do that." Calista brushes the litter's curtains aside and offers a hand to Oriana, who climbs in and promptly collapses into a corner.

"I'm going to look into relocating them, then," Antony says tightly.

Calista just laughs. "Where? You think they should stay with you? And *Keelan*? You think that'll be safer for them?"

"We don't want to be relocated. We've been comfortable with Calista," I add sharply, because Antony doesn't even like Calista, so he's certainly not going to listen to her, but maybe, just maybe, he'll listen to me this time. If he cares about keeping me safe, why doesn't he care about where I'll be most comfortable?

"Calista, will you give Lucia and me a moment?" Antony jerks a thumb at the litter.

Calista shrugs, pulls herself in, and closes the curtain behind. Sheer as it looks, I can't see her silhouette behind it, and I wish I could.

Antony may want to talk, but I don't.

CHAPTER TWENTY-FOUR

Facing Antony alone, my brain and body are simply a storm of confusion. Before coming to this island, I was confident in exactly how I should feel about him, even if my body didn't always comply with its instructions. I was free to be furious at how he'd treated me because it was nasty.

But now I see his actions were so much more complicated than that. How he lied to me was shitty—as was how he manipulated my interview and refused to give me information—but he was right about the dangers of the island. His methods were crap, but it was still kindness in the end. He *was* only trying to protect me. And I even understand why he would've lied—clearly, Estaralla is hiding everything that's happening here from Verigal City's council. If Antony had told me, and I'd passed that information on, I could've ruined him. I wish he could've just trusted me, but I understand full well why he wouldn't have.

I'm generally not all that trustworthy.

But still, he hasn't apologized. And as little else as I may deserve, I think I deserve that. Because well-intentioned or not, he was cruel.

"I thought you might understand by now," he says. "It's really not safe for you on this island. You can't just go around doing whatever you feel like. Why did you leave the Eliades Estate?"

"We were looking for Oriana's mother." It makes an excellent excuse for me while I bristle at his tone. "I understand it's not safe. I do. But Oriana's mother is in even more danger right now, and you expect Oriana and me to sit back and do nothing? Just because that's what we've been told to do?"

"Yes. Because the people who told you that know more than you do." Antony scrubs a hand through his hair. "Lucia, please. I know you're stubborn. I know that better than ever now. I just—you have no idea what it would do to me if you ended up hurt. If you ended up dead. And I don't think you understand how close you're getting to that."

My feelings play tug-of-war within my chest, and I feel like I might end up ripped in two. Part of me yells, *He cares about you! Forgive him! Embrace him!* But the rest of me says that he's still being pretty rude about this. "I do understand, actually. What you don't seem to understand is the danger isn't going to stop me. I can't let it. I have to figure out how to overcome it. Help me."

Antony hangs his head in his hands. "You're not listening."

I wish I could scrub my face because the muscles in my forehead are jumping, wired tight behind my mask. "*You* aren't listening. Calista doesn't seem to have a problem understanding that while she can advise us, Oriana and I are ultimately our own people."

"Calista doesn't care about you. I do!" Antony lifts his head at that, but I'm somewhat glad for the mask that blocks whatever expression he wears. His expression might just break me. As it is, my stomach flips, even while I'm still rent in half. He cares! But it stings to hear he thinks the only reason Calista's letting us go is because she doesn't.

I can only hope she can't hear us when she doesn't open the curtains to refute him. Otherwise, maybe, he's right.

"Lucia." He takes a step closer. "What can I do to convince you to listen?" He holds out his hands, and even though I shouldn't, I give him mine before I can stop myself. His hands envelop mine in warmth and stability, and I have to bite back the sigh of something like relief. Instead, the sensation shudders through me silently. Having him hold my hands again is like coming home at the end of a long day.

"You can apologize for trying to manipulate me," I say. "For not just telling me back in the city why you didn't want me here, instead of trying to lie and trick me."

"I'm sorry," Antony says, and this time, I can't bite back the gasp that escapes my lips. "I didn't feel like I could, but I wish I'd just told you the truth. I wish none of this had happened. You must see now that I was only trying to look out for you."

"I do. But I don't appreciate the way you did it."

"Right. I understand. If I could do it all again, I wouldn't do the same. I hate everything about what I did. I didn't even stop you, and I lost you."

I draw in another sharp breath as his grip on my hands tightens. My heart pounds hard, but I still don't know if it's fear or thrill. The apology does change my feelings, but I don't know how much. It doesn't erase what happened. I don't know if I can open myself up to truly trusting him again, and if I can't trust him, we'll never have a real relationship, no matter what might happen between us in bed.

"Do you forgive me?" he asks softly, his voice an invisible caress along my lips. I close my eyes.

"I don't know," I say because it's more than just forgiveness he wants. He wants us back together. I can feel it in the tenderness with which he holds my hands, the thumb that strokes the inside of my wrist right now. "I appreciate it, and I accept your apology, but it doesn't just erase the last several months."

I open my eyes in time to see him bow his head. He releases my hands, and steps back. "I accept that. Just—you know—think about it?" Even though I can't see through his mask, I somehow still manage to hear the lopsided grin in those words, that seed of hope he so hesitantly offers me.

I reach back out and give his arm a squeeze. Because maybe, just maybe, it's not impossible.

"You promise, though, you're not going to leave the Eliades Estate?" he asks, and it's a sudden bucket of ice water tossed over my head. I'm not sure how he ended up back there after his apology. Did he not understand what he was apologizing for?

"I can't promise. And I'm not going to lie. I'll do my best to be safe. Have some faith in the choices I make. I'm not so naive. If I choose danger, please believe that I'm not unaware and I've got a very good reason to take the risk."

Antony only keeps his head bowed, says nothing more, and as I clamber into the litter, I can only hope he understands.

Back at the Eliades Estate, after a plain, small dinner, Calista and I both wrap an arm around Oriana and together carry her to her bed where she promptly collapses again. A small pang of jealousy hits me, that she can sleep so easily. I shouldn't be jealous. It's only because she's ill. But energy courses through me, and I'm not sure when I'll next have a restful sleep.

Since Oriana and I got nowhere with our expedition, I turn to Calista. "Were you able to commission anyone to create us a trinket to find Oriana's mother?"

Calista busies herself, tucking the blankets neatly around Oriana's collapsed form in bed. "Unfortunately not."

The words stick in my throat as I watch Calista bustle about. There's something detached about her mannerisms tonight. Maybe she really is angry that we disobeyed her. But as much as her curt answer feels like it demands a follow-up from me, I don't know what that follow-up should be. If the answer's no, it's simply no.

But I can't accept that. I have to find the Shadow. But demanding she try again tomorrow—well, I have no reason to think that would lead to a different result from today's. I need to take matters into my own hands. That's always the safest way to ensure what needs to happen, happens, although when I think hard about it, I don't know how I'm going to convince someone to make one of these trinkets either. I'll have to consider the best angle: piles of money, sob story, both.

And then it hits me—*I* have magic. Maybe I don't need to hire someone else to do this at all. Maybe I can make the trinket Oriana needs. I don't know why I didn't think of this before. Perhaps because it's a harder spell than I've ever tried before, but I am on the island of Estaralla now.

By the time the idea's fully formed in my mind, Calista has left, and Oriana is settled, blankets tucked tightly around her chin, her eyes closed, and she looks peaceful as she ever might.

I need to talk to Calista, need to ask her how to perform such a spell. Since I've never done it before, I want to know if she has advice, pitfalls to watch for, anything, everything, so that it doesn't somehow go horribly wrong.

I whisper good night to Oriana and then race after Calista, but she's already gone, vanished into the night, as though she were never here, or never real, at all.

CHAPTER TWENTY-FIVE

I easily find Calista the next morning, at least, seated curled up in the courtyard with a book in hand. With her knees pulled into her chest, she looks smaller than usual, less like her polished surface of perfection, more like the girl I've glimpsed beneath the mask.

I clear my throat, and she looks up abruptly.

"Ah, Lucia," she says, and then immediately returns to her book. I'm not sure if I like the casual lightness in her voice because it sounds as though we've moved on from the icy conclusion of yesterday, or hate it, because there's a distance in that tone. It's the sort of tone I'd use with one of Mother's fancy acquaintances, distant, polite, and empty of any real feeling.

Part of me wants to ask if she's mad. But I can't afford to get mired down in these feelings. I have to find the ammiralia—really to find the Shadow and the Shadow's lair. So I launch directly into my question for her: "So the ammiralia."

Calista doesn't even look up. "What about the ammiralia?"

I clear my throat again. "You've already made it clear the Vessels will be no help. You couldn't find someone to help us, but would I be able to make Oriana the sort of trinket that we were looking for today? To help her find her mother?"

Calista snaps her book shut. "You could." Her voice is no longer hollow, but pointed.

"Why didn't you tell me that yesterday? You didn't need to go hunt for someone else to make it at all."

Calista gives me a long, unreadable scan with her shadowed eyes and golden mask. Then she drops the book onto the chair and approaches me, steps slow, with an almost predatory grace that doesn't match her hurried tone. "Even if you can, that doesn't mean you should. You must be aware you'll pay a price for every working."

With every step closer she takes, my nerves hum and my skin grows warmer, as though she's the rising of the sun itself, waking up my body. And when she finally stops in front of me, I'm torn between wanting to step away from her—and wanting to step closer. "Of course. I give up what I create. I make something hot, and I get cold."

Calista hums. "Right, so consider what that really means for what you're saying you'll make. If you're showing someone the path to a person they love, the magic will exact its own price. There'll be someone you love you'll never see again."

I think back to Antony's first warning, that warning I scoffed at so hard at the time. He told me to limit use of the magic. Maybe this was why. "But this island—" I start.

She leans in abruptly, pressing a finger to my mask, and though it's not my mouth, I freeze fast as if it were. "Shh. Speak quietly. Sometimes the island listens." Her gaze darts to the side, to the bur bling fountain in the center of this yard, and then she offers me an arm. "Walk with me."

I accept her arm, and she pulls me into stride beside her, her grip tight, keeping our bodies pressed together, heads close, and there's a foolish part of me that hopes she's doing this not only to keep the island from listening, but because she's also secretly enjoying herself so close to me.

"But there's all sorts of little magical trinkets here," I murmur. "You invite tourists here to experience magic! The entire place is built on magic. Are you telling me everything here has a price that was paid?"

"Yes," she says simply. Her stride doesn't break, even while I am distracted by the faint sweetness of the scent of her.

"The Pool of Dreams? Does that make people pay, too?"

"Oh, the pool is easy, which is why we like tourists to visit it. It doesn't require much we don't sacrifice anyway. How many people do you think get to live their dreams on this island? Dreams die so quickly that pool is never at risk of drying up."

My throat turns to sand, and I swallow. I'd never stopped to consider any of this. I don't know why I didn't. It makes sense, and I should have. Especially with Father's plan being what it was—to offer the gangs their own magical source.

"And the cave?" My voice rasps.

We step into the halls of the estate, and the cooler inside air is a relief against my hot skin.

"The cave is what it claims to be—mostly. A current of magic runs beside it, and the magic collects souls of those who've died on this island. They talk to guests and pretend to be whoever the guest wants them to be." Calista stops in front of a door. Her door, I realize, before she even opens it, and though I've been in her room before, that was before I'd realized she liked girls—and that I liked *her*. So even though I know she's just inviting me in for practical reasons, for privacy, my body seizes up and my heartbeat quickens.

"So are you saying that creating a trinket to find someone else's loved one would kill your own?" I ask, trying to stay on topic, but my voice comes out much rawer than I would like.

"Of course not," Calista says, and my nerves untangle a little—at least the ones related to if I can manage this spell. "If the magic is to take a life, a life would need to be granted. It only makes it so you never see them again. They can still lead a full and happy life."

I shiver. "So why would people create these trinkets to help someone else? Why would they sacrifice pieces of their own life in the process?"

"Because creating one will get them something more valuable than a loved one, they think. They need money. They want money. They love the person they're giving the trinket to, too. They think they care about nothing and want to see what'll be taken." She shrugs and pushes her door open. "I don't know. Doing nothing costs something, too. All we can do is pick the price we'd rather pay."

I see her invitation inside, but part of me says it's better for me to walk away. I have a spell to complete, a Shadow to find, magic to steal, so I can't bear to look at her.

The heat of her stare digs into me. "You're considering it. Why don't you answer your own question?"

I pause. I don't know if she wants the answer, but I do. And so I think. If I don't manage to get the Silverhands their magic at the end of this trip, the best that'll happen is I'll get a lecture and probably docked more money, thrusting us further in debt, and my life will be the same as before. The worst—they'll punish Severin to make a point to me. And so anything short of Severin's life, I'll willingly pay in order to succeed here. I have to because ultimately, that's what's on the line if I don't.

"You're right," I say quietly. "Sometimes the cost of doing nothing is just too high."

"For Oriana? You don't feel indebted to her, do you? What's happened to the ammiralia is tragic, but it doesn't belong to you alone."

I shake my head, and the words come out before they entirely mean to. I'd be flattered she thinks I'm so selfless—except, from her tone, I don't know that she'd consider such blind selflessness to be a good thing. "It's not Oriana I'm indebted to." I wait, heart pounding hard, tips of my ears hot, to see if she'll call me on the slip. If she'll ask what I mean. I don't even know that I don't want her to.

But Calista only hums. "I see. This debt—it must be large, then."

This is enough for me to push past all my swirling emotions and step into her room because practically, if I'm going to say even another word about this, the privacy is more important than my infatuation and all the overwhelming mixed feelings I feel in her presence—fear that she won't make a move in her own room, and I'll find myself rejected once again, nerves that she will and I probably won't even know what to do.

Calista follows me inside and shuts the door with a *click*. I stay beside it, like a safety line for myself. "It's from my father's failed business," I admit. It's vague, and, strategically, maybe it's not the worst to tell her. I'm floundering with how much compassion I feel toward her—perhaps it's time to try to win some from her for myself. That's the easier explanation for me to accept, besides the fact that maybe I just want to. "So, yes, it's been pretty hard for one lone kid to try to pay it off."

"You're not an orphan, though, are you? Why are you trying to pay for it alone?"

"My brother can't," I say. "He doesn't have any magical skill, so he's got no ways to make money that would be at all reasonable. You said you wouldn't want to sacrifice a sibling to the Vesselhood—well, I don't exactly want to sacrifice my brother to the gang. As much as I struggle, that would still be worse."

"What about your parents?" Calista asks. "Where are they?"

"My father left us—that's why we accumulated his debt. I haven't seen him in seven years," I say. "And Mamma—she won't help. She thinks, since I'm the one of all of us most like our father, I should be responsible."

Calista lets out a swift hiss. "That's not at all fair, to blame you for what he did simply because you're similar."

I shrug. I want to feel victorious in this moment. I think I *have* won some pity from her I can use. But instead, her indignation grinds within me. Fair, unfair, what does it matter? It's what Mamma wants from me, so it's the only way we'll be happy. "Well, other than really being just like my father and ditching them and letting Severin suffer all of the consequences, there's not a lot else I can do but take responsibility. It's a little like the price of magic in the end, isn't it? Someone has to pay."

She's silent for a long pause, and then she says, softly, maybe even sadly, "Perhaps *someone* must. But why, for all your concerns about the rest of your family, aren't you concerned about yourself? You can have a life that's more than just in the constant service of others' goals and dreams. You can matter, too."

The words dig deep, for a moment, their painful sting overwhelming the irrational giddiness I feel being back in her room. I feel like she's grabbed me, slapped me, pushed me back, and I'm reeling. Because she's right.

Here I am, lying, slinking, clawing my way across this incredibly dangerous island and—for what? Finding the magic would be a better future for the Silverhands, for my mother, for my brother, too, but for me?

The best it gets me is perhaps finally out of service to the rest of them.

She continues, "You can't really want to create glamoturas for others to play with for the rest of your life, spend all your time giving other people what they want, do you?"

I shrug. "No, I don't." But I can't manage more than that. Because even though I know I don't want to keep ripping myself apart for others' entertainment, always trying to give people what they want from me, I don't think I know what my own dreams even are. My mind briefly dances across the realization, and then pulls abruptly back because none of them matter. None of them *can* matter until I'm finished here. But with the talk of dreams, I realize I've still got one more thing to try before I give up and create Oriana's token. "Can the Pool of Dreams ever show you how to achieve a dream?"

Calista gives a little laugh. "Definitely not. It just shows you what they are and lets you feel a little like you would feel if you lived them. It's an escape, nothing more. A tourist attraction for people who've given themselves up to be what society wants to get a glimpse of what could've been instead." She leans in, voice growing warmer now, bringing that warmth right on back to my own cheeks. "Why—what're you looking for it to show you?"

"I need to find Oriana's mother," I manage to choke out because I can't make the mistake of saying anything different. No matter how close Calista steps to me, no matter how the gray in her blue eyes glimmers, no matter how honestly tempted I am whenever I'm around her to pull my mask from my face.

"That's your dream?" Calista's eyes squint beneath her mask. "Come on, Lucia, that's not a dream." Her hands flutter near mine, so close I feel their motion while her voice dances across my skin. It's playful, teasing, begging me to rise and follow her into this world of possibilities.

I can't. "I need to find the ammiralia. I can't dream until I get off this island."

"That's not how dreams work." Her voice is softer now, the playful lightness gone and replaced with something that might be sadness. "Dreams aren't supposed to be constrained by reality—that's why they're dreams. As a future Vessel, I'm not allowed to leave this island, but it's still what I dream of. It's still what I'd want if I could have anything in the world. It's still the main thing that gets me out of bed every morning because if I keep going, someday, somehow, it might come true. So what do *you* want?"

It should be an easy enough question to answer. I want to steal the source of magic to pay my family's debts. Of course I do. This has driven me forward for so long. It's what gets me out of bed every day.

But I can already imagine Calista saying, sadly this time, no longer teasing, *Come on, Lucia, that's not a dream.*

And she's right. A dream should be for myself, and I don't want the source of magic for myself. I want it so that Mamma will acknowledge that I'm *not* exactly like my father—and then let me go live as I please. I want it so the Silverhands will let me go live as I please. I just want these people to *leave me alone*, to stop feeling so entitled to everything I do. I'm tired of living to serve people, to please people.

But then, if I could do that, if I was finally free—what then? That, I suppose, would be my dream. But I haven't ever thought that far.

For all of the personas I donned and discarded like masks in the city, I made up little backstories, gave them something they wanted, something that mattered to them to pursue. I've been dozens of people with dozens of dreams and I'm not sure I've ever had one of my own.

"I don't know what I want," I admit quietly. "How do you? Why did you decide you wanted to leave the island? Is it because you hate it here? It's got to be more than that." Because I hate the situation I'm trapped in, too, but even though I want to run from it, I don't have a plan of where I want to run to.

"It is more than that. I suppose, for me, it was largely born of meeting all of our visitors. As a child it was—captivating." I close my eyes and just listen to the soft rise and fall of her voice. There's something captivating in that for me. A passion, a hope, a life. "To meet so many people who looked so different, who spoke differently, who dressed differently. Many of them were quite friendly with me, especially when I was a cute little child for them to dote on, and they'd tell me stories of how things were in their home over our dinners. And it fascinated me. I loved to hear the stories. I always imagined what it would be like when I could travel to them just like they traveled to me—because I thought, for a little while, that had to be what everyone did. Before I realized that most people can't and never will. But even after I realized that, I just couldn't let the idea go.

"There's so much out there beyond this island. I want to see the deserts, and I want to see the mountains—real mountains, not like these hills—and I want to see real snow. Don't you ever think about what's out there? Or perhaps you feel like you've seen enough.

I suppose I don't know. You *did* live in Verigal City, crossroads of the Aeditanian Sea and gateway to Estaralla."

"I did," I agree and wrinkle my nose, the stench of the city swimming its way up my nostrils with just the reminder, the sheer overwhelm of sweat, of spice, of sewage, of sea. With the reverie lost to the memory of unpleasant reality, I open my eyes. "I'm not sure it made me want to see more, though."

"Maybe you want solitude, then?" Calista suggests. Her eyes are wide—young and curious. They remind me strongly of the soft and girlish face I know is beneath her hardened mask. "A quiet little house far from anyone else all to yourself? Or with only whoever you've chosen as family with you?"

I know this isn't practical. I came to speak with her with a purpose—to ask her for advice on making a compass for Oriana to find her mother. But still, her words sweep me along because the realization that I, Lucia Arduini, know myself even less than I know my fake personas has opened a hole in me I hadn't noticed was there before.

And so I imagine a little house, tucked away into the rolling hills behind the city. I shake my head. "That might be nice for a while, but I think I'd get bored. But I—I like the idea of choosing my own family." Mamma, Father—while I can't say I hate them, I could never, they've also both brought me a whole lot of pain, dumped a whole lot of expectations on me I don't want to carry with me forever.

"You can start, perhaps, with that, then." Calista inclines her head. "You can think about who you want with you—and if you don't have a specific person, of course, just the type of person, or people, you want to be with. Your dream wouldn't have to be a place or an activity or any of that sort. It could just be a person."

"I don't know if it's just a person, though." My thoughts are swirling, a nagging pluck at the back of my mind saying that I might like someone like Calista. Someone with warmth and dreams, someone who encourages me to be myself and discover my own, someone who doesn't bury me with their expectations, someone who doesn't seek to control me, someone with whom we can both just be—free.

Calista shrugs at that. "Fair enough. It doesn't have to be that either." She reaches out and gently folds one of my gloved hands between her own. "That's the beauty of dreams. They're flexible. They can be whatever you want them to be, and they're just for you—not for anyone else—unless you want someone else involved in your dream, too. You can share a dream with someone, too, build it together instead of on your own." Her voice grows softer with each word, then, and my throat grows tighter.

"Did you?" I ask, and my voice comes out horribly raspy, and I've probably made a mistake letting these words slip at all, but her hands are a warm cradle around my own. "Share a dream with someone?"

Calista shuts her eyes, briefly closing me off from the one part of her I can read. "Ah," she breathes, a sigh that shivers. "I'm assuming someone passed on rumors about me. Yes, then, I did. There was a girl—a guide. I loved her, and we talked about what could be if we could run away from here. Together. And then she disappeared. As people do here."

I hold myself stiffly, not sure, if I let myself go, if I'd hug her out of pity or yank my hand away. Her halting tone bites into me, and I don't quite know why I chose to do this to myself—only that, even though I knew I might hate it, I wanted to know. And though I'm still pettily jealous of that girl, there's also a part of me that's glad Calista had a period of happiness in her life. "I'm sorry," I manage, because that's probably polite.

Calista waves one hand in front of our faces, as though swatting it off. "Oh, it was over a year ago now. So while I don't know that losing someone who meant something to you ever can mean nothing again, I have accepted it, you see. I don't love her anymore. Perhaps, even if she'd survived, the two of us and our shared dream might not have either. My dreams of travel are mine alone again—for now. Until, perhaps, I meet another woman who's interested in being a part of them with me."

It feels like a thread, dangling, close enough for me to reach. To pull, and see what happens. It feels a bit foolish because she's rejected me before, and it's not smart to assume a different outcome from the same situation. But I am stubborn. "What sort—" The words catch. I clear my throat, regretting already I've taken the bait. "—of woman— would you want?"

Calista leans in. Her eyes glimmer, so close to mine, and I really do wish I could see her expression in this moment. But maybe, for the sake of my dignity, it's better I don't. As it is, my knees feel weak, and I grip her hand still holding mine a little harder than I want to, just to keep steady. "One who wants to see the world. One who wants to be with me. One who wants, therefore, a life that's maybe out of the ordinary, that'll sometimes have to be a secret, but it will be *our* secret."

"I could—" *Be interested in travel. I am interested in something out of the ordinary. Something that's mine—ours—alone.* I snap my mouth shut, just in time to spare my pride and yet far, far too late at the same time. Because even if I haven't spilled all those words, I don't know what reasonable sentence I could've been starting. "Uh. Think . . about . . . my own dream." I can spin words into lies for days, but now, words seem beyond my grasp. I grimace, screwing up my flaming face behind my mask, but for once, I'm not glad the mask is hiding me. I want her to see how embarrassed I am by myself.

Calista gives a little shake of her head, a jolt I can only hope isn't a recoil. "Uh. I—see."

I doubt that because what I said didn't even make sense. "I mean everything you're saying makes me want to think of my own, too." A little better. Not great, but closer at least to something coherent.

"Right." Calista drags the word out, skeptical as she has every right to be. Distantly, I hear the eerie whistle that announced visitors to the estate in the past. But then she lifts a hand, trails her fingers down my mask, and even though the ceramic sits between our skin, an echo of the touch tingles my cheeks, and the sound is gone, and there's only this moment between us. I startle, barely stopping myself from my own jumpy recoil while she hooks her fingers beneath the bottom edge of my mask, and I briefly think she might rip it off. "Well, you asked how I know what I want, so perhaps another framing might help you understand it, too."

She doesn't remove my mask, though. Instead, her finger merely skims my jawline beneath it while I practically hold my breath because I'm afraid if I breathe, I'll gasp. "You see, dreams are another form of desires. And when you think of it like that—I think, at least—it becomes much easier to recognize. Because when you think of a dream, you should feel something." As her fingers reach the end of my jaw, she tucks a small, fraying hair behind my ear, never losing contact with my skin, and then she cups the back of my head in her hand, holding me steady. Captured. I can't move as she leans closer to me— not that I want to—until our masks nearly touch. Her other hand grasps my waist in a firm hold. "There'll be a physical longing. A pull. Telling you *that* is what you want."

And that, well, that I'm familiar with. I feel it now, where her fingers grip my dress, a warmth spreading, a tug pulling my hips to hers.

Part of me wants to demand if she's mocking me right now with her flirtation. Why she has to make it quite so taunting, why she has to make it quite so tempting, when she rejected me before.

Instead I whisper, "Don't your dreams ever make you *angry*, though? When you face the fact that you're not living them, that you're trapped here instead?" Like this, I mean. This tension between us, it's not all warmth and softness and joy. It prickles with its impossibility. She makes me imagine this other world and other life. She makes me want it. But I can't have it. All I have instead is this empty dream where our masks hover close, her fingers brushing where the plaster edge of mine meets my skin, but we'll never be closer than this.

I've never thought so much and so desperately before about what I can't have.

Calista pauses. "Sometimes. But I don't feel like the anger is a bad thing. It's good in its own way. It reminds me that I—the whole of me—am more than the role I play right now. I want more, and so I am more. The role that I've been forced into—Calista Eliades, glamorous host, future Vessel—is no more myself than the mask I wear is my true face. It's a comfort, in the end. Because even though the world may not see it, may not ever know it, I do."

The door beside us jerks open, and Calista and I spring apart with a speed that would suggest much more happening here than actually was.

Antony of all people stands in the doorway, a massive and stern shadow. Anger flares—why is he showing up now?

He folds his arms and says, "I've come to collect Lucia and

Oriana," while Calista simultaneously snaps, "Did you just break into my home?"

"I rang the bell, actually. Perhaps you heard it. Perhaps, I suppose, you didn't." His gaze flicks briefly to me, then, venom and pain leaking from his gaze. He lifts a ring of keys. "Borrowed these from Keelan. So then I let myself in, and I did check pretty much everywhere else before coming for your room, Calista, including Lucia's, because I thought you knew you're not allowed to bring the guides in here anymore."

"Forgive me for wanting to speak with Lucia without a million ears listening. Are you going to report me?" The ice Calista exudes raises the skin on my arms.

"I'll have to think about it." Antony thrusts a hand in my direction. "Come on, Lucia."

Calista shifts ever so slightly in front of me. "I wasn't informed of any scheduled trips. And I've been instructed to not let Lucia and Oriana leave the estate. Where are they going exactly?"

"Look." He glances over his shoulder, and then steps into the room as well, crowding us all in together in a stuffy circle. "I'm not here on behalf of the Vessels right now. Keelan doesn't know I took the keys. It's time Oriana and Lucia go back to the peninsula. You know they'll be safer if they leave. You know how dangerous it is for them here. You can't actually want them to suffer that fate, can you? You think Viola would like that?"

Calista hisses in a sharp breath, lifts a hand as though she's about to slap him, and then drops it again just as quickly. She folds her hands in front of her, knuckles turning white with strain.

My stomach flips because even though I shouldn't care, and Calista did say she was over it anyway, no one needs to explain who

Viola is for me to know. It's that obvious. "What about Ammiralia Rubellian?" I step back from them both because whatever they think, I can't leave yet. "We're just going to leave without her?"

"We'll continue the search for her on our own," Antony says.

My laughter escapes my lips, a harsh cackle, because I know that's garbage. "Oriana could be the key to finding her—the only way before it's too late. If she were given a compass to find the person she loves most, we could find her mother."

"No one is going to make that for you," Antony says. "You just need to go."

"Wrong. I'm going to make it." All my doubts vanish. If that's what I must bargain, I'll do it. I'll give up someone I love. Because whoever it is, they'll have a happy life still, even if I won't see them again.

"You're not." Antony steps toward me, placing himself between me and Calista.

"Why?" I lift my chin. "I could do it. Don't tell me I can't because I know that's a lie."

Antony bows his head and shakes it. "You shouldn't."

"Oh, yes, because you always know what's best for me."

Antony dares to set one of his hands on my upper arm. It's large, so large he can almost cup my arm in it whole. Once, it would've been an offer of safety, but now, it feels more like a threat. "I care about you, Lucia, more than I've cared about anything ever before. Why can't you see that? Don't you understand? I'm not supposed to be here right now."

"Then why are you? Because I don't want you here."

Antony recoils, releasing me briefly, but then, he reaches out again, this time curling a hand around my shoulder, and still, there's a familiarity that's tempting in it. "I'm choosing to risk it for you. Before I met you, this island was all I had—it and the duties it demands of all of us here. I knew exactly who I was going to grow up to be. I would live my entire life in service to the island, and that was fine with me. And then I met you, and I realized how much more could be out there in the world. It was as though I'd been living in the dark all along even though I hadn't known it, and the sun was rising for the very first time. All of a sudden, I felt things I'd never even realized were possible. Not just love, because I did love my family, but that was a love born of necessity. You were a possibility, a choice, and with you, at least at first, anything seemed possible. But then Keelan grew interested in you, and you grew interested in this island, and I realized that all those possibilities I thought I saw—they weren't mine. They were never mine, only yours. And I could either do what was expected of me and bring you back here, cage you, to be crushed by this haunted place—or let you go. So I let you go. Why is it so hard for you to understand that I tried to let you go only because I love you?"

I shouldn't flinch, but I do. He'd never said those words to me, and *now*, now, it just feels cruel. Even with his mask hiding his expression, I don't want to see any part of him as he says it. I'm furious and aching because he's saying he doesn't understand why I don't understand, but I don't get why he couldn't have said any of this sooner. When it would've mattered. When it would've made a difference to me. To us. Instead of dragging us through this miserable circle of lies and manipulation.

My gaze is pulled to Calista. She stands still to the side, her mask impenetrable as always—but that sight has never stung more. I need to see her face, need to see what she thinks of what he says, to see if she misinterprets and thinks it makes any difference to me—or if, perhaps, she's consumed by thoughts of Viola now, and her words before were a lie.

I'm on my own here. And so I say, not for Calista's sake, not for Antony's, only for my own, "You keep saying I don't understand, but I do. I get it now, why you tried to keep me from this island. The problem is, at this point, after everything that's already happened? I just don't care about that. Or you."

He recoils, but his grip on my shoulder tightens. His voice cracks, growing ever smaller, as he says, "I was only trying to protect you. I love you."

"I don't want you to protect me. I don't need your protection." I grab his hand that's now burning my skin and peel it off. "If you love me, *listen to me*!" He can't truly care about me if he doesn't see how much I hate his so-called protection that's really just condescending interference. "I'm not leaving this island. I can't leave yet!"

Antony yanks his hand from mine, and for a moment, the air hangs still between us, lanced by pain. Then he straightens, and when he speaks again his voice is steel. "Fine, you can hate me if you want, but you are leaving the island. At least you'll be alive this way. Now, the boat's waiting, and I don't know how much time we have."

"I'm not going." I fold my arms, stomp my feet into the floor as if I can shove them beneath the floorboards and never be removed from my spot. I glance to Calista for assistance, but her mask still hides everything. "I don't have to take orders from you."

"Actually, you do, because I'm your employer, and I'll fire you from your position if you don't come with me willingly."

I hiss through my teeth, "Now we're into threats, I see." I can't let him do it. If I get dragged back to the city now, Severin will have to drop out of school, be put to work night after night, and I will never get a second chance to make everything right.

"Are you coming willingly or not?" Antony asks through clenched teeth, his words short and curt.

"No." I will call his bluff.

"You're fired."

A lump forms in the back of my throat, but I spit the word out past it. "Fine." The longing stays thick in my veins. How I still, even now, even though nothing could ever make me his lover again *now*, wish he'd change. I wish he'd see that taking away my choices, no matter how right he turned out to be about the island's danger, was what ruined our chances together. It's not what he's done trying to protect me, but how, that's the problem.

"Well, now that you're no longer employed, or a paying tourist, it is illegal for you to be on the island of Estaralla. Lucia Arduini, you're under arrest, and being deported." He reaches behind his back and whips out a pair of handcuffs.

CHAPTER TWENTY-SIX

I skip back, dancing away from the swing of the handcuffs, away from his threat. After everything, after his apology, this is how things will end between us? He's going to forcibly drag me from Estaralla and back to my useless life in the city?

I'd thought I'd meant more to him than this. He'd apologized. I thought that meant he understood. He says he loves me, and I thought that would mean he cares.

But I'm just the fool. Again. There's a saying in the city: Those fooled once are merely innocent. Those fooled twice are gullible. And I've crossed that line all because I didn't pay close enough attention to what he's shown me this entire time. All because I wanted to believe in him.

"As of now, you're here illegally." His voice is hard, and there's nothing left but this command, no care, compassion, or pity for me.

"Antony, don't you think that's a little harsh?" Calista finally speaks again, and her voice, in contrast, is softer than ever, a fluffy cloud, a whisper of silk.

"It's the law. No outsiders are allowed on Estaralla except those working and those touring. She's now neither." He opens the handcuffs, the metal cracking as he does. His right hand shoots out, reaching for me, but I dance back.

Red sparks flash in the corner of my vision, burning away the last of my regrets. If he's going to force me to leave, I'll make him do it with force. "Make me."

He heaves a sigh, so dramatic his whole body shudders with it. "I'm sorry I've had to resort to this."

I scoff. "You didn't have to do anything."

He lunges for me. I dodge the swipe, but then he dives forward.

His arm catches me, and we fall. I land on my back, wind flying from my chest, and he lands beside me, arm pinning me to the floor. I twist to roll away, but his hand clamps over my shoulder and drags me back.

I shriek and swipe with my free hand at his face.

The cuff bites into my wrist as he slaps it on.

I never really had a chance to beat him in a fight unless he would get struck with regret at having to actually force me into the cuffs. But apparently, I'm not a weakness for him. Not at all.

His fingers clamp around my other wrist, followed by the cold sting of the metal. He bends over, his mask close to mine, but luckily, the masks are a wall between us.

"I will *never* forgive you this time," I snarl.

"I know. But you'll be alive. And that's what matters most to me." To him, still, not to me. It's never what matters to me that's important.

Antony grabs my hands and yanks me to my feet. I let my knees go weak, dropping to the floor. I skid forward on my elbows.

There's still part of me that hopes if I fight hard enough, he'll stop pushing me this way. That it will somehow finally make him see how much I don't want this even if he thinks it's better for me.

He hoists me up and over his shoulder. Blood rushes into my head, and my vision swims. With his shoulder bone digging into my chest, my stomach hurts, churns, and I half think I'm going to vomit all over his back.

I'd like to.

But I don't.

"Calista!" I turn my head to find her, which is easy enough. In her elegant green dress, she's a piece of finery that looks entirely out of place against the simplicity of the rest of her room; although upside down, her mask looks more monstrous than beautiful. It's something cruel, unfeeling, and empty. As close as we came so recently, she's a total stranger again. "Can't you do anything about this? Please!"

"Technically, it is the law. Antony and Keelan grant the island's visitation privileges—I can't reinstate you. I'm sorry." There's a note of regret in her voice, but it's wrapped tightly in stiffness. So tightly I might be reading too far into it. I don't know if she regrets not helping me now or just regrets having bothered to flirt with me—though if she still has fears Antony and I are a couple after watching this ridiculous display, she should know better.

I want her to regret my leaving, though. I feel it like a chilly prickle on the side of my neck where, so recently, I felt the brush of her fingers instead. I was just starting to think about what could be between us, and now, I'll never see her again.

Antony carries me away, each step jolting through me. I watch the floor rushing beneath us, catch sight of the corner of the hall I vomited on so many nights ago, but it's still pristine, hidden away, a secret never to be spoken of again.

He opens the door to Oriana's room. "Ammiraligna Rubellian,

you need to leave the island now—for your own safety. A boat is waiting. Why are you wear—oh, you know what, never mind."

I'm stuck with a vision full of the carpet in the room, the swirling flowers and glowing little bits that turn all colors of the rainbow. It's dizzying. I can't see Oriana, but I wish I could.

"Oriana, don't listen to him," I snap. "I'm going to help you find your mother. We need to stay to find her. He can't carry both of us away!"

"If Lucia and I leave, what's going to happen to my mother?" Oriana's voice is small but firm, and I could cheer.

"We're going to continue the search for her," Antony says. "I promise. But you're ill, and you won't get better until you leave this island. We need to go."

"Tell him you want to stay," I say. "Don't go with him!"

"It's your decision, Ammiraligna. But you'll have a new guide if you choose to stay. Lucia Arduini isn't working for us anymore. She's leaving, no matter what you choose to do."

The silence stretches on too long. Somehow, I think she's actually considering.

"I don't want another guide," Oriana finally says. "Keep Lucia."

"She's hired by the island of Estaralla," Antony says. "And we have decided to terminate her contract."

"That was an order," Oriana says.

Antony barks a laugh, and I wrench in his grasp, itching to slap him for his mockery. "You don't have the power to give me an order. Estaralla hired her, not you. Estaralla terminates her. Leave with her now, or you can stay alone."

Rustling sounds, and Oriana approaches. Upside down, she looks like a corpse even with the white mask covering her face, the skin of her neck so yellowed and gray and her eyes bloodshot and hollow. In truth, maybe it is better for her to leave now.

She touches my elbow, a question in her eyes. I don't exactly know what she's looking for, though. I'll fight however I can to not leave, but I also don't have a great plan, exactly, to follow through on that.

"I can make you a compass if we stay here," I say. "It can lead you to your mother."

Oriana's voice lifts with an almost painful note of hope. "Can you?"

"You're not making anything," Antony says. "Ammiraligna, she's not making anything. Are you leaving with Lucia or not?"

"I'll go with Lucia." Oriana gives me a firm nod, a conspiratorial nod. I hope that means she has a plan because I don't know how I'm going to fix this. Not this time.

Antony marches down the hall. Oriana trails him, more willing than I will ever be. Outside the gates of the estate, Antony dumps me from his back into a litter. It's not like Vessel Dionne's fancy little litter with its silken water curtains, but it has thick black curtains around the edges. It looks more like a jail wagon, which I suppose is exactly what it is.

After he and Oriana enter, the curtain folds back with an unnaturally loud *hiss*. Then we take off.

Unlike Vessel Dionne's litter, which glided smoothly and slowly, a strutting lady, this thing is a frantic racehorse. It shoots down the pathway, and I don't need to see outside to feel the speed. It bobs and lurches as it moves, so my teeth chatter and my bones vibrate.

Oriana presses a hand to her mouth, looking about to vomit. Antony faces the black curtains with his whole body turned away from us, paying no attention at all.

"Can't you slow this down?" I snap.

"No." Still, he doesn't look at us.

I grab Oriana's hand between my cuffed ones. She squeezes her eyes tight, and we race onward.

At least it's over quickly.

We slam to a stop, abruptly as we started. I pitch forward across the litter and land on my knees, head in Oriana's lap. She grunts, but somehow doesn't vomit on me. Small mercy.

Antony leaps out. He's in such a rush, and now that my head's no longer upside down, thoughts slip into my mind. He said to Calista he wasn't here on behalf of the Vessels. He may indeed have the power to have arranged this, but I think he's done this behind their backs.

He leans back inside the litter and thrusts a hand in Oriana's masked face. "Out." She gives her hand to him, and he yanks her right out.

"I got this," I say. If he's tossing me around like a parcel, it'll be faster than if I control my own movements and go. Nice. And. Slow. Maybe if I go slow enough, the Vessels will figure out what Antony is doing.

My best chance of staying might be to let them catch us.

I step out of the litter, avoiding his hand, stumbling on the first step and falling to my knees. Above us, dark clouds swirl. They're a strange color, a deep blue instead of gray, and small flashes of light dart between them. The air is chilly, raising ice along my skin, and it tastes like burning sulfur.

"Get up." Antony yanks me to my feet. "If you're going to walk, walk." At the end of the dock, a little sailboat bobs, looking rather helpless against the sea. I have no idea how he thinks that's going to bring us all the way back to the city. Even in the port, the rising waves toss it back and forth. Oriana walks ahead of us, her skirts whipping around her in the harsh wind.

"Is this safe?" I drag my feet as I walk, and Antony's grip pinches my arm as he tries to force me to move faster.

"It's safer than staying," Antony snaps.

I don't even have to fake a stumble as he pushes me onto the boat. The floor slides out beneath me, and I drop. But I'm aboard, so he just steps over me this time.

The slimy, salty deck freezes against my cheek.

Oriana helps me to my feet. "Thanks," I mumble. Antony storms past us, a frantic fury almost rivaling the tempest gearing up above. He unties us from the dock and leaps back aboard.

Behind, on the island, mist pours down through the green trees, rolling steadily toward us. Antony hoists the sail, and the gusting wind catches it hard. We lurch forward, and water spills up and over, soaking me to the bone. Oriana's teeth chatter.

The swirling clouds create a dark circle above us, a spiraling vortex, while the light crackles between them. Antony stands at the helm of the ship, and though he's too far for me to hear what he says, his lips move like he's mumbling to himself. But he's distinctly not turning us around. He's sending us right into the storm.

He'd rather get us killed than return to Estaralla.

CHAPTER TWENTY-SEVEN

Oriana grasps my arm. Her skin slips over mine, slick with seawater. "You'll make me something to bring me to my mother?" she whispers. "If we just get back to the island?"

"Yeah. If." I can appreciate her determination, but also, my goal has abruptly shifted from *stay on the island* to *don't drown*, and for now, that's my focus.

I stagger across the shifting deck toward Antony. I can't move with these cuffs. If we capsize, which looks awfully likely, I'll drown. If he's really so obsessed with me not dying, he'll remove these. I reach his feet, and I'm so small in his shadow, so helpless, and I hate it.

I hold my cuffed hands up. "You have to let me go!"

His gaze flicks down. He's pulled the mask from his face, so I see him again, and he looks shockingly tired. His strong cheekbones look gaunt, and his stubble says he hasn't shaved in at least a few days. Water streams down his face, and I can't tell if it's the drenching of the sea streaming from his hair or if he's crying. He grips the ship's wheel, no doubt the only reason he's still standing. His knuckles are stark white against the dark wood.

The next wave towers above us, a waiting threat, before it crashes down.

"If we capsize, I'm going to drown. Was everything you said about not wanting me to die a lie like everything else? Like your greatest lie of all—pretending to care?"

Antony reaches a hand into his pocket and pulls out a key. "I never ever lied about how much I care."

I don't understand how he's still saying that. But I only have so much energy to waste on anger at him this time because a wave rises behind us, larger than the last. Its edges are uneven, and it looks like a lifted hand. A hand commanding us to stop.

It crashes down. My legs fly out from under me, and I skid across the deck. Antony tumbles away in the other direction, and the key—the key slips out of both our reaches.

The next wave is already coming. I scream as the key slides across the tilted deck of the boat. "No!"

I lunge and fall the rest of the way to it. My fingers wrap around the key, its cold edges digging thankfully into my palm.

Then everything lurches back into motion, and I go tumbling across the boat once more. I smack into the railing, and with its temporary support, I jam the key into the cuffs and twist.

It clicks.

I'm free.

The fog has reached us now. Its tentacles crawl around me, blurring everything, and I squint into it. "Oriana!" I yell. I don't care what happens to Antony, but I won't run without her. If she's killed because he was trying to drag me away . . .

I don't see her—but then again, I barely see anything but a blobby mass of gray. My hands curl into fists. The railing of the ship presses into my shoulder blades. I try to step forward, but force slams me back into it. The bow of the ship lifts into the sky, pointing toward those deep dark clouds, tilting us near vertical, while a wave looms above us. Antony abandons the helm to frantically let out the sail, but it's much too late for that. Only moments remain before we're all in the water.

I fumble with the ties of my apron, thrusting it aside, and then shimmy free of the skirt and blouse both. Modesty won't save me, but less clothing to weigh me down will. So modesty can hurl itself from a cliff. I pause on my gloves because removing them feels somehow more revealing, but they're weight, they're clumsy, and they make it harder to work with the magic, so they come off, too.

The wave we're riding crests, and the water plummets. The railing behind me vanishes. For a moment, I'm weightless, flying in the midst of this magical tempest.

Then I fall.

The wind whips through my hair, and my nerves thrum. A small yelp escapes me.

I smack into the water. It's warmer than I expected but just as violent. It yanks on the fabric so hard that the mere undergarments I'm still wearing feel like stone, willing me under, while I flail and fight to the surface.

I break free and suck in a swift, briny breath above the water. Then I kick in circles, a desperate attempt to orient, while pitching waves roll all around me.

I quickly see I only have one direction in which to go. Behind me, which must be the direction away from the island, the waves rise up, so tall, unnaturally tall. They break, as ordinary waves might, but as soon as they do, new ones rise to take their place, forming a wall I'll never be able to climb. If I continue to fight the waves, eventually I'll drown. My strength, unlike theirs, is finite.

I am trapped.

I hadn't wanted to leave the island yet, but still, that realization sinks into me as a bone-deep cold. Even if I wanted to leave, I couldn't—and what does that mean for me, later, when I do want to?

That fear's nothing but a waste of energy now, though, so I catch one of the newly rising waves and kick to ride its energy, letting it carry me forward, back toward the beach. I squint into the gray and shout, "Oriana!" but I see no one, and my words are swallowed away.

The wave drops again, and I hurtle down with it. I hit the sea hard, a sharp punch to the stomach that seizes my breath. A rock rises before me, and I paddle forward. Reaching it, I thrust my fingers into its crevices and cling there while the wave pulls away.

In the brief space before the next wave hits, I scramble up the rock, skittering down the other side and out of the reach of the water. Only once I'm on the coarse rocks of the beach do I let myself drop to my knees. All of the control my lungs had gives up, and I cough and sputter and spit.

Fog swirls around me. It's thick, so heavy it tickles my cheeks and neck, like it's searching for a way to get beneath my skin.

Ahead of me where the beach meets the dock, a dark shadow looms, one arm lifted while their cloak whips around. Is it the Shadow? I'm too far to see any details.

I wonder if they see me, just a few steps away on the beach. But if they do, they don't care. They do nothing. I'd think they'd leap to kill me.

So maybe they don't see me. Or it's not the Shadow.

A shriek slices the air. It doesn't sound like Antony. I turn toward the sound yelling, "Oriana!" It was close, so I stagger in its direction, slipping along the pebbled beach back to the water.

A dark form bobs in the water. "Oriana!" I yell and hold my hand out, over the waves, while the rocks beneath me scrape into my knees. Foam sprays my palm—an abrupt reminder my skin's bare—but if Oriana's at all surprised to see the graying cracks across my palms, it's obviously nothing in the face of our current danger, because her expression registers only a sputtering desperation. The next wave pushes her forward, and I catch her hands as they hit the rock below me. Water streams down her face—her mask, noticeably missing—her eyes bugging out in their sockets, and she looks like a wild and terrified creature. Her mouth opens, but all that comes out is a pained groan.

The water recedes, but I hang on. Her weight yanks on my arms, making them feel like they're going to pop right out. I grunt and hoist, pulling her up onto the rock on her stomach. She lies there, still, face down and trembling, while the next few waves hit the edge, spitting remains at us. I set a hand on her shoulder and rub circles into her back. "We're alive," I say, because I'm not sure what else I could say that'd be reassuring and true. "We're alive."

The fog peels away, retreating from the water. Its edges slide by us, and then the cold lifts, and the sun breaks through and blinds me. I shield my eyes with a hand, squinting into the sparkling water, taking the opportunity to scan for Oriana's mask in case there's any chance it's floating somewhere we could grab it. Of course, as usual, there's no luck to be found for me. The overturned boat bobs a distance away, easy to spot amid the water reflecting light. Almost at its side, a person's arms flail. Antony.

A lump forms in my throat, but I don't even know if it's relief or disappointment that he's still alive. It doesn't matter either way.

I tighten my grip on Oriana's shoulder. "Come on. We need to get going."

I want to assume Antony won't think it's a fine idea to try to drag us away again. He has to realize the same thing I have: the storm lifted once Oriana and I were both back onshore. Something—or maybe someone—doesn't want us to leave this island.

He'd better not try to take us away again.

He might still be foolish enough to try.

Out in the quieting water, Antony swims with solid, large strokes toward the beach. Toward us.

"Where are we going?" Oriana rolls over and pushes herself to her elbows.

"Away, for now." I tug her sleeve. "Somewhere quiet I can create something that will lead you to your mother."

Oriana follows my gaze out to Antony and nods. She rises to her feet, a slow and labored movement, and then crosses the remaining rocks, with careful steps and arms stretched for balance.

When we hit the beach, we run.

CHAPTER TWENTY-EIGHT

I only half know where we're going as we stagger back up the path Antony's litter took us down. We didn't depart from the main harbor, but a deserted corner of the island. The stones beneath our feet are cracked, and the trees bend over, branches sweeping across the path in front of us. I just take us in the one direction I know, toward the one landmark that juts out among the green no matter which angle you're looking at it from—those white palace spires.

I check over my shoulder a few times, but only the wind follows. Antony hasn't caught up, and so I pull Oriana off the path.

Instantly, the air tightens around us, hanging thick with the smell of trees, rot, and moisture that gathers in a mist on my tongue. I push the curtains of branches aside, leading the way and inspecting each for thorns first so I'll take any hits they land. Oriana is ill enough already, and she doesn't even have the protection of her mask anymore.

When we've put enough distance between ourselves and the path, I stop.

"Before I do anything, you have to promise your mother is the person you love most," I say. "Can you promise? There's no one you love more? Especially since your relationship with her is . . . complicated?"

"I—I think so. I don't know who else. I don't have any siblings. I do love my father, but he's absent all the time, and he has even higher expectations for me than Mamma." Oriana's mouth twists to one side. "Both of them see me as the pinnacle of their work to rise in status, but in Father's case, that's going back through generations of his family. His grandfather was just a common seaman in the navy, and my grandmother was not even from the Tottian peninsula, but some village girl from Edalia. Mamma—my relationship with her used to be very good, actually, as a child. She would defend me when Father would be angry if I was less than perfect at a dinner party, if I got tired, if I whined. Things only fell apart with her more recently—after it became clear her dream of marriage for me was my nightmare."

I don't know why, but her words make my own chest hurt. In my life, that was Father. He stood up for me when I came home dirty from roughhousing in the park in ways little girls weren't supposed to. And then he left. He left us all, but mostly, he left me defenseless, and with even more fury from Mamma than ever before.

I *am* glad to help Oriana find her mother. I'm not sure I'd be willing to give up so much if I didn't need this for selfish reasons, too—who am I kidding, actually, I would never—but I'm happy our interests in this moment coincide.

"You didn't have any close friends?" I ask.

Oriana shakes her head. "I didn't have the opportunity. With the other daughters of naval families we spent time with, I had to be perfect at all times. My interactions with them weren't about me—they were about how they'd reflect on my parents. So I had to make sure they'd reflect well. None of those girls even knew me. My governess did, I suppose, but Mother fired her when I was fifteen because she included science in our lessons at my request and that was 'a useless pile of cold facts for a lady.' " She laughs, but it's weak, and it hits me hard that, just like Calista, she's had a lonely life.

"Never a secret lover?" I ask, because it's one I need to check.

"Ugh. Absolutely not." Oriana wrinkles her nose, and I'm not sure what to make of her distaste. It rankles a bit—I can't tell if she's one of the upper class who consider that for inferior women. But then, she sees my recoil, and blushes deeply. "Oh, I'm not against it. It's just people always ask me that—especially when they find out I'm reluctant to marry. I get tired of it. Everyone thinks the reason I don't want to marry must be because I already have my sights set on someone else. After all, they say, why else would I be opposed?" Her mouth tightens. "As if there could be no other reason but someone already waiting in the wings. As if *I'm just not interested* isn't enough."

Her embarrassment is so sudden and so complete I pause because I don't want to say another wrong thing about it. I did already make an assumption I shouldn't have. "That is incredibly annoying. I think not being interested is more than enough reason."

Oriana smiles faintly, and she looks back up. And though her smile is just a flicker, it feels so much deeper. "Anyway, have I answered your interrogation well enough, or do you want to know more about every thought I've had about every person in my life?"

"Well, what about me? Go on, tell me every thought you've had about me." I nudge her, and, just in case it's still not clear it's teasing, give her a wink.

She rolls her eyes, still smiling. "Well, you're clever, and I appreciate that, but you're also occasionally full of yourself. You're not so bad, but I do hate to break it to you that I certainly don't love you. Your feelings must remain unrequited."

"Unrequited?" I bark. "Now who's full of herself?"

Oriana flicks her hand in dismissal. "I thought we were just joking. Please, as if your real bumbling interest wasn't clear from practically the first day here."

I flush, real embarrassment this time. I was apparently so obvious even Oriana knew what was happening before I did.

"Now are we done?" she asks. "Or shall I tell you more about how you tripped over your own feet every time Calista entered a room?"

"Interrogation done!" I don't have much left to spell for her other than that knife I took from the kitchen. It'll have to do. That, or I'll be pulling my slip from my body and wandering in only my underwear, but even I'm not so immodest. I lift my knife. The handle warms against my slick palm, and I close my eyes. For this to work, the magic is going to try to take the person I love most in trade. I know exactly who it is. There's only one person in the world, really, I'd care if I never saw again. It's not my criminal father who's left me in this predicament. It's not my once wealthy mother, who I'll never be good enough for. It's not a friend—I lost most of the people I thought were friends years ago. It sure isn't Antony; whatever feelings I had for him have been squashed by the heel of reality. And it's not Calista either. She's gorgeous, enticing, has a pull I can't escape and don't want to either, but that's not love. I don't know her nearly well enough to love her.

But the thought of losing my brother—I hate it. Because he is the only one I'd care if I never saw again. Even though I'm doing this to save him, I don't want to lose him. I can't even bring myself to think his name, for fear that if I do, the magic is going to know it's him.

So instead, I go for the next person I think I can convince the magic I love. I imagine him when I loved him most—imagine the way the moonlight used to highlight his cheekbones and the strong line of his jaw. I imagine the way his lips felt against mine, soft, but strong and sure in all the ways I wasn't back then. I remember the warmth of his breath and the warmth of the words he would whisper against my ear, promises we would have a future together that was so very different from the present I was living. And I believed him. I believed him.

Bringing that all to mind stings a bit, like dragging my limp body through thorns, but maybe, just maybe, that pain will help convince the magic I love him. I love him, and he's betrayed me. Multiple times now.

I focus on the tingle of my fingers, and then, a tingle deeper in my chest. I think of love—Oriana needs to find the person she loves most. I focus and think and push. Oriana can have who she loves most, and I will give up mine. Antony.

My fingers grow hotter, a burning trail connecting them and my chest. An image flashes into my mind of the city docks. The smog of the factories rises behind while young men toil away, dumping nets of writhing fish across the cracked wood.

The image grows larger, like I'm flying above, flying closer, and the men on the dock come into focus. One of them, a wiry, tall boy straightens, brushing a flopping lock of dark hair out of his eyes. Sweat glistens on his forehead, and I catch sight of his hazel eyes. The same as mine. When he was bent over, he looked so much older—my poor little brother.

A hole opens in my chest. *Severin!* I want to scream.

No! I don't want to lose Severin. The magic was supposed to take Antony. I don't want to pay this price. I try to make my mind blank, shove the price back into the knife, because I can't let go of it yet.

But I don't have control anymore.

Once a spell begins, it can't be stopped. I already knew that. But still. I'd never really regretted a spell. Not until now.

Severin turns his head, lifts his gaze, and meets mine. A small frown pinches his brows, and I wonder if somehow he sees me. Or senses me. Or if any part of him knows I'm there.

Knows this is the last time I'll see him.

I pinch my skin, rake my nails down my wrist, desperate to think of anything else, anything to make this stop, but still, he's there.

Mist curls in around the edges of my vision, but I'm not ignorant enough to think this means I'm succeeding. This is the magic taking him from me. The mist obscures him now, leaving nothing but a silhouette.

That fades, too.

I'm alone.

I'll never see my brother again.

Now, I need to get the magic to release him from the Silverhands. This sacrifice has to pay off. Severin will be free. He'll have the life he should've had. And he'll be better off without me in the end.

That's the best I can do for him.

The connection rushes out of me, and I jolt back into my body, back into the tangled mess of the vines. A few roots have twisted their way around my ankles and begun to snake up my legs. Oriana stands back, watching, gaping, her hands clutched to her chest.

"What the hell?" I snap and slice down at one of the vines with my knife, sawing through, back and forth, until it snaps in two. I grit my teeth so hard my mouth aches as I do the next.

"Why didn't you help?" My patience is short, gone, and maybe it's not fair. But I just gave up my brother for Oriana to find her mother, and she couldn't even keep me safe.

Oriana unfurls her hands and holds them out to me. Blood wells across her palms, new lines of black spiking across her skin. Her bloodshot eyes pin me, accusing, and she doesn't need to say a word.

Guilt hits me, snaking around tighter than the vines. "I'm sorry."

Oriana shrugs, but it's clear that damage is done. She folds her hands back into herself, hiding the bloody streaks once more.

It's not fair the trees attacked while I was out. A wash of anger sweeps my strangling guilt away. What do I have to do to get things to go right here? To get the island itself to stop attacking me?

Probably make some sacrifice. Give up something huge. Apparently, that's how everything on this damned island works.

I hold out the knife. "This is for you." An outline of mist shimmers around it like steam rising from heat. The handle in my hand burns, and I hope it doesn't hurt her.

"What do I do with it?" She takes the knife, turning it over, and the mist shifts as she moves it, trailing after. "How does it lead me to my mother?"

"Think of her. See what it does." All of my body hums with hope. And desperation. If the person she loves most somehow turns out *not* to be her mother, all of this was for nothing. If it's someone not on the island, maybe it won't even react.

Maybe that's why nothing seems to be happening.

But I already yelled at her about the vines, and I was wrong about that. I'm not going to yell again, so I clench my fists at my sides and wait.

Slowly, the mist rises from the knife. It trails away from it, sweeping to the left. Oriana turns toward the trail. It fades swiftly, only a pointer. "Do you think we follow it? Or go away from it?"

"She's your mother. What does your instinct say? Whatever it says, do that."

Oriana's expression knots. "I think I should follow it. But there's—I don't know, there's part of me that's not sure I want to find her suddenly." She bites her lip. "Do you think that means it's trying to prepare me to find her . . . dead?"

The lie dances on my tongue, so much easier. "I don't know," I say instead. "But there's only one way to find out."

Oriana gives me a tight nod.

The heat and humidity are so oppressive it doesn't take long before slick sweat coats every inch of me. It drips into my eyes, stinging, as we walk. The one small mercy is that as the mist from the spelled knife touches the branches, they curl away, folding in on themselves. Leaves fall, leaving only withered twigs. It clears the path for us.

We trudge uphill, so steep my thighs burn. I can barely imagine how I'm going to feel tomorrow.

And Oriana.

She still wears her entire gown, buttoned to her chin, even though the lace around her neck and across her chest is browned and torn to bits now. She huffs as she walks but doesn't utter a single complaint.

The only good thing about the altogether too-long walk is it gives

279

me plenty of time to consider how I should approach the Shadow. Having no idea what the Shadow's build might be, and knowing that while I'm scrappy, I'm not a great fighter and could certainly be easily overpowered, trying a direct assault on them to remove their mask isn't my smartest approach. A better potential option could be an approach from behind when they're distracted. I have a distraction in play already: Oriana. She'll go right for her mother, no doubt, and if the Shadow goes after her to stop her from taking their prisoner, which is likely, I should have an opening.

However, I need an alternative if the Shadow, for some reason, decides to go straight for me instead and leave Oriana and the ammiralia for later. I suppose, if the Shadow is slight enough, maybe I can just make a run and grab for their mask, but I'll only do that if I'm completely confident. Otherwise, I'm best off hiding my intentions for as long as I can.

I haven't yet met anyone on the island who secretly thinks the Shadow is someone to be admired, but there always are devotees, even for the very worst people. I've certainly seen plenty of them in Verigal City, twisted and desperate people who cling to the heels of the most repulsive, often just because it makes them feel different from the masses and feel important. So that's what I'll do. I'll tell the Shadow I'm an admirer—which, even if they're suspicious, will cause them to lower their guard at least a little—and slowly move forward until I'm within range to grab.

We reach a flattened clearing. The path continues, now a sparsely green field of flowers and grass that looks like it's been burned, patchy and brown and short. It fades away into a wall of fog ahead.

Thoughts jolt through me, each one more unpleasant than the last.

What if the ammiralia isn't with the Shadow at all, and this is a waste of time?

What if I fail to unmask the Shadow and instead they kill me?

What if it's a trap for both *of us so the island can devour our bones?*

Oriana looks back at me. "Are we going into that fog?" The matching fog from her knife drifts in that direction, but it's not unlike the mist that swept over the cliffs and stole the ammiralia away in the first place. I'm not sure if that comparison makes me hopeful or terrified.

But all that waits behind us is Antony, and fates neither of us want. There's only onward.

We'll see what price we'll have to pay.

I nod. "We have to."

We enter the curtain of fog.

CHAPTER TWENTY-NINE

At least in the fog, the air is cooler. And strangely less humid. It's like whatever this fog is isn't water based at all. The sweat on my skin rises and evaporates into its own steam that fades into the clouds.

In the endless gray, there are no more of the trees that cluttered the rest of the island. A few dead stumps curl across the ground in hunched forms that barely reach my knees.

We haven't passed anything living in this fog yet.

Maybe nothing can survive it.

I wouldn't mind conversation at this point, but there's something about the utter stillness we're in that makes me afraid to open my mouth. That feels like if I make a sound, something will plummet from the sky and devour us whole.

We reach a rock wall blocking our way, so we're forced to move along the side of it. Brown stains fill the cracks between the stones, and an unexpected stench of rotting fish thickens the air.

A set of doors waits in the wall. They're taller than both of us, towering above our heads. Carvings swirl around the rims of the doorframes, a mix of rust and silver, like they once belonged to someone fancy.

The doorknobs are carved bird heads, beaks extended to make the handle. There's something about the carvings with their hollow, lifeless eyes that makes a shiver slink its way down my legs.

"Should we enter?" Oriana asks, whispering, as though she also fears the noise.

The smoke from the knife drifts toward the doors, vanishing into the wood. That's the direction we need to move. The question is if we want to keep heading around whatever this is—or go straight through. Maybe it's even trying to tell us the ammiralia is inside.

"Let me see." I grasp the beak and shove. The door sticks in the ground, until grinding open with a sharp and piercing whine. A deep smell of rot and death rises in its wake.

I cough and, perhaps against my smarter judgment, step through. Inside, the mist is thinner, and I can see the entire hall. It must've once been something grand—maybe a ballroom or a meeting hall. Beneath the dust on the floor are glittering tiles in a swirling pattern. The ceiling sweeps above, an arch stretching up to the sky. Broken glass glitters across the floor, presumably the remnants of the shattered window that makes up the entire back wall.

Alongside the glass and dust across the floor lie crumpled collections of bones. Skeletons.

People, once.

"Is it safe?" Oriana calls. "Lucia?"

"Uh," I say, because I'm not sure, but she takes that as good enough (it does mean I'm alive, at least) and enters.

She lets out a whimper. I set a hand on her shoulder, willing my own nerves to rise from my skin. The skeletons are dead. At least that means they can't do anything to us.

"Who do you think these people are?" Oriana whispers.

"Were," I correct.

She shudders beneath my hand. "What killed them?"

"I don't know, but we should go. Quickly."

Oriana hoists her skirts and all but sprints across the floor. There's no door on the other side, but there is an opening among the final shards of the former window.

"Don't let it cut you!" I holler and run after her. I don't watch where I'm going closely enough, and a bone crunches under my foot. I flinch from the sound, but keep going.

We can't look back.

Oriana swings one leg over the base of the window, and I hold my breath. The end of her skirt snags, and she yelps. I reach forward, tearing it free, and she tumbles over the other side. I swing my own leg over next, careful to avoid the glittering glass shards. They point up at me, a threat, but I make it over.

Oriana strokes the rip. "Mother won't be happy with me." She must be losing it, because really, how is this the time to mourn her dress?

"She won't have a chance to be unhappy if we don't find her first." I haul her to her feet.

Tears spill over her cheeks, and she falls into my shoulder. "I wish we'd never come to this damn island. I wish—there are so many things I wish I could change. I don't want to keep going. I want to go back—back in time. Can you do that? Take us back, erase our choices, let us just start again?"

"I can't." I don't think that's possible, but even if it were, I wouldn't. Because if I could somehow reset time, and Oriana never came to this island, would I? As terrible as things are right now, I need to be here. I set a hand on her back and awkwardly pat her. "We have to keep going."

Oriana swallows. Hiccups. She yanks away from me, thrusts the knife out, and marches in the direction of its smoke, her steps stomping, angry now.

Only a few steps later, the ground plunges away into a steep hill. We reach the precipice, and below sprawls a lake, glowing a sharp teal green.

There's lots of magic here in this water—or, well, liquid. It's probably not water, as I should know by now.

At the edge of the lake, a body bobs, skirts splayed out. It's too blurry for me to see more details, no matter how I squint, but Oriana leaps off the edge and skids down the steep hill.

Then her feet slip, and she tumbles the rest of the way.

I pick my way after her carefully. Oriana stands as I'm approaching the final steps, brushing herself off without glancing at me. She lifts her skirts and runs again, toward the body at the edge of the lagoon. Her gait is uneven now, more of a stumble, but it doesn't stop her.

As I near, the body finally comes into focus.

It's Ammiralia Rubellian. She floats on her back at the edge of the liquid, skirt billowing about, reeds wrapped around her wrists and neck. The dark veins are webs across her entire body, including her face. Her eyes are wide open.

And they are black pits.

CHAPTER THIRTY

Oriana plunges into the liquid with a gasp. It rises just above her ankles, shallower than I thought, and with a violent splash, she hurls herself beside her mother. Her mother rocks in the wave.

"Maybe don't—" I call, but it's too late. Who knows what this liquid will do to her? If it somehow immobilizes her like her mother, I'm going to be stuck alone with the Shadow. Plus, as much as guilt weighs on me for what's happened to the ammiralia, watching Oriana suffer would be so much worse. While the ammiralia was always a means to an end, it turns out that, as terrible an idea as it is to consider your mark a friend, I've rather grown to like Oriana. But she's not going to listen to me anymore.

She presses her fingers into her mother's neck beside a pulsing blackened artery, while I circle around behind her, carefully sticking to the shoreline. The liquid laps near the edge of my boots, but I don't step in. It glows with an unnatural green light. No way I'm touching it.

Oriana cries out—at least she's still moving—and throws her arms around her mother, pressing her face into her mother's chest.

"Is she alive?" I ask, tentative. I can't tell if the noise was joy or sorrow.

Oriana draws back from her mother. "Yes." She pulls the reeds taut and begins to saw at them with the knife.

"Don't!" I reach out, wavering. I'm not sure if I'm more afraid she's going to succeed in rescuing the ammiralia before the Shadow arrives and leave me to risk everything alone or that in rescuing the ammiralia, she's going to cause something even worse to happen. Quite possibly, given how obsessed this island is with its trades, the reeds will grab Oriana and pull her under in the ammiralia's place.

Oriana scowls, but at least she stops, holding up the knife. "Don't worry. It didn't even work."

That doesn't make me feel the least bit better. It's worse, really, because it means I'm right that those reeds aren't at all natural.

Oriana huffs and adjusts her grip as though readying to yank at the reeds instead.

"Don't!" I repeat. "You don't know what'll happen if you free her, and it could be bad."

"So then what do we do? Leave her? After we went through all this to find her?"

"No. Definitely not." That's hardly going to work either. I just need to delay Oriana until the Shadow arrives. For both of our sakes' really. I need to eliminate the Shadow, of course, but eliminating the Shadow also seems like it could be the best chance of safely removing the ammiralia from these chains she's been bound in.

Hopefully the Shadow is coming soon. I suppose I don't know their patterns at all. For all I know, they might not plan to return here for days. "We just need to be strategic." I kick the panic aside.

Nothing to do now but stall for as long as I can. And if that fails, well, I suppose Oriana and I both have the Shadow's markings as well. Perhaps I can figure out how to lure the Shadow to one of us as the next victim—with their prisoner missing, that should be easier.

Oriana narrows her eyes. "Strategic?"

"Yeah," I say. "You should look closer at the reeds. What are they attached to?"

"Why don't you come look at them?"

"I am concerned about that liquid, just like I'm concerned about the reeds."

Oriana rolls her eyes and throws one free hand into the air. "Ugh, you're wasting time! We have an opening. Stand back and be afraid if you want to. I don't care." She shifts, grip visibly tightening over the reeds.

As much as I didn't want to enter the unknown muck, that's enough to drive me forward into it. It's frigid cold, numbing the skin of my legs in a swift beat. "No!" I call out again, reaching forward.

Approaching, I can see more clearly. The vines aren't wrapped around Ammiralia Rubellian's wrists. They're stabbing into her skin, wrapped beneath it, and holding her tight. "Just—wait, just wait!"

"No," Oriana says, and then she looks up. Her gaze stops somewhere over my shoulder, and her lips part in frozen fear. "Absolutely not." She thrusts her fingers beneath the reeds and *yanks*.

"No!" I lunge to stop her, but it's too late. The reeds pop free from one of the ammiralia's forearms.

Released from its bind, her hand shoots forward, clamping around my wrist. Her nails bite into my skin and swiftly draw blood.

"No!" Pain lances down my arm, followed by numbness. I pry at

Ammiralia Rubellian's fingers, but they're cold and hard as stone. Blood wells around them.

"I had to. We have to get out of here!" She points over my shoulder.

And though I don't want to turn my back on Ammiralia Rubellian, I do.

At the top of the hill, the Shadow looks down at us.

CHAPTER THIRTY-ONE

Even though it was my plan to find the Shadow, actually *seeing* them up there sends a jolt of cold down my soaked legs. This is it.

I don't know if I'm ready.

Not now, while the ammiralia's hand is clamped around my wrist like a vise and Oriana is still trying to free her other. I was supposed to be able to sneak up behind them. I was supposed to at least be able to convince them I was an admirer, that I was on their side, but I very much look like I'm trying to steal their prisoner away while I'm also trapped knee-deep in muck.

Oriana grunts, and it's my only warning before a wet ripping noise squelches in the air. I whirl back. More reeds dangle in her hands.

"No!" I scream again.

Ammiralia Rubellian's other hand flies forward and clamps over my bicep. Her nails dig in again, and warm, wet blood oozes across my skin. Pain races up and down my arm, and blackness webs out from where her fingers touch me.

"Mamma!" Oriana shakes her shoulders, as if there's any human left inside that body. Ammiralia Rubellian doesn't budge. I stare into the dark veins crossing her face, and the inky blackness of her eyes.

Her body may still be moving, but the consciousness that was Ammiralia Rubellian is long gone.

I scrabble at her arms and hands, whatever I can reach, trying to push her away, but my nails slide uselessly over her waxy skin, while hers plunge deeper into mine.

A droplet of my blood slips from my skin and plummets into the pond. When it strikes and fades into the liquid, silver streaks shoot from where it landed.

The liquid shudders and begins to rise, crawling up my body, up my legs, up my waist, promising a cold, wet grave. I twist in Ammiralia Rubellian's grasp while her nails drag deep, slow gouges into my arms. A desperate scream finally escapes me.

The hooded figure runs down the hill. Their cloak flies behind them, robes whipping around.

"Oriana, the knife! I need it!"

The water slides up and over my neck now, and I don't have time. I'm trapped. Oriana slowly backs away, decidedly not passing the knife to me.

Shit, shit, shit. This wasn't how this was supposed to play out at all.

I slam my head into Ammiralia Rubellian's. Pain shoots through my skull and sparks dance. She doesn't even move. Her head feels as much like stone as the rest of her.

Oriana yelps, abruptly shifting from a slow walk backward to a full-on flailing jog through the water.

Her panic is my only warning.

Black gloved hands reach beneath the water and grab my arms. I twist, leaning back into folds and folds of clothing—but the Shadow is much smaller than the layers of robes make them appear.

I try to slam my head backward into them, but the hooded figure releases me just as swiftly. Across from us, Ammiralia Rubellian's mouth opens, and a gurgling howl tears from her throat.

I shift, trying to get an ankle out to kick her because I can't possibly fend off the Shadow as long as she's still got me in her death grip.

The hooded figure whips forward, drawing a knife with glowing gold carvings. The blade glows a bright green—just like the water—and they lunge for Ammiralia Rubellian.

A wave rises, a wall between them, and they thrust the knife through. The wave falls when the knife strikes it, but a second wave spins up from the side, catching the Shadow and sending them flying farther out into the water, away from me.

They twist and spin, slicing the water as it rises. They're like a whirlpool in the midst of it. As fast as they are, the water keeps rising, thrusting watery arms into the air, even as they cut them down. They slip between two, slashing at both with an arc.

Then they lunge forward, and the tip of the knife scrapes the side of Ammiralia Rubellian's cheek.

A line of inky black follows the trail of the blade.

The streak of opened skin begins to bubble. It hisses and spits, and burning droplets strike my cheeks. They sizzle on my skin, and the stench of acid raises tears in my eyes.

Ammiralia Rubellian pitches forward, and her grip on me finally slackens.

I scramble back, sloshing through the liquid toward the shore until mud sinks beneath my hands and air hits my skin. I gasp for breath while my head spins and everywhere the ammiralia touched turns painfully numb.

The Shadow saved me. Or, well, released me from the ammiralia at least. Still, maybe, just maybe it's enough that I can go back to my plan of being an admirer.

The Shadow jogs toward me, a hand outstretched, and I begin, "Thank you so much for saving me! I'm *so* grateful—I always knew you were—"

They say nothing. They don't change their pace at all—I can't even be sure they heard me. They seize my arm, yank me to my feet, and I don't fight them because one of my arms is free.

And now their mask of swirling smoke is within my grasp.

So I swing an arm forward, but my vision blurs with pain and they catch my hand in a tight clamp.

"Don't," she orders, and she doesn't even try to disguise her voice, the same that only hours ago crooned to me about wishes and wanting. My arm goes slack in her grip as I gape in disbelief.

I don't need to rip the mask off to know exactly who this is.

CHAPTER THIRTY-TWO

I should fight her. The fact that the Shadow is Calista doesn't matter. Just like nothing she said to me mattered, apparently. Everything she claimed to want, everything she promised, none of it was real. I'd laughed off Antony's concerns about her. But I was no more than a lovestruck girl who'd fallen into her trap, who'd let her seduce me and pull the veil right over my eyes. My stomach gives a little heave—I nearly gag. This was why she always drew away when we got too close. She was never interested, only wanted to make sure she had me thoroughly deceived, thoroughly wrapped around her finger, so I wouldn't catch on to the truth.

Antony had it right all along. No—not quite. She's worse than I think even he suspected her to be.

I might be able to move fast enough to startle her, rip her mask from her face, end this all. I can have everything I want, and she—well, I shouldn't care what happens to her because she deserves it all. But I can't do it. I can't breathe, can't make myself move—all I can do is whimper something pathetic because even having been punched with the truth hasn't quite broken all of her hold on me.

"You *lied*," I start, distantly aware of the ribbons of pain lacing my shredded voice.

Something small and dark flies across the corner of my vision.

It's my only real warning.

The ground *cracks* beside me, blasting Calista and me apart. Heat washes over me, and I go flying. Calista vanishes beyond the swirling cloud of smoke, while clumps of dirt and grass rain around me.

I shove myself to my knees, wincing as my hands dig into the ground. Blistering burns streak across my hands and up my arms, and I blink into the smoke. A dark form in a tattered dress, the shreds dangling from her body, steps through it. Deep tears mar the front, the worst of them a slash across her chest that shows a flash of the corset beneath.

Oriana.

Her expression is set hard. She lifts an arm, something small and round—probably another explosive—packed into her hand, dirt and her mother's blood caked on her fingertips around it.

"Thanks," I try, because maybe she thought she was saving me from Calista. Maybe she *was* saving me from Calista. Even now, I find it difficult to believe Calista would hurt me—but it's only denial, clearly. She lied to me about everything. She's been poisoning the magic. Killing all these people.

I thought I knew her, but I never did, all along.

I don't know why I keep being attracted to liars who'll betray me. As a con artist, I really should know better. Or maybe, that's the problem. I'm a liar, so I only like those who are, too.

Oriana's expression doesn't waver, but her lifted arm shakes.

Suddenly, I'm not sure she was trying to save me at all.

The smoke rises, revealing the empty clearing. Calista is gone. Oriana and I are alone beside the green, deadly lake. Ammiralia Rubellian's body has vanished like it's been swallowed away. Horrible as that is, it might be for the better. The human part of her was already gone. Now Oriana doesn't have to face the rotted husk that was once her mother.

In her free hand, she lifts the knife I spelled for her, but it's ordinary once more. The mist around it's gone. Even it knows the ammiralia is dead.

"She's not coming back," Oriana says, accusing.

"I'm sorry." I start to rise to my feet. "I'm so sorry, Oriana, really, I—"

"Stop. Just stop!" Oriana lunges forward, and I drop back to my knees. "I don't want to hear your condolences. I don't want your pity! This—this was never supposed to happen. It wasn't supposed to be like this."

I lift my hands weakly. I know she's grieving. Of course she is. And she has every right to be mad. But I don't know what my best approach is. I don't know what to say to her, and that's not good, because she has all the weapons, and I have nothing but words.

"No, it wasn't," I agree helplessly.

Her gaunt face sets into something hard and dark. Her lip curls and her eyes burn, as she slowly extends her knife in my direction. "We should've done this sooner, but it's reckoning time. Forget about Mamma and me—*you* should've wanted to flee this island as soon as we came across the corpse of a tour guide. Why didn't you? And do not lie. I'll know."

I weigh my options. Instinct tells me to lie anyway. It always does, and the truth doesn't make me look very good. But I don't know if I want to test her right now. Fury rolls from her in burning, acidic waves, and she towers above me with the explosive and my knife in hand. If Oriana does know something I don't realize she knows, if she knows enough to guess what's a lie, a lie could seal my end.

"Well?" she demands. "It's a simple enough thing to answer if you're not concocting another story."

"I'm sorry about your mother, Oriana." It's safe to start with—and to stall with.

"You said that already, and that's still not an answer!"

I'd bet she's bluffing. I don't see how she can know enough to call me out. But maybe after all of this, she deserves the truth. "I owe some—well, not very nice people a debt, and I came here to pay it." It's vague enough to not make me sound horrible, to not give much away, but it's all truth.

Oriana snorts, but her hand holding the explosive lowers a fraction. "Was that so hard?"

I allow myself to exhale and shrug one shoulder.

"Get up," she orders.

I wobble to my feet. She extends my knife, and for one brief moment, I think she might be about to give it back. But she just flicks her wrist. "Thank you. We're going back now."

I walk, and the ground sinks beneath my feet, clutching at me with every step. My legs burn as we ascend the small hill that spills into the valley. One final glance behind me lets me know Calista really is gone. Wherever she is, she isn't going to help me. Not again.

I'm on my own with Oriana.

Which should be fine, but the situation right now feels as slippery as the muddy ground I'm climbing. I'm missing something. Oriana knows—or thinks she knows—something she's not revealing.

I watch the hand at her side where the explosive is still balled up in her fist. "How long have you been carrying those?" It doesn't feel like an entirely safe question, but also, I doubt it's going to be the final straw to make her hurl it at me.

Oriana pats the back of her dress, seemingly, an empty space of air that must be some kind of illusioned pouch. I can only guess it's waterproofed, too. "Since Mother disappeared. It seemed for the better at that point, in case something came after me, too."

"But you didn't tell me?" Nothing said she had to, of course, but *I have an entire pouch of explosives hidden on me right now* seems like a major piece of information to skip. "Did you not trust me after I told you I'd been lying about the monster game?"

Oriana grunts as she hacks at the branches that dare to block our paths, a whirlwind of fury and pain. It's the only answer she gives, and I don't know what it means.

Sweat stings my eyes, rolling down my face, but I don't even want to lift a hand to wipe it away, afraid the wrong movement will send the grenade my way. "I'm sorry again. I really didn't know how bad it was here. I know you didn't either—or you wouldn't have lied to the Vessels about using magic."

I take the silence as acknowledgment I'm right, and walk on in an awkward truce, staggering back down the other side of the hill. Our footsteps crunch, unnaturally loud in the dead mist.

I don't know where we're walking. Back, maybe, but I don't know what waits for me there. I'm lost and stuck, more than I thought I would be. I thought, once I knew who the Shadow was, all that would be left was to undo what they'd done, find the source, take it, and run.

I shouldn't hesitate to attack Calista. It's not like me. I don't know if she deserves to be killed for what she's doing to the magic—but what someone deserves has never mattered much to me before. I need the magic and I need it clean. And she's blocking that. I should get rid of her. It's that simple.

Or it should be.

But I don't know why she's doing it. And though that shouldn't matter either, there's a little niggling feeling twitching around my chest saying it might. Maybe that part of me is delusional, hoping that some of the girl I thought I'd been getting to know was the real Calista. That she's got a reason, a good one, something more than just wanting to inflict pain on those who hurt her.

If she wants revenge against the Vessels, against the island, for hurting her lover, I get that. But then, how could she stand to hurt other tour guides, to sacrifice them just like the girl she loved?

But I still owe the Silverhands, and I don't know how else to escape their debt but give them the magic. Untainted.

"Sometimes I used to wish my mother would die," Oriana says softly. "If she died, I'd be free to do whatever I wanted. I could stop seeking a miserable engagement and go back to school to study. It feels like this tour was my dream vacation after all. This island reached deep into me and saw my soul's true wishes, so it stole my mother and killed her."

We enter the abandoned building again, stepping over the skulls across the floor. "I really don't think that's what happened. The—the Shadow's poison is killing all of the magic users, not just your mother." We pick our way across the bones, the many lives already lost. There's a pain in my lungs with each breath after that sentence—it hurts to say, hurts to think. That this is entirely *Calista's* fault in the end, that

299

Calista killed all those people we saw at the top of the cliffs, that she stole and killed the ammiralia.

But it doesn't quite add up. What about Viola? Even though I don't trust anything else Calista's said anymore, I still believe that she really loved her. It can't have been the Shadow who killed Viola. So then who—or what—did?

"Besides," I add, "you didn't even book the tour. Your mother did, didn't she?"

"Sort of." Oriana clambers through the doorway, and I follow. "I mean, she did. But I had to, let's say, convince her by sneaking the information about the conte's visit her way so she would oblige."

Warnings prickle across my aching, blistered skin. This doesn't make any sense with the information Oriana's given me about herself, her life, her goals. She doesn't want to marry the conte—does she?

She's a better liar than I realized, hiding behind her facade of awkward honesty.

Which means I don't know what else she's lied about.

Or what she hides.

"You see, about a year ago, Mother very nearly did broker an engagement for me. The only reason it was called off was because the man was caught literally murdering his whore's newborn baby." Oriana's mouth twists. "He was that quality a lord. Anyway, at the time, before it was called off, I was desperate. I went to people who were known for being able to make folks disappear—but I asked them not to make him disappear, but me. I wanted them not to actually kill me, but feign my death, set me free."

Everyone knows that anyone who makes people "disappear" isn't someone you want to work with. My throat is dry, but I scrape the words out anyway. "You didn't just think to run away instead?"

Oriana shakes her head. "My family would've hunted for me. If I was dead—well, Oriana Rubellian would just be *gone*. Plus, as much as my death would hurt my parents, at least then they'd never have to know I betrayed them. They could keep the memory of me as a good daughter, not a brat who threw her whole life away. And if I ran, they'd be the subject of endless nasty gossip, all kinds of rumors, made into jokes. But my death would gain them sympathy and honor from everyone whose opinion matters to them. So, no. I struck a deal." She gives a little squawk of a laugh. "But—and I know you knew that was coming—when I went to pay them the original fee, they told me they'd changed their mind. They had a better use for me, a better fee. They didn't want my money. They wanted me to do something for them instead."

"And?"

Oriana stops walking. Her mouth twists again, but she meets my gaze straight. Whatever she's going to say is bad. "No one's ever been able to remove magic from this island. They wanted a guest to try—to see if guests would have some sort of protection cast on them to make it possible." She folds her arms and looks around, the dead ground under our feet, and the mist that swirls. "Obviously that was a terrible idea. Guests—protected!" She barks a laugh.

I try to crack a smile in return, but my lips stick to my teeth. All I can really think is that she came here for the same reason I did. And she's deliberately omitted mentioning who sent her.

There are probably plenty of people who'd like to remove magic from the island for their own use. Plenty of those same people who were also in the business of "disappearing" others.

But the question beats in my brain: *Is it the Silverhands?*

"Did they tell you it was safe?"

"Of course," Oriana says. "But I wasn't foolish enough to believe them. I had my concerns. But when I told them that wasn't our original deal, they told me, if I didn't do it, they would disappear my mother instead of me. So I agreed. I would risk myself to keep her—and my own secrets—safe. I never thought the island would end up killing her instead." She glances back into the mist, and sadness softens her expression for only a minute.

"It's still not your fault," I say quietly. "It's theirs. Isn't it?"

"Yeah." She reaches behind her to stuff the explosive into nothingness, and her now free hand curls into a fist. "It definitely is. And you should remember that, too. You can think you have a deal with them, but if they want something else from you? They're not going to honor their word."

I know, now, deep in my churning gut that she was definitely working with the Silverhands. And then she confirms it.

"Are you still planning to take the magic to the Silverhands?"

Even with my suspicions, hearing the words from her mouth and the fact she's known what I've been doing here all along temporarily sends any strategy I might've had up into flames. All I manage is, "Are you?"

"Absolutely not." Her bloodshot eyes pin me with their force. "They threatened my mother, threatened us both onto this awful tour, and now she's dead because of it. They have no leverage over me anymore—if they try to kill my father, the entire navy will go after them, and they're powerful, but they don't want that kind of civil war in the city. As far as I'm concerned, they're never, ever, *ever* going to get what they want."

She lifts my knife, and I flinch back.

But then, to my shock, she flips my knife around and extends the handle back to me. I don't dare reach for it, only eye it warily. "You're not going to kill me, then? To stop me? You have to know I was working under the same deal."

"I did," Oriana says. "The man carrying our traveling trunk was one of theirs, escorting me to ensure I didn't run, and he recognized you. He told me that if you got the magic off and I didn't, my deal with them would be finished. He said it would be you—or me. And I'm telling you this because they wanted us against each other, and I am going to do everything I can going forward to make sure they get absolutely nothing they want out of this."

I lick my dry lips, swallow through the rocks in my throat. "Including the magic."

"Absolutely." Oriana narrows her eyes. "Are you really still going to give it to them? After all this? Are you not listening to what I'm saying? They backed out of the deal they made with me when they decided there was something else they wanted from me instead, and as you've pointed out several times, my family is rich. They're powerful."

"My family is in danger," I say quietly.

"Yeah, they are. But if the Silverhands backed out of their deal with me, whatever makes you think they're going to keep their word with you? You think, if you bring them the magic, they're just going to let you go?" She laughs, a harsh, scraping noise. "I really thought you were smarter than that."

I flinch. I don't know if it's the cruelty in her tone or the fact that she's right. What have I been thinking, assuming that once I gave the Silverhands what they really wanted, they'd let me go? That then I'd be free to make my own way, find my own happiness?

I am and always have been merely their tool, and they'll never let me go while there's something they can still gain from me. If I steal the magic for them, well, I'll have cemented myself as one of the top thieves in the world. They're not going to let such talent go. Not when there's so much more I could do for them.

Oriana gives my knife, still extended, a little shake. "I'm offering you an alliance. Together, we'll figure out how to address the Silverhands back in the city and the fact that neither of us brought what they wanted. I'll do whatever I can to help keep your family safe. They're offering you what they always have—threats and servitude. So, make your choice. I can't promise that even together we'll succeed, but don't you want to try?"

We stand on equal ground for the first time, and instead of seeing an enemy, I only see a girl just like me. I thought she was my mark, but she wasn't. We're equals, more like friends after all, than we otherwise ever could've been.

Oriana's right. Calista and her poison aside, it would be a terrible mistake to give the magic to the Silverhands. I have to figure out how to protect Severin another way. Because that's all I really want, and even if I turn the magic over to them, he won't be safe. Not when threats to him are such an easy way to manipulate me.

They'll use him against me again and again.

Like they've used my feelings of duty to my family against me for these past years. Like they've used my own guilt over my role in my father's schemes.

They'll use *me* again and again. Like they've used me until now.

But I'm done. I refuse to owe them anything anymore.

CHAPTER THIRTY-THREE

As we trudge up through the town, only the final hill remaining between us and Vessel Dionne's estate, I stop Oriana. There are probably rules against ordinary islanders taking in any of the tourists, but for now, Oriana will be safer among the crowd, however small, than going with me to confront Calista. "You should stay here."

"Just—on the streets?" Oriana waves a hand at the sky. It's bright blue and cloudless, and the soft wind is gentler than it has any right to be. There's no hint of the storm from earlier. "What's wrong with the Eliades Estate? Calista said that was our best place to be, didn't she?"

I pause, the way Oriana says Calista's name so casually ricocheting through me. Then I realize—she was standing far enough away she probably didn't hear Calista speak. She has no idea at all that it was Calista she tossed an explosive at not long ago. "Look, this may be a little hard to believe—*I* still barely do—but Calista's the Shadow. She spoke to me."

Oriana recoils. "What? I can't I don't—are you really telling me that Calista killed my mother?" Her voice lowers with every word until it rips into silence, both furious and confused. She shakes her head. "No, you're right, I don't believe it because it doesn't add up.

She told me to wear a mask, and she was right about that. It made a huge difference—I feel its lack, now."

I believe that—her usually bright copper skin has a strange ashen tone to it now. "I don't have an explanation. All I know is that it's definitely Calista's voice I heard from the Shadow."

Oriana tilts her head. "You don't think the Shadow might've disguised their voice to sound like her? To throw you off? What did the Shadow say, anyway?"

"She just said 'don't' to stop me." My face heats a little when Oriana nods, a quirk of her mouth that says if it was a trick to throw me off, it was a good one. It worked. And maybe, maybe, she's right. I was too thrown by it, too horrified, to consider that it wasn't Calista before me.

"Sure, that's possible," I say, even though I don't think it is. Something about her grip, the body that I could feel beneath the robes, even the scent—it was her. Oriana wouldn't know any of that, wouldn't know it even if Calista had grabbed her instead, but I do. "But the voice aside, I just really think it was Calista. And just in case I'm right, I think I should go on alone. What harm will that do? Do you think you're in danger here around these other people? No one here should hurt you. Here—I'll give you my mask so they won't even know you're not one of them."

Oriana's been wandering without her mask for the majority of the day. I should at least be able to make it up the hill without one, and I can grab a new one at the estate.

I continue, "And I'll come back and get you if—if I find proof I'm wrong. Otherwise, there's only a day left. You should lie low until it's time to get on the boat home."

Oriana extends a hand, and while part of me thinks she might be agreeing just because she wants to have a mask to put back on, that's good enough for me.

I approach the Eliades Estate with care, sneaking carefully around each corner so that Calista can't startle me if she's here. But the house rings with emptiness as I step inside, and I immediately know she's not here. The home is completely open, door and golden gate unlocked, which is what makes it feel most lifeless of all. And the snow that's been covering the courtyard this whole time has abruptly melted—or, perhaps, been removed. I'd bet the new bright green grass and cute patches of pink-and-yellow flowers that line the paths are fake, too, though.

Inside, the only doors open are the ones to Oriana's room and mine, and though I test the knobs on a few others after putting on a new dress and mask, they're all locked. I could pick the locks, but honestly, I'm not sure I want to see what's behind them. Calista's all I want to find right now. All I need to find. She's got all of my answers.

By the time I've circled the grounds six times, I start to wonder if Calista plans to return here at all. We're supposed to leave tomorrow, so maybe she'll just wait us out. The sun's sinking low in the sky, and I don't want to leave Oriana in the town at night. By day, I'm sure she's safe, but I have no idea what the streets are like at night.

But we can't sleep here. Maybe Calista's not coming back. Or maybe she plans to come back in the dead of night when we're not expecting her, when we're most vulnerable, to ambush us. And I don't want that.

It'll be safer if I'm the one to find and confront her, not just sit around, waiting, hoping and fearing. But I need a way to find her, a spell of my own to point the way like I made for Oriana to find her mother. Not, obviously, to point to the person I love most because I don't love Calista, let alone love her most. But some kind of spell to point to the person I'm romantically interested in would work.

Oriana can't help me there. I have no idea what the magic does if you can't pay the price, but that seems like a terrible thing to test after everything we've already been through. For all I know, it might well just kill her.

But.

I straighten.

I think I know who *can*.

CHAPTER THIRTY-FOUR

The massive double doors to the Key Vessel's palace intimidated me plenty when I arrived for the Island Ball with the safety of the Rubellians and Calista alongside me. Standing before them alone, I feel like a pebble in their shadow.

This time, of course, they don't open on their own for me. Instead, I have to force myself to step closer and closer, to take the knocker in hand. I hadn't noticed it on our first visit, but the door knocker is a golden dragon, wings outstretched, its curling tail the knocker.

One day left, I remind myself. I have no time to waste.

I check briefly over my shoulder to where Oriana crouches in the brambles nearby. I didn't want to leave her in the town or alone at the Eliades Estate, but I need to talk to Antony alone.

I knock.

And hold my breath. All I can do is hope Antony made it back from the ship, that he returned here, that it's not about to be Keelan who answers the door.

The door creaks open—to Antony, maskless and exhausted.

His high cheekbones I once thought were so handsome merely

look gaunt, his face hollowed out by the last few hours. His expression lifts when our gazes meet, filling with something raw and hopeful.

"Lucia?" He says my name like it's a question. "Are you . . . ?" he starts and then trails off. I don't know what he meant to ask, but I can't think of any sensible question that would start with those words. It's better he's realized it.

"I need your help." I step back, urging him out of the palace. Hope flashes in his eyes, and a smile begins to rise, but I shake my head, and his joy quickly drops. "You can take this as a chance to apologize to me for everything by helping me now like you never have before."

He obliges, stepping out from the doors with a heavy sigh. "I *am* sorry, Lucia. For everything. But you have to understand, I was only ever trying to protect you." His expression is like an open wound, bleeding between us.

"I do understand." It's not even a lie. I didn't at first, of course. But, now, having suffered this island firsthand, I get it. And with that understanding, I see everything that's happened between us in an entirely new light. He does care about me, as misguided as he is, and as poorly as he's shown it. All this time I'd been assuming he couldn't possibly care because he's hurt me so much, because he's lied to me, manipulated me, tossed aside my own requests and wishes again and again and *again*. I thought if he cared about me, he'd respect me.

But now I know both of those things were true all along. He does care about me, maybe even loves me as he says he does, and he also doesn't respect my decisions enough to just let me make them and face the consequences. Love doesn't always mean a willingness to treat someone as an equal, independent person. And love doesn't always prevent a willingness to hurt someone very deeply to protect what you think you have together.

Love alone doesn't make someone a good partner for you. Love alone doesn't mean you should be together.

"But you failed me," I continue, and he flinches. But I press on because the guilt is what might get him to act now. "You failed to protect me. You failed to even help me. So I'll ask again. Will you help me now?"

The doors groan closed behind him, and I take several steps back to put distance between us.

He whispers, "You never should have come here. You shouldn't still be here now. You needed to leave yesterday." He looks different than I remember. Like half of the man who used to make my heart race so. The same exhaustion that has slowly eaten away at Oriana is on his face, too.

"Speaking of, am I going to be in trouble because of your arrest?" I ask. One, it's quite well known that it's easier to get people to agree to a larger ask down the line if you ask for something small first, and two, I do need to know this. "Is there a mark against me somewhere? A record?"

Antony shakes his head. "There's a ledger of island visitors I keep. And their categories. But I didn't remove your name yet. You'd know if I had. I was only going to do it once we left the island. I didn't want to punish you, you know. I only arrested you to save you. What can I do to convince you to leave?"

"Tell me exactly why I'm in danger." I try my second ask of him. It's a large ask, but still smaller than the next. "The truth, this time. Stop with the bullshit and convince me with reality."

311

He steps in, but I jerk back, automatic. He shakes his head and barely mouths, "*No one* can know I've told you this."

"Are people listening?" I whisper back.

"Always," he replies.

Once I might've laughed at him for paranoia, but I believe it now. I'll believe anything now. On this island, my life isn't my own.

"Then come," I say, and when he steps closer, this time, I don't step back. He smells of smoke and fire, the flames that were once between us and are now just dusty ashes. I look at him and feel the cold of the cuffs digging into my wrists, and I don't know that I'll ever feel much else again. He's close enough it'd be so easy to close the distance between us once more.

But this distance won't be closed again.

"You and your family had used too much magic to ever come here safely," Antony says. "That's why I tried to stop you from coming the first time."

"The price of magic is that when we die, our bodies have to be returned to the magic."

Antony raises his eyebrows. "Someone explained."

"Yes." When Calista first said that, I didn't understand it fully, but the understanding is creeping over me now, slow, steady, burrowing into my skin. I thought she'd meant the surface-level interpretation— that those who died on the island would be returned to the magic. I hadn't ever imagined the magic itself would kill them to take the bodies back.

"Well, the more you use, the more desperate the magic is to recover you. There's been a . . . shortage of people paying the price. The magic has been unstable. Too many people left the island, used

312

magic elsewhere, and never came back here when they died. You'd used so much in the city. You should never have lasted a day here."

"Then why am I still alive?" I ask.

"I don't know. I really don't." He shakes his head.

Then I realize. At first, I wasn't going to survive. The first day, I felt so ill. Until Calista ordered me not to eat or drink anything but what she gave me.

She gave me alternative food. Food not linked to the magic. She gave me her magical charm at the most dangerous moment. She shielded me.

But why?

Hope, so delicate and fragile I barely even dare to glance at it, in case that might cause it to wither and die again, blooms. Because the obvious answer would be that Calista was trying to protect me, and this means she might not have been lying about *everything*. Part of her truly is the girl I trusted.

"Just to confirm in plain words, when you say the magic 'recovers' its users, you mean it makes them ill, then they die on the island's soil, and it gets the body back. Is that right?"

Antony nods. I suck in a sharp breath. The Shadow—Calista—was never the one killing people on the island. The island was. Calista is doing something else entirely, though I don't really know what.

"Since the first time I made the mistake of mentioning you to Keelan, he and the other Vessels were eagerly awaiting your arrival. They assumed you'd succumb quickly, and the power you'd return would be substantial. But then you didn't. And so they called on the magic to try to find you—at the Island Ball—but it still didn't find you. It took the ammiralia instead." Antony scrubs his face.

"So that fog—it had nothing to do with the Shadow?" I swallow, pushing down the now steadily rising tide of hope that Calista might not have to be my enemy.

Antony shakes his head. "The Shadow has been a convenient source of blame for the Vessels for the more visible effects of the magic's deterioration. And he is causing the magic to deteriorate, but the fog wasn't part of that. It was the Vessels trying to reverse the deterioration. I doubt you want to go seeking out the Shadow"— the side-eye he gives me makes me wonder if he's known I've been trying—"but he's not really your biggest concern right now, even if he is the island's. *You* need to be concerned about the Vessels. The fact the island hasn't found you yet—they think it means you're special, that you have the ability to withstand the magic's hunger in a way others don't. They think you belong as a part of the magic like them. They want you to become one of them."

"A Vessel? Me?" I start to laugh, but Antony's stony silence quickly cuts it off. He did say the Vessels were considering adding another.

I turn the thought over in my mind. A few days ago I wouldn't have pondered. I would've leaped. The Vessels know where the source of magic is. This will bring me there. But since I've already decided I don't want to hand the magic over to the Silverhands, I'm not sure I care to find the source of magic after all.

"That's why I tried to get you off the island. Whatever you think you can withstand, you do not want to be a Vessel. *I* don't want you to be a Vessel. I can't see you turn into one of those faceless monsters with that monotone voice and none of your spark. I just can't do that again." His shoulders shake and then collapse at that, and he drops his head into his hands.

I'm not so heartless as to not feel a brief wash of pity for him, for everything he's gone through with Keelan, everything he doesn't want to endure again. It must be an awful thing for him to live through. Maybe even awful enough for him to justify, at least in his mind, keeping me completely in the dark like a child.

But it's not enough to justify it for me. "See, I don't want to be a Vessel either. It wasn't my destiny, and it's not going to be. I can take care of myself." It's the one thing I've always needed him to believe, but he never has. It's the one thing that could've given us a chance together. "But I could use your help with something. I need you to make me something that will find me someone—someone I *like*." And there's my final ask, the largest one, the one that's going to destroy him. The final bow, though our dance has already ended.

Antony blinks a few times quickly. His throat bobs as he swallows, and I know what thoughts must race through his mind. *Who is it?* Because it obviously isn't him. "Like?" he asks quietly. "Like a friend?"

"No. I mean romantically." I wonder if he suspects at all it's Calista—if he's realized, like I have now, that I can be attracted to both men and women. He must have some idea because there's a limited number of people it could otherwise be.

If he does realize, apparently he doesn't judge. It's more generous than I expected from him, and it gives me just a little more respect for him. Not enough to change my mind, but still more.

All he says is, "I won't see you again if I make this."

"I know." I lift my chin. "I'm fine with that."

Around us, wind blows and the weeping trees surrounding the path dance, casting curling shadows our way, but he's still as a statue. For this moment, life has fled him.

"I—see," he says.

"You owe it to me," I say, no matter how harsh or cold that might

315

be. "If you care about me like you keep claiming, do something to help me. Help me how I want to be helped. And next time, with your next girl, actually listen to her when she asks for things. Don't just assume you know what's best for her and do whatever you want even if she explicitly asks you not to."

Antony laughs, a thick, wet sound. "Next girl. Sure, Lucia. Sure." He lifts a hand, and for a moment, I fear he might try to touch me. To kiss me goodbye or something foolish like that.

But maybe he has learned something after all.

He drops his hand and steps back. This is our goodbye instead. He pulls a small bracelet from his pocket made of uneven and strange green stones. I squint, wondering what is quite wrong with it before I realize.

I made it.

A long, long time ago. It was one of the first glamoturas I ever tried to construct.

And he kept it.

He squeezes it in his palm, and his eyes go distant. They watch me, but I know he's somewhere else, sucked into the magic, while it peels apart whatever strings have held us together.

Then the haze over him lifts. He opens his hand and drops the bracelet into my hand. It's warm and glows with a soft golden light that makes my heart floppy. "This is yours, anyway."

Words stick in my throat, so I lift a hand instead and give him a nod meant as farewell. I can't say goodbye, but I hope he knows that even with the bitterness between us, I hope he'll find happiness in the future. I hope he's learned something from this. I hope he finds another girl he loves and treats her better, and they have a long and happy life together.

He simply turns away, facing the weeping tree. His shoulders curl, and maybe he weeps with it, too, silently.

If I say nothing, he won't say any more either. This will simply be it, and we will part in silence.

I say nothing.

I leave.

And then, we are no more.

CHAPTER THIRTY-FIVE

A chill bites through the humid air, carving its own path, as I make my way down the island. Antony's bracelet, *my* bracelet, stays warm against my palm as it projects a golden circle of light onto the path in front of me, encouraging me forward.

I find Calista at the edge of the sea on a rocky, untamed part of the shoreline. A collection of stones juts out like teeth into the ocean's gnashing waves. She stands on one, calm and steady in the chaos that swirls around her. The foam from the ocean bursts up to her knees in a white spray, and her long, dark robes snap about her body in a tempest.

The scent of the salt and sea fills my nose, and I take in a long breath. It's the scent of freedom. Something other than this island and its curses and costs.

I approach her.

The clouds above us shift, and a beam of moonlight strikes the ground beside her. Its curve illuminates the edges of crushed and crooked skulls and bones, piled high.

My breath catches.

I stop moving.

She sinks to her knees, and black liquid oozes from the pile. It rises in thick tendrils, wrapping around her arms, and then she turns.

"Ah, Lucia."

Her mask of smoke still obscures her face in a hazy cloud. The blackness from the bones winds around her arms, her sleeves pushed back and bunched about her shoulders. The tendrils cling to her like snakes.

There's an entire rock that separates us and more than that, still, but I don't dare step forward and be the one to cross it. The golden light from the bracelet, though, expands. It fills the entire space between us.

She gestures at the light. "Someone helped you find me?"

"I came to this island for only one thing, you know," I say, even though that's not her question. It's my answer. "Not to be a tour guide."

"Your debt," she says. And takes a step. Waves crash, framing her briefly in foam. I wonder if she's picked this place, of all of the places on the island she could pick to access the magic, because the roar of the sea will allow a quiet conversation to go unheard by the magic.

I step toward her in turn so I can speak in a lower voice, beneath the violent vortex of the waves around us. I trust that if she thinks we're being overheard by the wrong entities, she'll say something. "The only way I can pay it is with the magic. And they're not going to call the debt paid if it's ruined."

She pauses, a long pause in which she must be processing what I've said. But if she's shocked, the only hint is the widening of her eyes that's so faint I'm not even sure it's real.

Finally, she barks a laugh. "Then forget your debt. It's better ruined."

I flinch. Somehow, the dismissal is worse than if she'd hated me for what I was trying to do. "I *can't*. Not just like that."

The moonlight glows behind her, lighting her in monstrous silhouette. "But you can't want to subject even more of the world to the magic. You know it's only here to steal people's lives slowly—or quickly, sometimes. Don't you?"

I swallow. "You make it sound like it's a living monster."

She steps forward once more. "No, it's not alive. It doesn't have a mind of its own to think."

The answer to my earlier wondering of what she's doing with the magic, if she's not the one killing the guides, strikes me. "You want to destroy it."

"I told you what I wanted this morning. I told you everything I wanted," she says, an oddly wounded note in her voice. "I want to escape this island. I want to live my own life, instead of wearing a mask every day until the day I have to take my mother's place as a soulless Vessel. I don't want to give my whole self up to the magic. But I can't run."

"Because the magic will stop you?" I ask. "The storm?"

Calista laughs. "Yes, but you should understand the storms weren't born from the magic alone. They were created by citizens. Everyone here isn't just an innocent victim—they're all complicit. Too many people were leaving the island and never returning to give their bodies back to the magic. The magic was growing unstable. Illusions were shaky. A mist crept across the island, and those who lived in its path and didn't flee their homes died. But these people—they think magic is their whole lives. So they forbade anyone from leaving again. And then that unfortunate tourist died, and they saw their chance to bring people back. They set up their little scheme to recruit glamorists from abroad to be tour companions. The job would bring them back to the island. To die. And strengthen the magic."

She crosses the final steps to me and lowers her arms. The tendrils unfurl from them and slide back into the ground where they sink into the dirt. I skip back, but she shakes her head as she watches the darkness ooze away.

"It won't hurt you. My poison may be in the ground, in the magic that then tries to poison people, but you misunderstood. My poison wasn't what was making you ill, and it's not what killed the guides before you. They were killed as the price of their family using magic."

"I know that now," I say.

A long moment hangs between us, taut in the sea-spray air. A wave crashes behind her in punctuation. Slowly, she lifts her gaze to mine, her eyes a mirror of the wild sea behind. "You could help me, you know." Her voice is small and uncertain, a contrast to her darkly terrible and wraithlike form. "We would be faster together." Swiftly, she adds, "You'll never leave this island otherwise. Surely you understood the storm that occurred when you tried to leave will happen every time you try—unless the magic itself is gone. You're never going to bring it back to the city, and believe me, you don't want to stay here. Not that you'll last much longer anyway."

Of course she's hesitant. She's asking me to do the literal opposite of what I came here for. I've already decided not to give the magic to the Silverhands, but destroying the world's only source of magic forever? That's a different thing entirely.

But if I don't, I'll never be able to leave this island. And is the life I would have trapped here forever really the life *I* deserve?

I haven't thought much about what I deserve in all of this.

Calista's the one who even reminded me it was possible to have dreams for myself—dreams that aren't just about serving a role for others. Wild, thrilling dreams, like traveling the world with another woman as my companion. I thought I would have the chance to dream if and only if I gave everyone else what they wanted from me, but I won't. I have to choose myself now. Or there won't be a later.

The reminder ropes itself around my heart and lungs and tugs, pulling me a step closer to her. I'll hear her out. "How would I help you? How have you been poisoning it?"

"Magic demands a price, so I make it pay a price that damages it. As I said, it's not sentient. So if you ask for something horrible, it will drag that from you in return without thinking of the effect to itself. There's a reason that everything here is pretty, that all our little attractions are about beauty and finding your dreams. The island likes those prices we pay. It doesn't like venom quite as much." She reaches into her pocket and draws something out, dangling it carefully in front of her. "Meet my little pet, Teri."

I skip back. It's a creature I've only heard of, a bug with a turtle's shell and a soft head and a curled tail full of venom. "It's poisonous to magic, as well as humans?"

Calista sets the little bug on her wrist. I flinch. Its tail twitches, but it doesn't strike her. "Not quite. I ask the island for poison. It gives me poison, and in return, it draws poison from my body as its price." She lifts a vial of inky liquid. "Then I dump the poison it's given me back into it. Two strikes for one price. Teri just helps me pay that price."

"You poison yourself first," I say, feeling slightly faint.

She nods. "You never asked me what would happen if you didn't have something to trade. You never asked if it always takes the same

322

price for the same transaction. You never asked a lot of questions about the magic you should have."

"So what are the answers, then?"

"If you have nothing to trade, the magic will keep searching you. You'll never leave the transaction state, and you'll slowly lose your mind," Calista says as she plucks the bug from her wrist and tucks it back away in the folds of the robe. "And it always takes the same thing for the same transaction. That's why poisoning it works. As much as it sometimes seems alive, it's not smart enough to learn what happens to it when I ask for poison."

"So the effects of your poison are just limited to you and the magic?" She makes it sound so simple, so harmless. "Those bodies all arranged at the top of the cliff above the palace—you had nothing to do with them?"

Calista gives a little snort. "Ugh, such an excellent scapegoat I made for Keelan there. He was just so thrilled with it. He—and the other Vessels—killed those people, not me. Didn't you wonder why they were all so close to the palace? Saying I had nothing to do with the deaths is perhaps absolving me from responsibility I do have, but I didn't kill any of them myself. As I poison the island, it fights back. It gets greedier. The mist creeps closer and devours people with potent magic in its path. The Vessels sacrifice tour guides and other people we can lure here so they don't get killed instead."

I flush a bit beneath the mask, feeling a little silly for having bought all of the lies so easily. The story of a shadowy villain poisoning the magic, slaughtering innocents, for no reason except evil was all too easy for me to believe. Even now, part of my mind is still thrashing against the concept that destroying the magic could be the better choice we have. It makes up so much of Verigal City—and almost the entirety of Estaralla. "Do you worry what'll happen to the island after magic is gone?"

"Not exactly," Calista says. "Certainly, I'm not naive enough to think there won't be a period of adjustment, and it may be a rough one. But what is the other option? Continuing to trade our happiness and our lives to an entity that devours us without a second thought? We're all nothing but sacrifices to the island in the end, every one of us who has engaged with its power. This will never end, never get better for us, unless we choose to end it."

Those words sink into my mind, into my consciousness. All along, I've been thinking about this all wrong, trying to pay my family's debts with my own blood and sweat. But in that way, I'll never really be free. The Silverhands are never going to really let me go, and the island won't either. But Calista has the way out.

She's not acquiescing to the murderous island she calls home. Instead of playing the role she was born to play, she's trying to destroy the chains that bind her down. She's going to shatter the mask she wears and be free.

I've played along with my chains for years.

But as long as I keep doing what they want, I'll always be under their control.

The sky before us is a strange, deep green-gray color, and the sea churns and spits at me. "So, if I did agree to work with you, how long would it take to destroy the magic?"

"Well, it's slow." Calista fiddles with her sleeves, suddenly sounding small. "I don't have a sure answer for you. I don't have a sure answer for if it's even possible. The island is trying to fight me, and I'm afraid the closer I get to success, the more likely it is to figure out how to take me out."

I take another step closer to her, an invisible tether between us tightening. I *want* to help her now, so much that it's a physical thing gripping me in an ever stronger hold. It tightens my chest, my lungs.

But I hear her warning. This could be a long time. And I don't have that time. Tomorrow, the Silverhands will declare my failure when I don't deliver them the magic and force Severin to start handing all of his wages over to them, too.

I need to risk everything to see it done now.

"Have you ever tried pouring the poison directly into the source? What do you think that would do for the speed of it?"

"I don't know where it is," Calista says. "That knowledge is restricted to the Vessels, but I assume it would do substantial damage."

"Enough to destroy it instantly?"

She twists a stray strand of hair dangling in front of her mask. "I don't know. Possibly not, as long as the Vessels still guard their own pieces of magic. The magic is embedded in them, in their minds and hearts, so it will always have somewhere to draw from if it's attacked."

"And if the Vessels died?"

"I think the magic would end up in very bad shape." Calista knots her fingers together in front of her. "Do you have a plan for this?"

My heartbeat rises above the sound of the waves. "I have a way to learn the source's location and maybe gather all of the Vessels at it. If that happened, do you think we could do it? Could we kill them all and end this?" The words come out of my mouth easier than I expected. I never really thought I'd propose so much murder all at once. But it doesn't sit as heavy in my stomach as I expected it might. Maybe someone else would have more of a conscience, but my thoughts are consumed by the people on top of the cliff, all of the murdered tour guides before me. Even if I manage to kill the Vessels, my body count will be nothing compared to theirs. I'll be saving everyone who would've come after me, and, frankly, I'll be saving myself. They wouldn't hesitate to kill me, so why should I hesitate for them?

Still, I ready myself to hear *no* from Calista. The Vessels are near strangers to me, but she's grown up among them. One of them is her own mother.

But this must have been an outcome she'd already considered, already come to terms with a long time ago in her fight to break free, because she says evenly and without hesitation, "I don't think it'd be a guarantee, but we would have a good chance. Probably a better chance than doing it slowly."

I take one step closer. I'm almost to her now. If I extend my hand, and she extends hers, our fingers could touch. But one thing still holds me back in its last, gasping clutches. If I destroy the magic, I'll never pay the debt to the Silverhands. Worse than that, they'll be furious at the magic's loss, since they have quite a lot of business built on it, and they *will* punish Severin to punish me. I know I can't give them the magic, give them this much destructive power, and I know the magic needs to be destroyed, but I also need a plan to deal with them.

"Do you think you'd be able—or willing—to poison people, not just the magic?" I ask.

Her eyes don't widen, and the swirling smoke of her mask face hides whatever she feels about this question. "I'd rather not hurt innocent people, but that's not what you're asking, is it?"

I take a deep breath, and then take the plunge. My whole body turns to ice, as if I might as well have thrown myself into the violent sea beside us. "My family's in debt to the Silverhands. If I help you destroy magic, I'll never be able to pay it back. So, in exchange for my help, I want yours. I want you to threaten and poison them into leaving me alone."

"It's a deal." Calista offers me a hand.

I take her hand and pull her in close to me, until our chests are just about touching. Beneath my thumb, her pulse beats in her wrist, and the press of her palm to mine is damp and cool. But between us, it warms quickly. "My plan to get access to the source is going to be risky—for you much more than me. Do you trust me?"

"Not really," Calista says, and it's so smart it doesn't even sting. I smile. Because she shouldn't. "But go on with it anyway. I'm not afraid."

"Good." I pull my hand from hers and hold it up between us. "First, I'm going to need your pet."

She doesn't hesitate in removing the little bug and setting it in my palm, and while she's said she doesn't trust me, the speed of her response brings me confidence. I slip the bug into the pocket of my apron, then lift my hands and let them flutter near the edges of her mask.

"And then?" she asks.

"Then . . ." A final step closes the space between us, and I lean into her swirling robes, until I feel the solid bend of her body beneath. When she doesn't pull away, I take it as acquiescence. I pause for one last breath because once this is done, there'll be no going back. We'll have no choice but to see this plan to its ending. The magic is right there—I know because she's been poisoning it—and so, Teresta and all of the Vessels are going to immediately know who she is. And come after her.

I pull her mask off first, dropping the billowing smoky form to our feet, and am treated to the sight of her actual face. It's so much gentler than the mask, so much warmer, as she gives me a soft smile I could never have seen beneath the smoke.

Then I toss my own mask aside.

Her brows furrow, and her lips part, probably to chastise me. Before she can, I press my mouth to hers. Her lips are soft beneath mine—but cold, chilled as the wind around us. She doesn't taste as sweet as I'd expected, not like she smells, but of salt and storm. The kiss sends a flash of energy through me, a strike of lightning that thrums through my blood and sets every nerve tingling.

It's a wild feeling, a sharp step off into the unknown. My body is no longer entirely in my control, and yet, it's also the most control I've ever had.

It's freedom.

We pull apart, and she says, "That was dangerous." But her cheeks flush a deep pink, and her lips curl in a tiny smile.

"Everything's dangerous here. It was worth it."

To my satisfaction, her blush deepens.

Really, the kiss wasn't necessary for my plan, but I wanted it, and there was no reason to deny myself. No reason to hide myself any longer.

A crackling noise sounds behind us, and I spin, wondering why Oriana's decided to emerge from her hiding spot now of all times.

But it's not Oriana emerging from the forest.

It's Keelan and Vessel Dionne.

CHAPTER THIRTY-SIX

Calista's eyes widen, and her lips slowly part as the realization of my betrayal sinks beneath her skin, burying itself in her veins, and she draws in a shaky, pained breath. I stagger back from her, shaking my head, begging her to understand. I warned her as best I could. I told her I was going to put her in danger. She agreed to the risk.

But her gaze swings wildly between me and the Vessels, just like her expression swings from pain to fury, and it's clear that when she said she didn't really trust me, she really didn't. And while I did need her to be convincing, to act betrayed in front of the Vessels so they wouldn't suspect us of conspiring together, this is so real it hurts.

I wish I wasn't here for this. I had no idea Teresta and the Vessels were going to be this quick. They can't have walked, but then again, for all I know, the Vessels don't need to walk.

Vessel Dionne heads for Calista. Calista slowly backs away, holding her hands up. "Mamma. Mamma, please, you've got to still be there somewhere." The smallness in her voice knots tight in me, but all I can do is watch. If I do anything else, it'll ruin everything. This has to happen.

Vessel Dionne lunges, an inhuman length to her motion, and

seizes her daughter. One hand grabs Calista's arm, nails digging in, and Calista drops her mask with a pained gasp. With her other hand, Dionne rips Calista's pendant from her neck and throws it into the sea.

"Mamma, *please!*" Calista screams. She swings an arm up, fist curled, but her mother catches it easily, holding both of her wrists tight. Calista sags, collapsing, while her mother holds her up by her wrists. I don't know if she's giving up because she understands this is part of the plan or if she doesn't think she can break free of her mother. Or perhaps, worst of all, if she simply doesn't want to fight anymore. If this is her surrender.

She whimpers still as Vessel Dionne drags her away. "Mamma, Mamma, Mamma, please."

It's all I can do not to flinch, not to grimace, because my mask is still in my hand, my expression naked and exposed to Keelan.

He approaches me.

"Well," I say with all of the slick pride I can muster and a little bob of a curtsy. "There you have your Shadow."

"Yes, thank you, Lucia." There's not even a ripple on his blank face to give me a hint as to whether that was sincere, or if he's skeptical of me, if I ruined my chances with the kiss.

I swipe my mouth with the back of my hand as if in disgust, an action I can only hope he's human enough to interpret correctly. "It was my pleasure—mostly. Except the end."

"I wasn't sure of your chances, but Teresta believed in you all along," Keelan says. "But I suppose, she is the wisest of us."

"I was happy to help you. The island is so beautiful, and it's a shame to see it crumbling like it is now." Antony already gave away that they're considering making me a Vessel, and that needs to happen in addition to Calista's sacrifice. I don't know if all of the Vessels will gather to watch her die, but I do know from that very first day with Keelan that all of the Vessels are present for an induction. If I agree to become a Vessel, they will all gather with me. Making them easy to slaughter.

So I need to display my interest, balance subtlety to not attract suspicion with eagerness. I need Keelan to be the one to suggest Vesselhood. "Will everything be better once Calista's gone? That decaying mist will lift?"

"Over time."

"There has to be a way I can help it clear faster." Even that feels too obvious, but I need to make this happen quickly. I don't know how long they're going to keep Calista alive, but the answer is probably not long.

"Another Vessel could stabilize things."

It takes a lot of control not to let out a noise of relief. "Another . . . Vessel," I repeat, slow and dense. "Wait. You want *me*?"

"There's a lot of magic lingering in you," Keelan says. "Teresta told us all she was shocked from the moment she felt you in the cave. She told us you were meant to be a part of this island one way or another, and she's never wrong."

"I don't know." I still don't want to seem too eager, and I figure I have a little leeway to push, because I doubt Keelan is really going to take *no* for an answer. "Is there a cost to being a Vessel?"

"There's a cost to everything," Keelan says. "You allow the magic to live in your heart, and in turn, you have power over all of the island and live forever."

"Would you make the trade again?" There's no way the magic will allow him to say anything but yes. He and the magic are one now, if I'm to believe Antony and Calista. None of the Vessels truly have control over even their thoughts anymore.

"Of course," he says.

"Well." A wave crashes, particularly large, stinging my cheeks with its salty spray. "Then I agree. I would be honored to be the next Vessel."

Keelan's face crinkles, skin folding where his mouth might be in the only smile he can manage. "Excellent, then. There will be no delay."

CHAPTER THIRTY-SEVEN

Keelan leads, and I follow, because it's impossible for me to back down from this plan now. Unlike when Oriana and I trekked, the trees bend away from us this time instead of blocking our path. They bow respectfully, instead of trying to fight us.

I'm no longer their enemy. At least, they think I'm not.

I do manage to sneak a look over my shoulder to check that Oriana's following us, and though I can't be *sure*, I think I see a flash of a gold dress through the trees. It's probably better if I don't spot her in full, anyway, because if I can, Keelan can, too.

We approach the palace, and then pass it, our path slowly climbing. We proceed by the ritualistic slaughter of the innocents that I found with Oriana next, still all neatly arranged. But of course, Keelan hasn't removed them, because it's his fault they're dead.

Just beyond them, there's a sheer rock wall, but Keelan walks straight for it, one step, then another, until he vanishes beyond it.

It's not real. It's just a glamotura. I had been so close to the source before.

I take a deep breath, step through the illusion, and then, I'm there. I face what I've been searching for all this time.

Estaralla's source of magic.

It's a small crater pool, a dark, viscous bubbling liquid. It spits and burbles a stench of rot and sulfur so strong I breathe through my mouth. The rocks around it have no life, just shining dark stains, though the area itself is lit with a warm, unseen, unknown light source that makes it all clear as day.

My gut says this must be the source from the way my stomach rolls. Energy courses through me as all of the stories said it would, but they didn't say it was going to be the sort of nervous energy that feels like the edge of a breakdown.

The rest of the island is nothing more than pretend with its glittering blue streams and springs and sweet-smelling flowers. This is its true face. The magic is poison, meant to trick people into thinking they have something special while instead it quietly sucks their lives away.

Keelan gives me two slow claps in return. "I was not sure you would make it here alive. But it seems the magic still trusts in you."

It's a small warning, giving me just two seconds to raise my defenses because obviously *he* doesn't trust me.

The Vessels step out from the other side of the bubbling pool, circling it in a single file line, heads bowed. They wear sweeping gowns and long robes that float around them in invisible breezes.

I only count four. I need all seven.

Vessel Dionne is nowhere to be seen and neither is Calista. My spelled bracelet glows on my wrist, confirming that she's nowhere nearby.

I clear my throat. I can't sound too desperate even though I am. "Where are Vessel Dionne and the traitor?"

"Vessel Dionne is dealing with her daughter," Keelan says.

"I thought they were going to be here," I say. "I thought I'd get to see the traitor sacrificed."

"And you will." Keelan's tone is clipped. "After you have taken the magic into your heart and become one of us. We decided it would be better if Calista were not here for this ceremony in case she turned out to be a distraction. She is good at causing trouble."

I probably shouldn't have kissed her. I'd hoped to play that off as just a trick for Calista, but perhaps the reality shone through in the end.

My gaze slides behind me, searching for Oriana again, but I don't see her. She must still be behind the glamotura, which is smart because there's nowhere to hide here. As soon as she steps through, the Vessels will see her. All I can do is hope she saw me enter. All I can do is hope she can hear us, even though she can't see us. If the glamotura is only visual, and perhaps it is, she will.

I touch the bracelet Antony spelled to lead me to Calista. It's still warm. The knife I spelled for Oriana returned to normal once her mother died. So the fact that my bracelet is still warm means Calista must still be alive. That much is good.

But without Vessel Dionne here, I doubt I can destroy the magic. Not while it would still live on in her, wherever she is. I could kill all the Vessels, but then the magic would probably swallow me alive before I could make it to wherever Vessel Dionne and Calista are now.

I need Vessel Dionne. I need to destroy the magic with one blow, or not at all.

Which means we must begin the ceremony.

I will get Dionne and Calista here—no matter the cost.

CHAPTER THIRTY-EIGHT

I don't know if anyone's tried to fake their way through a Vessel ceremony before. Probably. And the island probably caught them and killed them, as it does.

But they weren't me.

I turn to Keelan. "Let's go, then."

He lifts the gilded knife at his belt. As the unknown light in this area catches the blade, it casts rainbows in all directions. "You will cut yourself, let your blood drip into the source. Then you must submerge your arm, and you and the source of magic will be one."

I accept the knife from Keelan, take a deep breath, make a regular production out of it, and then swipe the blade across the top of my arm, following closely with my free hand. In reality, the blade doesn't touch my skin, and I lift a glamotura of blood in its wake.

I turn to Keelan. Even though I haven't drawn blood, my head spins. I've never had a performance this important before. This deadly.

He jerks his chin toward the bubbling, viscous pit at my side. I kneel before it, submerging my arm, and a stench rises from it. Something ashy, something burning.

Needles stab into my skin from all sides, and I can't bite back the yell. I yank my arm out, tumbling backward and landing at Keelan's feet, a pathetic quivering mess.

He looks down at me and nudges me with his toe. "What did you do?" he asks, but being him, it doesn't sound angry or shocked or anything. His face and his voice are as empty and emotionless as always. "I don't feel your power."

I twist at his feet, writhing around so that it maybe looks like *some*thing is happening right now. My arm still stings, the needles biting again and again, so the hiss of pain I let out isn't faked at all. This seems like it'd be painful. I don't know much about the ceremony, but I can't imagine something on this island that's not full of pain.

"This is not supposed to be painful." Oops. One of the other Vessels speaks, another man, even though his voice sounds entirely the same as Keelan's. He steps forward and grabs my arm, the one burning, with the glamotura of blood still lining my skin.

He yanks me to my feet, pulling me all too close to his blank face. Despite the fact I shouldn't be able to smell, much less feel him breathe, a stench of rot wafts over me in hot waves that I could swear is breath. "Please try again. Something is not right."

Of course, how could I truly trick magic with itself?

He yanks the knife from my hand before I can break free and drags it across my arm. I yell, the pain rising, but then it swiftly fades. My arm goes numb, no longer feeling his hand or the burning from the source.

"Hmm," he says, and it's still monotone, but I can't feel anything below my elbow now, and panic rises in me swiftly. He turns me and pushes me back toward the source, but I kick at him and break free.

"No!"

The Vessels form a semicircle around me, stepping into quick formation, a line of faceless, lifeless people. "Do not worry," one of the women says, her voice identical to Dionne's and just as flat. "Binding twice will do no damage. We need to ensure the bond is solid."

Keelan grabs me and shoves me to the ground with a heavy grunt. I don't fight back.

I need Dionne here to kill her with the rest. I must submit.

He yanks my arm forward, pulling me onto my chest, and thrusts it beneath the source. Instantly, my heartbeat slows. My panic lifts. My arm is numb, and I feel nothing, but I don't care. It's nice, the numbness, because there's no pain.

I lick my lips, and they taste like spun sugar. Keelan pulls me back, spins me toward him, and looks into my eyes.

For the first time, he's not faceless.

I see the boy he once was, a light-skinned boy with a dusting of freckles over a slightly crooked nose, with a pointed chin and full lips. He looks like a more roguish version of Antony, a personality that's long gone now. Eaten away by magic. And he smiles at me. "Now I feel the power in you."

A voice in the back of my mind whispers that I should probably panic at that.

But still, I feel nothing.

CHAPTER THIRTY-NINE

I feel much, much better than I expected I would. Following the numbness, a warmth creeps into my arm, down to my fingers, and then back up again. Keelan, the new Keelan, the one who has a face, gives me a nod, releases me, and stands.

I follow him to my feet and look around.

All the Vessels have faces now.

"Do you feel it?" Keelan asks, and his voice is different, too. It's softer, deeper, with what almost sounds like kindness, which is quite unexpected. I suppose the magic is in me now, the true bits of his soul that he handed over to it. That's why I see and hear *him* for the first time.

Which means my soul, whatever true self made up Lucia Arduini . . . she must be gone too, slipping away into the dark viscous pool, never to be seen again either.

I should be panicking.

I know it. My thoughts tell me so. But I don't feel it.

I just feel calm, almost tired, like my whole body is metal. It's too heavy to move or lift or bother with and barely feels like it belongs to me at all.

Because it doesn't, fool, a voice whispers, but I don't care. I can't care.

"Lucia! Lucia!" The girl's voice calling sounds so distant. I turn. A girl with copper-brown skin and long, silken black hair abruptly appears at the edge of the clearing as though she's stepped out from nowhere. I think I should know her.

The Vessels nearest spin toward her, one asking, "Who is this?"

Another echoes, "What is she doing here?"

Two Vessels close in toward her, but she falls to her knees and abruptly bursts into noisy tears, and they both stop, exchanging bewildered glances.

"It's one of the guests. Just don't let her interfere for now, and then we'll take care of her. Focus with me here. Lucia is undergoing transformation," Keelan snaps.

Whatever's supposed to happen to me, it hasn't finished yet. I still might have a chance to come out of this as myself.

But why? a voice asks, soft and androgynous, impossible to place. *You're nothing but a failure. Your scheme with your father failed. Your family hates you. Your former love will forget you. That girl you thought you liked is going to die because you revealed her treachery to us. Your new friend's mother is dead because of you, and she's going to die, too.*

Why do you want to go back to failing?

Stay with us, and you'll have power.

You'll be valuable.

You'll be safe.

You'll never have to fear or submit to anyone ever again.

It sounds appealing. So appealing. To not lose more people I love. To not have to worry about the Silverhands anymore.

But that's not quite true. I won't be submitting to the Silverhands anymore, but I *will* be submitting to the magic. I'll be the body of Lucia Arduini, but my mind will be controlled. I'll never get the chance to explore who I really am, what I really want.

The numbness creeps away, just a little, and I remember my last vision of Severin, the last time I'm supposed to see him ever. I remember the exhaustion on his face, the bent form of his body working on the docks, a life he was never supposed to have. I can't abandon him just like our father abandoned us.

"Where is Vessel Dionne?" I ask. It seems safer to act interested in her than in Calista. They have to bring her out, I swear. Unless Keelan lied that first day that all the Vessels need to be present for a new one to be inducted.

But if he didn't lie, and Vessel Dionne has to be here, maybe that means my transaction with the magic isn't complete yet. If it's not complete yet, maybe I can still undo it.

Keelan steps close to me and takes my chin in his hands. His gaze searches mine, and I wonder what he's looking for. Since I suddenly see his face, I wonder if he can see the magic in mine. He shimmers before me, while the mask of the girl behind him (*Oriana!* Her name is Oriana) blurs into something flat and featureless—like how the Vessels used to appear to me.

"Fetch Dionne," Keelan commands.

A spark flashes in me, a brief feeling of triumph, but it vanishes as quickly as it hit. I reach after it, but my chest is like a void, deep and dark and empty, and there's nothing to clutch at.

I should feel something.

As long as I can keep telling myself that, maybe I'll be fine. As long as I still realize there's something missing, I'll still have that much of myself left.

Feeling leeches out from my chest, inching back down my torso and up into my neck. Suddenly, prickles of pain strike, and heat boils. My skin burns in anger and in pain.

Let the past go, the voice whispers to me again. *You weren't happy, anyway. You weren't free. But you will be now. You will be.*

But that's not true. I won't be happy or free. I, Lucia Arduini, will be long gone. There'll be nothing left of me but a shell.

Keelan has lied and lied to me, thought from the start he could play me. No one plays me. I let them for a while, bent to the will of the gang, but I'm done. I'm done with them, and I'm done with Keelan and this devouring magic, too.

I am sick of playing along for him.

I am sick of playing along for *everyone.*

One more person joins the semicircle of Vessels. Her face is exactly what I might've pictured: an older version of Calista, but harsher, sharper, whose lips are bright red. She shoves a tied-up pile of a girl in front of her. Dark ropes wrap the girl's hands and feet and chest, and a gag binds her mouth. I squint at her. Something stirs in my chest, and for a minute, I think I must hate her too, because I hate everyone.

But no.

No, the warm rush in my chest for her isn't hate.

Her gray-blue eyes flash, wilder than the sea where I last saw her.

Vessel Dionne and Calista have arrived.

And I don't have to play along with anyone anymore.

CHAPTER FORTY

Calista stares at me, wide-eyed enough that I can read the horror there. If she's not furious at my betrayal, she's at least wondering how far gone I am. How alone she is.

The world spins, and numbness edges back into my neck, pushing away the temporary feeling I gained back.

You'll have power, the island tells me. *You'll be calm and happy and safe.*

But that's just another lie.

I thrust a shaking hand into one of the folds of my apron and am rewarded with a pinch to my finger.

The end of my arm begins to burn.

The poison from the little bug creeps into me, mingling with my blood and the magic I've taken in. It crawls up my arms like fire, wiping away all the numbness the magic forced into me.

I step forward around Keelan and toward Calista on the ground. "You traitor," I growl for Calista. Her brows pinch, but she looks more confused than furious.

Keelan takes my arm, his fingers cold on my stinging skin. He turns me toward him. His face blurs in mine, his already thin lips thinning once more to the nothing they used to be. The edges of my vision are turning gray. The magic is losing hold of me—because of the poison.

"I don't know if you should go near her," he says, because even now, I'm not safe and not yet free.

But the crawling of gray across my vision is the clock ticking down to where I pass out, and the poison takes me, and I die, and this all fails.

"Why?" I say. "I need closure."

"It shouldn't matter to you anymore." Keelan's brows are fading, too, but his eyes narrow beneath the faint shape of them that's left.

The traitor wouldn't matter to the magic?

She does matter. I remember how Teresta talked about her. That wasn't indifference. The magic hates Calista because she tried to defy it, tried to reject the price demanded, and no one dares to defy magic.

I place my hand on my chest, and the weight of my own touch feels so heavy, too heavy. I'm close to collapse. "It matters more to me now. She tried to destroy us."

Keelan's lips part with what might be surprise, but it's getting harder to tell. He lets go of my arm, and that's enough. I drop to the ground in front of Calista. My vision narrows until she takes up nearly all of it.

Bound by so many ropes, her shoulders slumped, and her hair a tangled mess about her face, she looks like when the polizia nab a beggar thief—seemingly so pathetic she probably should've just been released. She certainly doesn't need as many ropes as they've tied around her. I've seen so many different sides of her, some real and some just pretend: from prim and perfect to wild and vicious, but this is the first time I've seen her look genuinely pitiful.

I look back, and the motion makes my vision whirl between all the Vessels, finally landing on Oriana in the back. She tucks a hand behind her where I know she's got her invisible pouch tied.

My tongue feels like it's swelling into a thick wad of stuffing in my mouth, and my lips struggle a little to form the words around it. "I'm so much happier now," I say and give a small nod, something I hope Oriana can interpret as the signal it is. But she's quick, she's smart, and I trust her.

Then I grab Calista and shove her into the bubbling pool beside us. She yells, a muffled sound that's trapped by her gag, and sinks. Then I dive after her. As I disappear under the surface, Oriana's first explosive hits. The ground cracks, and a wave of heat follows me into the murk.

A sensation like a punch hits my chest. I taste blood and bile and rot.

I grab for Calista with one hand and reach for my knife with the other because I need to cut her free. I grab an end of the sinking rope and kick against the viscous liquid that wants to drag us both under.

I slide my knife through the ropes, and they fall away from her.

Poison, I think for the magic. *Poison, poison, make me poison now.* Calista had better be right, that the magic will draw the poison out of my body as the price for the transaction. That it takes the same price for the same transaction, even if the person asking is different.

My vision slides to a pinprick. Calista grabs me and pushes me over the edge of the pool, hauling my body out of the magic so my face presses into the ground. Her fingers pry at mine, unclenching them from around my knife.

I can't move my own fingers to help her.

Something bubbles in my stomach, strong and sour, and my body flashes between hot and cold. My limbs twitch, and I want to scream, but I can't control my lips and they won't open for me. Sticky warmth collects under my arms, blood and magic and poison all leaving me.

Beside me, the pool bubbles, a rolling boil now, and tendrils reach out for me. An unseen force wills me to jump backward, go backward, to drown in it.

I still can't move.

Above me, one of the Vessels appears. They're faceless again, lacking any features except their pitch-black eyes. He lunges out of the smoke for me, but Calista steps between us, and he impales himself on my knife in her hand.

It's followed by another punch to my chest.

That sensation must be the death of a Vessel. The magic still in me feels it. Or maybe it's just coincidence, and that's part of the poison.

Calista steps back into the wall of smoke, leaving me to stagger to my feet, trembling, by the side of the source on my own.

A third punch rips through me, and I cover my mouth with a hand as it fills with warm liquid, like my entire mouth has been sliced open. But it must be imaginary. It must be.

The fourth hits, and I spit. Actual dark liquid, a deep red but not quite blood, dribbles from my mouth. But now, my fingers are under my control again. So are my arms, my legs, all of me.

Someone jumps from the flames and tackles me.

I slam onto my back, and Keelan leers over me. His hands dig into my throat, and I kick my legs at nothing. *Calista!* I want to scream, but I have no breath left. Keelan's fingers squeeze it out.

I swing at his blank face, clawing at his cheeks. My fingers catch the shadows where his eyes should be, and I dig in.

His hands fly from my throat up to my wrists, and he hollers.

Too late.

My fingers sink in, and his unseen eyes burst beneath my nails. Hot, sticky blood slides down my fingers, down my wrists, and Keelan howls. I shove him back and stagger to my feet.

I'm no fighter, but I can be vicious.

A shadow emerges from the smoke, an arm raised, knife glinting. Calista sweeps forward, fluid as liquid, thrusting the knife through Keelan's back. His mouth opens, and a gurgle escapes. Then blood.

Calista yanks the knife out, and Keelan pitches forward. She dives after him, catching his feet as he dangles over the pool. "Don't let the magic have his body."

I grab his ankles, and together, we drag him back and away from the magic. The pool, roiling and spitting not long ago, has now sunk. There's barely any of the dark liquid left, just a smudge quite a ways down now.

My gaze locks with Calista's above his corpse. Blood streaks her face, glittering darkly, and her eyes are wild, her lips bright pink, and a smile breaks across my own lips.

She gives me a nod, then offers a hand, smudged with blood. I give her mine, just as slick. She squeezes tight, and then with her free hand, she leans over the source. My arm shakes, even as I try to hold her steady. Dark liquid drips from the end of her fingertips, and the little remaining source hisses below, like an angry animal.

The poison. "Where's my poison?" I ask.

"All over the ground," Calista says with a small hiccup that might be a laugh. The dark poison splashes into the dark magic, and steam rises from it. I reach into the folds of my apron, seeking the little bug's stinger there. It's a desperate, blind sort of scrabbling, fueled by the hopes that it hasn't fallen out with everything that's happened.

But luck smiles. The sharp pain of its sting buries itself in my finger, and I hold my hand out like Calista.

Poison, I think.

A burning sensation crawls up my throat, slinks down my arms, and out the ends of my fingers. I shudder, and my breathing turns rough. Still, it's not as bad as the way the deaths of the Vessels tore through me.

The smoke rising from the source reaches me, and it tastes of rot and burns my face, and I cough. And for a few moments, that is all the world is—rot and burning and coughing and stinging pain.

And then it clears.

And all that remains at the base of the pit are black flakes like ash.

And when I look behind me, there's no longer the haze of illusion that blocks us from the rest of the island. I can see all the way to the sea. And the ground that was, just moments ago, so lush and green is now all scorched, nothing more than ashes.

CHAPTER FORTY-ONE

It's a slow trek back to the harbor through the now dying foliage with Oriana limping in the rear. She even smiles, a nasty smile of triumph. The people who killed her mother are dead, and with Calista and me on her side, the Silverhands are about to be next.

And with her and Calista on my side, I feel the beginnings of hope, too. We just defeated the ancient Vessels of Estaralla, so maybe, just maybe, we'll be able to take the Silverhands on, too. Together.

Because with the magic's prices erased, I should be able to see Severin again after all. As long as, of course, we succeed. But if we do, he and I can truly be safe. Truly be free. And we can start our lives again.

"What do you think the islanders are thinking right now?" I ask Calista. "Do you think they've realized the magic is gone?"

"I'm sure they have." There's something somber in her voice that gives me pause.

"Do you regret it?" I ask.

"Definitely not." She's fierce enough for me to believe that's true. "But others will feel differently." Her gaze drifts across the land, the still-dead, still-brown ground around us. "Estaralla's entire economy was the magic. It was their entire identity." Calista shakes her head. "For most people here, trading their freedom for the power and money of the magic was a given trade. They won't feel free with it gone. They'll feel their lives are lost. People are going to hate us forever. We're going to be the villains in stories they tell."

"I don't care what anyone thinks of me now," I say. I'm done with all of that. And even as a faint part of me feels sorry for those people, it's more that I'm sorry they can't imagine something better for themselves. That they needed that parasitic magic to exist. "I never set out to be a hero. And I don't really care if I'm a villain."

EPILOGUE

What later came to be known as the day Estaralla's magic vanished was initially just called "the day of the black flash" in the reports that got passed around Verigal City. Because before everything shattered, there was a black flash in the sky, like a dark lightning bolt, followed by a crash not unlike thunder.

Then Verigal City's glamoturas vanished.

The gold in the city's welcome waterfall turned to ash.

The levees cracked, and the lower quarters flooded.

And all the homes of the wealthy turned ordinary again, all of the money they'd spent on glamoturas wasted.

But when they went to complain to the man who'd sold most of them, Julius, the boss of the Silverhands gang, was already dead.

Poison, probably, said reports and rumors passed around. But no one could name the exact poison. The effects on his body were unusual, something never seen before. His veins were blackened and popping, even while his skin was shriveled and graying, like someone had sucked the moisture right out of it.

Initially, there were also a few rumors of what—or rather *who*—might've caused the day of the black flash. A few people pointed out that there were several tourists on Estaralla at the time, including, of course, the daughter of a wealthy and powerful admiral whose wife mysteriously died on the trip. And then, there was the tour guide herself, who'd returned to the city with an Estarallan girl, something entirely unheard of, and made even more scandalous still when they left the city again promptly together with a younger boy in tow.

But those rumors didn't last.

They swiftly vanished, never to be mentioned again, except as a joke.

A little bit like magic.

ACKNOWLEDGMENTS

This book has been a very long time in the making (seven years!), so naturally, there are a lot of folks who've contributed along the way to its final form. I'm grateful for all of you here—and those I might have missed.

Sarah Fisk, my agent, thank you for all of the support you've given me over the years. Thank you for believing so strongly in my work that you picked me out of the slush pile not once, but twice. I feel so incredibly lucky to have an agent in my corner who understands my writing as keenly as you do and is willing to work tirelessly to find it a home in publishing.

Camille Kellogg, my editor, thank you for loving this book and for your sharp and insightful editorial guidance. You've taken this book to a new level that I could not have gotten it to on my own, and it has been an incredible experience to watch this book transform under your direction into a more glamorous, more romantic, and overall more complex version of itself.

Thanks to the rest of the team at Bloomsbury, Lily Yengle, Emani Glee, Jeanette Levy, Donna Mark, Oona Patrick, Laura Phillips, Sarah Shumway, Mary Kate Castellani, Alona Fryman, Erica Chan,

Beth Eller, Kathleen Morandini, Jennifer Choi, Andrew Văn Nguyễn, Erica Barmash, Faye Bi, Valentina Rice, Daniel O'Connor, and Nicholas Church, for the contributions that each of you have made to take this story from a computer file to a real (and gorgeous) book. And thanks to Manon Biernacki for the stunning cover art.

Rebecca Schaeffer, thank you for being this book's first champion in Pitch Wars. Your early insight brought this book to life, and your ongoing support since then ensured it didn't die on my hard drive. (Seriously, without you, this book would probably still just be a file on my computer.) Thank you for the seven years of encouragement and your unwavering faith that this book did belong on shelves and only needed to land on the right person's desk at the right time in order to get there.

Thanks to this book's earliest readers, Leigh Mar and Amanda Jasper. You were such a great help in launching the book into the next stage of its journey. Leigh, I will forever appreciate how quickly you read and the enthusiasm you showered on that really rough draft. It made all the difference.

Thanks to the next round of readers, Kim Smejkal, Sam Taylor, and Ian Barnes. It's been so long now that I'm not sure how well any of you remember this book, but I still remember your kind words for it.

Thanks to Becca, Courtney, Carrie-Anne, Jillian, and Ken for your fresh and thoughtful insights on the opening section that gave this book new life. I enjoyed having a regular time to get together and talk writing with you all and, in our meetings, gathered so many great ideas for both this book and others. I miss you all!

Thank you to my friends, Jess Essey and Laura Piper Lee. Jess, as my first ever CP, your influence on my writing is undeniable, and I'm so glad that you're still here over a decade later for writing sprints and industry chats—or just a drink at the gay bar. Laura, thank you for letting me beat you in all of the writing sprints that got this book finished. You're always there to cheerlead and (mostly lovingly) kick my ass and keep me on track when I veer off.

Thanks to the folks of the Submission Slog Comrades chat for all of your support and commiseration while I was on submission. I'm afraid of missing someone if I attempt to list you all here, but just know that if you've ever chatted with me directly, I am thinking of you.

Thanks to the other Bloomsbury 2024 kidlit debuts, Meredith, Kelsea, Leah, and Chatham, for your camaraderie. I feel so lucky to have you all as my debut-year imprint buddies, and I hope we share many publication years to come!

Thank you to my mom, dad, and brother for being there over the years and for all of your excitement for this book. Thank you for all of the copies you've preordered and/or pushed on the rest of the family (mom and dad) or your friends (James).

Last but not least, thanks goes to my wife, Karen. When I started this book, I didn't know you yet, but I am so, so grateful to have had you with me for the last part of this journey. Your support for me and my writing has meant the world.